MW00975246

WHISPERS
FROM THE
HAUNTED
WOODS

TERRY SWEATT

WHISPERS FROM THE HAUNTED WOODS

Copyright © 2022 Terry Sweatt.

All rights reserved. No part of this book may be used or reproduced by any means, graphic, electronic, or mechanical, including photocopying, recording, taping or by any information storage retrieval system without the written permission of the author except in the case of brief quotations embodied in critical articles and reviews.

iUniverse books may be ordered through booksellers or by contacting:

iUniverse
1663 Liberty Drive
Bloomington, IN 47403
www.iuniverse.com
844-349-9409

Because of the dynamic nature of the Internet, any web addresses or links contained in this book may have changed since publication and may no longer be valid. The views expressed in this work are solely those of the author and do not necessarily reflect the views of the publisher, and the publisher hereby disclaims any responsibility for them.

Any people depicted in stock imagery provided by Getty Images are models, and such images are being used for illustrative purposes only. Certain stock imagery © Getty Images.

ISBN: 978-1-6632-3494-0 (sc)
ISBN: 978-1-6632-3495-7 (e)

Print information available on the last page.

iUniverse rev. date: 01/25/2022

CONTENTS

CHAPTER 1

THE CAMPING TRIP

"This is the last stake", Les told David as he tied the cord around the metal spike. "Tent's up."

Several feet away three other pairs of scouts finished setting up their two-man pup tents and the campsite was taking shape in fine fashion.

It was Friday afternoon, June 1984. The eight boy scouts, all life-long friends, were hiking a remote stretch of the north Georgia woods near the Appalachian Trail. Their destination was Springer Mountain about five miles away. The overcast sky and an occasional warm breeze offered only small relief from the stifling heat.

Les Harrison, fifteen-years old and one of Georgia's most decorated boy scouts, scanned the surroundings momentarily with his steel-gray eyes. An owl hooted from somewhere in a nearby tree. David Branish, his best friend since grade-school, tossed his sleeping bag into the open doorway of the tent.

Billy Vance and Steve Yarborough, the two youngest of the group, had their tent unrolled and were tossing the stakes on the ground around it. Undoubtedly, one of them had his Dungeons and Dragons game pieces with him and they would soon be trying to get a fantasy game going. That plan would be quickly squashed by the others.

A dozen-feet away Ken Northington, the only African-American member of the troop, and Mark McFarland, nicknamed "Blondie" for his near-platinum hair color, were having their usual argument about tent placement. Ken liked having the doorway face the outside of the campsite and usually further from the others. It gave them more "solitude" he said.

"Whenever you find the exact right spot," Mark said to Ken as he stood waiting with the small hammer in hand. "Maybe some time today, bro?"

Ken froze, looked at him momentarily and laughed. "Face it Blondie, you'll never be black like me so just stop trying with the lingo. Why don't you just talk like a normal white person and tell me to get moving so you can get a spot of tea brewing or something." Ken smiled and awaited a retort.

Mark thought momentarily. "Fresh brewed tea and some whoop ass. Sounds good to me."

Ken gave him a quick exaggerated glare, then smiled. The two of them had been trading light-hearted racial innuendos all summer and had gotten quite good at the practice, much to the chagrin of the others.

"Hey David," Don said, holding his pup tent in one hand and several tent stakes in the other. "Can you give us a little room?"

"Huh," David said absent-mindedly, only then noticing Harry two feet away from him. Harry was holding one of his tent stakes like a dagger, acting as if he were planning to stab David in the neck if he didn't get out of his way.

"You're standing in our living room, dude," Don said. "This long hike has worn us all out. Let's get these tents pitched so we can start relaxing."

Don Dixon and Harry Richards were the leaders of the group, more because of their age and years in the scout troop than for their expertise. The only high-school seniors in the pack, their remaining time in the boy scouts was now down to its last few months.

Les sometimes thought the two of them had let their status as the longest tenured troop members go to their heads. They were the oldest scouts now but not the wisest ones. Nor the tallest. Neither of them stood over five-feet five and both could stand to lose about twenty pounds. Les also suspected Don had taken up cigarette smoking although he wasn't sure.

None of those factors stopped Don or Harry from taking charge of every situation whenever the opportunity came up. Whether it was their pride or vanity, Les didn't know. He usually just tried to ignore their bossy boastfulness as much as he could.

When it came to scouting, Les was more experienced and knowledgeable than Don and Harry combined, despite being a year younger than either of them. For now he was just biding his time. He would become the new troop leader in one more year and David, who was five months his junior, would then be his co-leader when that time came.

All of that aside, Don was in charge on this day, if for no other reason, because his father's company van had provided their transportation that morning.

"I've got something really great to tell you guys after dinner tonight," Don told them. "It's the real reason I wanted us all out here a night earlier than the rest of the guys."

"What is it?" David said.

Don looked at him with a slight smile. He didn't reply.

"You guys will just have to wait until tonight to find out," Harry said. "But trust me, It's really cool!" He looked over at Don and smiled. "Ain't that right?"

"It sure is," Don said, pulling his mess kit from his pack. "Well worth the wait."

The campsite they had chosen was some fifty feet off the main trail and afforded quick access to the stream. They all took a dip to clean up and, about an hour before dusk, fire wood was gathered and a small bonfire started. They then cooked and enjoyed a hearty supper. As darkness encroached, they started telling jokes and stories around the campfire like usual.

After a few minutes Don looked over at Harry. "Twenty-one thirty. I think this is a good time for our announcement."

Harry nodded. "Alright everybody, listen up."

"Is it time for your big announcement?" Les said loudly and with a great deal of fake enthusiasm.

"Yeah, it is," Don replied with a snide grin. "So shut-up."

"I already know what the announcement is," Ken said in an even more excited voice. He waved his hand like he was a contestant in a really bad game show.

"Well why don't you just tell us, smart ass," Don said sternly.

Ken grinned. "You two pretty boys are getting hitched."

All of them except Don and Harry exploded into laughter. Both turned red with anger.

"I'd hold my horses if I were you, Ken," Steve said between chuckles. "You're about to be asked to be one of the bridesmaids. And you're going to have to wear a dress."

"Yeah Ken," Billy said. "A sexy one. I think your best color is lavender. Wouldn't you agree, Steve?"

Steve laughed. "Yeah. Ken would look sweet in lavender."

"Oh, shut-up!" Ken said with a wave of his hand.

Les looked over at David. They were both laughing so hard they were having trouble catching their breath. "These guys are a riot," Les said.

"Alright, shut-the-hell-up, all of you," Don shouted. He and Harry both were furious. The others slowly settled down and resumed gazing into the fire. They were all having a great time.

"Can we be serious for one minute here?" Don said tersely. They all were quiet a moment, taking some time to gather their collective composure.

"Tonight is really more than just another night on the trail. I mean think about it. All of us out here alone with no adult leaders. Tonight we're not boy scouts, we're men. On our own and in control of our own destiny. This did not happen by accident."

"Hey Mark," Ken said. "Did you happen to bring your brother's violin?" More laughter.

Don glared across the fire at him. Ken grinned back. "Hey, you need some soft music for this love story".

"Or some banjoes", Steve said. The rest of them laughed.

"You wimps shut-up and listen," Harry shouted. "Each one of you is lucky as hell to be here with Don and me tonight. If all of you just want to act like a bunch of eleven-year-old queers at a slumber party then take it somewhere and lose it in the woods."

"Yeah you sons-of-bitches!" Don added. That got the group quiet in a hurry. He looked over at Harry and laughed.

"Alright, alright!" Les said, waving his hands palms-down. "Cut all the crap. Let's get this over with. Don, you have our undivided attention." He looked around at all of them. "Scouts honor."

Don gave him a serious, genuine look. "Thank you Les."

He paused a brief moment. "Look guys, what I'm about to tell you is no story. We're men now, out on our own. I don't know about you guys but I like being out here without the rest of the troop. And there's a reason I specifically chose each of you to be here with Harry and me tonight."

"Uh-oh," Ken said.

"Save it Kenny!" Harry said. "Maybe Don should have said except for you."

The smile quickly faded from Ken's face. "What is that supposed to mean?"

Don stared him down for a brief moment. "It means you are here with us tonight by chance, nothing more, nothing less. Evidently some of the other guys here like you. I personally don't feel I really know you so the jury's still out with me."

"And also with me," Harry added. "And it's not looking so good right now, bro."

Les sat up and leaned forward. "I said you had our undivided attention. But not to be jerks. That goes for you too, Ken."

"I'm cool," Ken said innocently. He smiled and looked at Mark, Steve and Billy for approval. They all gave him dirty stares.

"Look Don, correct me if I'm mistaken," Les said, "but I thought we were here alone tonight because we were the only ones in the scout troop that wanted to get an early start on tomorrow's hike. We are meeting up with Scoutmaster Thomas and the other guys at the base of Springer Mountain tomorrow at 1300, right?"

"Yes, that's right, Les," Don said. "But everybody is in on the group gathering tomorrow. Tonight is different. It only happened because I worked it out with my dad to have one of his van drivers deliver us up here."

"And not everybody in the group was invited," Harry said. "You all are here by special invitation so act accordingly."

"Well, I'm truly honored," Les said, glancing at his wristwatch and then briefly in the direction of the clearing. "You want to get to your point, now? It's getting late and we've got a long hike tomorrow."

"I'm aware of that, Les," Don said. "What I don't think you guys realize is that we are alone out here for a whole night by ourselves only as a result of careful planning on my part."

"Okay, we get the careful planning part," Billy said. "So what have you guys got up your sleeves?"

Don looked over at Harry and they both chuckled. "Something more awesome than you can imagine," Harry said.

Steve placed his elbows on his folded knees and planted his chin into his palms, letting his body language tell Don he had his total attention. "Fire away Don. We're listening."

"It took a lot of negotiating to get my dad to agree to diverting one of his delivery vans to bring us up here," Don said. "That was the first step."

"Then came the part where Don's dad agreed to work on Scoutmaster Thomas to let us meet him at Springer tomorrow," Harry said. "That was the really tricky part."

"That took some doing," Don said. "Mr. Thomas was really hesitant about our being up here alone tonight. He let my dad know he wanted no responsibility if we mysteriously didn't show up at Springer at the appointed time. He wanted us to meet at the church tomorrow morning at eight-o'clock with everybody else."

"Yeah," Harry said. "Don leaned on his old man and got him to lean on Mr. Thomas."

Les laughed. "Mr. Thomas told me about that phone call when I talked to him on Thursday. He still wasn't too keen on the whole idea. I had to assure him I'd keep a close eye on you guys tonight." He looked over at Don and chuckled. "Apparently your dad leaned-on him pretty hard."

"I guess it didn't hurt that you were coming along, Les," Billy said.

"Oh, we were coming whether Les made it or not," Don said.

"Yeah," Harry added. "Les just helped clear the way for the rest of you wimps."

"So you guys pulled a few strings so we could get an extra night on the trail," David said. "That's supposed to be some big accomplishment?"

"You'd better believe it," Harry said.

"Alright, listen up," Don said. "Stage one was arranging transportation. Getting old man Thomas to agree to the plan was stage two. Stage three was up to you guys to see if you could get it past your parents to join us. Obviously you succeeded. That's why we're all here right now."

"Are any of your parents looking for you right now?" Harry asked them. "See any scout masters or other adult leaders? No. Admit it guys. Tonight is a first for each of you. Well, except you Les, of course."

"Okay, you got us up here, you got us up here," Billy said. "Are you ever going to get around to telling us why? I'm dying over here!"

"Okay," Don smiled at him. "What I'm about to tell you guys is to be kept only among us. This night in the woods tonight is just a dry run. I'm going to plan another hike for all of us this fall just like this. No scout leaders, no parents, only us. It'll be the ultimate hike."

"Count me in", Harry said. He looked around the group. "It will be the first test of manhood for some of you."

"When's your first test going to be, Harry?" Ken said. They all laughed.

"In about five minutes when I kick your ass," Harry said. He and Don laughed.

"So let's say we all get up here again this fall on your ultimate hike," Les said. "Any special reason?"

"Oh yeah," Harry said. "It's going to be the coolest hike ever."

Don looked around at the surrounding trees, now appearing as a curtain at the edge of the firelight. Les thought the expression he wore was one that anticipated the arrival of another person. It was theatrical and false, able to fool some of the other guys but not him. He knew Don too well.

"Is this the part where I'm supposed to get scared and wet my pants?" Ken said.

"That's how you handle everything else," Harry said. He looked over at Don and grinned.

Don smiled. "There are places out in these woods that no white man has ever seen. Or a soul brother either," he said, glancing at Ken.

"Hidden out in these woods are some old Indian camps. Abandoned, forgotten, and still intact. They've remained completely untouched since the very day the Indians that lived in them were rounded-up and sent west to reservations. The right person looking in the right place could find one of them. That somebody is me."

"And me," Harry added.

"Why would anyone want to find them?" Billy said. "There wouldn't be anything left of those old Indian camps."

"You're wrong there, friend," Harry said. "Arrowheads, tomahawks, spears, pottery, stone carvings and no telling what else. Probably some valuable stuff too. You guys really should read more."

"I'm not big on reading comic books," Ken said. They all laughed.

"Ha," Harry said. "You're not big on reading, period." He looked over at Don and they both laughed.

"Valuable stuff?" Steve said. "You act like Indians had gold and jewels or something. They were all poor, remember?"

"They made jewelry," Mark said. "But it didn't have any value."

"They left behind entire encampments," Don said. "Just picture yourself walking into an Indian village that nobody has set foot in for over a century. It doesn't matter what's there, it would still be a cool thing to do. All we'd have to do is start turning over rocks, maybe dig a foot or two here and there. In a pretty short time I'll bet we'd find quite a few interesting things."

"I think you've been smoking a peace pipe," David said with a laugh. "Even if you could find an old Indian camp there would be nothing there to find that's worth having."

"Yeah," Mark said. "And even if there ever had been it would be washed away by the elements after more than a hundred years. Sounds like a waste of time to me."

"You couldn't be more wrong, pal," Don said. "All over the country, particularly in the southwest, people are finding Indian artifacts and selling them for big bucks. Bigger money than you can imagine."

"Selling them to who?" David said. Suddenly, Don had his full attention.

"Black market thieves," Les said. "Lowlife scoundrels, future cell mates, that's who."

"Not so fast, Les," Harry said. "There are plenty of legitimate museums that buy stuff like that. And you guys won't believe the prices they're paying."

"Tell me more," David said.

Don gave Harry a quick smile. "Indians left behind all kinds of artifacts. Clay pots, masks, dolls, tools, all kinds of things. I even read in the newspaper a few months ago that some guy found a large basket that had been buried for two-hundred years in Arizona that fetched five-thousand dollars!"

"Wow," Ken said. "For one basket?"

"That's right," Harry said. "Just think how much we could get for a whole bunch of stuff if we can find it. We'd all make a killing."

"You aren't going to find anything like that in north Georgia," Les said. "Arizona is arid enough that a basket could last a couple of hundred years buried in the back of a cave. But here in the east the humidity is too high. Nothing like that is left."

"But pottery is," Harry said. "If we managed to dig-up an intact clay pot that dates back before the Civil War, it could be worth a fortune."

"Harry's right," Don said. "I've studied Indians from this part of Georgia and there were plenty of them around. Some, like the Cherokee and the Creeks were here for hundreds of years. Mark my words, there are plenty of old Indian camps in these woods. You can't tell me you wouldn't want to find one and spend a weekend there. If we just go to the trouble of looking there's no telling what we'll find."

"You guys don't have to come along," Harry said. "Me and Don can handle it. We'll show up at school one day with a jar full of arrowheads and old jewelry and beads and every kid in the hallways will be asking us why we didn't invite them along. You guys don't know what an honor it is to be included in this."

"So why is it so important that we get up here alone for this proposed hike of yours?" Steve said.

Ken laughed. "Because Scoutmaster Thomas would freak-out if he knew about it."

"I'd say that is a likely possibility," Don said. "And I don't need him or any of your parents getting up in arms about it."

"Mr. Thomas can be a real wimp," Harry said. "It doesn't take a rocket scientist to figure out how he'd react if we tried running something like this past him."

"Yeah," Don agreed. "Just look at how bent-out-of-shape he got over my dad's phone call about this trip."

There was a momentary pause while the others pondered what Don and Harry had told them. "This is a once-in-a-lifetime opportunity," Don said at last. "It's up to you if you want in or not."

"Look," Les said, "I don't mean to rain on your parade, but what you are talking about is highly illegal. About five years ago Congress passed a law called the Archaeological Resources Protection Act that prohibits exactly this type of activity. In extreme cases violators can get up to five years in prison and a quarter-million-dollar fine."

"Well, now you're just talking stupid," Harry said. "Have you heard of even one person in those five years who got caught and prosecuted? No. People all over the country are doing this and getting rich. Why should we miss out?"

"We won't be doing anything illegal," Don said. "And besides, even if we did they'd have to catch us first. This isn't stealing. Anything we find would never be found by anyone else, ever."

David looked at Harry and smiled. "This really does sound cool."

Harry grinned. "Yeah man, it's a no-brainer. We're in and out slicker than snake shit. It'll be a blast!"

"We could sell anything that's valuable and keep the rest as souvenirs," Don said. "Here's a chance for us all to make a few bucks and have a great time doing it."

"So just where are these places?" Billy asked.

Don gave him a prideful smile. "I was waiting for one of you to ask that question."

"Don's got a map," Harry said. "It'll lead us right to a camp."

"It's not just "A" map," Don said, "it's "THE" map. Spotted it in my grandfather's bureau when my old man and I were cleaning out his house after he died last March. It's a hiker's guide to the Appalachian Trail, printed in 1939. One of the locations listed is an Indian Burial Ground."

"Oh, cool!" Steve said. "Do you have the map with you?"

"No," Don said. "I couldn't take a chance of losing it or the wrong person seeing it. I've got it taped to the underside of a drawer in my desk at home. My old man never saw it and doesn't even know it exists. I want to keep it that way."

"So you're the only person who has seen it," Billy said.

"I've seen it," Harry said. "The map is so old that it's falling apart. But in the lower right-hand corner the words 'Indian Burial Ground' are clearly printed on that map."

"The Burial Ground is actually identified on the map?" Mark said. "You're joking."

"No," Harry said. "There's even a small dot showing the exact spot."

"It shouldn't be hard to find either," Don said. "With all our scouting skills combined we could probably locate it with only an hour or two of searching."

"Well if it's on a map then every hiker in the state has already been there," Les said. "There goes your fortune."

"Hold on there, Mr. Negative," Don said. "They don't print the location on maps anymore. Haven't for decades. I've researched it. No map the National Park Service has printed since 1940 has the Indian Burial Ground location on it. This old map my grandfather had was the last one that showed it."

"Maybe that's because there's nothing left of it," Ken said. "Did you ever think of that?"

Harry gave him a nasty look. "Yes, we considered that."

"And we also considered that there may be another reason," Don said. "Maybe they don't want to advertise the fact that there is treasure in there waiting to be found."

"Don and I figure that's the real reason they don't print maps with its location on them anymore," Harry said. "There weren't that many people backpacking in the 1930s so it really didn't matter that much at the time. Now, millions of people hike for recreation. We're living in a different era."

"That's right," Don said. "And the difference between them and us is that we're the ones with the map. The accurate map."

The eight of them sat in silence a moment. As the fire crackled and the tree frogs sang, the summer night seemed to pulsate around them like a big, cohesive organism.

"This idea of yours sounds so cool," David said at last. "But we'd better make sure nobody knows anything about what we're doing."

"That's why we waited until we could get you guys together out here alone to tell you about it," Harry said. "Don and I have been sitting on this for months."

Don looked at him and nodded. "As I said, this is a special night."

"Well you can count me in," David said. "I wish we could start tomorrow. What do you think, Les? You're the scout with all the badges."

"I really don't think there would be anything worth finding other than a few arrowheads," Les said. "I'm quite sure there wouldn't be anything valuable enough to sell. But you guys all know that I'm always up for a good camping trip. It would be different from what we're used to. It sounds interesting. I'll come along."

"That's the spirit," Don said. "I always knew you were cool, Les." He gave Les a broad smile.

Les smiled back at him. "I think you're going to need me along on this trip of yours, Don. Even if it's for nothing more than to watch your back."

Ken chuckled. "That's for sure."

"What about you, Ken?" Harry said. "You up for a weekend in the red man's camp with a bunch of white boys?"

Ken darted his brown eyes, winked and then smiled. "It sounds interesting but I think I'll decline. I'd never get it past my mother to let me spend a weekend out in the woods playing Cowboys and Indians with a bunch of white boys."

"You can probably count me out too," Mark said. "My dad would freak if I tried it."

"Steve, Billy, what about you guys?" Don said. "Think you could arrange it?"

"I'll have to get back to you," Steve said.

"Same here," Billy agreed. "This is no simple plan."

"You guys are just wimps," Harry said. "Why did you bother becoming scouts in the first place?"

"Cool it, Harry," Don said. "If we are going to do this and do it right then we're going to have to carefully plan every detail. It might be necessary for one or more of us to tell our parents a few fibs to get us all free out here."

"I can't believe I'm going along with this," Les said. "It almost sounds like you are proposing a bank heist or something, Don."

"Well, we have to remember that none of us has a driver's license yet," Don said. "That means somebody is going to have to drive us. I think I can handle my dad in that area."

"But one thing we don't need is any of your parents getting nosy and screwing everything up for the rest of us," Harry said. "That means all of you stay tight lipped about it whether you end up coming along or not."

"That's right," Don said. "No talking to anyone else in the troop about it either. The last thing we need is some kind of a rumor going around."

"Yeah," Harry said. "So whether you are in or out you keep our plans secret. Got it?"

The other guys all nodded.

"Don, you and I will work on this over the next several weeks," Les said. "I just hope you guys won't be too disappointed when we don't find any of these treasures you're dreaming about."

"I hope you won't be mad when we're saying 'I told you so'," Don said. He looked over at David. "So you're in, right?"

"Oh yeah," David said, his light blue eyes and a few pimple heads reflecting the campfire light in a way Les found amusing. His dark hair appeared red in the light and somehow caused him to resemble a 1950's ventriloquist's red-haired dummy, with acne for freckles. "I've pretty much got my parents trained to fully trust Les. If he gets to go, I get to go."

"Good," Don said. "Then it's the four of us for sure. You other guys can get in later if you want. But not a word about it to anyone. I'm serious. Scouts' honor."

The conversation changed to other subjects and continued for the next few minutes. Around ten o'clock they began making their last bathroom trips to the woods and then to their respective tents for the night. As planned, David and Les were the last to retire.

"See you cats in the morning," Don said. Les and David gave him several minutes to get settled-in. Then began shoveling dirt onto the remnants of the fire to douse it completely. Once the fire was out the camp site became pitch dark. David led the way to their tent by flashlight.

Once they were in their sleeping bags David and Les talked for a few minutes as they always did before falling asleep. "I was surprised when you said you were in for Don and Harry's burial ground expedition," David said, keeping his voice low so nobody else would hear him. "You were such a Doubting Thomas during the whole discussion that I thought there was no way you'd go along with it."

Les chuckled. "I'll admit I had some major concerns about it at first but then I remembered whose idea it was to begin with. Those two clowns and their harebrained ideas never cease to amaze me. It might be fun to go along if for no other reason than to watch them dig a few holes and find nothing more than some worms."

David thought a moment. "So you don't think they'll find anything?"

"No," Les said. "This is just a silly plan for Don to get out into the woods without any adult supervision and pretend he's his father in Vietnam twenty-years ago. That's all it is."

"I don't know," David said. "It sounds to me like they've done some pretty good planning. They may really be onto something."

Les thought a moment. "Well, you can believe that if you want to and that's okay. I'm mainly coming along to make sure none of you get into real trouble. That, and to satisfy my own curiosity."

"Well, I for one think it's going to be really fun," David said. "Probably better than you think. Just don't do anything to spoil it for the rest of us, okay?"

"Oh, don't worry about me," Les said. "Remember, I'll go on a hiking trip any month of the year. I'll play along with you guys so it goes exactly the way Don and Harry have it planned. Just don't be disappointed if you come home exhausted and empty-handed."

"Oh, I won't." David turned and looked at Les although it was way too dark to see him. "Either way we'll have a good time, right?"

"Right," Les said. "Goodnight."

CHAPTER 2

THE MIDNIGHT RAVE

About an hour later, Les awakened to the sound of a loud engine approaching from somewhere in the distance. After a moment he realized someone was driving on the dirt road toward the clearing and his eyes shot open.

"Somebody's coming," David whispered. They lay silently as the sound grew louder. Soon the approaching vehicle was so close Les could see light on the surrounding trees through the thin nylon mesh of the tent. A moment of panic struck him and he sat up to listen.

Through the sounds of tree frogs and crickets, he could distinguish at least three different vehicles, each emitting enormous vibrations of engine noise and, no doubt, air pollution. They're coming this way, he thought. He quickly got his boots on and crawled out of the tent. David was out right behind him.

"Let's take a closer look," Les said. They walked a short distance up the trail and saw three pick-up trucks, two cars and a motorcycle amble up the dirt road and turn into the clearing. When the bright headlights shined right toward where the two of them were standing, they both ducked instinctively. A few seconds later the engines were turned off and a group of people began piling out. From their voices, it sounded like there were about twenty of them. Some were laughing and others were shouting into the dark wilderness.

"They sound drunk," Les said. "That or crazy, or both."

"How can you tell?" David said.

"Just listen to them."

An instant later someone turned on a radio and the piercing sound of heavy-metal rock music filled the forest. "What's going on?" Steve said from somewhere behind Les.

"Quiet!" David whispered. "We don't want them to hear us."

"Who?" Steve said, his voice a bit lower now.

"Don't know," Les said. "Some sleazy characters are setting up a party in the clearing."

Don and Harry walked up with the others right behind them. The eight of them stood and strained to see what was going on. In the light of one set of headlights they could see several people moving about. They could hear objects being removed from the backs of the trucks and thrown onto the ground.

"They're piling a bunch of stuff in the middle of the clearing," Ken said. "Hey, maybe it's 'dump your garbage in the woods night'." Nobody laughed.

In the faint moonlight a lone figure could be seen pouring liquid onto the heap. He paused to light a match and a moment later a bonfire roared to life. They could now see the group of people and their vehicles very clearly.

All eight scouts immediately ducked down so as not to be seen in the bright firelight. "What have we got here," Ken whispered, "a bunch of gypsies?"

"I wish that's all they were," Les said. "I'd say more like convicts."

"We'd better keep an eye on them, that's for sure," Don said.

"You got your large knife handy?" Les asked him.

"Of course," Don said. He reached down to his thigh and withdrew the foot-long U.S. Army issue knife from its sheath. "Never go into the jungle without it."

"Good," Les said. "Why don't we keep a watch as long as they're here."

"Yeah," Harry agreed. "And the watchmen will keep the knife handy."

"Okay, it's settled," Don said. "Harry, why don't you and David take the first watch." He handed Harry the knife, now back in its sheath. "Billy and I will relieve in an hour or so. Then Les and Ken."

"Works for me," Les said.

"Yeah," Ken said, "and I'll hold the knife." He threw Les a quick grin.

Les glanced over but didn't reply. "I'm going to try to get some more sleep. Wake me if anything happens."

David and Harry took seats against trees on opposite sides of the trail with a clear view of the bonfire. From there, the strange group of visitors was about two-hundred feet away. The others returned to their tents about forty-feet back down the trail.

"Maintain silence," Harry whispered. "As long as we stay quiet we should have no trouble with these freaks."

Les lay in his tent with his eyes open for several minutes, listening to the distant noise and convinced he would never even doze this night. In a short while, however he drifted into a deep sleep. To his later surprise, he wouldn't awaken until Don called his name from just outside the tent when it was his turn to go on watch.

"Les, get up. It's your watch with Ken," he heard Don's loud whisper. "Oh-one-hundred, rise and shine."

"Okay," he said. "Keep your shirt on."

Les got up on his knees to crawl out and almost kicked David, who had come in after his watch and was out cold. Once he got outside, Don motioned him over for a private conversation. Les had never seen Don so serious.

"Listen, there's this one creepy dude that you're really going to have to keep an eye on. I overheard some of the others call him 'Snake'." Don handed Les his knife, then put his hand on his shoulder, pulling him close to be sure Ken couldn't hear him.

"During my entire watch this freak was running his mouth nonstop. Some of the stuff he was saying was really creeping me out."

Les glanced up the dark trail and saw Ken in the faint light stepping gingerly toward their vantage point. "What was the guy saying?"

"I only caught bits and pieces over the music but I think he's some kind of psycho. And he's got this sword in a sheath on his belt. He must have pulled it out ten times in the last hour. Waving it around like he's fencing against an invisible opponent. He was playing with it constantly."

"Maybe he thinks he's a reincarnated Confederate soldier or something," Les said. "Like some of those Civil War reenactment buffs."

"It's a sick obsession whatever it is," Don said. "He even pointed the sword at one of the others like he was going to cut off an ear or something." Don gently tapped the knife Les held in his hand. "Les, he's killed a guy with it!"

Les's eyes grew wide. "Are you sure?"

"That's what he told the others," Don said. "He was bragging about it. I heard him say a guy named Earl cheated him out of some money over a drug deal a year or so ago in Alabama. Snake stabbed him and threw the body in a trash dumpster behind a strip mall. Nobody else said anything for awhile after that. I don't think they doubt him. Neither do I."

Les thought a moment. "Maybe he was just trying to scare the others so they'd never cross him."

"Yeah, maybe," Don said. "But with that much detail in his story I doubt it. Whether he's making it up or not, admitting to murder is pretty serious."

Les again looked up the trail. Although it was pretty dark, he could see Ken looking back at him. "I'd better get up there. I think Ken's getting edgy."

"I didn't mention it to him and I don't think Billy heard what I heard," Don said. "I'm not sure we should tell them all this right now. We don't need anybody getting panicky."

"I agree," Les said. With that he started toward Ken.

Don grabbed his arm. "Hey, first sign of trouble you wake me at once, okay?"

Les patted his shoulder. "You can count on it."

Don went to his tent and Les walked cautiously up to accompany Ken at his outpost on the trail. He glanced at his watch, it was seven minutes past one.

"I don't know about you, man," Ken whispered, "but I'll surely be glad when these hobos leave."

"You and me both pal," he replied as the two of them found seats. Les took a moment to assess the situation. Several of the vehicles and their occupants had left. Only a car, a truck and the motorcycle were still there and the bonfire was down to a small inferno. Music was still blaring from the truck and occasionally voices could be heard shouting over it. Les counted seven people still milling about.

He scanned from person to person in the faint, distant light of the fire. It didn't take long for him to spot the one called Snake. He appeared to be about twenty but could easily be forty. Les's eyes locked-in on the scrawny, tattooed man with long, dark hair wearing long pants, cowboy boots and no shirt.

"Snake," he heard someone shout over the music. The long-haired man turned and looked toward the others.

"Snake", Les whispered.

"Oh hell," Ken said. "Where?"

Les glanced over at Ken who had jumped to his feet and was looking around on the ground in terror. "No, man," he said. "I mean that weird guy over there." He pointed toward the bonfire. "Right there."

"The man looks like a snake, I get it," Ken said as he sat back down. "Very funny."

"That's what someone called him," Les said. "I don't know, maybe it's a nickname or one of his tattoos or something."

"Now how the hell do you figure that?" Ken said. "You psychic or something?"

Les glanced over at him a moment and then looked back toward the bonfire. "Something like that."

The volume of the music faded and Les realized that it was a tape that had been playing. One of the people in the group walked over to the truck's cab and reached inside.

"How long before you guys want to head for home?" one of them said. "It's getting late and it's two hours back."

"We'll go pretty soon," the one called Snake said. "I got what I came for." He patted one of his pant's pockets.

"I wonder what it is he came for," Ken whispered.

"Probably drugs of some kind," Les said. "He looks high as a kite to me."

At that moment a loud sigh came from behind them as one of the scouts rolled over in his sleep. Les and Ken were both startled by its loudness and became even more so when they realized Snake had heard it too. An instant later the blaring music resumed. Les saw Snake yell at the man over by the pickup truck to turn off the music.

Les jumped to his feet, turned toward the tents, put his hands together to project his voice and yelled: "Red Alert! Company's coming!" At that moment the music, the woods, and the world went silent.

He dove to the ground in the middle of the trail and Ken quickly slid over next to him. The two of them watched as the freakish-looking man called Snake stood glaring in their direction. Without taking his eyes away he felt around the ground until he got his hand on his sword. A moment later he began walking slowly toward the woods.

"Oh Hell," Ken said in the faintest whisper, "he's coming this way. What do we do?"

Les placed his finger to his lips to tell Ken to be totally silent. Then he reached down and unsheathed Don's knife.

"Where you going, Snake?" somebody by the fire called out. "You got to lay some cable?" The others laughed.

"Shut-up all of you," Snake said in a deep and powerful voice. He unsheathed the sword and held it up to admire it momentarily. "I heard something."

"Probably just a owl," a drunken woman's voice added.

Snake turned and glared back at the fire, then pointed at her with the sword. "Dint you hear me say shut-up?"

Snake turned and walked a few more paces before stopping again. With a lit cigarette and a quarter-full bottle of Tennessee sour mash in one hand, the sword in the other, Snake stood and stared into the dark woods, listening for human movement like a rabid wolf.

Les could swear Snake was looking him straight in the eye, despite the fact that he was crouching motionlessly in almost total darkness. For several long seconds, neither of them moved. Something about the guy told Les he was probably not unfamiliar with the inside of a jail cell.

"I think Snake's hearing things," a guy by the fire said, and he started toward the cab of the truck. "Things are getting too quiet out here."

Snake turned and pointed the sword. "You touch that stereo before I say and I'll cut off your hand." The guy froze and looked at the others with a puzzled expression. Snake continued to glare at him. "You hear me, Dooley? Do I look like I'm shitting you?"

Dooley held up his hands and ambled back toward the fire. "I'm cool, Snake," he said. "I'm cool."

"Nice fellow," Ken said to Les in a quiet whisper. He was now so close to Les in their prone position that Les thought he could feel the ground vibrating from Ken's heartbeat. "What do we do if he comes over here?"

Les glanced over at him. "We'll have to take him out."

Ken's eyes widened. "You're not serious."

"As a heart attack," Les said. "Wait for my signal then find a large tree limb you can swing like a baseball bat. Find it as fast as you can. If it comes down to him or us, it's going to be him."

"I don't know, Les," Ken said nervously. "I'm not sure I can move."

"Listen to me very carefully," Les whispered. "See that maple tree over there? If I give you the go signal you run over to it and start pulling on limbs until you find one you can pull loose. Then I want you to crack his skull, got it?"

Ken's eyes were firmly on the clearing. Snake continued to stand completely still, staring in their direction. "What are you going to do?"

Les looked Ken in the eye for a long moment. "I've got Don's knife here but it's no match for that sword. If we work together, we can take him down. Remain calm, Ken. Remember, if either one of us fails we both die."

"I'm not sure this is necessary," Ken said.

"I wasn't going to tell you this but Don said he heard this guy bragging earlier about killing someone. I'll bet there's even some reward money on his head. A few thousand dollars maybe. That could do a lot to pay for Wilderness Unlimited if I don't win that scholarship next month."

He continued staring out toward the motionless Snake. "This guy's a serious criminal. I'd love the chance to take him in. Dead or alive."

Ken stared at Les, barely able to make out his face in the dark. "You're just making all this up, aren't you?"

"No," he said, "I'm not. We may find ourselves having to defend ourselves against this psycho freak."

Don and Harry had crawled up on their stomachs and were now just behind the two of them. "I've got a canister of mace in my hand here," Don whispered. "I brought it for defense against bears but it works fine on weirdos too. If he gets within fifteen-feet I'll douse him. Harry and Ken you guys knock the sword loose with a tree branch. Les, cut him if you have to."

"Oh shit," Ken said in a loud whisper. "You guys are serious!"

"You just do your part with the tree branch and shut-up, Ken," Harry said. "We'll do our parts and you do yours, got it?"

Ken paused a moment while the seriousness of the situation continued to sink-in. One look at Les told him he was in agreement. "Yeah," he said at last.

Les sat perfectly still, holding the knife firmly in his right hand while he studied Snake's face as best he could in the faint light. He was holding the sword and pointing it toward the woods, almost as though he was using it as some kind of listening device. The fire crackled loudly and no one spoke. After another moment Snake started looking up at the trees overhead, then back toward his companions standing by the fire.

"Relax guys," Les said. "He's getting bored."

The four of them continued to stare at Snake, now eerily silhouetted against the orange smoke billowing from the ground a dozen feet behind him. He turned and started walking back toward the fire, taking a moment to put the sword back in its sheath.

"Guess I was just hearing things," he said. "Alright Dooley, you can turn the music back on."

"You sure, Snake?" Dooley said.

"Don't make me tell you twice," Snake said. A moment later, the loud, southern rock music resumed, the heavy bass-guitars echoing off the surrounding wall of trees like the heartbeat of a massive animal.

"Man," Ken said. "That was close. I don't want to tangle with that guy. He's insane!"

Don and Harry rose to return to their tent. "You guys keep your eyes peeled," Don told them. "Call me if anything happens. If we have to, we'll cut his throat. We'll take them all out if necessary."

Ken and Les watched the two of them leave and then looked at each other. Neither spoke.

A few minutes later, Ken went and got both their sleeping bags. They spread them out on the ground and laid down on them, watching for more trouble. The watch continued uneventfully. Sometime around three o'clock, someone pulled out a gun and started shooting beer bottles. Les jolted awake from a doze. "Oh great," he whispered, "they've got a gun."

The other scouts emerged from their tents and huddled into a group low to the ground. Out in the clearing, three people were getting into the car and two others into the truck and preparing to leave. "You coming, Snake?" somebody asked.

"In a minute," he said. He was putting the sword in its place next to the saddle bags on the back of his motorcycle. "Got to bleed the lizard first. You guys go on. I'll catch up to you on the interstate."

"Ten-four," one of them said. The engines then started and the two vehicles drove noisily away.

Once the car and truck had disappeared into the dark quiet of the woods, only Snake and his motorcycle remained. Snake again started walking toward the trail at the end of the clearing. Once he reached the edge of the woods he continued walking. The eight huddled scouts remained motionless and watched as Snake came closer and closer.

When Snake got about forty-feet away, he stopped, unzipped his pants and began urinating. The whole time, he looked all around the woods before him. When his eyes fixed on the trail where the eight scouts lay on the ground, he stood staring. He finished his business and zipped-up, continuing to stare directly at them.

"He detects something out of the ordinary," Les whispered. "It's too dark for him to see us but he still somehow knows we're here."

"But that's impossible," Billy whispered. Les thought he sounded terrified.

"Who's out there?" Snake demanded in a loud voice. He walked several more steps toward them and stopped. "Answer me dammit!"

Les crawled over to a large tree and carefully stood up behind it, gripping the knife tightly. He then motioned Don to get over beside him.

"This guy is some kind of predator," Les whispered. "He can't see or hear us and yet he still knows we're here. I've read where serial killers sometimes can operate like that."

"That's so freaking weird!" Don said.

Les peered around the tree and looked Snake squarely in the eyes. He was so close he could hear him breathing. For the first time all night, Les felt himself trembling slightly.

Suddenly, Ken, who had pulled his oversized nightshirt over his head, jumped up and began screaming. The move caught Les completely by surprise, and when he first looked in the direction of Ken's screams, he thought he was seeing a ghost.

David, immediately realizing what Ken was doing, jumped up behind him and turned on his flashlight so it shone through Ken's flailing white shirt. Ken waved his arms frantically and screamed at the top of his lungs, galloping wildly as he hopped down the trail toward Snake.

Les could tell that Snake was momentarily baffled, undecided as to whether or not to fear this strange apparition approaching him from the woods. He thought he could see Snake's hand searching for a weapon in his pocket. There didn't appear to be one. Ken had managed to catch him momentarily unarmed. Still, his sword was on his bike just a short distance away. Play on his fears, he thought.

"Snake," he shouted in an angry, deeply southern voice. "It's me, Earl. I'm back from my shallow grave in the garbage dump good buddy. And your skinny ass is mine!"

A look of utter terror overcame Snake's face and he began taking a few slow steps backward. Hearing the name Earl from a strange voice in the forest stopped him cold. "No way," he said in a weak, quivering voice.

"I'm back from the dead for you, Snake," Les said, this time louder. "It's time for you to come join me and the maggots."

The scouts watched from their hiding places as Snake backed further away from them, instinctively feeling his belt for his sword. Les realized he didn't remember where he had left if. We've got him on the ropes, he thought.

Ken, who was now less than thirty-feet from Snake, jumped up as high as he could and let out a blood-curdling scream. His nightshirt slowly drifted back down over him, descending in a ghostly fashion. David carefully pointed his flashlight through the nightshirt from behind, revealing the parts of it not occupied by his courageous buddy to make it appear as eerie as possible.

"I've come for you Snake," Les shouted again. "Time to die!"

Snake suddenly turned around and bolted for his motorcycle. Ken continued screaming and jumping up and down, hopping toward Snake like an angry ghost dancing at the end of a rope.

Snake took a running leap onto his bike, desperately kicked four or five times to get the motor started, and gunned the engine. The bike jumped out from under him and Snake landed on his behind. He jumped up, ran over to the bike, climbed onto it again and roared out of the clearing, narrowly escaping a crash into a grove of trees. In only a matter of seconds the bike motor could be heard no more.

There was a moment of silence to allow the eight of them to digest what had just happened, then they burst out laughing. "Did you see how close he came to crashing into those trees?" Billy said. "That was classic."

The sense of relief Les felt was nothing short of euphoric. "You took an awful chance doing that," he told Ken, shaking his hand. "Absolutely brilliant. You sir are our hero."

Ken laughed and started a round of high-fives. "I couldn't let you kill him, Les. That would have messed up your whole life."

Those words shook Les back to reality. It had never occurred to him.

"That was really risky, Ken," David said. "What made you so sure it would work?"

"He was all alone," Ken said. "Without his friends around I figured his red neck would turn yellow."

"Luckily for all of us you were right," Steve said.

"Hell," Don said, "I was right behind you with Harry's hatchet. The only life you just saved was that freak's."

"Well he's gone now," Les said. "Let's hit the sack." With that, they all returned to their tents.

The next morning, just before getting back on the trail, they strolled over to the clearing to examine what easily could have become a crime scene. Empty beer and liquor bottles were scattered everywhere, as well as plenty of other trash. Don looked at his watch. "We've got to meet Mr. Thomas and the guys in about four hours. We'd better get going."

"Just one more thing," Les said. "Let's not tell Mr. Thomas or anyone else about any of this. If anybody asks, the evening passed uneventfully."

"What are you talking about?" Billy protested. "We've got some serious bragging rights here. Let's ride it for all it's worth."

"Are you crazy," Harry shot back. "If Mr. Thomas or any of our parents hears about this we won't get to go hiking unchaperoned again until we're forty."

"That's right," Don said. "You'll shoot our planned Indian relic trip right out of the water. This is a secret we'll all take with us to our graves. Scouts' honor. Everybody with me?" The other guys all nodded.

They loaded on their backpacks and started walking up the trail. For the next two hours hardly anyone spoke.

At a few minutes past noon the eight of them arrived at the small parking lot where the highway met the trail to Springer mountain. They found a shady spot to sit down and relaxed while they waited. For each, it was a good chance to rehydrate. About thirty minutes later Scoutmaster Thomas and the rest of the scout troop emerged from the hiking trail and joined them.

That night, now part of a group of twenty that included three adult scout leaders, they were finishing dinner and sitting around a big camp fire. The guys were all talking and laughing, creating plenty of noise amongst the usual quiet of the deep north Georgia woods.

Les had been sitting between David and Ken as they ate the evening meal of Mr. Thomas' special camp chili. David got up to get some more water and Ken leaned over to say something to Les.

"Don't hurry off to sleep tonight," Ken told him. "There's a big rock we can sit on about fifty-yards up that trail over there. I need to talk to you alone."

Les looked at him with a curious expression. "What's on your mind?"

"Last night," Ken said. "It's been bugging me all day."

"I thought we weren't going to talk about that again," Les said. "I didn't get much sleep after all that and I'm ready to hit the hay."

"I heard you yell at that Snake guy when I was running at him," Ken said. "My little trick wasn't working until you piped-in. What I want to know is: who's Earl?"

Les looked at him a moment and sighed. "You're not going to let me off easy on this are you?"

Ken nodded his head. "I've got to live with this too. And I really need to spend some time talking with you about it."

"Sure, whatever," he replied.

An hour or so later everyone was in their tents. Les whispered to David that he was going out to use the bathroom and David didn't reply. Hopefully he's asleep, he thought. He climbed out of the tent, zipped the flap closed quietly and headed up the trail. Ken was sitting on a large rock on the left side of the trail that overlooked a small valley. Les walked up and sat down.

Les told him what Don had overheard and what the two of them had discussed privately. The whole story took about three minutes. "I just went with my gut," Les concluded. "Luckily everything worked out fine."

"Looking back I don't know what came over me," Ken said. "I guess I was just ready to end the ordeal and that seemed like a way to do it that we all would find amusing."

"Thankfully it worked," Les said. "That guy could have shot you. He wanted to shoot you. What were you thinking?"

"Snake wasn't the one with the gun," Ken said. "The people in the car had the gun. When they left, it went with them."

"You sure about that?" Les couldn't remember anything about who had the gun. Then again, he was asleep when they first started using it.

Ken paused a moment to chuckle. "Oh, I'm positive. There's no way in hell I would have charged that guy if he'd had the gun. And he had already put the sword away on the bike. I knew he was unarmed."

"He could have had a knife on him," Les said. "Did you consider that?"

"Yes," Ken said. "It was a calculated risk I felt I had to take."

Les rolled his eyes. "Luckily, you gambled and won. But I don't advise taking risks like that in the future."

"I realized you were serious when you said you were willing to kill him if necessary," Ken said. "That was the risk I wasn't willing to take. That ordeal had to end right then and there. I honestly believe I did the right thing."

Les took a moment to ponder what he was saying. "I have to admit you've got a point there. Especially since your plan worked like it did."

"I couldn't believe the drastic measures you and Don were considering," Ken said. "You two white boys were a heartbeat away from doing something that would have affected you the rest of your lives. All of our lives. Whether we got away with it or not it would have haunted me the rest of my days. I didn't want that. I don't think you did either."

"Believe me, I didn't want to get violent with the guy either," Les said. "I just knew it was a possibility that we might have to kill him if he pushed us. I was just preparing myself and everyone else for the worst-case scenario. I've never had thoughts like those before. Thank heaven they didn't become a reality."

"An ice-cold reality," Ken said. "And I think Don actually wanted to kill him. Unlike you, he's a loose cannon waiting to go off. We'd better keep an eye on that guy."

"Is something up between you and Don?"

"Nothing in particular," Ken said. "He and I have barely had conversation since I first joined the scout troop earlier this year. It's mostly a gut feeling I get from him. But he and Harry were the only ones in the group that didn't high-five me at the end last night. I found that a bit odd."

They sat silently for a few moments. The cacophony of crickets and tree frogs surrounded them with a curtain of pulsating noise that at times was almost deafening. Les liked the way it drowned-out their voices long before they could be heard back at the camp behind them.

Les had also noticed some changes in Don's personality over the last year or so, but he attributed most of it to simply going through the teen years. Then again, Ken may be seeing something that he himself wasn't. Ken had plenty of wisdom, Les had to give him that.

"There are plenty of white guys like Don around," Ken said as he stared at the meadow at the bottom of the valley that lay some thirty vertical feet downhill below the rock on which they sat. The moon was right overhead now, and the tips of the high-grass were blowing gently in the evening breeze, creating a sea-like surface that resembled a neon-green lake.

"They're people without dreams."

"Now what in the world does that mean?" Les said.

"Dr. King used to talk about dreams. You remember Dr. King?"

"Of course," Les said. "He delivered that speech beside the reflecting pool in Washington, D.C. about twenty-years ago." He looked over at Ken and remembered some of the history from school that had really caught his eye when he read it. "I got an 'A' on a paper I wrote about that speech."

The two of them sat quietly for a moment. "Have you ever read that speech?" Les said. "I mean sat down and read every word?"

Ken thought a minute. "No, not every word. I've seen it on film though."

"A great speech," Les said. "I get plenty of inspiration from it."

Ken looked over at him with an amused smile.

Les looked back at him and smiled too. "Yes, it's possible for a white guy to do that. Anyone with common sense, regardless of their color, would too. He was speaking to all Americans. I certainly felt like he was speaking to me. I have a dream too."

"What's your dream?"

"I want to climb Mount Everest."

"What?" Ken said, a little careless with his volume.

"Keep it down," Les said softly. "Yeah, I want to climb Mount Everest one day. Then I want to climb one even harder, its next-door-neighbor, K2."

Ken laughed. "That's cool, man," he said. "We all have our dreams."

Les patted his shoulder. "Thanks, Ken."

Ken looked over at him. "That's what buddies are for. I sure hope you win that Wilderness Unlimited award. That will make all that we went through last night worth it."

"Me too," Les said. "I've got my hopes too high and keep telling myself that I probably won't win. Another worst-case scenario I'm trying to prepare myself for."

"You don't give yourself enough credit," Ken said. "It's in the bag." The two of them got to their feet to return to camp and their respective tents.

"I'll say 'good night' here," Les said. "Total silence from this point. We don't want to wake anybody."

When Les got to his tent he found David still asleep. It appeared that nobody else in camp was aware he and Ken had been missing.

The only significant event to occur during the remaining three days of the camping trip came on the final night as the entire troop sat around the campfire. As usual, Mr. Thomas gave them a brief speech as they finished eating the evening meal. Les always liked hearing what his scout master had to say and also appreciated the way he always referred to them as "men". Never "young men" or "guys" but always "men". It meant a lot more hearing it from him than when Don said it.

Mr. Thomas was in his early fifties, balding, and a little chubby, with a broad grin and glasses that were tinted yellow just a little. He had a deep, bellowing voice but usually spoke softly once he had everyone's attention as they wrapped-up dinner. He always wore his uniform neatly too. Every minute of every day that he was outside his tent his uniform was perfect. Les really respected that.

"Just a quick note to congratulate all you men for another successful hike with no injuries or fatalities," he said.

Several of the guys laughed as they always did since they had never had anything close to a fatality, although no trip went by without his mentioning it. Les had noticed before and was noticing now that Mr. Thomas got a brief look of anger on his face as he looked around at the snickering fellows.

"Question, Mr. Thomas," Les said.

"What is it Les?" Mr. Thomas liked Les a lot and always smiled when he spoke to him.

"I'm just curious about your last comment. Have you ever had a hike where someone died?"

There was total silence at that moment, even from the campfire. Mr. Thomas stood looking at him for a long moment. "You know Leslie," he said at last, "I've been waiting a long time for one of you to ask me that."

The boys all watched him as he walked slowly to the wood pile and gathered a few small sticks to throw, one by one, into the fire. This was one of the subtle things he did when he was about to tell them a story.

"I've been lucky enough throughout my scouting career that such a tragedy hasn't happened to me or any of my comrades," he said. "But it's something we all have to keep in the backs of our minds because it can happen at any time, not just out here but everywhere else our travels take us.

"But actually Les, the answer to your question is 'yes'." He paused a moment, tossing more sticks into the fire.

"I had a teacher in high school that liked to spend the summers in the Rocky Mountains," Mr. Thomas continued. "Mr. Traschel was his name. He taught English Lit and Phys Ed. He was by far the most liked teacher at the school.

"I read in the local paper just a few years ago that he was killed by a 20-year-old kid who got high on acid and decided to go hunting. A hiker came along the trail and saw the kid cleaning and gutting him like a deer. The kid got 25 years in prison but nothing will ever bring Mr. Traschel back." He paused as he looked around the campfire. "Not a day goes by that I don't think about it."

Les sat staring at Mr. Thomas. "Wow, I never saw that coming."

"That's just it Les. We so seldom do."

Ken leaned over from his right. "Some dangerous people out in these woods," he said.

Les nodded thoughtfully.

"That's why I always congratulate you men on the last night of every trip we make," Mr. Thomas said. "Hopefully, that will never change. The woods are very dangerous and always will be. Never take anything for granted. Help is a long way away when you're out here. You always have to be thinking, even when you are asleep."

"You didn't tell him about what happened to us the other night, did you?" Ken whispered to Les.

"Of course not," Les whispered back. "Why would you even ask?"

"Because he almost sounds like he knows about it."

"He doesn't know about it," Les said. "He just gives a speech like this on every trip. After you've been with us awhile longer you'll get used to it."

The conversation around the fire gradually relaxed and a couple of hours later they were all asleep. The following morning they broke camp and returned home.

The only odd thing Les noticed about the trip home was that for some reason, Don and Harry rode in the other van, not in the one with Ken, David and himself. He dismissed the thought and they were soon back at scout headquarters, which was the parking lot of a Presbyterian church about a mile from the high school.

CHAPTER 3

SCOUTING: ADVENTURES FOR LIFE

Les first became a Cub Scout when he was in the second grade. From the start he demonstrated great talent for leadership and teamwork. He won his district's "Pinewood Derby" model car championship just six weeks after joining. The following week he was elected den leader, a post he held through various Scout troops until joining the Boy Scouts when he was a seventh grader.

Now, four years later, he was positioned to take the leadership role in the troop once Don and Harry left after their senior year of high school in the spring. This was a mostly honorary post he and David would share. However, since Les had started scouting a year earlier than David, he would officially be the leader of the pack. The two of them had discussed the issue from time to time but neither really gave the matter much importance.

Since its announcement in early January the Wilderness Unlimited contest had been the talk of the entire north Georgia scouting district. The competition was open to Boy Scouts all over the country and offered a once-in-a-lifetime opportunity. Two scouts from each state would win an all-expenses-paid trip to the camp in the Sierra-Nevada mountains of eastern California. The two-week event was open to boys thirteen to seventeen years of age and promised the finest hands-on survival training available outside the U.S. Army.

Although the contest itself held a great deal of interest for virtually every one of the guys Les knew, most of them seemed to realize that qualifying to win would require more merit badges and accomplishments than many of them could muster. Most lost interest as they read the long list of submission requirements and realized that they just couldn't qualify.

Les had more than just a passing interest in winning the contest. He had asked his mother two years earlier if she would send him to a Wilderness Unlimited camp. She told him that she would if she could but, since she was a single parent, she couldn't afford the $2500 price.

When Les heard about the scholarship program, he immediately began his campaign to be the scout chosen by his district to compete for one of Georgia's two spots. He already had acquired every merit badge that had ever been within his reach and met or exceeded virtually all of the contest's requirements. All of this had come before he even knew the contest existed. His mother told him as she read one of the promotional flyers that she felt the contest was designed for scouts just like him. "It's time to take things to the next level, Les," she said. "Go above and beyond and you can win this thing!"

Over the next several months Les dedicated himself fully to winning the campaign. He began contributing written submissions for publication in various Scouting newsletters and even created one of his own. He spent countless hours researching topics about which to write and then carefully typed up his stories.

Scoutmaster Thomas copied and distributed his newsletters to scout groups all over Atlanta as well as some neighboring towns. This vastly increased his reputation as an exceptional Boy Scout.

He wrote articles about many topics including emergency trail food sources, how to prepare creek water to make it safe to drink, how to tell a poisonous snake from a safe one, and how to build an emergency shelter in a dark forest. He also crammed as much emergency medical knowledge into his head as he could find.

As the contest submission deadline reached its final two months, Les tried to think of any other way to increase his visibility in the local scouting community. One night he had a sudden idea to create a comic book serial, something he had always wanted to see in a scouting magazine.

He started that very night and within a week had four episodes written about a fictional scout named Duke and his dog Bo who trekked the virgin forests of pioneer America. Duke and Bo dealt with one survival crisis after another in the 1850's Midwestern American forests using crude tools to build shelters and foraging for their food.

One story had the two of them hiding from hostile Indians and avoiding freezing to death in a blinding snowstorm. Another had Duke and Bo struggling for survival on a log-raft in a raging river. Those two pieces appeared in a national scouting magazine and Les quickly became well-known.

He studied hard to make good grades in school and did volunteer work at his church and in the community, all of which was included in his various submission letters for candidacy. Finally, at the quarterly recognition dinner in March, it was announced that Les had won the title of "North Georgia Boy Scout of the Year."

The District office of the Georgia Boy Scouts submitted his name as their lone representative for the scholarship along with piles of documentation of his accomplishments. At a scout banquet a month later they all learned that he had won.

Just one week after getting home from the camping trip that had started with Don and Harry's Indian burial ground announcement, Mr. Thomas gave the crowd the good news. "This is an incredibly proud moment for me," the Scoutmaster said. "Les Harrison, please come forward."

Les stood and approached the stage of the church's Fellowship Hall, pretending not to know what was happening.

"Les, and ladies and gentlemen, we heard from the National Wilderness Unlimited headquarters earlier today," Scoutmaster Thomas said. Les looked his mom in the eye and she gave him a smile and a wink.

"You're going to the Sierra-Nevada, Les!" the Scoutmaster said. "You've won the scholarship!"

Amidst applause and cheers from his fellow scouts and all the other troops present, Les stepped to the microphone and gave a brief speech he had prepared just in case this happened. When he took a moment to thank everyone that had helped him, most notably his mother, he noticed her crying just a little. After his speech the one-hundred or so scouts and their families gave him a standing ovation. It was a night he'd remember the rest of his life.

"I knew you were going to win all along!" an elated David exclaimed as he shook Les's hand when he rejoined them at their table. "You sir are the North Georgia Scout of all time."

"Yeah, Les," Ken said, giving him a quick, hard hug. "You're a Hall-of-Famer!"

"Thanks so much guys," Les said as he shook dozens and dozens of hands. "It's a great honor. I'm truly blessed!"

One month later in late July, Les flew to Reno, Nevada to meet up with some four-hundred other scouts and leaders for a two-week wilderness experience in the Sierra mountains that would change him forever. At a remote, high altitude site in eastern California, Les would truly begin to grow into the man he would become.

Wilderness Unlimited was a local California mountaineering, white water, and remote training outfitter, made up mostly of current and former western ski resort workers who were looking for ways to make cash during the summer months. There were numerous similar operators throughout the American and Canadian west, but this particular outfitter catered to the high-end, dedicated, eco-tourist. They charged big money, and used the latest equipment and most efficient techniques available. Les was truly delighted that a scholarship existed for such a fine experience.

Each day started with reveille at 0600, followed by a hearty breakfast and then two hours of meetings. Les and the crowd of other scouts would sit on the ground or on tree stumps or rocks, listening to the teachers that lectured on everything scouting. Then they would venture out into the wilderness for various instructional activities, each more fun than the last.

As the days went by the intensity and level of instruction increased. By mid-week, Les and the other young men had met war veterans, Army infantrymen, and a Navy Seal. One day they were introduced to an Air Force Captain who had survived a week-long ordeal alone on the run in Vietnam. After being shot-down, the airman had avoided capture and survived off the land before being rescued by some frogmen at the mouth of the Mekong river.

On another day two Texas Rangers lectured them on tracking techniques used on elusive human and drug-smugglers along the Mexican border. They then got hands-on training sliding down ropes to the ground from several stories high in a redwood tree.

On Saturday two soldiers jumped from a plane into the large meadow in the middle of camp to begin their lectures about the paratroopers. The campers stood watching in utter astonishment.

The quality and level of the instruction was amazing. Each passing day brought more surprises and new activities. Les was having a better time than he had ever imagined possible. He frequently wished to himself that this adventure would never have to end.

Sometimes during a morning lecture his thoughts would wander as he gazed skyward into the magnificent canopy of towering redwood trees and firs, some of which produced cones the size of footballs. Countless native Americans had hunted these woods over the centuries, he thought. At times he felt he was amongst them, their spirits and his at one with the rocky cliffs and rushing streams, the eagles and condors that soared so majestically above them. The magnificent scenery that surrounded him was as timeless as it was beautiful.

Just a few miles away from where he sat lay Donner Pass, the infamous site of the snow-bound pioneer wagon train disaster of the mid-1800s. The tragedy had ended in cannibalism. What a harsh climate, he thought. A place where a snowstorm in April can paralyze a whole community of people and slowly snuff them out completely. These woods are dangerous, he thought. And they must be respected every minute you are in them.

The instruction continued every morning and was followed by lunch and an afternoon of various activities. In the second week, after every scout had experienced each of the activities offered at least once, they were given a daily choice of how to spend the afternoon. Les quickly learned that he had a passion for white water.

He mentally became his storybook character Duke as he learned to cut logs and build rafts using tree bark for twine. He practiced starting camp fires with wet wood and how to get safe drinking water from the streams. He even learned how to catch crawfish and minnows with his bare hands, then putting them to use as bait for brook trout. He went to sleep each night amazed at how much he could learn in just one day.

The first ten days at Wilderness Unlimited were spent learning to live off the land and survive in the wild. The last three days of the camp were spent demonstrating what they had learned under test conditions.

Each boy was weighed before the test began. Then, they were sent into the wilderness with a hunting knife, a canteen, a sleeping bag, a flint and a compass. Some of the boys chose to stay in small groups but Les opted to go it alone.

Shortly before sunset on the first day, Les reached a remote pond in the woods and set up a campsite on its banks. He gathered some berries and firewood, built a fire and slept on the ground.

At first light the next morning he got up and initiated a deer hunt. First, he cut down a straight tree limb, whittled the end to a sharp point and fashioned a crude spear.

He then walked the pond's shoreline for an hour, gathering the freshest and most pungent flowers he could find. Once he had a nice bouquet, he tied them into a bundle and placed them at the water's edge. Then he climbed into a tree above the spot and hid amongst the canopy of leaves. He got seated as comfortably as possible in the tree, then sat listening to his growling stomach.

Two hours later a large deer strolled slowly out of the woods and drank from the pond about forty-feet away. He then turned and noticed the flowers. It took about eight long minutes for the stag to finally get in range for Les to take his shot. As quietly as possible he lifted the spear and then fired it straight down. It was a clean hit.

He jumped down from the tree and used his knife to finish the deer. He then gutted and cleaned it, and roasted it over a fire. For the next two days he ate deer steaks and read a book. When the wilderness trek ended, he emerged from the woods weighing ten pounds more than when he went in. Just for show, he even brought the antlers out with him.

At the weighing session, Les ended up being the only scout in camp who had actually gained weight during the ordeal. This won him the National Wilderness Unlimited merit badge. Upon his return home, his troop honored him at a special banquet just for him and his picture and story ran in the local newspaper. People were still talking about it in late August when Les arrived for his first day as a junior in high-school.

"Hey Les," David said as he walked up to him in the hallway. Les was trying out the combination to his new locker. "You missed a great hike over the weekend. Where were you?"

"My mom always takes me down to her sister's farm in central Georgia the week before I start back to school," Les said. "I spent most of the time fishing in their private lake. Did you guys have a good time?"

"Yeah," David said. "There's a new kid in the troop named Tommy. He took your place in my tent. He's a pretty good guy for an eighth-grader."

"Not good enough to take my place in the tent permanently, I hope."

David chuckled. "Don't be an idiot. Anyway, Don and Harry have put the planning of our big hike into full gear. We're aiming for the first weekend in October."

Les thought a moment. "Oh, you mean the trek to the Indian camps? Are they still on that kick?"

David smiled and Les noticed a gleam in his eyes. "Oh yeah, big time. Don's got it all set-up with his old man's company van. We'll get dropped off Friday afternoon and picked up on Sunday."

"What about those other guys?" Les said. "Can any of them make it?"

"No. Steve, Billy and Mark can't make it. Tommy's coming though. Looks like it will be just five of us."

"What about Ken?" Les said. "I know he said he was doubtful, but why don't we see if he's changed his mind."

David frowned and quickly looked around to make sure Ken wasn't nearby. "Not a good idea."

"Why not? I could talk to his parents for him. Maybe they'd let him come along."

"That's not the issue," David said. "Don and Harry both have been pretty cool towards him lately. I think they felt he took away some of their thunder with that dancing ghost routine he did to get rid of that Snake guy that night. And Ken's smart comments around the camp fire didn't help his cause much either."

Les tossed his English book into his locker and closed it. "Those two can be such jerks!"

"I know, I know," David said. He took a moment to study Les's facial expression. "Look, I'm not any happier about their attitude toward Ken than you are, but I really do want to go on this hike. And since Don is the one making all the arrangements, we pretty much have to do it his way."

"Yeah, I know," Les said disgustedly.

"I don't think Ken's available anyway," David said. "He told me his parents would nix it so he's not even going to ask their permission. So it'll work out for all of us."

At that moment the one-minute warning bell rang. "We'd better get to class," David said. "I'll tell Don you're in. He'll give us more details as the date nears."

"Okay," Les said. "See you later."

At lunchtime Les spotted David sitting in the school cafeteria with Harry and Don. As usual, there was an empty seat waiting for him. "Hey guys," Les said as he sat down.

"Les, this is Tommy," David said, introducing him to the kid sitting to David's right.

"Nice to meet you," Les said shaking his hand.

"Hey Les," Tommy said. "Congrats on the Wilderness Unlimited merit award. That's really awesome!"

Les smiled sheepishly. "Thanks."

Tommy was a small fellow, only about five feet tall. Les figured he couldn't weigh more than 75 pounds. His short black hair was combed back and held in place by some sort of hair gel. It made his whole presence come off as a nerd. It was obvious he was thrilled to be spending time with some upper-classmen.

As they sat eating, Les noticed that Don and Harry didn't seem too interested in conversation with this newest member of the scout troop. The two of them were busy trying to talk to the four girls at the next table and getting nowhere.

Something Don said to one of them made David laugh. "You think those two will ever get girlfriends?"

Les nodded with a smile. "I doubt it, but who knows. Sometimes persistence pays."

David grinned. "I'm saving myself for college."

Les looked at him and laughed. "Yeah, so am I."

"Hey Don," David said. "Tell Les the latest on the camping trip."

Don and Harry turned back toward them and Don got an excited tone in his voice. "Okay, here's the deal. I'm going to get my dad to drive us up near Woody Gap and drop us off Friday after school. I figure we'll have about an hour of daylight left to hike when we get there. That will get us a good ways up the trail before we have to stop and set-up camp."

"Let's do it this weekend," Tommy chimed in.

"Forget it," Harry said. "Don's dad can't take us until next month. Besides, it'll be cooler then and the underbrush will be thinner."

"Woody Gap," Les said. "Is that close to the burial ground?"

"Would you mind keeping your voice down?" Don said, looking around nervously. "I'd like to keep this out of the media if possible."

Les looked over at David and laughed. "Oh, okay Don," he said a little quieter and with feigned seriousness. "I didn't realize this was a top secret mission."

"I've done months of planning on this hike all the way down to the finest detail," Don said. "And one of those details is complete secrecy." He looked over at Tommy. "And that goes double for you, twerp."

Tommy was about to take a bite of his pizza slice and looked over at Don with a hurt expression. "Hey, what did I do?"

"I know your mom and my mom are big buddies," Don said. "But I'll bounce you out of this unit in a heartbeat if you start screwing up."

"What are you guys talking about?" Les said.

"Don's mother suggested to him that he invite Tommy to come along with us on our hike," Harry said. "After some lengthy discussion between the two of them, some of it rather heated at times, they decided together that little Tommy needs nice older boys like us to influence him in manly things like scouting and keeping off drugs."

"Oh, I get it," Les said, carefully wording his response since Tommy was hearing every word that was being said. "He's your insurance policy against an abrupt cancellation."

"That's not the situation at all," Don shot back. "My mother doesn't tell me what to do." Neither Harry nor Les could tell if what he was saying was genuine or not but both chose to end the discussion at that point.

Don reached over and put his arm around Tommy's shoulder, giving him a gentle shake and patting his back a couple of times. "No, Tommy here is my mom's sweet little nephew. Not the family kind of nephew however."

Harry's seedy grin made its way again to his round face. "More like the pain-in-the-ass kind." He and Don both laughed.

"Hey guys," Tommy said. "If you don't want me coming along then just say so."

"But we do want you along Tommy," Don said in his most gentle voice. "You just do everything we tell you and we all will have a peachy time. Won't we guys?" Everyone else at the table nodded in agreement.

Les looked over at David and saw him suppressing a laugh. Something about that made him a bit leery but he quickly dismissed it. "So, Don, why don't you bring the map to school with you tomorrow. Then we can all take a look at it."

Don looked around momentarily. "Can't do it. It's too risky to bring it to school. We'll all take a look at it when we get to the campsite on Friday night. Not before."

"Why not?" David said. "You afraid you'll lose it?"

Don gave him a quick glance. "Yeah, to the wrong hands. Some teacher could confiscate it or it could get damaged in my book bag. There's no reason to show you guys the map until we are on that trail."

"Yeah," Harry agreed. "We know where we're going. You guys just need to trust us."

"Go ahead and mark your calendars for the first weekend in October," Don said. "We'll fill you in on details as the time nears. And in the meantime, not a word about our plans to anyone. We've come too far in this to screw it up now. Everybody okay with that?" They each mumbled in the affirmative.

"And do me a favor, Tommy," Don said. "Limit what you say about all of this to your mother. We're just going on a simple little camping trip. We're not going to be doing anything dangerous or risky, okay?"

"Oh sure, Don," he said. "She knows how much I'm looking forward to going with you guys. She's cool with it."

"Good. Let's keep it that way." Don smiled and took a bite of his hamburger. Harry turned and said something raunchy to a girl at the next table. She responded with a sneer and stuck out her tongue at him. They all laughed and lunch returned to its usual routine.

CHAPTER 4

THE SEARCH FOR THE RED MANS LAIR

On Friday afternoon at just before four o'clock, David and Les were waiting with their loaded backpacks in David's driveway when the van pulled up. Don, Harry and Tommy were already aboard.

An hour-and-a-half later the van pulled over to the side of the two-lane highway and the five boys got out. As they donned their backpacks, Don's father gave them the expected lecture about being careful. "Find a pay phone and call me if you need to come home before Sunday."

The other four of them moved away from the van and began preparing to hike while Don finished placating his father's concerns. "That won't happen, Pop," Don told him through the open window. "We'll be fine. Be careful driving home."

Les was bending down securing the zippers on his pack when he heard David chuckle. "That Don sure can lay it on thick," he said.

Les glanced up and smiled. "It's that charm that makes him such a good leader of the pack."

David gave a surprised look before realizing that Les was kidding. "Oh yeah. He's my hero."

At that moment the van pulled back onto the highway and drove away. The five of them stood and watched it disappear down the mountain road. Once it was gone and the quiet of the surrounding forest enveloped them, Don let out a sigh of relief.

"Ah," he said, "the sweet smell of freedom. I want to take it all in for a moment."

"Well make it quick, dude," Harry said. "We've got some tracks to make."

Don smiled. "Hey, the hard part just ended. I knew my old man would make it difficult right up to the last minute but all the negotiating I've been doing has paid off." He patted the map in one of the side pockets on his backpack. "This is going to be the best hike ever."

"Can we get moving now?" Les said. "We don't have a lot of daylight left."

"Doesn't matter," Don said, taking a quick look at his compass. "Okay men, let's move out." He started down the trail and the others fell in line behind him.

Les nodded to Tommy to go ahead of him as he took his place at the rear. He looked around as he walked and admired the surrounding mountain countryside. It was a beautiful early fall afternoon. The trees were just starting to turn and the temperature was in the upper-sixties.

For the next hour there wasn't much conversation as each young man seemed to be in his own mental state of solitude. Don led the way with Harry right behind. Tommy followed along behind David and periodically looked around at Les. "I'm still here," Les would say each time he did.

At around six o'clock, with a glorious red sky forming under the sun that would set in less than an hour, Don stopped and pointed to a small trail that led into the woods to the right. "That looks like a good spot to camp," he said.

The others agreed and dropped their packs. In only a few minutes, all three pup tents were up and the evening firewood was being gathered. "Harry and I will cook dinner tonight if you guys will handle it tomorrow night," Don said.

"Okay with me," David said. "Do we need more wood?"

"You can never have too much firewood," Harry said. He reached into his pack and pulled out three packets of freeze-dried beef stew while Don got out his camp stove.

The last remnants of sunlight dropped from the horizon as Tommy, David and Les made several trips into the forest for wood. Les then got a small flame going and the others began adding twigs. In a few minutes they had a bright, warming camp fire.

"Supper's ready," Harry said a few minutes later. He began spooning out the stew, serving Don first. "You go ahead since you have the big speech." He and Don both laughed.

"Thanks, Harry," he said. He looked around at the other three. "Get ready to hear about what a great weekend I've got planned for you guys."

Tommy was next in the chow line. "I'm ready to hear it, Don. Man, I'm so ready for this!"

"Not so fast Tommy," David said with a laugh. "You haven't tasted Harry's cooking yet."

"I mean about the weekend," Tommy said with a big smile.

Les laughed. "He knew that. He's just messing with you."

They sat and ate in silence as the crackling fire warmed them from the encroaching evening coolness. When Don finished he got up from his seat by the fire and walked over to his pack. The others watched as he carefully pulled out the tattered yellow map.

"That your grandpa's map?" Tommy asked.

"Where did he get it, his grandpa?" Les said.

"That's actually a possibility Les," Don said as he carefully unfolded it and spread it on the ground. "I think you will be quite pleased when you see this thing. Grab your flashlights and step over here."

As they gathered around and shined their lights, Don squatted down and pointed to the lower left corner. "There it is, 'Indian Burial Ground'. And we're approximately right here." He pointed to a curve in the trail about two-inches from the burial ground on the map.

"We're only a couple of hours away at the most. If we head out first thing in the morning we should be there by nine-thirty or ten. Then we can spend the entire day and camp there tomorrow night. That way we'll have time to find all sorts of things."

"Man," Tommy said, "that's really neat! Cool idea, Don!"

"Yes it is my friend."

"Let me see that," Les said. He leaned forward and stared at Don's map for several long seconds. "That spot is actually outside the boundary of the National Forest. You guys know we aren't supposed to go there. It's considered trespassing."

Don looked at Harry a moment and sneered. "Don't be a party-pooper, Les. Where's that old sense of adventure of yours?"

"Yeah, Les," Harry said. "Try not reading the map too closely. We don't want you straining your eyes."

"I'm not trying to spoil anybody's good time here," Les said. "But what you guys are suggesting is illegal and risky. If we run up against some zealous land-owner we might get shot at."

"We're not going to get shot at because nobody's going to even know we're in there," Don said as he glanced over at Tommy. "You're talking nonsense, and besides you're scaring the boy."

"Yeah, Les," Harry said. "I think you've been attending too many of Mr. Thomas's scare speeches. You're getting paranoid."

Les glanced over at David and Tommy and could tell by their facial expressions he was going to get no support from them. They were hooked on the idea of going to that burial ground. Deep down, so was he.

"I've never been in an Indian burial ground before," Tommy said. "I'll bet it's pretty cool."

David looked over at Les and tried to read his thoughts. He felt a little more convincing wouldn't hurt. "I think if we're careful we'll be okay," he said. "The nearest road is miles and miles away. There won't be anybody else anywhere around. Besides, it's not like we're going to hurt anybody."

"That's right, David", Don said. "This is a chance to get a real-life history lesson. Sure beats learning about it in a classroom."

"I'm just saying we need to plan our steps carefully," Les said. "Trespassing is risky business, especially for me with that boy scout of the year award still fresh in everybody's mind." His argument against the plan was losing its appeal, even to himself.

"Just like I told my old man, I never do anything without being careful," Don said. "But since I found this old map in my grandfather's attic last summer I've been counting the days until I get a chance to go to that burial ground. Tomorrow is that day. You guys can stay out if you want but I'm going in."

"So am I," Harry said. "I've been waiting all summer for this too."

"I'm in too," Tommy said. "This is going to be fun."

They all looked over at David who gave Les a brief glance before replying. "I'm with you guys," he said at last. "What do you say, Les?"

"Alright," Les said. "Despite my reservations, I'm in too."

"Great," Don said. "It's quite a hike so we'd better get some shut-eye. I've got my alarm watch set for 0600. I'll wake you up then."

Les made a quick trip to the stream to brush his teeth before heading to the tent. He found David already bundled-up in his sleeping bag when he got back.

"You don't think there's really any danger of someone shooting at us, do you?" David asked him. "I mean we are in the middle of nowhere out here. I don't even remember seeing another hiker today."

Les was rolling-out his sleeping bag and stopped and thought a moment. "I don't think we'll have any problems really," he said. "But then again, there's something that kind of bugs me about this whole thing. I can't put my finger on it but it's a little more serious than I was expecting."

He unzipped the sleeping bag and crawled into it. Then he turned-off his flashlight and set it down next to his pillow where he could easily find it again. "Don has really put a lot of thought into this and pulled-off an amazing number of successful steps to actually make it happen. That's a big accomplishment for him. And frankly, it's a little scary."

The two of them lay still in the total dark for a moment before David broke the silence. "Is it really scary for you?"

"I have to be extra careful about everything I do these days. If someone sees me somewhere I shouldn't be and recognizes me then it could be quite embarrassing."

"I guess fame has it's drawbacks," David said with a chuckle.

Les smiled. "Yeah, I guess it does. Good night."

Nobody stirred until they heard Don's voice at six o'clock sharp. "Alright troops," he called out. "Time to get up and move 'em out. This is the day we've been waiting for."

Les sat up and reached for his boots. It was still dark so he had to turn on his flashlight. After he crawled out David did the same.

The mountain air was cold and the wind added a chill. Still, it looked to Les like it was going to be a nice autumn day.

The others were out of their tents within a couple of minutes and they scurried to eat a quick breakfast and break camp. By seven-o'clock, the five of them were donning their backpacks and heading down the trail.

At around nine-fifteen they came to a stream. "Here's the first indicator that we're getting close," Don said excitedly. He stopped and pulled out the map to study it a moment.

"Okay," he said, "we go about another two-hundred yards or so and see the stream again. When we do, we know we're near the place where the side-trail branches off."

"What if there's no side-trail?" Tommy said.

Don thought a moment. "There very well may not be. In that case we'll have to make one. Come on, let's keep moving."

As they proceeded down the trail, the shallow stream disappeared into the woods to the right. Then it reappeared some distance ahead and crossed the trail again. The five of them stepped from stone to stone as they traversed, trying to keep their boots as dry as possible. Once they were all on the other side they began looking for a path into the woods to the right.

"Hey," Harry said, "there's something in the grass over there." The others watched him walk along the stream a few feet from the trail. "It's an old rowboat."

They all walked over to take a closer look. "I'd say that thing's been here a while," Don said. "Most of the paint is chipped off."

"I wonder what it's doing here," David said. "Kind of a strange place for a rowboat."

"The depth of that water varies greatly depending on the amount of summer rainfall," Les said. "There must be a lake or a pond just downstream from here. Somebody probably paddled that boat here back in the spring and then went off and left it. When they came back the stream must have receded too much to get home the same way."

Harry looked at Les with an amused expression. "Yeah," he said, "I'm sure it happened just that way."

"Maybe," Les replied. "I guess we'll never know."

Harry had just pulled a large bag of gorp out of his backpack and opened it. After taking a handful he handed the bag to Les.

"Thanks," Les said, trying to sound nonchalant. Even though tensions were high right now between them he was glad to see that Harry was still holding onto the troop's age-old tradition of sharing. He took a handful and handed the bag to David, who then passed it to Tommy.

"Snack Don?"

"No thanks," he said.

Tommy then handed the gorp back to Harry. They all ate in silence as Don continued to study his map.

"Alright, listen-up," Don said. "Here's where it starts to get tricky. The stream path has changed a lot in the fifty-five years since this map was printed. Some of the places where the trail crosses water could be off by a hundred yards or more now."

"And there could be some new ones that aren't even on the map," Les said. "That will make it harder to use them as benchmarks."

"Maybe we shouldn't even use them at all," Harry added.

"You may be right," Don said. "We're just going to have to sniff-out the trail we need."

Tommy had wandered away and was walking around the high grass near where the rowboat had been found. "Here are the oars," he said. He held them up for the others to see. "Oh gross, there are animal bite marks along the handles." He tossed the oars into the boat.

"Makes sense," Les said. "The handles are the part the small animals find the tastiest since they are the places the salt from sweaty hands remain most prevalent."

Harry sealed the bag of gorp and zipped it into a pocket on his pack. They all awaited Don to finish studying his map.

"Alright," Don said, glancing up at the trail ahead. "Just a little farther."

He resumed walking and the others followed, the dry leaves crunching loudly under their feet. About a quarter-mile farther up the trail he stopped and studied the map some more. "It's right along here someplace," he said excitedly. "According to this map the burial ground is off the southernmost part of the trail along this loop. This looks like the exact spot."

"Let's spread-out and walk along the trail looking to the right," David said. "Maybe there's an open area where a trail once was."

"Good idea," Don said. "Alright everybody, fan-out."

Once they were about another fifty-yards down the trail Don cried out: "I see it!" They all rushed over to where he stood.

Les followed Don's pointed finger and saw what looked like an overgrown footpath. He could follow with his eyes its route through the trees and up the hillside. "This might be it," he said.

The closest tree to the trail had a badly rusted yellow sign on it indicating the boundary of the National Forest. The five of them knew very well that crossing the boundary constituted trespassing.

"I was afraid there might be a sign like that somewhere around here," David said. "You guys know we aren't supposed to go any farther. Especially in the places where they place a sign."

"I didn't come this far to halt because of some sign," Harry said. "Too much planning went into this to stop now."

"Breaking the law wasn't what I had in mind when I came out here with you guys," David said. "If we're caught in there we could get into trouble. The kind of trouble that keeps you from getting into the army or college."

Harry laughed loudly. "Why would you care. You planning to go to some pansy cooking college and then go work on an army base as the mess tent bitch?"

He and Don laughed and David noticed Tommy laughing too. Even Les was grinning.

"Caught out here by whom?" Don said. "There's not a living soul within three miles of us right now. I think you and Les have been sharing your tent too long. You both are turning into a couple of nut cases."

"I don't know," Les said. He was standing at the edge of the trail staring back into the woods. "If someone went to the trouble of putting that yellow warning sign on a tree at this particular spot then there might have been a special reason."

"I think you're onto something there, Les," Harry said. "It's telling us we're in the right place."

"This may just be a popular place for hikers to take little side trips," Tommy said. "There could be a cliff or some other dangerous terrain back there."

"Good thinking, Tommy," Don said. "And we don't need to worry about it since we're experienced scouts."

Les thought a moment. "Or there could be some reclusive land-owner back there with an affinity for sniping at trespassers with a deer rifle."

"Now you're talking crazy," Don said. "Who could possibly live in a place like this? It's six miles to the nearest road and twenty to the nearest town. I assure you there's nothing back in those woods but virgin forest."

"Yeah," Harry said, "and buried Indian treasure."

"There's no treasure back there," Les said. "It's time for you to face reality and stop imagining things."

"Well, we'll find out when we get there won't we," Harry said.

Les stared into the thick grove of trees that lined the side of the trail with a dazzling array of bright yellows and burnt reds. "I have a feeling there's more back in those woods than just a bunch of trees."

"Is it the sign that's bugging you?" Harry said. "Because if it is then I can take care of that." He picked up a fist-sized rock and hurled it at the sign. The rock struck the rusty metal plate dead-center, sending it flying off the tree to the ground. Don then walked over to it with his hands in his pockets, gave a perfunctory glance skyward, whistled momentarily, then kicked the sign into the brush where it disappeared.

"Problem solved," he said. "Now we can all say 'what sign' if anyone asks. I assure you nobody ever will."

"You know that won't qualify as a legitimate excuse," Les said. "If we're caught back there by a Forest Ranger or land owner we can get into a lot of trouble. Whether we saw the sign or not."

"They've got to catch me first," Don said. "And they'd have to catch you too. I do hope you'd at least have enough sense to run away."

Les sneered. "I guess I'd have to. If I got caught doing something illegal after all the stories in the newspapers about my scouting awards, then I'd get written-up in the paper again. Only this time with my mug shot."

"Let's vote and get it over with," Tommy said. "Majority rules."

"Fine," Don said. "Just for the sake of clearing the air, let's vote."

"I say we don't do it," David said. "There are plenty of other things we can do and still have a great time while we're here. Why don't we just pitch the tents and play poker or something."

Harry laughed, mostly from sarcasm. "Play poker, are you kidding me? David, you've been talking about this trip for a month now. Ever since we first told you about it you've mentioned it at least once a week. We'll have all winter to play poker. You wimping out on us?"

"No," he said. He glanced over at Les and tried to read his face. "I'm just having second thoughts."

"And well you should be," Les said. "It's really not safe or smart."

"Well, I say you're wrong," Harry said. "And no matter how we vote, I'm going in."

"Me too," Don said. "I'm in this jungle for a reason. So what do you say Tommy? Which side are you on?"

"I'm in," he said.

"Alright," Harry said. "The vote's three to two in favor. Let's quit wasting time."

"You guys going in or staying out here?" Don said. "If you're staying we'll need some of the food."

"I didn't think about that," Les said.

"Come on," Harry said. "Dividing that stuff up is going to waste valuable time. This isn't like those summer hikes when we've got daylight until nine o'clock. We've got to keep moving."

Don glanced at his watch. "You guys decide. I'm waiting exactly ten seconds."

"Come on, guys," Tommy said. "Nothing's going to happen to us. It'll be fun."

"What do you think, Les," David said. "We haven't seen anybody on the trail today."

Les looked around and saw no one. "I guess we should be okay if we keep our presence low-key. But at the first sign of trouble I'm out of there. And all of you guys need to be out right behind me."

"Yeah, whatever," Harry said.

Don smiled. "Then it's settled. Let's move out." He started up the trail with Harry one step behind. Tommy fell-in behind them. David and Les then tagged-up the rear.

CHAPTER 5

TRESPASSER AWARENESS 101

The five young men charged up the hill and into the thick woods. Les wasted no time catching-up to Don and Harry at the front. Tommy soon fell alongside David at the rear.

"Why were you on Don and Harry's side back there?" David asked. He and Tommy were now far enough back so as to be out of earshot from the others.

"I joined the scouts for adventure. Nothing against you and Les but I like the way things have quickly gotten exciting. My father wouldn't let me join the scouts for the longest time but since he and my mom are getting divorced he doesn't have much of a say-so anymore. A few weeks ago she finally caved-in and agreed to let me join the troop. Maybe she figured I need some male role models. The way I look at it, days like today are opportunities for me to make up for a lot of lost time."

"One thing you need to learn, kid, is to respect the views of smart people," David said. He watched Tommy's still-childlike face fall, then looked up ahead to make sure none of the others could hear him. "And Les Harrison is one of the smartest people you'll ever meet. I'm not so sure about Don. And as for Harry, he's totally brainless."

"Barbed wire fence ahead," they heard Don call out. The five of them came to a halt and looked into the woods on the far side of the wire.

"That thing's a little rusty," Harry said.

Les looked at him and smiled. "A little? This fence is older than we are."

"No matter," Don said. "As long as nobody gets cut on it we're okay." He placed one heavily-booted foot on the lowest two strands and pushed them down to the ground. Following traditional scout procedure, he then pulled the top two strands up using a small log to protect his arm, creating an opening two-and-a-half feet high. "Keep it moving guys," he said.

Harry bent down and stepped through. Tommy went next. David looked at Les a moment. He shrugged and gave a sheepish 'why not' smile. David stepped on through and Les followed close behind him. Harry then held the jagged wires apart for Don.

Once they were clear of the fence they began hiking at a quick pace. Within moments they were in a tight, single-file formation. No one spoke.

Fifteen-minutes later Don stopped near the top of a ridge where he could see about a hundred-feet of trail ahead. He was a knowledgeable scout and checked his compass frequently. Les checked his too as a back-up. They were in unfamiliar territory now and had to be very careful to not get lost.

The hike continued due south for about a mile, going over rolling hills and circumventing massive oak trees, some of which were five-feet wide at the base. It was a dense forest and the colorful tree canopy provided so much shade that the ground beneath it was almost dark. It seemed to be getting cloudy as well. Even though it was just past noon, it felt like early evening.

Don stopped and got out his map again. A worn corner broke off and fluttered to the ground. They stood silently for a moment, taking in the view of this unfamiliar and somewhat eerie place.

"Listen to the quiet," Les whispered. "Nothing is moving. There isn't even a breeze."

He looked over at Don and saw that he was mesmerized by his old yellow map. "It's got to be here," he said. "According to the map, we're standing right on the letter 'R' in the word 'Burial'."

"What's that?" Tommy asked. They all looked in the direction he was pointing. There was an object in the woods about thirty-feet away that Les could have sworn upon first glance was a tiny human head on a stick. As they slowly approached it they saw that it was a gnarled tree stump, carved to look like a human head.

"A burial ground marker!" David said.

They slowly approached and got close to it, each careful not to touch it. "Wow," Harry said. "You can still see the details of the Indian face on it with the eyes closed like a dead man."

"I saw one of these pictured in a book in the school library once," Don said. "It's a burial ground marker alright." He looked at the others and smiled. "Looks like we're getting warm!"

Les looked at him a moment. "Did you bother to read what the book said about markers like this or did you just look at the pictures?"

Don glared at him. "Yeah, I know what you're getting at, Les."

"Do you mind sharing with the rest of us?" Tommy said. "Is it valuable?"

"Hell yes," Don said. "This thing is worth some bucks." He and Harry high-fived.

Les looked over at the smiling Tommy. "To correctly answer your question, this marker is valuable. But not in the monetary sense. More so for the information it gives us."

Tommy frowned. "What do you mean?"

"Markers like this are put up as a warning," David said. "Tribal legend says that only Indians from that particular tribe are allowed to enter. Anybody else who does is cursed!"

"Cursed?" Tommy said. "That's not good."

"No, it isn't," Les said. "And since none of us are members of any Native American tribe then it certainly applies to all of us."

Don laughed. "That's a bunch of crap. They just spread that shit around to scare wimps like you away!"

"Maybe," Les said, "But I'm not an advocate of trashing other people's cultures and beliefs. If we step past that marker we may be making a big mistake."

"I just don't buy that stuff," Don said. "It's a carved ornament, nothing more."

"Yeah," Harry said, "and we've come an awful long way to start worrying about nonsense stuff now."

"I'm not so sure it's nonsense," Les said. "I've just got a really bad feeling right now. I just think we need to give this some careful thought."

"Alright," Don said. He paused for about three seconds. "Okay, I've thought about it. Now let's get moving before it gets any later." He looked over at Harry. "We'll saw-off the marker and take it with us on our way back out."

Harry smiled. "No telling what else we're going to find back here." He and Don stepped past the marker and headed deeper into the forest.

At that moment Les thought he heard a twig snap a few yards away from somewhere behind them. He jerked his head to the right and looked into the empty woods. "Did you guy's just hear something?"

"No," David said, "where?"

"Right over there," Les said pointing.

"I don't see anything," Tommy said. They stood silently, listening. The only sound came from Don and Harry's footsteps as the two of them disappeared up the trail.

"Must be just hearing things," Les said.

"You guys coming?" they heard Don call out.

Les hesitated a moment, then began walking. "Yeah, hold-up." The three of them went a dozen steps before encountering Harry as he stood on the trail waiting for them.

"What are you guys so worried about?" he said. "You think some big, mean forest ranger is going to jump out from behind a tree and arrest all of us?" He turned and started walking. "There isn't another person for miles around."

A moment later they caught-up with Don. "Lead on, Colonel," Harry said.

Don stepped forward and began the gradual uphill trek. It was now obvious to Les and the others that he wasn't interested in any more protests. His lack of respect for Indian culture was becoming painfully obvious now that he was getting tired.

Les stopped and watched as the other four started making their way into the thick underbrush. Something about it was really worrying him now.

David turned and looked back at him. "You coming, Les?"

Before he could reply, Harry turned and added his observation. "You can stay here and stare into space if want to, Les", he said. "We won't think any less of you." He chuckled and looked over at Don who was still walking into the woods. "Will we Don?"

"Of course not", Don said. "Lots of great American explorers started out that way."

"So this is where we've ended up," Les said, more to himself than anyone else. An undercurrent of hostility had been festering all day and was now reaching the surface. It had never been this pronounced before between Les and the other two on any of the hikes they had taken together over the last four years. Even the week-long ones.

We're getting into new territory, he thought. In more ways than one. The predominant feeling he seemed to be getting now was one of survival mode. He was being pulled by a need to concentrate on watching everybody else's back. In Don and Harry's case, he wasn't sure he even wanted to do that.

Then again, he thought, it was exactly what he came on this trip to do. For now however, he had to at least give the impression he was still enjoying the adventure.

"I'm coming," he said. "My curiosity is peaked just like everyone else's."

"Good", Don said, stepping through a thick patch of grass that stood two feet high. "Try keeping up with the rest of us for awhile."

Les took his place behind David. They walked in silence for several minutes.

Approximately two-hundred yards up the trail they came to a small clearing. Don removed his backpack and laid it on the ground. "We can move about more freely without the packs", he said. "Then, if necessary, we can pitch our tents here."

"I don't think we should camp here", Les said.

"Me neither," David said. "There's no way I could sleep in this spooky place."

Both Don and Harry glared at them but neither spoke. The five of them got their packs off and stood admiring the surroundings and catching their collective breath.

"Something worrying you about this clearing Les?" David asked.

"Nothing in particular," Les replied.

David paused and took a couple of deep breaths. "I guess that's good."

Don reached into his pack and pulled out a small collapsible shovel. With a flip of his wrist he snapped it into working position. "What are you going to do with that?" Les asked him.

"I'm going to scratch my ass", he replied. "What do people do with shovels, Les? Row a boat?"

Les thought of several responses to his sarcastic question but held his tongue. He was too tired to waste any more energy arguing with him.

"You guys get whatever tools you've got, there's no telling what we might find", Don said. "And remember, time is growing short."

It was obvious now to Les that Don expected them all to follow his orders without question. He also figured that any hint of insubordination from any of them would be met with an immediate threat of not getting a ride back home the following day. That was an idle threat at best, but one that had at least a hint of upper-handedness to it. They all seemed to realize that this was Don's ball game, and they were going to play along whether they liked it or not.

Don took his machete out of its sheath that he had tied to the side of his pack. The others watched as he held it up in his right hand and inspected it momentarily. "Let's go this way," he said, and with a wave of his hand he started into the woods, clearing a trail by swinging the machete from side to side.

He had taken off his drab-green army jacket, and his white t-shirt stood out starkly against his fatigue pants and heavy, shiny black boots. Don's dad had served in Vietnam and junior was strictly military from head to toe, at least as much as any sixteen-year-old could be.

Everyone else wore jeans, sweat-shirts and standard hiking boots. They were just typical hikers, but Don, who often prided himself in his vast knowledge of the outdoors and then sprinkled-in some military protocol, was going to play this scenario to its rightful conclusion, whatever it was. He was a young man of destiny, determined and strong. And this was his day.

Once they had walked a few dozen more steps, they reached the crest of a small hill. Don stopped walking and stood looking down the gradual embankment ahead of him. When Les reached the spot and took in the same view. "This is it," he said.

All the others looked at him except Don, who stood silently, surveying the bottom of the hill. What lay ahead of them appeared normal to David, Harry and Tommy. Les saw it differently however. Don did too.

"This is what?" Tommy whispered.

"What we came here looking for," Les said.

"This is some kind of strange place," Don said as he looked above and around him. "Everything is different in this part of the woods."

"It just looks like woods to me," Harry said. "Are you guys sure this is the place on the map we're looking for?"

"Yeah," Don said, "this is it alright."

"See how all the trees in this area are bare," Les said. "Look at the leaves on the ground. They haven't fallen recently, they look like they've been here for years. And look at all the dusty places in the caves of the tree trunks. It's as if some presence has changed the landscape slightly."

"Sort of like a graveyard," David said. The others looked at him but nobody spoke.

Don started down the hill and, after several seconds, the others followed. Moments later they were moving as a pack down the heavily forested embankment.

Les suddenly became aware of something moving quickly through the underbrush and coming toward them downhill to their left. He turned just in time to see a large rock, almost as big as a bowling ball, roll from the woods at a rapid speed.

"Look out Harry!" he yelled.

Harry spotted the rock coming right at him and quickly jumped aside. It missed him by about a foot and continued to increase speed as it raced down the hill. The five of them stood and listened as it came to a noisy halt against a tree somewhere far below.

"That thing came at me!" Harry said. He looked up the hill into the dense brush. "Who the hell is up there?"

They all froze in their tracks and stood looking anxiously up the hill. "That rock sure picked a peculiar time to come rolling down," David said.

"Yes it did," Les said. He knew nobody was out here with them, they were too far off the main trail. Then again, he couldn't really be sure.

"Maybe the vibrations of our footsteps shook that rock loose somehow," he said at last. "I guess it was just a million-to-one-shot."

Harry was just now getting his wits back about him after the near miss. "I'm sure glad I wasn't wearing my pack," he said. "I don't think I could have gotten out of the way of it in time."

"Well, whatever it was watch your step," Don said. "All of you."

One minute later they were at the bottom of the hill, surrounded on all sides and above by massive, mostly bare trees. The limbs, which creaked loudly during the occasional wind gust, provided a thick canopy under the cloudy sky overhead. The shady woods were cool and dark, and appeared totally lifeless.

"Hey," Don said, "look down there." He was pointing ahead to the flat area that made up the floor of this small valley. "There are a whole bunch of indentions in the ground."

"Indentions," Harry said. "Maybe graves."

"Could be," Don said. "I think we've found what we're looking for."

Walking in a tight group and seemingly unaware of their own growing fear, the five of them walked to the edge of the flat, muddy area that appeared to be a burial ground.

"These indentions are the last places that dry up after a rainfall," Don said. "The ground is softer than the surrounding area. If there was anything lying on the ground around these hillsides the rain would have washed it down here."

"This is the creepiest place I've ever seen," Tommy said. Somewhere a crow squawked loudly, causing all of them to jump.

"Yeah," Harry said. "It's like a big cemetery. Just without the headstones and wrought iron fence surrounding it."

"It's some other kind of fence," Les said as he looked all around them. "I can sense it."

Without a word, Don walked over to one of the indentions on the ground, tapped the earth with his toe to find the softest spot and started to dig. "Hey, you shouldn't do that!" Les yelled.

"Shut up, Les," Don shot back without breaking his rhythm. "What's going to happen, some dead Indian chief is going to come out of the woods and scalp me? I'm really scared!"

"No, listen," Les said. "Something's wrong, I can feel it."

"Oh yeah?" Harry said. "I got something you can feel right here Les." He turned and jabbed his shovel into the ground and gouged out a clump of earth the size of a soccer ball. Two more similar jabs revealed several arrowheads.

"Hey look," David said. "You've got something there!"

Les watched in amazement as Harry and Don quickly enlarged the hole. Tommy and David then started digging alongside with their knives.

"What in the hell do you think you are doing," Les said. "You guys need to stop and think about this."

"We're doing exactly what we came here to do," Don said. "Either join in and help or stay the hell out of the way."

Harry managed to snare a long root and began walking along the ground, pulling it up as he went. As the long, snaking line of root came free, it brought with it large amounts of dirt. About a dozen arrowheads of all shapes and sizes came out with it. So did a large number of small yellow bones.

"Hey, check this out," Harry said. "I think I've found something big." He picked-up a piece about six-inches long and brushed-off the dirt with his hand. "It's a leg-bone!"

"Let me see that," Don said. Harry handed it to him and Don blew off some more dirt. "Wow, it is a leg-bone. This knob on the end is part of a knee or hip. This is amazing!"

He looked over at Les. "See what I've been telling you? What do you think of my excavation trip now?"

Les stared into Don's eyes as his mind raced through a number of ways to respond to his question. "I don't think you want to know."

Don and Harry ignored him as Harry continued pulling the root three more feet until it snapped. He tossed it away and started kicking dirt out of the small trench he had created. His boot struck something hard and firmly embedded. "Come here, Don."

Don walked over and together with their knives they dug around the site. "There's something in there alright," he said.

Les started backing away, looking above and around in all directions. He went from nervous to scared in two seconds. Somehow, he expected himself and his comrades to be attacked by someone or something at any moment.

After reaching a line of trees twenty-feet or so away from the others, Les stood and watched. Don and Harry were squatting and digging.

David and Tommy stood behind them, leaning in and looking over their shoulders.

The ticking alarm clock in his head suddenly started to ring. It wasn't as loud as he had feared it would be, but it rang just the same. It rang and rang and rang, finally playing out as it wound completely down. Once the little clock that was buried somewhere in his mind went silent, a cold, terrifying realization came to him. Whatever it was that the five of them were doing and whoever it was they were wronging, the point of no return had officially now been crossed. Only one coherent word came to mind: unthinkable.

Les was so overwhelmed with fear that he had almost no emotional reaction at all when Don cried out in excitement and held up a sickening, black, dirt-covered human skull. "Pay dirt!" he shouted.

"Whoa, look at that thing!" Harry cried out in amazement.

Don held the skull in his hand and smiled foolishly. Suddenly he bolted at Tommy and started trying to touch the skull to his face. Tommy screamed and started running. He tripped over a tree stump and fell to the ground.

"Initiation time," Don cried out as he put the skull against Tommy's cheek. "Kiss the chief."

"Quit it!" Tommy yelled, and Don walked away laughing while the younger boy on the ground began to sob softly. "You're nothing but a bully!"

Don looked around at him. "What did you say?"

"That's enough!" Les yelled. He was glaring at Don with a scowl.

Don turned his attention away from Tommy and toward Les. "Maybe you'd like to kiss Chief Dirtface yourself Les," he said daringly, wiggling the dirty skull back and forth in his hand and making it look like it was laughing.

"Only if you want him shoved up your ass," Les replied. Harry and David laughed nervously. Without taking his eyes off Don, Les walked over to Tommy and gave him a hand up. "You alright?"

"Yeah," he replied softly, rubbing the dirt off the back of his pants. "I'm fine."

Les looked over at Don who was still glaring at him. "You going to kiss it and make it better?"

Les replied with the same line, delivered with his best childlike voice and a lisp. "You going to kiss and make it better? Why don't you kiss my ass, Don."

Don gave him the finger. "Why don't you two ladies go find your backpacks and set up the tents. Us men still have some excavating to do."

"Hey Don," David said, "I don't think we should spend the night out here. Maybe this is a good time to head back to the main trail."

"Are you crazy! We've come this far and you want to leave in our moment of glory?" Don looked over at Harry for approval. "We pull-up a few more roots and we could find something, big like a cooking pot. If it's still intact it could fetch thousands of dollars. And you losers want to walk away now?"

"Yeah," Harry said. "We thought you guys were grown-ups when we asked you on this hike. I guess we'll have to tell scoutmaster Thomas that you three still need some development. Maybe a demotion to the gay troop would work for you pansies."

"There's no such thing as a gay troop," Tommy said.

"Oh there isn't?" Harry said. "Obviously you checked to be sure."

"You shut-up," Tommy said.

"You shut-up," Harry said, mimicking Tommy's voice.

"You finished, Harry?" Les said. Harry stood glaring at him. "Scoutmaster Thomas would be horrified if he knew what you were doing right now. In fact, he'd probably kick you two out of the troop."

"Well ain't it a shame that we're getting out soon anyway," Don said. "Harry and I are ready to branch out on our own. We don't need losers like Scoutmaster Dumbass telling us what to do. As far as we're concerned we're already out of the troop."

"Yeah", Harry said. "And you can tell him that next time you see him."

Les, David and Tommy all shared a silent moment of shock at that statement. "You've changed," was all Les could think to say to Don at that moment. "I think this place has gotten to you."

"No, I've grown-up," Don said. "And it's getting high-time you did too, mister boy scout of the year. When are you going to become a man scout?"

Harry laughed as he picked-up the shovel. "Now are you girls going to help excavate or did you just come along to enjoy the scenery?"

"Hey Les," Don said. "Seriously, it would really help us if you guys went back to the packs and started unloading the tents."

"What?" David said. "You expect us to do all the tent set-up? I suppose you want us to do the cooking too?"

"Might as well make yourselves useful," Don said as he resumed digging in a nearby bare spot. "Who knows, we might find enough trinkets for us all to take some booty home."

"Spare me," Les said. He turned and looked back up the trail. "The shadows of the trees are starting to get long." He glanced at his watch. "Quarter-past-four. Wow, the day is passing fast."

"It sure is," David said, looking up. "It'll be dark before you know it."

"Why don't you guys go back to that clearing where we left the packs and start setting up," Don said, his tone much calmer now. "We'll be along to help you later."

"Spend the night here in this Indian graveyard?" David said. "Are you crazy? There could be anything lurking in these woods at night."

Don glanced over at him and chuckled. "There's nothing in these woods at night that isn't here during the day."

At that moment Les heard another twig snap from somewhere nearby. There it is again, he thought. He didn't bother to look around, just dismissed it.

"I hate to say this but I have to agree with Don," he said. David looked at him in disbelief.

"I'm afraid we don't have much choice." Everyone's eyes were on Les as he glanced at his compass. "We're a good three miles off the main trail. We skipped lunch and I for one am tired and hungry. The only open space big enough for all three tents within miles of here seems to be that clearing back there. And for some reason it feels to me like the most peaceful part of these woods."

"Well you're finally making some sense," Don said. Les ignored him.

"David and I will go set up the tents and start dinner. Tommy, why don't you come with us and gather fire wood. Don, you and Harry just come along when you're done here."

"That sounds great," Don said. "Welcome back to the team." He and Harry resumed digging. Without another word Les turned and started walking back toward the packs. David and Tommy fell in line behind him.

When the three of them had gotten out of Don and Harry's earshot, David looked over at Les. "You sure changed your tone in a hurry. Why are you dropping the protests and going along all of a sudden?"

"I just realized I needed to distance myself from Don and Harry as much as possible. Maybe you guys do too. Something happened to the two of them the moment we entered this part of the woods, I saw it in their eyes. Don in particular." He paused, looked around them and lowered his voice. "And what's more . ."

David's eyes grew wide. "What?"

Les looked back at him. "I wanted to distance myself from them out in the open. In plain view."

David and Tommy looked at each other and then back at Les. "You mean they are possessed or something?" Tommy said.

"Wait a minute, Tommy," David said. "What do you mean, Les? In plain view of whom?"

Les leaned closer to the two of them and kept his voice just above a whisper. "Ever since we came across that marker on the trail I've had the strange sensation that we're being watched. I haven't seen anybody, haven't heard voices or anything. It's just a feeling." He saw shock on both of their faces. "A real creepy feeling. It's like I'm reading someone's thoughts. And they aren't good."

"Who could be watching us?" Tommy whispered, looking around nervously. "You think there's a forest ranger somewhere out there?"

"I'm not sure," Les said. "I doubt there are any forest rangers this far off of public land. There could be a land owner tracking us. Every now and then I hear a twig snap somewhere in the woods but nobody else notices so it could just be my imagination."

"Or it could be something else," David whispered.

Les gave him a brief stare. "Yes, it could."

Tommy was looking around with terror in his eyes. "Are you sure about all this, Les? These woods are mighty quiet."

"I don't know. All of a sudden I started seeing hate in Don and Harry's eyes. I've never seen either of them like that before. I realized I couldn't reason with them so I simply backed off. I'm glad you guys stuck with me."

Les slowly resumed walking toward the clearing and the others got on either side of him. "I got really creeped-out the moment they pulled that skull out of the ground," he said. "It's scaring the hell out of me."

He glanced over at Tommy and saw the fear in his eyes. He was only thirteen but to Les suddenly looked much younger. Something in the back of his mind told him bringing Tommy along on this hike was a huge mistake. He had to dismiss the thought quickly.

"What are we going to do?" David said. Les thought he sounded more terrified that he had ever been in all the years he'd known him.

"Let's just stick to the plan," Les said. "We've got wood to gather and dinner to cook. Treat this like any other Saturday night on the trail. I'll let you know if that changes."

They walked without speaking for a minute before Tommy broke the silence. "That Don sure can be an asshole."

David chuckled. "I know."

"Let's just hope nobody catches us out here or we're all going to feel like assholes," Les said. The thick woods remained silent and still. Five minutes later they reached the clearing.

Les and David began setting-up the tents as Tommy started gathering firewood. "Stay where one of us can see you while you gather wood, Tommy," Les told him.

"Don't worry," he said. "I'm too scared right now to get more than ten-feet from you guys."

Tommy stayed close to the perimeter of the clearing and gathered a good supply of dry wood while Les and David got all three tents set-up. Then they all gathered wood as the last of the daylight faded into twilight. In less than an hour they had the campsite in good working order.

"This place is really creepy," David said as Les lit the fire with his lighter. He was keeping his voice low, hoping Tommy wouldn't overhear. "Now I've got the feeling somebody is watching us."

Les looked up into David's eyes. "You okay?"

"Yeah," he said. "But several times I could have sworn I saw someone or something in the corner of my eye standing a few yards away. But when I looked around there would be nothing there. I started getting really nervous."

Les looked him in the eye momentarily, then turned back to the camp fire. "But you didn't actually see anybody, right?"

"No," David said. "But I remembered something else now that I read in one of those Native American history books. About the watcher."

Les whirled back around. "A watcher? What on earth is that?"

David paused to make sure Tommy was out of earshot. "Advance scout. Quiet as a church mouse. Comes and goes like the breeze. If you ever see one it's never straight-away. Just a glimpse beside a bush or peering from behind a tree. Then it's gone."

Les took a deep breath and blew life into the fire. Its flame lit-up the entire clearing for the first time at that moment. He decided to change the subject a bit. "I think we're all a little edgy. Try not to worry about it."

"I wish I could believe it was all in my head," David said.

"Let's just get dinner started," Les said. "I'm really hungry."

"I'm for that," Tommy said. He had just walked up with an armload of assorted sticks and dropped them by the fire pit. "It's getting too dark to see now."

Les pulled out the camp stove and got it going. Soon the aroma of beef stew filled the air.

A few minutes later Don and Harry came marching up the trail, their footsteps crunching through the dry leaves. They were talking excitedly and could be heard well before their flashlights came into view.

"Look at what all we got," Harry said, holding up some beads and arrowheads in one hand while shining his light on them with the other.

"Yeah," Don said, "we also found some more bone pieces but they were all shards. The leg bone was kind of big. But we got this cool head. This was the best find." He held up the skull that was a little larger than a softball.

"You're not going to take that thing home with you are you?" Les asked him.

"Hell yes," he replied with a smile. "Can't you just see the expressions on the girls' faces when I whip this thing out next week in the school cafeteria."

"That's gross, Don," Tommy said.

"Who asked you?" he shot back.

"Don," said David, "sometimes you amaze even me."

Don put the skull and the other trinkets next to his backpack and sat down on a log to eat. "I'll take that as a compliment."

After eating, the five of them sat beside the warm fire and talked as the stars filled the crisp, autumn sky. Although there had been a lot of tension earlier, the food seemed to help get things somewhat back to normal between them.

"I hope we haven't done something terrible here today," Les said.

Don gave him an exasperated look. "What do you mean by that?"

"You know," Les said. "Coming in here and desecrating these Indian graves. I just don't feel right about it, that's all."

"Don't start that shit again," Don said. "Only a superstitious fool would believe that bull about Indian spirits guarding the graves and bad luck falling on intruders. It's a bunch of nonsense."

"What about spirits and bad luck?" Tommy asked.

Don looked at Tommy a moment and then at a grinning Harry. "Don't play dumb with me. I'm sure you've heard about Indian curses. It's just like medicine men, Santa Claus and voodoo, it's all make believe."

"Yeah," Harry said. "Good thing too. Indian legend says that the spirits of the dead come after anyone who trespasses on their sacred burial ground. Ole Chief Dirtface is going to show up at Don's house next week to pick up his head." He and Don burst out laughing.

"Yeah," Don said, lifting up his knife. "And when he shows up I'm going to take another vital part of his anatomy off too." With that the two of them laughed and laughed.

"Geez Don," Tommy said. "You've got no conscience at all."

"Shut up wimp," he shot back. "Or I'll start practicing on you." He and Harry laughed again.

Don made a quiet comment to Harry about it being sexual but Les ignored him. He was too nervous to get mad.

"My mom dated a really nice guy up until a few months ago who taught me a lot of things about Indians," Les said. "He collected Indian relics, arrow heads, and anything else he could find about them. Plus he had a nice book collection too. He was a smart guy. He knew a lot and also spent time with me."

"Who was this guy?" David said. "Did I ever meet him?"

"I'm not sure. His name was Bob but my mom and I called him Frosty. He got that name because he had white hair."

"I do remember him," David said. "He played ball with us in your back yard once."

"Yeah, that's him," Les said. "They dated for a year or so and then they broke-up. She never told me but I think she realized he was just too old for her. Too bad. I really liked him."

"Anyway, one time he told me about an Indian legend that was so creepy I didn't sleep that night. He said there are many such legends and some of them are true. He sure believed in one in particular."

"What was it?" Tommy asked with a crack in his voice.

Les looked at him a moment. "The one about the Little People. Frosty showed me some drawings in one of his books of what they supposedly looked like. Black and white sketches of small, demonic creatures attacking a wagon train full of settlers. They were everywhere, behind rocks, in the trees. Some were attacking people with tomahawks and others were setting fire to wagons. I know they were only drawings but they scared the hell out of me."

"Little people?" David said.

"Yeah, midgets," Harry said. He and Don laughed.

"Small people are called 'dwarfs', not 'midgets'," Les said. "And I'm not talking about dwarfs. Little people are small Indian warriors that live on tribal lands in the woods. They occupy and defend sacred ground. They can be very dangerous if you cross them."

Les looked around and saw that he had everyone's full attention. "Indian legend says that there are little Indian people that hide underground in lodges where no white man can find them. When the Indian people are wronged, they come out under the cover of darkness or sometimes even in the thick underbrush in the daytime and take their revenge."

Don laughed. "Don't tell me you believe any of that shit."

"I'm not saying whether or not it's true," Les said. "I've never seen supporting evidence one way or the other, so I'm not drawing any conclusions. All I'm telling you is what Frosty told me."

"He just made that story up," Harry said. "Was he a drinking man?" He looked at Don and snickered.

"No, he wasn't," Les said. He was determined not to let Harry anger him.

"Calm down both of you," Don said. "This might be interesting. I need a good story as a lead-in before I pull the skull out at school and startle everybody. Hey, with any luck at all I might scare somebody so bad they'll faint."

"I'm glad you aim high," David said. "You'll go far in life Don."

Don smiled. "Damn straight."

"Go on Les," Tommy said. "What else did Frosty tell you?"

"Not much more. But he peaked my interest in the subject so I started doing some research at the library on my own. Some of the things I found out are quite intriguing."

He paused momentarily to glance all around them. "The legend of the little people sounds a bit farfetched, but throughout North American history, there have been a number of strange occurrences that can't be explained any other way."

"Like what?" David asked.

"A lot of them aren't documented," Les said. "It's mostly legend, handed down orally through the generations. But a few are pretty convincing.

"I'm sure you all know that when the white man came to America he killed virtually all the Indians that were here. Between wars and famines, mixed-in with the many viruses and diseases the European settlers brought with them, the red man didn't have much of a chance.

"All told, about ninety-four percent of the North American Indian population was wiped out by the European settlers in one way or another. It's the worst case of genocide in the history of the world, at least in terms of percentage. Any Indian victories were few and far between. Most of the time the white man killed at will and took what he wanted by force. It's a sad commentary for the country where all men are equal and free."

"Will you get to the point," Don said. "I've got an important announcement and there aren't enough violins around here for this sad story of yours."

"Your sympathy is overwhelming Don," David said dryly. Don smiled broadly and Les noticed for the first time how much he was starting to look like the bully he was becoming. A dangerous bully.

"The legend of the little people is basically a series of stories where the white man has had to go to enormous lengths and sometimes extensive loss of life to accomplish goals," Les continued. "There were all kinds of unexplained events during the days of the pioneers. Settlements were destroyed without explanation, literally vanishing into the wilderness. Everything from mines caving-in to droughts and storms have been blamed on the legend of the little people. But the most convincing of all is the disappearance of the first English colony in America, Roanoke Island, North Carolina, also known as the 'Lost Colony'."

"I've heard of the 'Lost Colony'," Tommy said. "But I don't know anything about it."

"Sir Walter Raleigh led a group of settlers to Roanoke and left them there to colonize the island and plant tobacco for export," Les said. "He returned to England to get more supplies and ended up being delayed by a naval war between England and Spain. When he finally got back to Roanoke Island two years later there was no trace of the settlement to be found. It was as if no one had ever been there at all. There were no ashes, no ruins, no graves, nothing. Just some meaningless carvings on a tree.

"The mystery will never be solved officially, but some historians think it could have been something from the Native American spirit world. Not only was it the single plausible explanation but it made sense. White settlers had never really encountered the red man before. They didn't know who or what they were dealing with.

"The little people may have attacked the settlers in their sleep and massacred them. Attempting to forestall the inevitable invasion of the white man for as long as possible. If that's what actually happened then they kept America free from European domination for an additional few years.

"The English investigated the incident but came up with no answers. There were only a few isolated Indians living many miles away and those tribes were known to be peaceful. None of them had even known the colony existed. Whoever or whatever wiped out the Roanoke Island colony left no trace behind.

"Frosty told me he believed the legend of the little people started with the incident at Roanoke Island. And it could still be around in some form today: dormant, lying in wait until called upon again."

"Look!" Don yelled pointing. "There's one of them now!" Startled, everyone looked around.

"I don't see anything," Les said calmly.

"That's because they don't exist," Don said laughing.

"Say what you want," Les concluded, "but what we did here today was wrong. I feel bad about it and if you had any conscience, you would too."

"Yeah, yeah," Don said. "Spare me the song and dance. Come Monday, I'm going to be the most popular guy in school with this skull."

"You mean the most popular guy in the principal's office," David said with a laugh.

Les decided to give the subject of Indian curses a rest, and the conversation soon became much more light-hearted. Soon, some of the day's tension began to subside.

The five of them now sat close to the warm fire, talking for awhile and never sticking to any one subject for very long. Les drifted away mentally and was soon deep in his own thoughts. He was completely exhausted and felt his eyelids droop momentarily. Slowly, his mind drifted back to the conversation around the campfire.

"You guys can say what you want about Vietnam," Don was saying, "but I feel sorry for the suckers that go against us in the next war. We'll kick ass!"

There was silence for a moment before Don spoke up again. "Well," he said, "basically you boys have been pretty good about this whole thing and it's time to celebrate with some good old fashioned Indian fire water." He reached into his backpack and pulled out a pint bottle of whiskey. "A few spirits will liven things up a bit." He unscrewed the cap and took a big swig. "Ah, that's good," he said, handing the bottle to Harry.

"Alright!" Harry exclaimed, taking a big swig of his own. The others watched as Harry grimaced and then swallowed. A moment later he coughed loudly. Everybody laughed.

"How is it?" Don asked him.

"Smooth as a baby's behind," he said, then he laughed too.

"Where did you get this stuff?" Les asked as Harry passed the bottle to him.

"Swiped it from my old man's liquor cabinet," Don said. "The way he puts it away, he'll never miss it. Go ahead, take a snort, it'll make a man out of you."

Les held the bottle up and sniffed it. "Smells terrible."

"Tastes worse," Harry said. "But the taste isn't why you drink it."

Les took a small sip. Indeed, it tasted worse than it smelled. He almost spit it out but knew if he did he'd never hear the end of it. He managed to get it down, then passed the bottle to David sitting to his left.

David held the bottle up and studied it for a long moment. Don looked on with a mixture of amusement and anger. "Are you going to drink it or just memorize the label?"

David took a small sip and grimaced as he swallowed, then held the bottle up to inspect the label in the firelight again as he recovered from the taste. "That's not so bad," he said after a moment. Both Don and Harry laughed.

"Then let's see you drink it like you mean it," Harry said.

David looked at him for a moment and then smiled. "Thanks," he said, holding up the bottle. "Here's mud in your eye." With that he took another swallow, this one bigger, grimaced, then handed the bottle to Tommy. He immediately handed it back toward Don.

"Take a sip Tommy," Don said without taking it. "Don't be the lone holdout. Where's your spirit?"

"I don't want any," Tommy said.

"Take a sip you little fairy," Harry said. "It'll make a man . . big boy out of you." He and Don broke up laughing again.

"Why don't you two just finish it," Les said. "That way you'll not only be men when you wake up tomorrow, you'll be hung-over men."

Don looked at Les a moment, then took the bottle from Tommy's hand. "Wimp," he said. He and Harry each took another drink. They offered it to David again and he joined them. In a short time the little bottle was empty.

For the next hour they sat around the fire, talking some but quiet most of the time. At some point Les realized that he had just tasted fire water for the first time in his life. A little later, during a long period of silence, he suddenly realized that the pulsating sounds of crickets they had been hearing around them all evening now sounded more like faint, distant drumbeats.

He jolted alert. Am I imagining that? he thought to himself. As he listened, the sound faded back into the rhythmic chirp of crickets and tree frogs. After another few seconds it vanished completely.

The sounds from the surrounding woods were brief and soft on this fall night. They were merely whispers compared to the cacophony that had been heard all summer.

Les looked around the campfire into the faces of the four other guys. They all stared into the flames, each apparently deep in his own thoughts.

Don got up and walked over to his pack. He pulled out his knife, picked up the dirty skull, walked back to the fire and sat down. Everyone else sat and watched him as he began scraping the dirt out of the eye sockets.

Just as Don flicked out the first chunk of caked dirt, Les felt a bold of panic. Immediately he got nervous and started looking around. It was pitch-black dark now. The firelight extended out about ten-feet in all directions. Beyond that there was nothing but invisible forest. He looked over at David and saw that he was looking into the woods too.

"Did you hear something?" David asked. Les didn't reply. The other guys sat motionless so as not to make a sound. They sat and listened for a minute or so, but nothing could be heard.

"You guys are nervous nellies!" Harry suddenly blurted out loudly making everybody jump. He and Don snickered.

"Yeah," Don said. "Too bad you didn't drink enough fire water to clear your heads and relax yourselves." He resumed scraping the skull with his knife. "You sure are an ugly bastard, Chief Dirtface," he said to it. "Don't worry though, a week in a jar of bleach and you'll be smiling like your old, war-paint-wearing, red-assed self."

At that moment Les distinctly heard a twig snap somewhere in the woods, this time really close-by, and whirled around to look. He was certain he had heard something. He looked back at the other guys who were still just sitting and watching Don scrape away.

Les looked back into the forest again. He felt a strong, eerie presence. Then he remembered what David had told him about the watchers in the woods. He trembled momentarily as chills ran down his spine. They felt like cold clammy hands with a potentially firm grip.

He grabbed his flashlight and shined it into the woods. The other guys were alerted by his sudden move and grabbed their own flashlights. All of them shined the lights into the woods but saw nothing but trees.

"What is it Les?" David whispered. "Did you hear something?"

There was a long silence before Les replied. The five of them sat shining their flashlights in all directions into the empty woods.

"I guess not," Les said at last. "Must have just been my imagination."

"Maybe it's Chief Dirtface's spirit," Harry said. He and Don both acted scared but were faking it.

"Hey Chief Dirtface," Don yelled out at the top of his lungs. "I've got your head right here. Why don't you come and get it?"

At that moment Les could have sworn he heard a loud whisper from the forest reply: "Not Yet."

"Did you hear something?" he asked.

"You mean from out there?" David asked nervously. "I don't think so. Did you?"

"I'm not sure," Les said. "I don't know if I heard something with my ears or my mind. Sounded like a voice."

"Man, I don't think we should be here," Tommy said. "Maybe we should have gotten out of this burial ground area when we had the chance."

"A little late for that now," David said.

"Oh no," Don said, "you're not going to cry again are you?"

Tommy crinkled his nose at Don. "No."

"Just relax, Tommy," David said. "We're going to be okay."

A cool, steady breeze blew through the camp a moment later and all of them felt a chill simultaneously. Each of them instinctively moved closer to the warm fire. Several minutes passed and nothing more was heard from the woods.

"I'm tired," Don said at last, standing up to stretch. "I'm going to crash, see you guys tomorrow. Oh, and by the way, I hope I don't hear any strange grunting noises coming from your tent, Les."

"You won't as long as you stay out of it," Les said. Tommy and David laughed. Harry and Don went to their tent.

Once the three of them were alone, Les couldn't help but mention how different this camping trip was from all the others they had experienced together over the last four years. "I can't remember ever having so much hostility between us on a hike before," he said. "Things settled down after dinner but it got really tense at times this afternoon."

"I know," David agreed. "We've always had little skirmishes, but never like today."

"Maybe you two and those guys are just growing apart," Tommy said. "That's what happened to my mom and dad. They both told me it was nobody's fault. I guess those things just happen."

"I'm not so sure that's all there is to it," Les said. "We're foreigners in these woods out here. That's a factor that normally helps scouts to bond. But something about this place seems to be dividing us."

"I wouldn't worry about it," Tommy said. "You two guys still have each other. Don't worry about those two jerks."

Les looked at his young friend and smiled. "You're alright, Tommy."

"Thanks," the younger boy said.

"Hello," David said waving one hand in the air between them. "Have I turned invisible over here?"

Les looked over at him. "You're okay too, David. Even if you are a drunk slob."

"What?"

Les smiled. "Just kidding."

"Hey," Tommy said. "We need to build up that fire before it goes out."

"Why don't we just let it die," Les said. "It's a good time to turn-in." He stood up and headed for the tent. "See you guys in the morning."

"I guess I'd better call it a night too," David said. "We've got a long hike back tomorrow." He and Tommy said goodnight and David followed behind Les, who paused momentarily to watch Tommy crawl inside his tent and zip the doorway shut tightly.

Once they were in their sleeping bags, Les heard David snicker. "I was beginning to think you and Tommy were sharing a moment out there."

Les rolled over and faced him. "I expect crap like that from Don and Harry. But not from you. Are you feeling okay?"

"Well I have to admit I got a rush from that whiskey," David said. "It kind of made the fun around the fire even better. It even made Don and Harry seem a little more tolerable."

"Well I'm not having much fun," Les said in a lowered voice. "I think we're in too much danger here to be having fun. I'd like to hit the trail and get the hell out of here at first light."

David lay silent a moment. "Sounds like a good idea to me."

Moments later Les heard him snoring lightly. He lay awake for a while longer, listening to the faint sounds in the woods. David's insight now had him more than just a little concerned. Thinking about it would delay his sleep for another half-hour. Eventually he drifted off.

CHAPTER 6

THE NIGHT IN THE
BURIAL GROUND

Sometime later, Les was stirred awake when he heard something moving around outside the tent. The sound of twigs snapping underfoot as well as loud breathing just a few feet away made him snap alert. He lay motionless in the total darkness, trying to figure out who or what he was hearing. Then came the unmistakable sound of a tent doorway being unzipped.

Suddenly there was a loud roar, like that of a bear or a lion. David sat up an instant later. "What the hell is that?"

Without a word Les crawled out of the sleeping bag and reached for his flashlight. A few seconds later came a loud, terrifying scream. "That's Tommy," Les said. He and David both were out of the tent in less than thirty-seconds.

Les shined his flashlight on Tommy's tent and saw a great deal of movement going on inside. More screams came. "Something's attacking him in his tent," David said. "He's trying to tear his way out the back end."

He reached for one of the remaining sticks from the wood pile and handed it to Les. He then picked out another for himself. Instinctively, they got on either end of the tent and shined their flashlights on it.

A faint amount of light could be seen through the nylon. Suddenly, Tommy burst out the back of his tent and scrambled dazedly to his feet. He screamed loudly, then spotted Les.

"There's a monster in my tent!" He ran to Les and got behind him.

Les and David, both now wielding large sticks, stood several feet from the back of Tommy's tent with their flashlights illuminating the torn nylon. They watched in terror as something crawled out. At first it looked like a small bear, only with an elderly man's face. At that moment there was a flash of bright light and the three of them quickly realized they has just had their picture taken by a flash camera. Don emerged from behind a tree a few feet away laughing loudly. The monster in Tommy's tent removed a rubber mask to reveal Harry's face. He rolled on the ground laughing.

"That was great guys!" Don exclaimed. He walked over to Harry and gave him a hand getting to his feet. "I got a good picture of it too."

"Very funny," Tommy said sarcastically. "You made me tear up my tent. It's ruined!"

"We'll help you repair your tent," Harry said.

"You shitheads!" Les said. "What the hell are you thinking?"

"Just having a little fun," Don said. "We've got to initiate the new guy. It's tradition."

"There's no such tradition", David shot back. "You guys are just being idiots!"

"Who are you calling an idiot!" Harry said.

"You Harry," Tommy said. "Now my tent's torn-up and it's cold out here."

"Don't be such a wussie", Harry said. "Just zip your sleeping bag all the way and curl up with your teddy bear. You'll be fine."

"Alright, enough already," Les said. "Let's just get back to sleep. Tommy, try to make do with your tent tonight. We can try repairing it tomorrow afternoon when we get to the next campsite."

Tommy sighed. "Okay I guess."

Harry headed back to his tent and Don followed him, looking back over his shoulder. "Come on guys," he said. "You've got to admit it was a funny prank."

"Sure was," Les replied with a smirk. "I'll be lying awake for the next hour laughing about it."

"Yeah, me too," David added. "Jackass."

They each got back into their sleeping bags and all was quiet again within a few minutes. Les fell back to sleep in mere moments.

About two hours later the silence was again broken by another of Tommy's loud screams. Les shot awake and paused momentarily as Tommy screamed repeatedly and could be heard thrashing about in his tent.

"Dammit!" David yelled. "Aren't you two ever going to grow up?"

"Let go of me!" Tommy could be heard screaming. "You're hurting me you sons of bitches!" Then came a loud thump, like someone being hit with a large object.

"No," they heard him cry out again. Then came the sound of him running into the woods.

Les scrambled out of the tent with David right behind him. Both were shocked when Don and Harry emerged from their tent and rushed over to them. "What the hell is happening?" Don said. It was obvious to the rest of them that they had just been awakened as suddenly as were Les and David.

The four of them turned their attention some distance away where Tommy could be heard screaming hysterically as he ran headlong through the pitch-dark woods. "Help! They're after me!" he shouted frantically. "Help Me!"

"He's lost his freaking mind!" Harry said.

"Hey Tommy", Don shouted. "It's okay, we're not chasing after you. Get back over here before you get hurt."

Not seeming to hear him, Tommy continued to scream as he ran blindly through the forest. "No! No! No! Get away from me you sons-of bitches! Get away! Get away!"

"What is he running from?" David said. All four of them were shining their flashlights in Tommy's direction but they revealed nothing in the distant darkness.

"Whatever it is he needs to lead it back this way in order for us to help him," Les said. "Tommy, come back to camp."

As they stood helplessly beside Tommy's tent, trying to follow his movements by the sounds of his footsteps, they heard him fading further into the wilderness. A moment later they heard a loud thud as he hit something hard. Les thought he could actually distinguish the sound of the very breath leaving Tommy's body as he stopped suddenly, crashing through brush and sliding to a halt in the crisp leaves of the ground. After that there was only silence.

"Tommy!" Les called out. "You okay?" No reply came. "Tommy," he called out again, this time more frantically. "Tommy, where are you?" He looked at Don and then back at Harry. "Oh shit!"

"Listen!" Don said. The four of them stood motionless, straining with their ears. What sounded like muffled footsteps could be heard moving about faintly for several moments. "Who's out there?" he yelled.

No reply came but Les thought he heard the footsteps disappear into the woods. "Everybody get your boots on fast," he whispered loudly. "We've got to get to him right away. Don, grab your knife and the bear repellant."

"Got them right here," he replied.

Les reached inside the tent and grabbed his boots, then sat on the ground, holding his flashlight in his mouth as he tied them. David sat nearby doing the same thing. The whole process took less than a minute. Les then reached into his backpack and pulled out the small first-aid kit.

"It sounded like he ran somewhere over this way," Les heard Don say. He and Harry were in the woods about twenty-yards away, shining their lights in all directions.

"Anybody see him?" Les called out as he stood up.

"Not yet," Harry said. "If he's here we'll find him."

"If he's here?" David said. He gave Les a puzzled look.

Les was standing next to the back of Tommy's tent, inspecting it with his light. "I think it's a bear we're dealing with," he said. "I don't see any animal fur in here though. An no tracks on the ground. Very strange."

He took a quick glance up and saw Don and Harry's flashlights being brandished about a hundred-feet or so away. They were calling Tommy's name and having no luck finding him.

"I'm going to get those two assholes thrown out of the scout troop when this is all over."

"I hope that's the worst thing that comes from all this," David said. "Do you really think it's a bear?"

"Don't you?"

David paused. "No tracks or fur, an attack so quiet that none of us heard a thing? Tommy attacked when there wasn't any food in his tent?" He glanced up and all around. "In an Indian burial ground?"

Les studied David's face for a moment and felt a cold chill run down his back. He could see genuine fear in his friend's eyes.

"Let's go see if we can find the poor kid."

They headed into the woods and began combing the area, gradually moving farther and farther from the campsite. Soon they were retracing their steps and checking the same places a second time. Sometime later Les looked at his watch and was astounded to see that they had been searching for over an hour.

"Does anybody see any trace of him at all?" Les said.

All three of the others replied negatively. "I can't believe this," Harry said. "It's as if he walked right off the face of the earth."

"I don't think we're going to find him until the sun comes up," Don said. He walked over to the campfire and began stirring it with a stick. Harry joined him and added a few small pieces of wood. Moments later it popped back to life.

Les and David took seats beside the fire and began warming their hands. Les hadn't realized how cold and exhausted he was until that moment.

"What time do you have?" Harry said.

Les, his brain working in slow-motion, paused a moment before looking at his watch. "4:32."

"It's going to be another hour-and-a-half before we start to get any morning light," Don said. "Not much point in looking further until then."

"What the hell was it that attacked him?" David said. He looked around nervously and was obviously trembling. "Whatever it is it could still be out there."

"I think it's gone," Harry said. "Must have been a big bear."

"Black bears don't usually attack like that unless they are trying to steal food," Don said. "Unless it was a Grizzly."

"There aren't any Grizzly bears in this part of the country," Les said. "I don't think we're dealing with an animal." The others all stared at him.

"Well if it's not a bear then what is it we're dealing with?" David said.

"Whatever it is it's walks on two feet," Les said.

He glanced at his feet and spotted his first-aid kit where he had set it on the ground sometime earlier. In it were smelling salts, bandages, antiseptics and aspirin, none of which could do him or Tommy any good at the moment. He felt overwhelmed by helplessness.

The four of them sat silently around the campfire, each constantly watching the dark woods over the shoulder of his buddy across the campfire. Occasionally someone would toss a few sticks into the fire or take a drink from a canteen. The minutes passed like hours.

Now and then Les would look into Don or Harry's faces. They both sat staring blankly into the flames. He could only imagine what might be going through their minds. Suddenly David put into words exactly what he had been thinking for the last two hours.

"I just can't stop thinking that this whole mess could have been avoided if you two hadn't decided to pull that rubber mask stunt. There's just no place for that kind of crap out here in the deep woods."

Don shot him an angry look. "So what are you saying David? You think this is somehow our fault?"

"We were in our tent the entire time," Harry said. "Don't you two jerks come out of these woods trying to blame this on us. It was an accident!"

"A very preventable one," Les shot back.

"He'll be fine once we find him," Don said, looking up at the dark sky. "We just need some daylight. Maybe in another hour or so."

Les resumed staring into the fire and they all went silent for awhile. He found himself not wanting to look Don or Harry in the eye. He could think of at least a thousand places he'd rather be right now than here. It was a new all-time low in his lifetime of camping experiences.

There was no point in discussing blame and fighting about it. That would do little more than waste their limited supply of energy.

There were so many things he wanted to say to the two of them, not just about tonight but the entire last year in general. They were no longer his scouting buddies but something totally different. In the last year, ever since they became seniors and got driver's learning permits they turned into teen punks. Bigger boys than before physically but smaller mentally.

They had gone from somewhat smart to complete smart-asses, with matching bad attitudes and grossly inflated egos. Potential thieves, cheats and cell mates. Virtually all traces of respect and trust he once had for them were fading like the weakening voices of the crickets and tree frogs into the cold, wintering woods that surrounded them.

Les had to keep his wits about him and bury his feelings as much as he could. In reality, he wanted to scream at them and punctuate it with continual blows to the face with his fists. After years and years of scout trips, safety lectures, merit awards and team-building exercises, Don and Harry had broken practically every rule in less than 24-hours. They had soiled everything scouting stood for and it made him sick. He knew his life would never be the same again after this night. It was going to be his introduction to manhood, just never in the way he had ever imagined.

He glanced around the fire at the three of them, then into the direction where he last heard Tommy scream, now over two hours past. He hoped to hear moans, or crying, or anything that would lead them to him. All he heard was the eerie silence of the woods.

Les felt sick and somewhat ashamed. They had deep trouble on their hands. Somewhere, probably less than two-hundred feet away, Tommy lay unconscious, maybe dying, and there was nothing they could do about it.

Les felt a quiver from somewhere deep in his throat as his mind flashed memories of other hurtful experiences he'd been trying to bury for years. He remembered from childhood the familiar first sign that he was about to burst into tears. Then, like now he stifled it with all his might.

The last time he remembered feeling the quiver was the night right after New Years two years ago when his mother told him she and Frosty had decided not to see each other anymore. She gave him no further details.

Les took the news in stony silence. After a moment he realized he would never even have the chance to tell Frosty goodbye. That had hit him like a bean-ball. And he never saw it coming.

Over the next several months after that he secretly hoped Frosty would just drop by one day while he was out cutting the grass or walking home from school but it never happened. Maybe it was just as well. Although Les played the scenario over in his head many times, he still didn't know what he'd say if the situation ever came up. It was perhaps the first time in his teen life that he realized the normal human need for closure.

As Les sat looking into the campfire he felt alone, even though David was only inches away to his left. Depressing thoughts have a way of gathering in the human mind, he thought.

He would just have to try and forget about Frosty. But at the moment, he just needed to keep the quiver in his throat from becoming chattering in his teeth and tears on his cheeks. He took a quick look around the camp fire and saw that nobody was noticing. That offered the faintest amount of relief.

His thoughts then drifted back to some of the many things Frosty had told him about the plight of the red man and how the European settlers had at first befriended them before turning on them. Attacking and killing them, taking their farmland, their animals, their way of life, and finally shuffling them off to the barren land of the Midwest, out of sight and out of mind.

He had known all this Native American history for years, but for the first time it was all coming together in his mind, making him sad and angry. And, for the moment at least, ashamed.

That's when he remembered the most frightening thing Frosty ever told him about Native American warriors. "They didn't always attack in a loud charge like they did in the old black and white movie westerns," Frosty had said. "They were crafty and meticulous, creeping in at night and silently killing one opponent at a time while they slept. By the time the victims knew there was a danger their numbers had already been severely shortened. Then the final charge was an easy slaughter."

Les felt a pang of fear as he looked around them in all directions, wondering if they were being watched from behind the trees. Earlier he had felt that the danger had passed and they were alone. Now, he wasn't so sure.

The fears and bad memories continued for a long time, and somehow Les kept himself from sobbing. He was finally brought back to reality when he heard Don say: "there's the first sign of daylight."

They all looked up toward the east and saw redness in the clouds at the horizon. "Maybe in a few minutes it will be bright enough that we can find Tommy," David said.

"Yeah," Harry said. "We'll find him."

Les looked at Harry, then Don. "You guys sure have a crummy way of initiating new guys. Or is this just how you cash-in your insurance policy when you're done with it?"

Don looked up at Les and appeared almost too tired to speak. "I feel terrible for Tommy," he said at last. "I wish we could have saved him from whatever it is that attacked him. But he never should have been here with us in the first place."

"Come again," David said.

"Don tried everything he could think of to get Tommy left at home this weekend," Harry said. "But his mom was never going to go for it."

"It was like negotiating with a stone wall," Don said. "It finally boiled-down to Tommy comes along or no hike."

"None of us should be here right now," David said. "This whole hike idea was a mistake."

"Nobody forced you to come with us," Don said. "You're he because you wanted to be. And if Tommy's mother had just said no then we wouldn't be in this predicament."

"Pretty smooth negotiating," Les said. "Tommy's mom deals out the cards and we all lose." He stood and removed his jacket. "Well, no use arguing over it now, our fate is sealed. Whatever that's going to be."

"I'm just wondering what we're going tell them when we get back," David said.

Les looked at him a moment. "We tell them the truth."

"Yeah," Harry said. "It was a tragic accident."

"That's not exactly the truth," David said. "You guys played us for fools. Especially Tommy."

"Our little prank had nothing to do with what happened to him," Don shot back.

"What happened was an accident involving some kind of wildlife," Harry said. "It could have happened to anybody. Any further details about what we were doing out here won't change the outcome one way or the other so let's just keep our mission to ourselves."

"That's right," Don said. So when we get back you guys just let me do the talking."

"Oh, I get it," Les said. "Just as long as we all say the same thing then everything's cool."

Don looked at him for a long moment. "Yeah, that's about right."

Les stared at him in shock and disbelief. He wanted to say so many things he couldn't decide what should come first. "Listen to you," he said finally. "You act like Tommy is just a prop, like a tent-pole. You got what you came for so you're satisfied. So what if it got Tommy killed."

"Who said anything about him getting killed!" Don said. "He's fine out there wherever he is. He just got knocked-out, that's all. We'll find him and get him on his feet in no time. You're just paranoid, Les."

"Yeah, well I guess we'll find out when the sun comes up, won't we," Les said.

"That's right," Don said. "He'll be fine, you'll see."

Les could now make out some of the landscape around them in the faint morning light. Without another word he began walking back into the woods. The others joined him and began searching for their fallen friend. Less than ten minutes later David cried out: "I found him."

They all rushed over to where he was standing. "There," he said, pointing down an embankment. Les spotted Tommy lying motionless in a heap against a large rotting tree. They were standing on an outcropping of rocks that formed a shelf about five-feet above the ground below. Tommy had apparently run off the end of it and fallen face first to the ground. Les rushed down to him with the others close behind.

"I can't believe he's so close to camp," Don said. "I could swear I looked down here at least three times."

"I thought I did too," Harry said. "It's almost like he wasn't in that spot until now."

"Do you guys realize how crazy that sounds?" David said.

Harry and Don looked at each other, then around the surrounding woods nervously. Meanwhile, Les was slowly rolling Tommy over.

"Oh shit," David said. "Look at his face."

Tommy was pale white, his lips colorless and pallid. His left eye was badly swollen and the whole left side of his face was dark purple. He had been sleeping in his pajamas, which were now tattered and dirty. His right leg was bloody from the knee down and the buttons on his shirt were torn off. Tommy's bare chest was scraped and bloody from an apparent run through a briar patch and his hands and feet were covered in dried mud.

Les couldn't help noticing that Tommy's facial injury was on exactly the same spot that Don touched him with the skull the day before. He put his ear to Tommy's chest.

"Is he alive?" Harry asked softly. "Please tell me he's alive."

"His heart's beating," Les said, "but just barely. I'm pretty sure he's in shock. We've got to get him to a doctor and fast."

"How?" David said. "We're a long way from the road, it'll take forever."

"Hey," Harry said, "remember that old rowboat we saw back at the stream? Let's take it and go wherever the current takes us."

"What if it doesn't float?" Don said. "What do we do then?"

"I think you're on to something Don," David said. "I doubt it will hold all of us but it sure would be a good way to move out of these woods fast."

"I know how we can do it," Les said. "We all four have air mattresses. And I've got a spool of about thirty-feet of nylon cord. We'll carry those with us and put them under the old boat. Then we lace it up nice and tight. We'll be able to make a raft that will really move by doing that."

"Then that's the plan," Don said. "Let's get moving."

"First things first," Les said. "Let's start by making a stretcher. Follow the procedures from the emergency manual."

Don gave him a confused look. Les realized he was the only one present to have gotten a merit badge in that particular discipline.

"We'll need two poles about six feet long," he said. "A couple of young dogwood trees should do. David, assemble your little hand saw and start cutting. I'll get Tommy's sleeping bag."

"What about the tents and stuff?" Harry said.

"Never mind them," Les said. "We can come back and get those later."

"How much later?" Don said.

Les looked at him and had to hold himself back to keep from punching him. "How about next May? Is next May good for you, Don?"

Don and Harry seemed to both realize at that moment that it might just be best to do what Les said and not make any comments or suggestions. "Any more stupid questions?" Les asked. They both shook their heads.

From that point on they worked as a team mostly in silence, broken only periodically by instructions from Les. A few minutes later they carefully rolled Tommy onto a crude stretcher and donned their back packs. "Don, you and David carry him first," Les said. "I'll use the compass to get us back to the trail. They picked up the stretcher and began the long hike.

The going was slow at first. The terrain was uneven and Les had to make frequent checks of the compass. He and Don traded that duty several times as they took turns carrying Tommy.

It took over an hour, but they finally made it back to the main trail. From there it was a short hike to the stream. Harry ran over to the old boat and dragged it to the water. Remnants of spider webs and clumps of dried mud tried to come off as he slid it out into the open.

"Harry, start wiping the crap off the bottom and sides of the boat," Les said. "That will make it a few pounds lighter."

"Me?" he replied.

David and Les had just set Tommy down. They had his stretcher covered heavily with sleeping bags and only his closed eyes could be seen under his stocking-cap.

Les looked over at David, then at Harry. "Oh, I forgot. Don, you get over and help him."

"What do I use to wipe it with?" Don asked.

"Try Harry's face," David said. Don gave him a nasty glare. Harry held up his fist and scowled.

"You two jackasses got us into this mess and you're going to do everything you can to get us out of it," Les said, actually losing his temper for the first time. "Now reach down there with your bare hands and wipe down the damn boat!"

Without another word they both did as they were told. "Come on David," Les said. "Let's get these mattresses inflated." He pulled the foot-pump out of his backpack.

Once the blowing-up process was done on the floats, Les tied them together in a square using the cord. They then put the old rowboat on top of the air mattresses and tied it down at the corners.

"Okay, let's see how well she floats," Les said. He pulled the boat along the beach to the water and waded away from shore.

"Looks good from here," David said. Then to Don and Harry: "Get Tommy and come on."

Together the four of them set the stretcher in the boat and tied it down. Then they started wading downstream. After a short distance the water got deep enough for them to get into the boat as well. Soon after that they were sharing duties with the two oars in a mild current.

Several creeks on either side spilled into the waterway that had now become a small river. The oars were worn and gnawed, making it difficult to row fast. Luckily, the current was helping to move them along.

"I think I see a cabin up ahead," David said a few silent minutes later. There was a heavy mist rising from the water and the sky overhead was cloudy and dark. A distant porch light was now visible as they realized they had finally come across a hint of human civilization.

"There's a dock over there," Don said. "Let's see if we can row over to it." Les and Harry had the two oars and together they managed to maneuver the boat up to the end of the small and somewhat dilapidated wooden structure.

"I'll go see if anybody's home," David said, and he carefully got out of the boat. He ran to the house and knocked on the door. An elderly man in a bathrobe answered. Les could see David talking to the man and pointing back toward the boat. After a minute he came back to the dock. "He said there's a doctor that lives a couple of miles up the road. He's phoning him now. Let's get Tommy inside."

It took all four of them to get the still-unconscious Tommy out of the boat in the stretcher. They then carried him up to the house.

"Let's take him in this room and lay him on the bed," the man told them. "The doctor said he'll be here in about ten minutes."

They carefully rolled Tommy onto the bed, then went into the living room and took a seat on the couch. A short time later there was a knock at the door. The doctor, a man of about fifty, came in and greeted the homeowner. "Thanks for coming, Pete," he said. "The boy is in the bedroom."

"Who is he, George?" he asked. Then he noticed the other four.

"Those boys brought him here," George said. "They told me they were hiking in the area and the boy fell. He doesn't look good."

Pete headed for the bedroom. "Let me look at the injured boy first. Then I'll want to talk to them." The two of them went into the bedroom and closed the door. A minute later the homeowner, George, came back out.

"Who are you boys and what brings you way out here?"

"We're boy scouts," Les said. He introduced the four of them as well as Tommy in absentia. "We've been out on the trail since Friday."

"What happened to Tommy?"

"Bear attack," Les said. "It sprang into his tent around 2:30 this morning. We all heard him screaming as it chased him into the woods. I think he ran into a tree and fell down an embankment. We weren't able to locate him until dawn."

"I see," George said. He made no effort to introduce himself or try to make them feel at home. The four boys sat while he stood. He looked at each of them, then stared out the window for a moment. He seemed to

Les to be deep in thought. Then he turned to face them with a puzzled look on his face.

"Why were you boys hiking this far from the national forest trails?"

"Like I said," Les replied, "we're scouts . . ."

"I know that," George interrupted. "I mean, why are you here instead of over at Blood Mountain or Springer or Amicolola Falls?"

"We've already been to all those places," Don said. "We came here because it's a place we've never been before. We just followed a map."

George glared at him. "A map! If you've got a map then you should be aware that you're nowhere near public land. Every acre around here is privately owned."

"Well, sure we are now," Don said. "But we weren't when we got the boat into the water upstream."

George looked at him but didn't reply for a moment. Then he asked the question that would shock Les so much that he'd remember it the rest of his life.

"You boys weren't anywhere near that Indian Burial Ground, were you?"

Les felt his heart jump into his throat. He searched his brain for a response but Don beat him to it.

"What Indian Burial Ground?" He acted puzzled by the question. The response seemed to placate George and Don smiled slightly. That made Les even more nervous.

"There's an ancient Indian Burial Ground a few miles from here," George said. "It's a bad place! People go in there and don't come out. You never want to go there. They used to put its location on maps but don't anymore. Good thing too. Not after some of the things that have happened up there."

Les and David looked at each other but neither spoke. George continued to pace slowly across the living room, occasionally glancing in the direction of the closed bedroom door where Pete was examining Tommy. "That tribal graveyard is an evil place. An evil place."

Les was shocked that George even knew about the Burial Ground. He was beginning to realize now how bad their judgement had been.

"My dad's a Nam vet," Don interjected suddenly. "He told me bad things happen to people who trespass in native people's burial places."

Les glared at him. He couldn't believe his ears. Don was being the ultimate smart-ass and everyone but the old man knew it.

George gave him a thoughtful glance. "That's true son. Indian Burial Grounds are sacred places. No white man should ever go into them. Indians leave symbolic statues behind to guard the grounds when they leave. Some of those statues carry evil curses that take on a life of their own against trespassers when they are disturbed.

"That's why the National Park Service doesn't advertise the existence of such places. The fewer people that know about them the better. You play around in a place like that and you can end-up with a lifetime of trouble. Or no lifetime at all."

George returned his gaze out the window toward the misty river. "The best thing that could happen is for that evil place to remain hidden in the woods, forgotten and ignored forever."

Les looked over at Harry. Unlike Don, the old man's point of view seemed to hold more value to him than it did when Les had said the same thing the night before. Les thought Harry almost looked scared. Only one day too late, he thought.

At that moment the bedroom door opened and the doctor emerged. Without thinking, Les stood and the other boys followed suit. The expression on Pete's face told the whole story, even before he said anything. "I'm sorry boys. It was too late."

"You don't mean he's dead," Harry said. Unlike Les, he appeared to have no idea such news was coming. "But he was only knocked-out."

"He was in shock long before you boys got him here," Pete said. "He'd lost some blood and the overnight chill dropped his body temperature to hypothermic levels. There was nothing any of us could have done for him."

Les felt his heart sink to a new low. Tommy was dead. Deep down, he'd known it was coming for hours, and yet it still didn't seem possible.

"I need you boys to come with me," Pete said. He turned and walked back toward the bedroom and the four of them followed. Les led the way.

Tommy was lying on top of the bed sheets with his mouth slightly open like he had died in the middle of a scream. The massive bruise on his face had turned a sickening yellow, and the cuts on his bare chest and stomach were a criss-cross of bloody streaks.

"You said he was running from a bear in the dark, hit a tree and fell into a ravine. Is that right?"

"Yes," Don said. "Then we couldn't find him with our flashlights. We searched for over two hours."

Pete looked at him for a long moment. "You sure it was just one bear?"

"We're not sure what it was," Les said. "We never actually saw a bear."

"I was thinking it might have been a hornet's nest," David said. "He just kept running through the woods like he'd lost his mind. But I didn't see any stings on him."

"Bees wouldn't have swarmed into his tent," Pete said. "And there's not a single sting on him. Or a claw mark or a snake bite. He was running from something else. Was there somebody else out there in those woods?"

"No," David said. "Just the four of us."

"Nobody else that we know about," Harry said. "And the rest of us were asleep in our tents when it happened."

"These injuries don't look to me like they were inflicted by an animal," Pete said. "I think this is the work of a man. Or maybe several." The four of them were speechless.

"There's something you boys aren't telling us," George said from behind them. "What are you hiding?"

"Nothing," Don said. Les thought he sounded close to tears. "He fell in the woods in the dark. That's all we know."

Les stood staring at Tommy as he lay still on the bed. His feet felt like they were caked in blocks of ice. The familiar quiver in his throat reappeared.

The doctor reached down toward the foot of the bed and pulled up the sheet revealing Tommy's right leg. "Look right here," he said, pointing with his gloved hand. He gently twisted Tommy's leg outward to reveal three deep slice marks in a neat row along the inside of the calf just above the ankle. Dried blood was caked around the gashes that were half-an-inch deep and of uniform size.

"What caused those?" Harry said.

Pete glanced over at George who wore an expression of horror on his face. "I was hoping you could tell me. It looks like someone tried to cut off his foot with a blunt instrument like a hatchet."

"Or a tomahawk," George said.

The doctor looked at the four boys sternly. "Are you sure nobody else was out in those woods besides the four of you."

"No," Les said. "I . . . I don't see how. Nobody could have operated like that in total darkness." He looked around at the others.

"I didn't see anyone either," Don said. "Still, he was out there where we couldn't find him for over two hours."

"It's was the Little People," George suddenly cried out. Les turned and looked into his face. The man was terrified. "You boys went into that Burial Ground didn't you? You've unleashed an unholy curse! Do you know what that means? You all are dead! Dead I tell you!"

"Calm down, George," Pete told him. "That's nothing but an old wives' tale."

"It's more than that and you know it, Pete," George said. "You remember that couple that disappeared up that way about six or seven years ago. All that was ever found of them was their heads. And what about those three punks two summers ago . . ."

"Those incidents had nothing to do with the Burial Ground, George!" Pete said.

George stared at him for a moment. "The hell they didn't." He turned and looked from boy to boy with an expression of anger mixed with fear. Les even noticed his chin quivering slightly. "You've unleashed that evil Indian curse. It's going to track you down. All of you. There's no escaping it. You're all as good as dead!"

"That's enough George!" Pete said. That startled him and he looked at the doctor with fear in his eyes. The four boys waited to hear what he was going to say next.

"I'll go call the sheriff," Pete said. "I'm ruling this a tragic accident. You boys better go call your fathers. And when you get home you all should make appointments to see your school counselor. Something like this can cause psychological problems later if you don't get help right away."

"You boys have much bigger problems on your hands than any school counselor can fix," George said, pointing at them with a trembling finger like a one-man jury. "You are going to need more like a mystic, or a voodoo man. Hell, a miracle is what you're going to need, you stupid punk fools!"

"George, please!" Pete said.

George gave him a brief startled look. He then turned his gaze back to the four boys. "Go call your fathers right now. Collect. Then I want you out of my house. All of you. You can wait for your rides outside."

Pete, seeming to realize there would be no reasoning with George, whom he'd known some seventeen-years, sighed. "I've got a better idea. You boys help me get your friend's body into the back of my station wagon. We'll go over to my office. I have a refrigerated storage facility there. You can call your fathers then. I'm afraid it won't make any difference to Tommy."

"I'll help you with the dead boy," George said. "You four go on outside right now."

"Alright, we're going," Don said. "Come on dudes. We know when we're not welcome." He headed for the front door and Harry quickly followed.

"George," Pete said, "their friend just died. Be a little more understanding."

"You be understanding, Pete," he said. "I'm telling you they're cursed. And I don't want them anywhere near me."

Don turned and started to respond but Les grabbed his shoulder. "Don't say a word," he whispered. "You either Harry."

Once outside Don had a few choice words for the others about George. "Man, is that guy a prick or what? I wonder where he grows whatever the hell it is he's been smoking."

"Really!" Harry agreed.

"Don't let him hear you," David said.

"What's he going to do? Make us start walking?"

"I wouldn't put it past him," Les said. "Look guys, let's just go up his driveway a ways and sit on a log or something while we wait for the doctor. They should have Tommy loaded in just a few minutes."

They walked a hundred-feet or so from the house and spotted a large log that had seating room for all four of them. Once they were comfortable they began reaching into their packs for a snack.

They sat eating silently for the next several minutes. The day remained cloudy and cool.

"Do you suppose it's true?" Harry asked. "You know, about that curse."

Don chuckled sarcastically. "Hell no! That's all a bunch of crap. How many times do I have to say it?"

David was just finishing the last bite of pita bread smeared with peanut butter. "I don't know, Don. He seemed pretty convinced. And that stuff about incidents that have already happened up there. I'd sure like to know more about them."

Les didn't bother to join the conversation. As the other three talked he sat and ate the last of his trail mix and sipped from his canteen.

"What do you think, Les?" David said at last.

Les looked around the others and struggled for something to say. At that moment Pete's tan station wagon pulled up and stopped. "Okay boys, climb in."

It was only about a twenty-minute ride to Pete's office. Hardly anyone spoke. Occasionally, one of them would turn and look back at Tommy's body lying under a sheet in the back of the car.

"Are we in trouble?" David asked. He was sitting in the back seat on the passenger's side. Pete looked up and made eye contact with him in the rear view mirror.

"You mean legally or morally?" The doctor paused a moment to allow a yellow jeep to drive past before turning left into the parking lot of his small office. "No, I'll explain it to the sheriff and your parents. This was just a tragic backpacking accident. Such things are really more common than you think."

He pulled into a parking space and cut the engine. "Okay, let's go get on the phone. The sooner we call the sooner they'll get here."

After a brief discussion the four of them decided it would be best to call Don's father and David's father. The doctor would handle contacting Tommy's mother. Luckily Don knew how to reach her.

Once the calls were made the four of them took seats in the waiting room. Les got comfortable on a large leather couch and immediately began to doze. He was soon interrupted, however, by Don, who suddenly seemed to be feeling the effects of a guilty conscience.

"Listen guys," he said, "for what it's worth, we never intended for Tommy to ever get hurt out there."

Les opened his heavy eyelids and looked at the two of them. It took a long moment for him to gather the strength to reply.

"I know."

"I still can't believe all this," David said, shaking his head. "This is like the worst nightmare I've ever had."

"Worst nightmare for all of us," Les said. He closed his eyes again and dozed-off within moments. About an hour later he awakened when he heard David's father enter the front door. The sheriff came in right behind him. Pete invited both of them to the back for a private conversation. Ten minutes later Don's father arrived and joined them.

Les continued to snooze on the couch and basically slept through the entire debriefing process. Sometime later David came and shook him awake. "Come on Les. Let's go home."

Without a word he got up and walked to the back seat of David's family car and set his pack on the floor. The three of them left without any further conversation with Don or Harry.

As Les dozed in the back, David sat up front and answered his father's relentless questions. Although he paid little attention to their conversation, he did pick-up bits and pieces of it.

"I had a chance to talk to the sheriff when he first arrived," Les heard David tell his father. "Don and Harry were in the back at the snack machine and didn't know he'd gotten there yet. So I told him all about how those two jerks led us off the main trails so we could visit a real Indian camp. I also told them about the rubber masks and scaring Tommy out the back of his tent earlier. I wanted him to know right off the bat that Les and I had nothing to do with how it turned-out."

"Good thinking," his dad agreed.

The entire way home Les slept almost all the time. When he fluttered awake for brief moments, and the severity of this awful situation hit him again, he found himself repeatedly thanking God that they had gotten out of the doctor's office before Tommy's estranged parents arrived there.

Sometime later they reached the driveway of Les's house. He got out, paused briefly to thank David's dad for the ride and said his goodbyes.

The rest of that Sunday passed for Les like he was in a daze. He would later learn that the sheriff had talked to Don, Harry and Don's father before allowing them to leave. They got a stern lecture from him about how he would have arrested the boys for trespassing on private land if they were eighteen. It would have gone on their permanent record and they each might have gotten some jail time. But, given the circumstances, he figured they had learned a pretty good lesson in the worst way. That was probably punishment enough. So he figured anyway.

Harry was relieved that the morning finally ended without anyone getting a rap sheet out of the deal. Don was even more relieved that it ended without anyone even suggesting they inspect the contents of his back pack.

Les lay awake that Sunday night for some time before finally falling asleep. The weekend had started out with such promise on Friday afternoon. That day seemed a month ago now.

Tommy was laid to rest two days later. Les and David sat near the back of the small church during the funeral and basically kept to themselves the whole time. They never saw Don or Harry.

Although Les and David hardly spoke during the funeral, both felt some comfort from having the other one there. It didn't make things any easier for Les, however. He had never felt so low in his whole life.

Over the next few days Les began to notice images that popped into his mind for no apparent reason. While studying in the quiet of his bedroom one night he suddenly thought he heard Indian drums from somewhere far away outside.

The next night he awoke in the early-morning hours from a nightmare about being attacked by an Indian brave who had entered his tent with a large knife. As he lay awake, trying to calm his racing heartbeat, he thought he heard something scratching at the screen in the window above his head.

He knew the neighbors had a cat that sometimes came around. But he'd never known the cat to scratch the window screen. And besides, the window was four feet above the ground.

Am I hearing that or just imagining it? he thought. The scratching was faint, but he was almost sure it was there. Scratch, scratch, scratch. There it was again. He pulled the sheet up to his ears. It came again. Scratch, scratch, scratch. Les wasn't sure if he could muster the courage to get up and look out the window. He lay awake for a long time but didn't hear it again.

The nightmares got worse the next night when he dreamt that he was part of an 1800s U.S. Army unit. He was witnessing a firing squad that was executing several blindfolded Indian braves who had participated in a failed attack. In the dream an evil-looking sergeant with only part of a face ordered him to light a torch and burn down a small village while the terrified Indian women and children stood at gunpoint and watched, each sobbing fearfully. He awoke from that dream in a cold sweat.

His dreams seemed to be taunting him, making him wonder if there was something to all that curse talk after all. As he struggled to come to grips with the after-effects of the previous weekend, he considered taking the advice of Doctor Pete and making an appointment with the school counselor. Then he thought about how he would try to explain his dilemma to the her without looking like a complete jerk, or a criminal. He finally decided to wait a few more days to see if things would get any better on their own.

There was no doubt in his mind that the night in the Burial Ground had made a significant impact on his mental stability. With each passing day he believed more and more that there really was an Indian curse that they had awakened in the woods. It worried him constantly.

CHAPTER 7

A RAINY DAY AT THE FISHING HOLE

In the days that followed the harrowing camping trip, Les withdrew somewhat from the other boys. He aimlessly trudged the hallways at school, shuffling from class to class like a man who wanted to just be invisible. He didn't know how many of his fellow students even knew about what he had been through and didn't really care. All he wanted was to be left alone and those around him seemed to detect it. He had very little conversation with anyone the whole week.

David lived about four miles from Les and a get-together between the two of them required some planning. Either a lift by car from a parent or a lengthy bike ride was required for one to visit the other.

They talked by phone a few times in the days following the tragedy and saw each other at school, but neither suggested getting together. Les spent most of his days after school at home, helping his mother around the house and studying. With the nights came the nightmares.

Meanwhile, David was dealing with the tragedy the best he could by withdrawing somewhat as well. His brother, John, who was three years younger, wasn't much fun to be around and David found John's friends, who seemed to be visiting their house constantly, annoying at best.

David began searching for things to do away from home in the afternoons after school, and ended up hanging-out mostly with Walt and Robert, two guys in his neighborhood that he had played with since he was in grade school.

On Saturday afternoon after helping his dad rake leaves, David walked over to Walt's house to see if he might want to play a little one-on-one basketball. Walt's mom answered the door and told him that Walt had gone with Robert down to the end of the street to fish in the creek.

David knew the place well. The street they lived on dead-ended at the bottom of a hill into a cross-street. The row of houses that stood along that street were backed by a large creek that formed the rear boundary of their properties.

There were a couple of places where storm drains ran into small ravines that fed rainwater from the street into the creek. Over the years David and all the other kids in the neighborhood had used the ravines to access the shore-line of the small waterway.

There was a particularly wide spot on the creek where the water reached a depth of around six feet. The "pond", as the boys called it, was some thirty-feet across from one bank to the other and about fifty-feet long. A large pipe ran the width of the pond with two cement support platforms at the one-third points. The section of the pipe between the two supports was a perfect place for the boys to sit and dangle their feet.

In the pond were bream, bass, catfish, crappy and all other kinds of natural creek and pond life native to the southeastern United States. Of course, an occasional snake showed up as well and the boys always had to be alert for copper heads and water moccasins.

For the last seven or eight years, David, Robert and Walt had come to the creek almost every day of summer to fish. Armed with fishing poles made from bamboo stalks with six feet of fishing line, a hook, sinker and float, the three boys had spent countless hours talking, laughing and joking as they caught and released the pond's collection of small game fish.

Sometimes one of them would catch a few worms or some grasshoppers for bait, other times they would get a piece of raw bacon out of their mother's refrigerator. Whatever the circumstances, the summer days of youth had drifted by with many hours of pleasure in this isolated spot on the outskirts of the city.

The three of them often talked of going fishing together in some exotic location like the Caribbean or the Gulf of Mexico, or of getting a boat and heading to a lake together. It was all talk of course, nothing more than sharing a dream as they fished in their private little pond.

About one-hundred-yards past the creek was an embankment with railroad tracks at the top. Sometimes, as they sat fishing, they'd hear the steady beat of the locomotives coming up the tracks. A few minutes later the sound would build to a crescendo and the train would roll past and above them, making the pipe on which they sat vibrate just a little.

The three of them would always look at the engineer, sitting inside the open window and preparing to start blowing the horn as the train approached the cross-road a half-mile or so ahead. Occasionally the engineer would look their way and they'd all wave. He'd smile and wave back, sometimes giving them a short blast on the mighty horn. It made for a memorable moment for three kids fishing in their neighborhood pond of dreams. It was southern living at its best.

As they had grown older, the three boys found themselves fishing less often. What had once been a daily activity was now a rare and special occasion. When Walt's mom told David that the other two guys were down at the pond, he quickly retreated back home to see if his fishing pole was still in the spot in the garage where he had left it after the last time he had used it back in July or August.

He went into the garage and spotted it right away. Grabbing it, he turned and headed for the half-mile walk to the bottom of his street and an afternoon of reliving his childhood one more time. About ten minutes later he stepped from the road into the familiar ravine that ran between two houses and headed to the fishing pond.

When David emerged from the trail through the woods he spotted Walt and Robert sitting on the big pipe. "Hey guys," he called out. The two of them looked around with startled expressions on their faces.

"Oh, it's only David," he heard one of them say.

David stepped onto the pipe and carefully walked out to the fishing platform. "Catching anything?"

"Not much," Walt said. "I hooked a catfish a little while ago but he got off before I could pull him in." He reached to his right and pulled out a coffee can with punch-holes in its lid and passed it over to David. Inside were several grasshoppers.

"Don't let any of those get loose," Robert told him. "They're the only bait we've got."

David carefully extracted one of the grasshoppers and replaced the lid on the can. He then baited his hook and lowered the line into the murky water. Once he was settled he looked over at the other two. They both sat staring blankly at the floats on their lines.

"You guys are kind of quiet today," David said.

The two of them looked at him and started laughing. Then they both caught themselves, looking a bit embarrassed.

David smiled. "What's with you guys?"

Walt laughed again. "Should we tell him?"

"No," Robert said. He turned his attention back to his fishing.

David's smile faded a bit. "Tell me what?"

Walt broke-out laughing, uncontrollably for a moment. "We're shit-faced!" Robert started laughing too.

David was still puzzled. "You're what?"

"My mom's brother just left our house today to head home after visiting for a week," Robert said. "I went into the guest bedroom to see if he'd left any spare change or anything lying around and found a bottle of bourbon about a third full sitting on the floor of the closet. I think he forgot he had it and just walked out without it."

Walt laughed. "Good old Uncle James."

"So you guys drank it," David said. "I guess I showed up too late."

"You want some?" Robert said. "There's still a little bit left."

"Sure," David said. He looked over as Robert reached into the brown bag that was sitting on the flat surface of the support and pulled out a bottle of Kentucky bourbon. About three to four ounces of the brown liquid remained.

"There you go," Robert said. "I don't think I need any more."

"I know I don't," Walt said. "I'm shit-faced."

Robert laughed. "You're not shit-faced. If you were you wouldn't be able to stay on this pipe."

"Well," he said, "I'm not feeling any pain."

"Me neither," Robert said with a smile.

David held the bottle up so he could read the label. "Made from the finest ingredients. This looks like some good stuff."

Both Walt and Robert snickered. "You wouldn't know good stuff if it bit you," Robert said with a noticeable slur.

Carefully holding his fishing pole and the screw-off top in the fingers of his left hand, David took a big swig. It tasted awful, but this time he knew what to expect and swallowed it down with no problem. He glanced over at the two of them who were watching him eagerly. Without a word David took another swig, this one bigger.

"Ah," he said with a smile. "Like I said, good stuff."

"You mean you've had it before?" Walt said. There was a great deal of respect in his eyes.

David smiled, trying to look wise and experienced. "Oh sure. My friend Don had some whiskey on the camping trip I got back from a week ago. I'm no virgin."

He looked over at them awaiting another laugh but this time one wasn't coming. "Is that the trip where that kid got killed?" Robert asked.

David felt the smile drop from his face. "Yeah," he said, "I don't want to talk about it." He looked at the bottle, now with only about one shot left in it. He turned it up and finished it, then screwed the top back on. "What do you want to do with this bottle?"

"Throw it somewhere," Robert said. "We sure can't take it home with us and put it in the trash."

"Hey, I know," Walt said, "let's go up onto the railroad tracks and smash it."

"Hell no," Robert said, "just smash it somewhere around here."

At that moment they heard a distant rumble of thunder and noticed that it was getting quite breezy. "I've got a bite," Robert said. "I think it's that big catfish again."

He stood up and almost lost his balance, managing to place his right foot on the narrow cement platform before tumbling into the cold water. Once he steadied himself, he carefully stepped over Walt and then David to try to lead the fish toward the narrow stretch of beach that ran under the left end of the pipe.

Walt stood up and went through the exact same routine to follow. David ducked down to allow him to step over him, then watched them jump over to the beach.

"Well Robert was right about one thing," David said.

"What's that?" Walt said.

"You're not shit-faced."

He and Robert both laughed. "Told you," Robert said.

"Well," Walt said, "give me a little time. I'm only thirteen you know." They all laughed.

David was sitting with his fishing pole in his left hand and the empty bourbon bottle in his right. He looked over at bank to his left and tossed it onto the ground. Another rumble of thunder could be heard in the distance but they all ignored it. A moment later the wind picked-up and the surrounding trees began to waft a bit. A large number of yellow and red leaves fell from above and landed softly in the water.

"I think we've got some rain coming," David said. "And I've got to pee."

He rolled most of the fishing line around the end of his pole, laid it carefully on the platform and stood up. He then walked five paces to the right support. The last two steps were awkward, and he reached the safety of the platform just an instant before losing his balance.

I hope the guys weren't watching, he thought. He looked over and saw the two of them pull a foot-long catfish onto the beach. Robert placed his right foot on the fish and Walt began trying to extract the hook.

"Don't let that damn thing sting you," Robert said.

"I won't," Walt said with a laugh. "I wouldn't feel it if he did though."

David turned around and assessed his situation. He really felt the bourbon now and wasn't sure he was going to be able to get off the pipe without falling in. He wanted to get over to the bank on the side from which he came but it was much farther away than the other bank. At this point, getting onto solid ground was a priority and he really had to pee. Besides, he thought, the bushes we've used as a bathroom for years are on this side.

He took a moment to plan his strategy for walking the five steps or so across bare pipe to reach the bank. A few light raindrops began falling. It had been a warm autumn day until now, about seventy-degrees before the clouds and wind showed-up. Don't fall in, he thought, or there will be nothing at all warm about this day.

"Here I go," he muttered and he began hurrying across the pipe toward the waiting hillside where it vanished underground. The first two steps were fine but on the third his foot slipped just as he was planting it. David realized he would have to leap toward the bank with this last step as his momentum was about to carry him over the water to his right.

He stepped, leapt and reached for the foot-tall grass that jutted out toward him from the hillside. He landed on it but couldn't hold on, sliding down the hill on his stomach until his feet dropped into the water up to his knees. The cold was numbing.

"Oh shit," he cried out. He knew the other guys must have heard his fall and were probably laughing at him but he couldn't hear them over the sound of the heavy wind. Without looking around he clamored up the hill and proceeded to the bushes.

Just as he walked up to them and unzipped, the rain started in earnest. He had to go too badly to worry about it now, and began the satisfying relief of emptying his bladder. By the time he finished the rain was pouring. He was getting soaked and was glad to see that the rain was much warmer than the creek water. He zipped-up and looked back, just in time to see Robert and Walt hurry up the trail on the far side of the creek and into the woods, headed for home.

"Hey guys," he hollered, "wait up." Neither of them gave him so much as a look back. Just like that, he was alone. "I need your help to get back across this pipe," he said, more to himself than anyone else.

The rain continued to pour as David stared down at the pipe. There was no way he was going to make it across as tipsy as he was and as wet as it was. What he needed now was some temporary shelter to try and protect the limited amount of dryness he still had. If nothing else, there was a bridge about two-hundred yards upstream where Garrison Road crossed the creek. It would be out-of-the way, but it did offer a safe passage back to the other side and in the direction of home.

David looked toward the rail-road tracks and spotted a big oak tree that still had most of its reddish-brown leaves on its massive limbs. Figuring it was the driest place around, he decided to run to it, first stopping to pick up the empty liquor bottle and toss it into the brush.

He hurried to the oak tree and stepped under the canopy of its cover. Standing with his back against the massive trunk, he looked around at the pouring rain. Guess I'll just have to wait this one out, he thought.

Suddenly David heard a somewhat-familiar voice call his name. It was a voice he had not heard in a long time, but was familiar just the same. "David," he heard again. "Over here."

He looked across the creek and saw that Walt and Robert were long gone. There was nobody around the creek. He looked all around the other side of the tree and in all directions but saw no one.

"Over here you chubby dumb-ass," he heard. David looked up at the rail-road tracks and saw a kid about his age standing there. "Come on up here, I've got something to show you."

David couldn't believe his eyes. It was Gene Ameson, he recognized him from school. "Gene?" he said. "Some other time when it's not raining."

David hadn't seen Gene in at least a year, maybe two. He had been in a couple of his classes back in eighth and ninth-grades, but Gene didn't go to his school anymore. In fact, David thought, it seemed like he had moved-away.

"This won't wait," Gene called out. "There's a dead body on the side of the tracks."

"A dead body?" David hollered back. "What, a skunk or something?"

"No, a person," Gene called back. "Better get up here now or you'll never get to see it."

"I don't really want to," David said. The bourbon had him a little dizzy now and a climb up the soaking wet hillside to the tracks had very little appeal.

"You mean you're a pansy," Gene called out.

That got David's attention. "I am not," he yelled back. "I'm just drunk. And in case you haven't noticed, it's raining like a bastard out here."

"You're a pansy," Gene yelled. "You always were. I'll bet you're not even drunk. You're a pansy and a liar."

David stood staring up at Gene and tried to remember him. It had been so long since he had last seen the guy that he had completely forgotten about him. Then he remembered what a bully he was. Gene was a jerk.

Gene was older than the rest of the kids in his class since he had been held-back a year when he was in elementary school, and seemed to like to use his size-advantage as a tool to push other kids around. In fact, David couldn't remember Gene ever calling him by his name before. To Gene,

David's name had always been: "Dumb-ass". And David usually had heard it while getting shoved into a locker or onto the nearest floor.

"Come on David," Gene called again, this time waving his arm in a big sweeping motion. "Prove you aren't a pansy for once in your life."

David thought a moment about being tipsy on alcohol for the second time in a week. He was starting to like it, it made him feel more courageous than usual. And for some reason, Gene looked to him like he hadn't gotten any bigger since David had last seen him, which seemed strange since it had been awhile.

"Maybe all those cigarettes are starting to catch-up with you," David said in a low voice where Gene could never hear. David used to be afraid of him. But now with a size advantage things were different.

"Yeah, I think I will come up there," David muttered softly. "And when I get there I'm going to kick your jerk ass."

"Alright," he called out to Gene, "give me a minute to get up there. I'll show you who's the pansy."

He began walking quickly toward the tall pile of gravel rocks that made-up the bed of the train-tracks. When he reached the base of the hill he looked up at Gene. David figured he must have had a few snorts of something too to be out on these tracks in the rain like this. All the better, he thought.

Gene stood looking down at him, his face darkened by the shade from his shoulder-length, straight, blonde hair. David didn't need to see his freckled-face up close to know it was he. Gene's straight-from-shoes-to-collar stature and his obnoxious voice gave him away. David began climbing on all-fours up the hillside. Save some energy for Gene's ass-beating, he thought to himself.

"You know that kid that got killed in the Indian burial ground last weekend?" Gene said, pointing to his left up the tracks. "His body's on the ground at the bottom of the hill just up ahead here."

David had crawled part-way up the embankment and stopped to look up. "What?" he said. "That's impossible."

Gene had walked several steps in the direction he had been pointing. All David could see of him was his dirty, torn shirt and his mop of oily hair, both blowing in the swirling wind. The rain continued coming down steadily but the climb had taken the chill away. He reached the summit and stood on the tracks. Drunk or not, he was determined to get to Gene for face-to-face talk.

David instinctively looked in both directions to see if a train was coming. All he saw was the long, straight line of empty tracks that ran a quarter-mile one way and a half-mile the other, before disappearing around curves. Colorful yellow, red, and brown trees stood amongst the pines that lined both sides of the tracks, blotted out by rainy-fog in the distance. The dense forest on both sides of the tracks gave the area a remote and isolated feel.

Gene was standing down near the short trestle that spanned Garrison Road and the creek underneath it. David saw a car drive down the hill, through the underpass below the tracks and up the hill on the other side. Apparently the driver had taken no notice of them.

"The kid's body is down this way," Gene said, waving his arm again for David to hurry. David couldn't see Gene's other arm and the shirt he wore was torn so badly that it was hardly staying on him. That seemed strange but David quickly dismissed the thought. He was just happy to have the opportunity to give Gene some pay-back.

"It's not Tommy," David said as he jogged toward Gene. "I went to his funeral just a few days ago. He's buried in the cemetery ten miles from here. You see somebody else. Where is he?"

Gene was standing with his back to David, pointing with his left arm down the steep hill that lay on the left-side of the gravel mountain. The tracks were very high here. It was about thirty vertical feet down to the roadway and another twenty to the creek bed beyond that. David began mentally planning how to do this without pushing Gene to his death. He wanted to hurt him, but not fatally.

"It's the same kid alright," Gene could be heard saying from behind the veil of his long, messy hair. "I know for sure that it's him!"

David was trembling now. He had stopped walking and stood ten feet away from Gene. It couldn't possibly be Tommy lying down at the bottom of the hillside, he thought. In fact, there can't be a body down there at all, can there?

"Come on!" Gene said without looking at him. "You have to come over here to get a good look." Again he waved his left arm several times, the movement somehow awkward and strange. David thought he could hear a loud creaking sound coming from Gene's shoulder.

He also couldn't help noticing how filthy Gene looked. His shirt was torn into ribbons and he was covered with dirt. His pants legs were ripped and stained with what looked like patches of dried blood.

Gene stood pointing toward the side of Garrison Road below them. With the car that just passed now gone, the only sound was of the rain and the water rushing over the rocks in the creek.

In his teen-aged, intoxicated state, David for some reason really wanted to see the body Gene was telling him about, if for no other reason than to prove it wasn't Tommy. He started walking toward Gene to stand beside him and look at whatever it was that he was pointing out, ready to dismiss it as nothing more than a garbage bag that somebody had tossed from a passing car.

"He's right down there," Gene said, still pointing down the hill, "see him?" David walked the last few steps toward Gene and followed the point of the one finger he could see on Gene's hand. Sure enough, there was something there that resembled a human body.

David's eyes grew large as he stared down at it. From this distance it was hard to be certain, but it did look like a motionless body, lying face-down on the ground at the water's edge near where the creek disappeared under the bridge.

It appeared to be wearing a twisted red shirt and blue jeans. David couldn't tell if it was an adult or a child, a boy or a girl, but as his eyes focused, he saw what looked like hatchet buried in its head.

"Oh shit!" David cried out. "Tommy? Is that you?" He was terrified. He looked over at Gene. "That's not really Tommy, is it?"

Gene slowly turned to look at him, almost as if in slow-motion. "No, it's not really Tommy," he said in a now-raspy voice that David barely recognized. The wind blew Gene's dirty hair away from his face and David got a good look at him for the first time. One of his eyes was missing, gone along with half the skin on his face. The other eye was solid-white and dead-looking. Gene's right arm was nothing but a stump, and there was dried blood all over his chest.

David's eyes grew wide with sudden terror and he began backing away, staggering to keep his feet on the uneven rail-road ties. He watched in horror as Gene turned his rotting face up at the sky and began laughing in a howling sort of way. Large roaches started crawling out of his mouth and the rotting smell of a decomposing human body overcame him like a steamroller. The wind howled and the ground seemed to vibrate.

David screamed and turned to run away. He lost his footing and fell on his face. He rolled-over and looked up to see Gene approaching him, scowling with his half-a-face and waving his arm and stump like a bizarre scarecrow.

"Stay away from me, you freak bastard!" David screamed. He struggled to get back to his feet, preparing to run if Gene got any closer. Gene stopped walking toward him and now stood ten feet away, laughing in a guttural, haunting way.

Suddenly David's mind found the bottom of the file in his head on Gene Ameson. The high-school year-book this past spring had been dedicated to Gene because he had been killed in a car accident with two drunk buddies the summer before. David hadn't even noticed his absence from school the next year. He had forgotten all about Gene until he saw the yearbook.

One of David's classmates told him that she went to Gene's funeral and that it was really bad. Her eyes were wide with fear as she told him the gruesome details.

"He was so torn-up in that accident that they had to have a closed-casket ceremony," she told him. "I heard that the car was going over sixty when they spun off Garrison Road and into the creek. Gene flew through the windshield and sailed fifty-feet. His head was smashed and one of his arms was torn-off. He died at the scene."

"Wait a minute," David said. "You're dead! This is the very spot where you died!"

"That's right you chicken-shit dumbass," he heard Gene say in a voice that sounded like it was coming from the bottom of a tomb. "It isn't Tommy lying dead down there. It's you! Come, I'll show you."

Gene lunged at him, grabbing his collar with his one remaining hand. His gray, lifeless fingers were cold and clammy. His two-inch-long fingernails were caked with dirt. Coffin flies crawled and flew about his foul-smelling, rotting torso.

David screamed as he tried to pull away. "Let go of me you asshole!" With a wave of his arm he shook Gene free and clambered to his feet, struggling to keep his balance between the rails and not let himself fall down the embankment on either side.

Gene stumbled backward several feet away from David and again looked skyward, laughing in an evil, haunting way. He then turned toward David and peered at him with his milky-white eye. His half-a-face creaked and skin tore as he tried to smile. "Goodbye, Dumb-ass."

At that moment David heard the deafening sound of a train's horn right behind him. He turned and looked around just an instant before the speeding locomotive hit him. The last thing he would ever hear was a fading blast from the train's horn as he sailed into the air and then down the embankment into the creek, his body finally landing in a heap just inches from where Gene's dead body had been found a year-and-a-half earlier.

Les first became aware that something was wrong when David's mother called his house at a little after seven o'clock that night. She was frantic.

"Les, have you heard from David?" she asked when he answered the phone. "He went to the creek this afternoon to fish with a boy in the neighborhood and didn't come home. I was hoping he might be over there."

"No, he isn't," Les said. "I haven't seen or heard from him since last Friday. How long has he been missing?"

"At least six hours," she replied.

"Notify the police right away," Les said. "Tell them to start a search around that creek."

David's mother began to cry. "I already did that," she said. "They're on the way there now."

After several silent moments, they said goodbye and hung up.

The following morning at just after sunrise, their worst fears were confirmed. The county coroner concluded that David had been walking along the railroad tracks when a train came along and caught him by surprise. Nobody that knew David, especially Les, bought that story. Still, it was what was listed on the death-certificate as the official cause of David's senseless demise.

A small article in the local paper mentioned the tragedy. It quoted an unknown source from the railroad stating that the engineer had seen

David alone on the tracks well before the train reached him. Unable to slow the speeding locomotive, the engineer frantically blew the horn numerous times. Apparently David never heard it.

Two days later, David's funeral was held at the small Methodist church he had attended since his baptism when he was an infant. David had a lot of friends and most of them were there.

Les hadn't slept more than a few minutes at a time since the phone call from David's mother. Not only did he feel horrible for David, the situation was worsened by the fact that he had heard the drums in his head all that day. He was now certain that there was more to David's death than his simply not using common sense while walking down the tracks.

There was no one sitting within ten-feet on either side of Les in the pew as he awaited the start of the funeral service. He felt an enormous sense of relief when he looked up and saw Ken walk into the church. Ken spotted him and came over and sat down next to him. "Hey Ken," Les whispered as he shook Ken's hand. "I can't tell you how really good it is to see you."

"I'm really sorry, Les," he whispered back. "I went to Louisiana to see my family and just got back yesterday. I just can't believe all that has happened. When I heard about Tommy, and now David, I thought it was some sick joke."

"You've got the sick part right," Les said. "This is like some kind of nightmare."

"What in the hell . . .", Ken looked around the church and caught himself. "What's going on around here?"

Les shook his head. "I don't know. They say he was just walking down the tracks when a train came along and hit him. Nobody knows what he was doing out there. It messed him up really bad too. That's why the casket is closed."

"There's no way a train just hit him," Ken said. "He was way too smart for that. I think somebody killed him on purpose."

Les stared into Ken's face for a long moment. "I think so too," he said.

At that moment the preacher began speaking and the funeral commenced. Les looked across the aisle and saw David's mother and grandmother wiping their eyes with tissues. His dad and younger brother just sat motionless, staring blankly at the preacher. The words were kind and compassionate, but did little to ease the pain of the tragic circumstances.

"Man," Ken whispered to Les, "white people sure do grieve quietly!"

Les came out of the pitiful thought process he was in and looked over at him, wondering if Ken was making some twisted attempt to lighten-up the mood like he did sometimes out on the trail. He quickly saw that he wasn't.

"If this was a black funeral the kid's mother and grandmother both would be wailing so loud you could hear them two-blocks away," Ken said. "They'd both be screaming like banshees."

Les didn't reply to Ken's comment but realized at that moment how true it was. Tears were rolling down his own face and he was struggling to keep from sobbing, yet the thing he was trying hardest to do at the moment was remain completely quiet. Apparently David's family members, and everyone else in the chapel, were doing the exact same thing.

A short time later the service ended with the preacher walking over to David's family and leading them toward the rear of the chapel. The organist played soft, somber music as the mourners began to stand and walk slowly to offer condolences.

After a few minutes, almost everyone present was outside. David's family walked from the chapel toward the cemetery. Two of the funeral home employees rolled the coffin away from the front of the chapel and into the adjacent hallway. Les, who was standing about twenty-feet from the coffin at the time, decided to follow them.

"Where you going Les?" Ken said. "The grave-side is this way."

"I know," Les said. "But I really need to spend a moment alone with him if I can."

Ken stared into Les's eyes trying to understand. Les figured he needed further explanation.

"Hey, I shared a pup tent with him at least a hundred nights out on the trails," Les said. "I need some closure."

"I understand," Ken said. "Go with him and take all the time you need. If anybody says anything to you about it tell them to come talk to me."

"Thanks man," Les said. "But I'm sure everything will be fine."

"I'll be outside," Ken said. "Just come out whenever you're ready."

Les looked down the hallway and saw that the two funeral home employees were wheeling David's coffin into a room to the left. He slowly began walking toward them.

"Leave him here for a minute," Les heard one of the young men tell the other. "We'll go get the hearse and pull it around front and then drive him down to the grave-site." They then walked past Les without even looking at him and exited the front door. Les looked around to see that everyone else had left the church and were walking in a big group toward David's final resting place.

Les stepped into the room and found himself alone with David's closed coffin. Bracing himself, he opened the lid. David's face had been pounded badly by the fall, in fact, his injury looked a lot like Tommy's. David didn't look good, but certainly not bad enough to be dead.

"I don't know how to say goodbye, old friend," he said through tear-filled eyes. "We had so many more places to explore." He paused a moment, realizing that this really was the last time he'd ever see David. He gently placed his hand on David's shoulder. At that moment he had a sudden memory of the doctor at George's house asking him what had happened to Tommy's leg. The thought shocked him. Check David's legs, he thought.

Les took a quick look around to be sure he was still alone, then opened the lower half of the coffin, revealing David's bare feet. Les reached down and lifted his left leg. He pulled up the cuff of the pants leg terrified of what he might see. The leg was undamaged. He then did the same to the right leg. What he saw there sent cold chills down his spine. David had three deep slash marks above his right ankle, just like Tommy. They looked identical. He couldn't believe his eyes. Somewhere far away he heard steady drumbeats. He jumped away and almost screamed.

At that moment he heard footsteps approaching. Les quickly closed the coffin and stood silently. A young man walked in and rolled the coffin out as Les followed a few steps behind him. When Les reached the sanctuary, he paused a moment to collect his wits before starting the long walk outside to the cemetery.

He sat next to Ken and trembled as they listened to the prayers and watched the coffin being lowered into the grave. All he could think about was the curse. Somehow it had gotten David too, there was no doubt in his mind now. The curse is real and it still had some unfinished business to do.

Although he hadn't spoken to Harry or Don since before Tommy's funeral, Les felt it his duty to warn them about the curse. He also felt there might be some degree of safety in numbers since they were all in this together. He immediately made plans to talk to them. He also wondered how long it would be until the curse came after him.

CHAPTER 8

THE HAUNTED HOSPITAL
PART I

Harry was not around the day David's tragedy at the fishing hole occurred. He wanted to get a new pair of sneakers that day so he rode his bicycle over to the local mall. As he walked through the crowded food court he noticed a large banner at a booth where a couple of attractive young women were handing out leaflets and talking to passers-by. Figuring it a great opportunity to have a pretty girl talk to him, he headed over to see what it was all about.

The banner had the name of a fraternity from the local medical college on it and said that they were raising money for the children's burn unit at the adjacent hospital.

"Hi" a brunette who looked to Harry to be about twenty said to him as he walked up. "Would you like to participate in the Sigma walk-a-thon for us tomorrow?"

Harry thought a moment as he quickly came up with an excuse. "Oh, I'm visiting my grandmother out of town tomorrow," he said. "But I'd like to help out on some other occasion. What other activities are you guys planning in the near future?"

"Well" she paused, as she tried to think of something. "We are sponsoring a Haunted House around Halloween. Maybe you could come to that."

"Oh, that sounds great," Harry said. "I have a couple of scary masks and costumes. I could be a monster or something."

The young lady, now seeing that she was well off track from the walk-a-thon recruitment, realized she needed to get Harry sent on his way before he did something really embarrassing like ask her out. She glanced around and spotted the fraternity president, Squirrel, talking to one of the pledges a few feet away.

"Hey Squirrel," she said. "Can you come here a minute?"

Squirrel walked over and gave Harry a quick look. "What is it sweetie?" he said with a smile.

"This young man wants to be a part of the Haunted House team," she said. "I don't know if you can use him or not but I've got to get back to handing out leaflets."

"No problem," Squirrel said with a smile, and he reached out to shake Harry's hand and gently steer him a few feet further from the walk-a-thon booth. "We've pretty much got all the helpers we need since we're one of the largest fraternities on campus, but you can come see us as a customer. Maybe even bring a date."

Harry remained silent a moment, allowing the disappointment to show on his face. "So, how many guys are in your frat?"

Squirrel suddenly remembered the letter he had received just days earlier from Sigma national headquarters warning him about his chapter's dwindling membership. National had become concerned that over half their members were upper-classmen and that there had not been many freshmen joining their ranks since Squirrel took over as president the previous fall. Rush was just around the corner now, and it was his responsibility to keep fresh pledges coming in for future generations. The letter made it clear that National was keeping an eye on his progress.

He took a moment to size-up Harry and suddenly realized he might be future pledge material. Maybe he could find Harry a job in the Haunted House after all. Just make certain he's actually planning to come to State next year before wasting any more time with him, he thought.

"You in school around here?"

"Yeah," Harry said. "Just started my senior year over at North Falls High. I haven't decided about where I'm going to college next year but I'd kind of like to stay in town and live at home. That way I'd have more money to spend on tuition, and I just live a couple of miles from campus."

"Good answer my friend," Squirrel said. "Maybe you'd like to go Greek too."

"Oh yeah," Harry said, making a mental note to suppress the smile that he'd been told many times appears on his face when he fictionalizes. "I've got a good friend named Don who's always telling me about how he can't wait to get to college and join a really cool fraternity. I know he'd like to help out with the haunted house too."

Squirrel grinned. "I didn't catch your name."

"Harry."

"You know, Harry," Squirrel said, "we just might be able to use you guys after all. We're having a planning meeting next weekend with all the guys and little sisters to discuss how we're going to pull-off this haunted house fund raiser. If you and your friend are interested in coming I could introduce you to the rest of the guys as quote-unquote future pledges. It would be a great chance for you two to get involved, and next year at this time you'll be shoo-ins to get voted-in as pledges to join the Sigmas."

Harry couldn't believe his ears. "That sounds great sir", he said.

"Call me Squirrel."

"Okay, Squirrel," he said with a smile. "I know Don will be thrilled as well."

The two of them talked for a few minutes as Squirrel filled him in on all the details of the planning meeting. He finished his sales pitch in typical fraternity fashion by swearing Harry to secrecy. When Harry left the mall that day he was all smiles.

A recent class schedule change had altered Les's lunch time so he no longer saw Don and Harry in the school cafeteria on a daily basis. He spotted both of them from a distance at school that week but didn't get a chance to talk privately to the two of them together until Thursday afternoon. As Les was walking through the food court at the mall he happened to notice Don sitting at a nearby table. Harry was a few feet away at a counter getting them sodas.

No time like the present, Les thought to himself. As he was heading toward Don's table, a girl walked over and sat next to Don. Les recognized her as one of the new students that had just transferred to the school that year. She was in his English class so Les felt that he sort of knew her.

"Hey guys," Les said, pretending to be just passing by.

"How's it going, Les," Don said. His enthusiasm diminished rapidly when Les walked over and sat down.

"Not so good," he said. "There's something really important I need to tell you and Harry."

"Hey Les," Don said. "We're on a date. It can wait."

"This can't. Besides, it'll just take a minute. It's about David."

Harry walked over and, to Les's total shock, had a girl with him too. "Harry, I'm glad you're here," Les said, pulling out a chair for the girl.

"Sorry Les," he replied as they sat down, "I've already got a date." He looked at Don and they both laughed. A moment later Les laughed too. Loudly and sarcastically.

"Good one dude," Les said. He glanced around the table and noted that he wasn't getting any welcoming looks from the four of them. That told him he had their attention.

"Listen, in all seriousness, I've got to tell you about David."

"Oh yeah," said Harry, "we heard already. Poor guy."

"Well, wait until you hear this," Les tried to continue. "I was at the funeral home right before they buried him and . . ."

"What was he doing on the train tracks in the rain?" Don interrupted, lighting a cigarette. "I thought he was smarter than that. You backpack with a guy for years and you think you know him. Then he pulls something stupid like that. Go figure."

"Wait," Les said, "there's more to this than you realize. I think he was lured out there. Or else something chased him in front of that train."

"He was just doing something stupid and ended up dead," Don said. "That's the long and short of it." He wasn't going to come right out and tell Les to get lost in front of the girls but he was using his body language as strongly and clearly as he knew how to send the message. Les refused to take the hint.

Realizing this, Don decided to try ignoring him. "So Harry," he said, "what time are we hooking-up with the Sigmas on Friday night?"

"Eight o'clock," Harry replied. "I've got my brother, Skip lined-up to drive us over there. We'll pick you up around seven-thirty and head over to meet the fraternity boys."

"Fraternity boys?" one of the girls asked.

"Yeah," Don replied, flicking his ashes into the small metal tray. "Harry and I are going to help the Sigmas with their annual haunted house this year. It won't open for a couple more weeks, but the guys want to get together and plan. We told them we'd be there."

"You guys are actually going to set foot on a college campus?" Les said. "You've got to be kidding me."

Don shot him a nasty look. Les could read his eyes. Don wasn't liking the tone of his voice one bit. Les was pushing all of Don's hot buttons. And there wasn't a thing he could do about it.

"No, we're not going to be on the campus. The haunted house is going to be somewhere nearby, in an undisclosed location that won't be made public until next week when the official announcements come out. We're meeting there, not at the college."

"Yeah Les," Harry said. "And maybe if you promise not to act like a wimp we'll even tell you where it is. Eventually."

Les realized he wouldn't be hearing any of this if the girls hadn't been there. He decided to remain quiet and let them ask the questions. He just hoped they'd ask the right ones.

"How did you guys get in so good with the Sigmas?" one of them asked.

"They like our style," Harry replied with a grin. "And there's a chance we might be pledging next fall if we end up going to school there. The Sigmas already have their eyes on us."

Les could barely believe his ears. He knew neither Don nor Harry was fraternity material. And they certainly didn't have the grades to get into State. He remained silent, however, despite his shock, in hopes of learning more.

"Can we come along on Friday?" one of the girls asked.

"Not this time," Don said. "But once it opens we'll need dates for all the parties, so keep your calendars open."

The conversation was starting to make Les sick. "Listen Don," he said, "about David."

"What about him?" he demanded.

"I saw his leg right before they buried him," Les said. "He had the same gashes . . ."

"You saw his leg?" Don said loudly and with a glare. "What were you doing checking out his leg? You into dead guys now?"

"You're getting a little perverted in your old age, aren't you Les?" Harry said. He and Don laughed loudly. The girls chuckled nervously.

"Real funny," Les said. "I'm trying to wise you up. David had the same marks on his leg that Tommy had. I think there's a correlation."

"There's no correlation," Don said. "You're imagining things. Stupid things!"

Les looked over at Harry and saw the slightest glimmer of fear on his face. He then looked Don straight in the eyes and smiled.

"If you never hear anything else I ever say, Don, hear this," Les said. "Tommy and David have two very distinct things in common. First, they both wound up with three deep gashes in their legs that matched to a tee. Second, they were both chased by something. I don't know what it was because the only time I saw it in action it was too dark for me to make it out. But whatever it was, it was evil. Evil as hell. And both of those two guys were plenty scared by it before it killed them. And unless you two are the world's biggest idiots, which very well may be the case, you'll be plenty scared too."

Don blew smoke toward Les and remained his usual, cocky self. "We're not interested in hearing about your leg fetishes, Les. Or your idiotic theories about invisible killers chasing people through the woods. Or, for that matter, your former best friend's inability to avoid an oncoming train. Basically Les, I'm done with you. Get it?"

Les gave Don a nasty look. "Don," he said, "do you think it's possible for you to get any more stupid?"

He and Don sat staring at each other for several long seconds before Harry spoke up. "Hey Don, maybe there's something to this stuff Les is saying. It was too dark to see what was really happening with Tommy in those woods out there. Maybe he really was being chased by something."

"I think you're finally getting the idea, Harry," Les said.

"Will you two morons listen to yourselves!" Don said. "This whole story is full of crap and you're full of crap too, Les! Now, weren't you on your way somewhere?"

Les stood, his chair tipping backward and falling noisily to the tile floor. "Yes I was," he said. "But don't ever say you weren't warned. You guys are in serious danger. Not from me but from something a hell of a lot worse. The handwriting is all over the wall. I'd come down off my high horse and read it if I were you."

Don put his free hand down to the front of his pants. "Yeah Les, I've got your high horse right here."

Les took one step back, glaring at him for a long moment. For an instant the whole mall seemed as silent as the deep woods. "I don't believe you."

He looked over at Harry who was wearing a look of serious fear for perhaps the first time in his life. "I'd at least hope you're going to wise-up, Harry."

"Why don't you wise up," Don said. "Tommy and David both got killed because they were stupid. You need to learn from their mistakes a hell of a lot more than I do."

Les picked-up his chair and returned it to the table. "You heard what that mountain man, George said. I don't believe in curses anymore than the next guy, but David had the same marks on his leg that Tommy did. Maybe that doesn't bother you but it scares the hell out of me."

He waited a long moment for a reply but got only stares from all four of them in response. Don snuffed-out his cigarette in the ash tray and sat glaring at him. His eyes begged the question; "what are you going to say next? Let me guess, nothing intelligent."

Les decided now was as good a time as any to be on his way. "In case I don't see you again," he said sarcastically, "it's been a real pleasure knowing you."

"Yeah, likewise Mister Boy Scout of the Year," Don said.

Les walked away and headed outside. Anger soon gave way to sadness as he thought about the friendship that was now gone from his once close-knit group. Just the previous April, before he knew he'd be going to Wilderness Unlimited or had even met Tommy, the four of them, David, Don, Harry and Les, had gone camping together in the woods nearby. They had made a deal to always be friends and stick up for each other no matter what. It was as if that spring night had been in another lifetime. Tommy and David were dead and the other two had become total strangers. Les couldn't remember ever feeling so alone.

The following Friday was cool and blustery, and the peak colors had finally reached the lower elevations of northern Georgia. Fall's golden gown was starting to cover the grass and streets like velvet. The sunset was unusually beautiful that night, leaving a purple and red patchwork of clouds against the stark night sky.

Harry and his brother Skip were five minutes late picking up Don. Usually, Don, who was very meticulous about being prompt, would comment. This time he chose to be quiet with his teasing, mainly because Skip was not one to listen to a punk run his mouth and he and Harry were privileged to be chauffeured in such royal fashion.

Skip's Charger, which roared like a pack of lions when given the slightest amount of gas, squealed around the corner and into Don's driveway at seven thirty-five. Don ran out to the passenger side door and squeezed into the back seat behind Harry. Saying hellos, Don belted himself in.

"I didn't hear a seat belt being put on back there I hope," Skip said in an accusatory fashion. "What's wrong, Don, don't you trust my driving?"

"Of course Skip," Don said. "It's those idiots we're going to be on the road with that scare me." Skip smiled and drove on. Don thought Skip was one of the most dangerous drivers in the United States. At least he used to be. But Don wasn't going to be the one to tell him so.

The Sigma's had managed to rent an old four-story building that was scheduled to be demolished sometime in November. The brick structure had been built as a hospital during the 1920s but had become obsolete by the 1940s due to its small size. The old hospital was rectangular in shape, with a long hallway running its length on each floor joining about a dozen rooms on either side.

The elevators had been removed for salvage long ago, their doorways now crossed by two-by-fours that had been nailed to the walls on either side. Access to the upper floors was now possible only by a stairway at each end of the building.

With more than eighty rooms and only about three dozen Sigmas, the place was much too large to be used in its entirety, so tonight's meeting was set up to decide which rooms to use, how to use them, and other various details. The college's legal secretary had also added a clause in the thirty-day lease agreement stating that nobody was to enter the third or fourth floors of the building due to their deteriorated condition.

"That's fine," Squirrel had told her while he was signing the paperwork that would give the Sigmas legal ownership of the doomed structure until the fifteenth of November. "This fund-raiser will be too small an operation to move any attractions beyond the first two floors anyway."

Tonight's meeting would double as a charitable event for the fraternity and a kegger for their party-sides. Unbeknownst to Don and Harry, it was also going to be a meeting to initiate the new helpers. It was an old fraternity ritual intended to make the evening a little more fun.

When Skip's car pulled into the parking lot the headlights shone on a large group of Sigmas and their dates standing around enjoying two kegs of beer. Everyone present took notice. Don and Harry jumped out and quickly eliminated any further attention Skip and his dragster might have otherwise elicited.

It was just as well. It would have taken the numerous pre-Med, Chemistry and Biology majors among the crowd about thirty-seconds to realize that Skip, a part-time attendant in the local department store parking decks and full-time C-student, did not fit into the Sigma mold. Unless, of course, they should happen to one day get a parking deck of their own.

Harry looked around for a minute before spotting Squirrel up near the front of the Hospital building. "Hey Squirrel," he called out.

Squirrel, whose real name was Roger Townsend, was talking with two other guys and their dates when he heard his name called. The three girls in the group looked at Harry and Don, then gave Squirrel a look that plainly asked the question; "you don't know those two creeps, do you?"

"Hey guys," Squirrel said with a perfunctory smile. "You here to help with the haunted house?"

"Yeah," Harry replied. "This is my friend Don. He'll be a freshman next fall too."

Don stuck out his hand to shake but was too slow, Squirrel had already said "hi" and was looking back at his five friends and explaining the new helpers. "Why don't you guys get yourselves a beer and we'll get started with the orientation in a few minutes. I'll find you when we're ready."

"Sounds good," Harry said. He and Don then looked around for a moment before spotting a nearby keg.

"Man," Don said, "this is great! Nobody to card us or anything."

"Damn straight," Harry replied as he started pumping the keg. He and Don poured themselves a beer and wandered away. They soon found that there wasn't anyone else in the crowd that they knew and Squirrel was too busy to talk to them, so they drank and talked between themselves as darkness finished falling around them.

A few minutes after Harry and Don had gotten their third beers, someone turned on a car's headlights illuminating the middle of the crowd. There was a sound system set-up near the front of the building and the radio feeding into it was turned off. Squirrel stepped up to the microphone and asked everyone to give him their attention. A hush fell over the entire parking lot. The only sound other than the night creatures in the woods was that of a train whistle somewhere off in the distance.

"I'd like to welcome you all to the site of the first annual Sigma Haunted House," Squirrel said, his amplified voice echoing off the brick building behind him. "This year we'll be raising money to help the children's burn unit at the University Hospital a few blocks away. We also hope to have enough left over to pay the rent on this building for the month and to cover a few of our fraternity debts. We're glad you're here brothers, little sisters, pledges and friends."

The sixty or so people present erupted into a boisterous applause. From somewhere in the crowd, Don noticed the unmistakable smell of burning marijuana. Behind him a girl dropped her beer and several people around her laughed and teased her about being drunk. Her date wore a smile that said that everything was proceeding along exactly as he had planned.

Squirrel continued from the microphone with feigned seriousness. "As some of you are aware, we have asked for the assistance of some future Sigmas that are currently doing time in high school. Will you guys come forward please?"

"Guess he means us," Harry said to Don, and they began to stroll toward Squirrel. Another fellow about sixteen-years old or so joined them and the three of them were soon standing next to Squirrel.

"Okay, let's introduce these guys and then we'll get the Sigma future pledge initiation ceremony underway," he said.

Don looked at Harry. "What's this about an initiation?"

"Beat's me," he whispered. "But whatever it is it'll be fun, you'll see."

Squirrel got each guy to introduce himself, the other boy's name was Jim. "Alright," Squirrel said, "here's how the ceremony works. One man at a time, you'll each be given a beer and a flashlight. You'll have thirty seconds to finish the beer. Then you will walk by yourself into the haunted hospital using this door behind me."

Harry looked over at Don. "He expects us to go alone into that creepy place?"

"Now there are four floors in the building," Squirrel continued. "There is a stairway just to your left as you enter the door. You will walk, armed only with your flashlight up all four flights of stairs. When you reach the top of the stairwell there will be a large window to your left. It's that window right there." Squirrel pointed up to the dark window on the top story of the ancient building.

"When you get to the window, shine your flashlight out so we can all see it. We'll applaud to let you know that we've acknowledged your arrival there. Then you simply return back here where we will dub you an official Sigma future pledge." The crowd cheered.

"Now remember," Squirrel said, "should you fail to complete the mission, you will be labeled a coward, and you not only won't get to participate in the haunted house, but you will be banned for life from Sigma membership and all Sigma related activities." The crowd rustled and stirred. Many individual conversations erupted, and the parking lot took on a festive atmosphere.

"If you don't shine your light out that window boys, you will shame our fine organization. Return a failure and you will be asked to leave the party immediately. No chances for a do-over."

Squirrel's fraternity vice-president, Frank, took the break in the action as an opportunity to offer some advice. He gently pushed Squirrel's microphone downward and leaned over to whisper in his ear. "Don't forget about the clause in the lease about us staying below the third floor."

Squirrel looked at him a moment, then smiled reassuringly. "They're only going to be on the stairs. It'll be fine."

Don and Harry stood looking at the large crowd, then at each other. "Talk about peer pressure," Harry said.

Don nodded. "I just hope there aren't any Sigmas hiding in there, waiting to jump out at us when we pass."

Night had completely fallen now and the car headlights that were shining on the four of them was the only illumination. That, and the occasional spark of a cigarette lighter.

A chilly breeze made its way through the woods and crispy leaves could be heard hitting the cracked asphalt some distance away. After a moment a gust of wind sent them skittering noisily across the pavement in a large pack, resembling a group of tiny rats, fleeing the scene before something bad started happening.

"Okay Gentlemen," Squirrel said, "who's first?" There was a moment of silence as the three young men looked at one another.

"Now guys," said Squirrel, making like a game show host, "you aren't hesitant because you are aware of the countless people who died in this building, are you? Surely you don't hold any belief in that old story about the disgruntled man that took revenge after his wife died during a botched hysterectomy exactly thirty-years ago tonight! The same man that came back and cut the power at midnight, then slaughtered three nurses and a doctor with a machete. The same man whose ghost is said to prowl these woods sometimes late at night."

One of the Sigmas in the back of the crowd howled loudly at that moment, sounding momentarily like a wolf. Everyone jumped, then laughed nervously.

Squirrel smiled. "Certainly big fellows like you would never believe the stories about ghostly screams echoing up and down the hallways. And bloody stairs. Those same stairs where two of the nurses ran to escape their killer and fell in the darkness, breaking their legs; those same stairs where the machete-wielding madman slowly approached them and cut off their arms and legs before cutting off their heads; those same stairs gentlemen . . . that you will be ascending alone in the dark tonight."

One of the Sigmas walked quietly up behind the three candidates and yelled: "Boo!" All three jumped noticeably. The crowd howled with laughter.

Another Sigma walked up to them with a fresh cup of beer and held it up. "Who's it going to be?" asked Squirrel.

"Me," Don muttered.

"What was that?" asked Squirrel, "did I hear one of you say something?"

"Me," Don repeated, this time louder. "I'll go first!" The crowd roared its approval.

"Alright Dan," Squirrel shouted.

"Don," he corrected him.

"Don," said Squirrel, "you're starting to show Sigma potential already. Here's a beer for you my man." The other Sigma handed Don the beer and he took it in a trembling hand. "Now," Squirrel said, putting his arm around Don's neck, "before you chug that baby down, let me ask you something. What made you volunteer to go first?"

"Because I'm no wussy!" Don shouted into the microphone. The crowd began howling with laughter and applause. Don suddenly felt like a hero. This would make his fourth beer and he was borderline drunk. He felt like he had the courage of a lion, a big lion.

First, he'd pull-off this little stunt for them and prove he was mature beyond his years. Then he'd be welcome to drop by the old frat house whenever he was in the neighborhood. And soon after that, he would be partying with them like this all the time. Harry's little stunt to get the two of them into this new group of friends was starting to work out nicely. Nothing was going to stop him now. Certainly not four flights of dark, abandoned, rickety stairs.

"Okay Don," said Squirrel, "hold that beer in your right hand and wait for the signal. Let's sing . . . Here's to Sigma Don, Sigma Don, Sigma Don, oh here's to Sigma Don who's with us tonight. So drink chug-a-lug, drink chug-a-lug, drink chug-a-lug . . ."

As the crowd sang in unison, Don drank like a dying man in the desert. Within twenty seconds the beer was gone. The crowd applauded boisterously.

"I think our first candidate is ready," Squirrel said and the crowd cheered again. The chant of "Don, Don, Don," started somewhere in the mob. With a big stupid smile on his red face, Don turned and started toward the door to the hospital. The car headlights were turned off and the only remaining light was that of Don's flashlight.

"Let's be silent, Sigmas," Squirrel whispered into the microphone, "we may hear some screams from the ghosts, or maybe from Don." Everyone laughed. Faintly, Don's footsteps could be heard as he entered the creaking door and began climbing the dusty stairs.

There was a small window at the midway point, and Don's flashlight appeared faintly in it for just an instant. He continued up the stairs and, less than a minute later, shined his light through the broken lower pane of the topmost window. The crowd cheered, he had done it!

As Don left the window, the car headlights were turned back on and some of the people in the crowd got themselves another beer. They were ready to give Don a big hand when he emerged from the building. Minutes passed. Don didn't come out. More minutes passed. One of the Sigmas walked up to Squirrel and whispered in his ear. "Why is it taking so long? Did you have somebody hide in there and grab him or something?"

"No," Squirrel said, "nobody's in there. At least nobody I know about."

When it had been ten minutes since Don's flashlight had last been seen, Squirrel realized that the crowd was growing impatient and decided to proceed. He grabbed the microphone to continue the show. "Well Don," he said, "you've passed the test and evidently passed out as well." The crowd howled. "Okay, next candidate please."

"Hey Squirrel . .," Harry said in a worried voice.

"Alright!" said Squirrel, "our next brave man is ready to go." He lifted Harry's hand in the air like he was the winner of a heavy weight prize fight and the crowd cheered.

"Squirrel," Harry said in a panicked voice, "don't you think we should wait until Don comes back out?"

"You think we have all night?" Squirrel shot back. "Get ready to chug!"

"He may need help or something," Harry protested.

"You can help him when you get inside," Frank said. He looked over at Squirrel and grinned. "Don's an honorary Sigma now. What about you?"

Harry stared blankly at the crowd a moment, then looked back at Squirrel. "But Squirrel . . ."

"Hey pledge," Squirrel replied, "you're not chickening out on us are you?" Harry realized with horror that the whole crowd had heard the question.

"No, of course not Squirrel," he said, "but it's not like Don to stay gone like this, especially when there's a crowd waiting to meet him!"

"I'll bet he's just waiting to scare you when you pass him on the stairs," Frank said. "You'd better be on your toes."

"Be careful not to wet your pants Harry," a guy in the crowd shouted and everyone except Harry laughed.

Harry was plenty scared, and he now realized that he was in this thing way over his head. There appeared to be no backing-out now. The Worthy Keeper of the keg handed Harry a fresh beer and he stood staring at it while the crowd began to sing. "Here's to Sigma Harry, Sigma Harry, Sigma Harry . . ." When they got to the word "drink," he continued to stare bewildered into the cup.

Squirrel covered the microphone with his hand and leaned over to Harry. "You'd better turn-up that beer you little twit or you won't live this down before you're a hundred years old."

Harry suddenly remembered that Skip wasn't due back to pick them up for at least two more hours. That's a mighty long time to be standing around out in those creepy woods alone, he thought.

As the crowd finished their little song he began drinking and chugged it all in five painful gulps. He paused momentarily as his stomach tried to throw it right back up. The sixty-plus students in the mob waited patiently for him to spew the beer out his nose before they burst into laughter. Somehow, Harry managed to hold it in.

"That-a-way Harry!" Squirrel shouted into the microphone as he smiled that hateful perfunctory smile of his. The crowd roared its approval. Harry was handed a flashlight and pushed toward the door.

Slowly, he walked to the building like a condemned man. The large metal door that hadn't been oiled in years, let out an eerie, loud creak when he pushed it open. The pungent smell of rotting wood and ancient, peeling paint hit his nostrils with roughly the same amount of force as a cattle prod. He stepped on inside and thought this must be what it's like entering a tomb. At that moment, now safely out of view from the crowd, a long-overdue vomit came with a blast.

"Don," he called out, wiping his face with his sleeve. He aimed his light up the dark, cobweb-encased stairway. "Hey Don!" Only his echo replied.

The lights were turned-off in the parking lot and Squirrel told the crowd to be quiet again, this time so they could hear Don's ghost repeat that he was "no wussy."

"That is probably what awaits Harry tonight too," he added. "No wussy." The crowd laughed and Harry, who heard every word being said about him, felt the sting of humiliation added onto his fear as he began climbing the creaky steps.

When he reached the second floor he paused and looked down the long hallway. His flashlight faded into the dark abyss long before it reached the wall at the far end. Harry thought he heard faint rustling sounds coming from somewhere. Rats, he thought, probably huge rabid ones. He continued up the stairs, half expecting Don to jump out from somewhere and scare the daylights out of him any second. He knew he'd faint if that happened, sending him careening down the stairs to a painful death.

"Don, where are you?" No reply came.

He got a good pace going up the stairs and didn't slow down at the third floor landing. When he turned the corner around the railing to continue up, he thought he saw something pass across the hall a few doors down. He froze, and backed-up a couple of steps to take another look. "Don, that you?"

The flashlight reached only a dozen-feet or so into the darkness and the hallway seemed empty. Harry stood listening. Suddenly a noise, sounding perhaps like someone hissing, passed across the corridor near the far end. "Oh shit!" he exclaimed aloud and he jumped back toward the stairs. It's probably one of the Sigmas, he thought. Waiting to scare me on the way back down.

He started to head for the exit when the crowd outside began to sing. "Oh here's to Sigma Harry, Sigma Harry, Sigma Harry . . ." Then he remembered what Squirrel had said about him living to be a hundred. I'll be happy if I just live through tonight, he thought.

Another hissing sound came from somewhere down the hallway, this time closer. He shined the light again but saw nothing. Then he realized there was dust swirling in the air about fifteen-feet into the darkness.

I wonder what stirred up that dust, he thought. Not waiting to find out he rushed up the last set of stairs and spotted the dirty window. When he got to it he shined the flashlight out and downward. The loud, boisterous singing stopped and was followed by loud cheering.

"Well what do you know," Squirrel told his date and their friends as they stood looking up with the rest of the crowd. "Looks like the little dipshit actually made it!"

"Are we really going to pledge those two?" Frank asked him.

Squirrel looked at him and smiled. "Maybe. But I wouldn't hold my breath if I were you. I'd say those two losers are fifty-to-one shots to get accepted by our fine university." He took a long sip of beer. "We'll worry about the rest after that."

"Okay Bobby, you can cut the headlights on now."

"Okay, Squirrel," he replied. Bobby reached into his convertible and pulled the lever. The lights came on for several seconds, then suddenly went dark on their own.

"Get those lights back on!" Squirrel yelled.

"They don't work," Bobby yelled back as he flipped the switch on and off several times. "Now how the hell am I going to see to drive home?"

At that moment a long, low groan began to emanate from somewhere deep inside the crumbling old hospital. At first it almost seemed like the cry of an animal somewhere in the surrounding woods, getting louder quickly and coming closer. After a few seconds every person present realized with horror that it was coming from one of the upper floors of the building. The sound then trailed away.

Everyone in the parking lot stopped their conversations mid-sentence and looked puzzled at the person nearest them. Before anyone could speak the sound came again. And everyone heard it this time.

It started out softly, then grew quickly into a hideously loud, guttural moan. It echoed hauntingly through the corridors of the hospital, vibrating the walls and releasing enough force to make one think the building was exhaling. It reached a mid-range pitch, then suddenly went quiet, the sound disappearing into the innermost reaches of the building like it was taking refuge in the very cracks of it's dirty, decaying walls.

Whatever it was, it had caught everybody's attention. Not a sound came from anyone in the crowd as they all reached the same conclusion that what they had heard was neither from Don nor Harry, nor from anything human. All sixty or so people were collectively too terrified to move. They stood frozen in the almost total darkness.

The only illumination came from a dim street light at the end of the parking lot about fifty-yards away. Almost instinctively, the members of the party standing along the perimeter began to move slowly inward, tightening their space. The night suddenly became a little colder.

They turned their attention in unison to Squirrel as if expecting some kind of explanation. He stood speechless for a brief moment, then shrugged. The sounds had been as much a surprise to him as it had to the rest of them. A moment later, the car headlights came on like normal. But normal didn't describe what was happening.

The silence was finally broken by Jim, the third initiation candidate. He looked over at Squirrel and leaned forward to make sure his words were heard. "I'm out of here!" he said. Before Squirrel could make any kind of reply, or even realize he was the one being spoken to, Jim ran to his car and started the engine. The loud squealing of his tires as he peeled away seemed to bring everyone else out of some sort of trance.

Jim's hasty departure took with it any interest anyone present, especially Squirrel, had in staying another minute. "This is a good time for us to leave," he said to his friends.

Squirrel picked up the microphone and addressed the crowd. "Looks like we have two winners," he said, turning and facing the dark building. "Don, Harry, you guys are in. Congratulations!"

Then to the crowd: "be here next Friday at sundown for the grand opening. Now, let's continue the party at the Sigma house, move out!" With that he took his date by the hand and headed for his car.

"Hey Squirrel," Frank said, "aren't you going in to check on those two kids?"

"Who do I look like to you," he shot back, "frigging Sherlock Holmes? You go look for them if you like, I'm leaving!"

Squirrel led his date by the hand to his car and opened the door for her. A moment later he was driving out of the parking lot with a long stream of cars right behind him. Five minutes later the parking lot was totally evacuated.

CHAPTER 9

THE HAUNTED HOSPITAL
PART II

Hours passed. At around midnight Skip arrived to pick-up Harry and take him and Don home. Harry had told him to come by around eleven-thirty and Skip was running a little late. He had been at the high school football game with several friends he had graduated with the previous spring and had just dropped-off the last one.

"Where the hell is everybody?" he said to himself when he pulled into the empty parking lot. He drove slowly up toward the front entrance and stopped with his high-beams pointed into the doorway Harry and Don had entered earlier. "Anybody here?" he called out. There was no reply.

"Well, Harry," he said to himself again, "looks like you've already gone home." He reached for the gear shift and put the Charger in reverse. As he turned and backed-away from the building a thought crossed his mind about what his father would say if he got home and Harry wasn't there.

I know how that conversation will go, he thought. He'll tell me to get my ass back over here and not come home without him. He put the car in park and decided to give Harry one last chance.

"Hey Harry," he yelled out the open window. "You here?" Then to himself: "hell no you're not here, nobody's here." He grasped the stick-shift again but paused when he realized his headlights were now pointed straight at a keg rocking gently in a shiny metal washtub. "Hey, I wonder if there's any beer left."

He turned off the engine and got out of the car. Walking over to the keg, he took a plastic cup off the small stack that remained and tried the nozzle. Nothing came out but a faint hiss of air. He rocked the keg back and forth and heard a sloshing sound inside. Grabbing the air-pump, Skip added some pressure, then tried the nozzle again. Cold, foamy beer began to trickle out.

"Excellent," he exclaimed. After pumping for about another minute, the cup was two-thirds full of liquid and one-third full of foam. Skip blew off the foam and took a drink. "Ah, that's good!" He finished it off and pumped the keg some more. Then he stood alone in the parking lot and drank down several more cupfuls. "Nice of you frat boys to let me join you tonight," he muttered, holding the plastic cup toward the decrepit building in a toast.

As he started pouring one last one for the road he heard what sounded like his name whispered from somewhere behind the partially open door of the building. He whirled around. There was nobody anywhere to be seen.

"Harry?" he called out. No reply. "You'd better get your butt out here right now or you're walking home." He had finished pouring the beer and began walking toward the car.

"SKIP," came the whisper again. He turned and looked around. The open door moved ever so slightly in the night breeze. The rusty hinges made a creaking sound that resembled human laughter.

That sounded like Don, he thought. "You little pricks," he shouted as he set the beer on the roof of the car. He decided to grab his flashlight and take a quick look around the grounds before leaving. The rarely-used light hung from a magnet just under the dash.

Standing next to the Charger and shining the light up at the numerous broken windows that dominated the front facade of the hospital, Skip could see how this place would make the perfect setting for a fraternity haunted house fund-raiser. I'll bet there's been some serious making-out taking place here tonight, he thought. Who knows, even those two little punks may have gotten lucky.

"Get out here now if you guys want a ride. This is the last time I'm saying it!"

The faint sound of laughter came again. He looked toward the door. It didn't move. "What's going on in there?"

Someone's playing a prank, he thought. Maybe if I play along I'll get invited to a party.

He took a step toward the building, then stopped and walked around the car to get into the glove compartment. Better take the switchblade in there too, he thought. Just in case the voice calling wasn't Harry's.

Skip took his beer off the car and finished it as he approached the hospital door, tossing the empty cup on the asphalt. A lone owl hooted three times in the nearby woods. A train horn blew somewhere far away too.

The door groaned as he pushed it open and his mind immediately told him that the noise he had heard from just inside the building (or thought he had heard?) didn't match the sound of the rusty hinges. He shined the light down the long hallway and it faded into nothingness. A couple of rats scattered past his feet and he felt the slight thump of a tail brush against his shoe. His initial thought was how something like that would have made him jump if he didn't have a few beers in him. I'm feeling no pain right now, he thought.

"Hey Harry," he called out. "Last chance." The echo vanished down the hallway.

"Hell," he said, "he's probably home already." He turned to leave when from somewhere overhead there was a soft thud and what sounded like faint, unintelligible talking and laughing. He strained to hear.

"Up here," came a whisper from the darkness above. Skip reached into his pocket and pulled out the switchblade that he had smuggled across the US-Mexican border in his back pocket three years ago when his family visited Juarez. With a push from his thumb it snapped open.

He listened a moment longer but now heard nothing. He knew it was pointless to proceed but he couldn't help thinking there might be a whole room full of Sigmas somewhere up there passing around a joint. He definitely wanted to join the party if there was one, so he headed cautiously up the stairs.

The batteries in the flashlight were starting to weaken somewhat but a periodic shake gave him a brief blast of light he would need only part of the time. Enough so that he decided to continue. His light was too faint to reveal the drops of fresh blood, numbering in the thousands, that were making the stairs sticky under his feet.

When he reached the second floor, he paused and listened again. He heard a faint shuffling sound overhead, like someone moving a chair across the floor. In his mind he saw a dozen or so people drinking, smoking, eating and being merry. He continued up the stairs, pausing at the third floor landing.

He shined the dim light down the hallway but could see nothing. What was left of the batteries was almost gone. "Come on, dammit," he said, giving the light a good shake. A brief burst of light came, then faded quickly to very low. During the momentary brightness his eye happened to catch sight of something metallic lying on one of the stairs ahead of him. He reached for it and quickly realized it was a flashlight. He switched it on. Bright light illuminated the last row of stairs before him. He looked up and could see where they ended at the fourth floor. "Harry?" he called out as he continued ascending. "You up here?"

He reached the fourth-floor landing and shined the light on the ceiling, or what was left of it. The roof was full of holes and weather damage. Old pieces of dank shingles hung like rotted cardboard drapes and a strong draft chilled the air with each gust of wind outside. Through the many gaping holes he could see the distinctive blue nylon fabric tarp with which workmen had covered the roof years before. It sagged and dripped water in many places. It was obvious that nobody had been here in a long, long time.

Skip shined the light down the hallway. Piles of dusty debris lay here and there, thick cobwebs lined the corners of the ceilings and floors, as well as the doorways. What looked like had once been a flimsy gurney was on its side about thirty-feet down the hall. Its two remaining wheels jutting toward the ceiling like hands in a rusting surrender.

"What a filthy place," he said. "Nobody could be desperate enough to party in a creepy place like this." He turned and headed down the stairs. When he got to the third floor landing he walked quickly across it and proceeded toward the next set of stairs. From the side of his eye he got the brief impression of someone standing a few feet down the hall. He thought he heard him whisper loudly the word: "yo".

Skip took two more steps before what he had just seen registered and stopped him in his tracks. He stepped back in front of the hallway entrance and shined the light. He saw no one. "Hello?"

He remembered that his previous check down this hallway was with the weak light. Now, this healthier one showed him much more. There was dust swirling in the air. "Is someone there?"

Skip stood in the total silence and looked down the long hallway. Then he realized that a lone figure was sitting in a chair toward the far end. "Hey," he called out. The person didn't turn and look his way. Then he realized who it was.

"Hey Harry, is that you?" he called out. He began walking toward him. It was Harry alright. "Man Harry," he said as he got closer, "you must be drunk as a skunk! Where's everybody else?"

Harry did not look in his direction or acknowledge him an any way. He just sat with his eyes closed.

Skip walked closer and closer. When he got within ten-feet he began to realize that something was very wrong. He walked up to Harry and shined the light on his face. "Hey, wake up!" he said. Harry sat motionless, eyes closed, and wearing the slightest hint of a grin.

"Mom is going to kill both of us if you come home drunk you moron. You hear me? Wake up!" Skip reached over and gave him a mild slap on the back. Harry's head tumbled free from his shoulders and rolled into his lap. Skip jumped back several feet and watched in horror as it fell from his lap to the floor, landing with a thud like a rotten pumpkin.

Skip took a deep breath and screamed. He shined the light on Harry's face. His eyes had opened and he was smiling. Skip screamed and screamed and screamed. A full-body tremble began somewhere in his legs and crawled up his spine like a swarm of spiders, numbing his mouth and making his teeth chatter. He was too terrified to move.

Suddenly the door ten feet to his left creaked slowly open. He could do little more than turn and point his light at it. There was nobody in the doorway. But there was something else.

A long Indian spear had been driven into the floor. Don's head sat on top of the spear. His eyes were open and gazing upward. His mouth was wide and agape, like the last thing he saw before he died was the blade that would behead him descending from above and behind.

The spear rocked gently from side to side, and Don's head rode it like he was on a children's ride at the county fair. Skip dropped his flashlight, now trembling like a man with his finger in a light socket.

He began staggering backwards down the hall toward the stairs, trying to somehow get hold of himself. After a dozen or so steps he spun to start running and his feet went right out from under him. He fell onto his seat and splashed in a massive puddle of blood. It splattered all over his pants and covered both hands up to the elbow.

"SKIP, Skip, skip," came a whisper from somewhere down the hall. Skip sat petrified, quickly darting his gaze from side to side and all around. From the floor Harry's head smiled up at him in the dim light coming through a window. Don's head continued to rock on the spear. Skip even thought he heard Don's tongue slapping against his cheeks with each swing.

Then he heard the shuffling of feet in the darkness about twenty-feet down the corridor. The sound lay between himself and the stairs he had just ascended.

That's not the sound of rats, he thought. Tightening his grip on the switch blade that he had somehow managed to hold onto, he got to his feet. How he had been stupid enough to come in here he would never know. Slowly he began to step toward the farthest end of the hall, hoping there was an exit that way. The shuffling feet came closer. He heard faint snickering and whispering. The voices sounded childish.

For an instant he thought again that this was all a set-up, some kind of sick joke. Instantly his brain reminded him that Don and Harry were dead, worse than dead. And he was wearing a large amount of their blood on his clothes and skin. A joke this was not!

He crept further down the hallway, now in total darkness. The sounds came closer. In a moment they would reach the faint light that shined in the window. Skip would finally be able to see once and for all what was approaching him.

His mind continued to give him information that he could have used five minutes earlier but was now useless. Whoever it was had hidden in one of the rooms and waited for him to pass. It had obviously worked on Don and Harry, and it would work on him too if he couldn't get out the other end.

Keeping his eyes on the chair in the hall ahead of him where Harry's headless body sat, he continued down the corridor. The sounds behind him grew closer. Suddenly the source of the sound began to emerge into the light. He stopped and looked back.

"It's a child!" he exclaimed as he saw a short figure step into the light. It was only about three feet tall and made a giggling sound. Skip saw a bloody tomahawk in its little hand and a vicious grin on its wrinkled dark red face. There was blood on its teeth and it uttered another of those eerie whispers.

"Skip," it said. Even though he was standing in total darkness Skip knew it could see him. Once Skip could see his pursuer, the most intense anger he had ever felt overcame him. He gripped the switchblade tighter, so tight that it now felt like a part of his hand.

"I'm going to dice you up like fish bait you little shit!" he exclaimed as he started toward it. Two more little people stepped into the light, each identical to the first in size and weaponry. Skip froze in his tracks. He had taken about five steps and could see them more clearly. They weren't children after all. They looked like tiny old men, red men. They were little Indians and looked to be at least a hundred-years-old. They raised their tomahawks and began to approach.

Skip could read the expressions on their faces. They weren't laughing at him. They were smiling revengeful smiles, ones that said they were going to even a score they had been waiting centuries to settle. Skip still had some semblance of hope he could take them until three more appeared. He could hear still more behind them. He turned and bolted for the other end of the hall. Behind him dozens of feet shuffled in his direction.

After a short distance he came to a dead end. Skip pounded on the barrier before him and realized that it was a closed door. He fumbled for a door knob and his fingers found one. He turned it and pulled. It wouldn't budge! The footsteps were only a few feet away now! He pulled with both hands and realized that some fool had gone to the trouble of nailing the door shut at the top of the frame.

He pulled the knob again. It gave a little, revealing a thin crack. He yanked as hard as he could and quickly jammed his right hand into the crack that appeared briefly during the height of his pull. His fingers went in an instant before the door snapped back on them. The pain was excruciating, and Skip thought he heard his fingers cracking.

The footsteps shuffled closer and the giggling became louder. He pulled at the door with all his might, trying to widen the crack as much as possible. His fingers were numb and the pain shot up his arm. In another time and place he would be screaming from the agony, but now his fear was far more succinct. He pulled as hard as he could and the rotting door began to come loose. A couple more good yanks should do it, he thought frantically. He pulled again. The door loosened a bit more.

Then the first tomahawk sliced into his left ankle. At first he felt a jolt, then the cutting pain screamed up his leg. There was another blow, just above the first, then another just above that. They were trying to cut off his foot!

He yanked at the door and it burst open. It flew from the hinges and came down on top of him. He struggled to get out from under it. Don't go down, his mind screamed, or they'll start on the throat next!

He hobbled to his right and let the door fall. One of his attackers was crushed by its weight. He/it screamed momentarily from under the heavy door. Skip jumped onto the door and felt just the slightest twinge of pleasure as the sound from underneath went silent before he scrambled through the doorway.

Suddenly something grabbed him around the right leg and held on. He looked ahead to see a dirty window one floor down. There was faint light coming in and he could barely make out a stairway. He shook off the thing on his leg but felt tiny fingers and arms trying to take hold in its place. Skip started down the stairs, his ankle crying out in protest. He took one step, then two at a time.

The window, he thought, it's my only chance! He ran at the window, which was too dirty to see through, and dove head first with outstretched arms through it. He could feel the glass splintering around him. The criss-crossed wooden frame gave the slightest resistance before giving way. He sailed through and into thin air, falling for several long seconds. Then there was a hard thud as he hit a grassy slope some one-and-a-half stories below. There was intense pain in his head, his back, his neck, his arms. He then drifted into unconsciousness.

Sometime later he awakened. It was daytime and he was being loaded onto a stretcher. He felt pain from head to toe. He only had enough awareness to wish aloud that he was dead.

"You had quite a nasty fall there, son," someone was saying to him. He opened his eyes and saw it was a paramedic. "Your mom called the police around three this morning and said you might be here. Luckily we spotted your car."

They loaded him into an ambulance but, before they could close the door, a police detective leaned in and looked at him. "You kill those boys?" he asked him.

Skips eyebrows raised. "You crazy?" he said. Blood flew from his throat in tiny droplets. Some of the droplets landed on the detective's shirt.

"Somebody sure made a mess in there," the detective said. "Was it you?"

Despite the intense pain the smart-ass in Skip still somehow found its way to the surface. "You think I cut myself up like this for laughs?" he exclaimed. His anger just made the pain worse. "Ow!" he cried out as they belted him into the stretcher. "I think they broke every bone in my body!"

"Who did?" the detective demanded.

"Those little shits," Skip cried out. "Must have been twenty of them. They have to still be in there, hiding in a hole or something. Look for them, they've got to be around here somewhere. They should be tortured for what they did to my brother, the little bastards!"

The detective was taken aback by Skip's outburst. "Who are you talking about?" he demanded. "Those fraternity jerks?"

"No!" Skip said. "It was a bunch of midget Indians or something. They were little monsters is what they were!"

The detective's eyes grew wide and he took a step back. He found himself unable to think up another question. He then turned and took a menacing look at the old building. Skip thought he saw fear on the man's face.

The paramedic told him he could talk more to Skip at the hospital in a couple of days. "He's lost a lot of blood and needs medical attention fast." He rolled Skip in and closed the door. The ambulance drove away.

There were fifteen police officers on the scene. The detective blew a whistle and they all stopped what they were doing and looked at him. "The killers may still be around here," he shouted, "search every inch of the building!"

"Any idea who we're looking for, Chief?" one of the officers asked.

"I'm not sure," he replied. "Maybe a bunch of kids in Indian costumes."

That comment was met with several blank stares. "Just police the entire area!"

Over the next twenty-four hours they searched the old hospital building from top to bottom. They searched the grounds, the surrounding woods and even set up a road block for a brief time. No trace of anything ever turned-up.

The following Tuesday the haunted house plans were canceled by order of the police department. A thorough search of the Sigma fraternity house turned up no evidence to implicate Squirrel or anyone else of any wrongdoing. They found no bloody clothes and no weapons or other implements that could have been used to commit the type of crime that occurred.

When questioned, everyone at the fraternity house claimed to have left at the same time and that the two boys were very much alive when they were last seen. Nobody saw anything out of the ordinary and no one mentioned the eerie groans.

Squirrel and Frank met briefly and determined that the little "initiation ceremony" should simply be deemed a private fraternity event that had gone terribly wrong; therefore, it was no business of the police, county or campus. With the limited crime scene evidence appearing to be Native-American in origin and no similar artifacts found in the frat house, the case quickly went cold.

The old building was officially condemned later that week and "no trespassing" signs placed all around the perimeter of the property. An occasional police patrol through the area was then scheduled to keep visitors out until the building could be razed three weeks later.

Skip would lie in the hospital for a week. He had escaped with no broken bones, a sprained left elbow, a badly-gashed ankle, a concussion and numerous minor cuts on his shoulders and back from the broken window glass. The doctors treating him told him repeatedly how lucky he had been. Had he selected one of the side windows instead of one at the end of the building he'd have dropped three stories onto hard pavement.

Skip didn't feel very lucky though. His injuries even kept him from attending Harry's funeral.

Besides the spear where Don's head was found, the only weapon of any kind found in the hospital was Skip's switchblade. This led to his being considered a suspect for a short time, but he was cleared before he ever even knew it. Forensic specialists spent several days at the scene and determined that Skip could never have done such a barbaric act alone and armed only with a cheap Mexican can-opener. Plus, it appeared unlikely he could have done such injury to himself as the ones he sustained.

Whoever had decapitated the two boys had used a large sharp instrument and hacked away a number of times. Harry had been tied to the chair, but post-mortem analysis led to the conclusion that he was already dead when the restraining took place.

Don had not been tied up at all. His body was found in a room one floor below his head. It appeared that the killers had dragged his headless body down the hall, using his blood in an attempt to make it slippery for subsequent victims.

The county coroner concluded that both Don and Harry had been held by several attackers while an apparently strong individual cut off their heads with a machete or similar weapon. The killings also appeared to have been ritualistic in nature.

It was by far the most notorious crime anyone on this police force had ever encountered. Whoever or whatever it was that had done it apparently left the scene after Skip jumped out of the window. Luckily for him they didn't decide to finish the job. They easily could have gone outside and killed him too if they had desired.

The fact that no trace of blood or anything else was found outside the building led the investigators to wonder how the killers could have made such a clean get away. It appeared that they had never left.

Skip's brush with death made him an instant local celebrity, much to his chagrin. When news broke about the tragedy, the medical campus became a media circus. Reporters were on Skip's hospital floor day and night, hounding everybody in scrubs for information. The police even had to post a guard at the door to his room to keep them from just walking in whenever they saw the need. This led to numerous unpleasant conversations between hospital employees and media personnel. After a few days, and once the police had pretty much eliminated Skip as a potential suspect, the reporters and cameras disappeared.

Les's mother felt a great deal of sympathy for Don and Harry's parents and urged him to go visit Skip. It didn't take her long to realize that he didn't really want to.

"Regardless of the circumstances between you and Harry prior to his death you have to put it all aside," she told him. "You and Skip once had at least a semblance of a friendship. Now go over and spend a few minutes with him. It's simply the right thing to do."

Les considered educating her on some of Skip's recent escapades that he was aware of including truancy, underage drinking and an episode or two of vandalism. For some reason that seemed to be bad idea.

"I guess you're right," he said. "It wouldn't kill me to go see him I guess."

"That's the spirit," she said. "The poor guy could probably use a friend right now."

Les smiled but didn't reply. He and Skip had never been what one would call "friends". He had never really known Skip that well, and from some of the things he had seen and heard about him over the last couple of years, figured he didn't really want to.

The last time the two of them exchanged words was a few months earlier when Les and Harry were making last minute preparations the afternoon before a camping trip. The two of them were assembling their gear and Les had made the mistake of leaning his backpack against Skip's car while he rolled-up his sleeping bag. Skip came out of the house and froze in his tracks when he spotted the backpack.

"Get your damn backpack away from my car before you scratch the paint," he yelled.

"Okay," Les said, still in the middle of cramming his sleeping bag into its stuff sack. "I'll get it in a second."

Without a word Skip took the backpack and tossed it several feet into the yard, never even looking in Les's direction. He then jumped in the car and backed out of the driveway.

Les stood and stared at him as he squealed away. "Your brother's a real jerk, Harry."

"Don't I know it," he said. "Just be glad he was in a hurry or he might have thrown you over there with it."

Things hadn't always been so testy between them. Back when they were eleven, Les and Harry were on the same baseball team in Little League. Sometimes he'd go over to their house on summer afternoons and Skip would hit the two of them fly balls in the back yard. No doubt Skip did it only because he was bored but Les became a better player from all the practice. Trying to keep that positive fact in mind, Les approached the door to Skip's hospital room.

"Hi Skip," Les said, sticking his head in the door. "You welcoming visitors?"

Skip, obviously still dazed from all the medication, slowly turned his head and stared at Les with no hint of recognition. Suddenly his face lit up and he smiled.

"Les? Good to see you man. Come on in."

Les wore a concerned expression as he walked closer and shook his hand gently. There were several cuts on Skip's face and a nasty bruise under his left eye. "Man," he said, "you really got banged-around. You holding up okay?"

"They tell me I am," Skip said. His speech was slowed by medicine and fatigue. "A couple of days ago I was in so much pain I was just hoping I'd die."

Les sat down and Skip named off some of the injuries he had sustained and the medicines he was being given to combat the pain. "So excuse me in advance if I fall asleep on you. I think it'll still be a few more days before they let me go home. So what brings you here?"

"Just came to see you," Les said. That seemed to please Skip a great deal. "Remember when you used to hit fly balls for Harry and me during baseball season? I got to be a pretty good ball player after that summer Skip. I never told you thanks."

"Hey, no charge man," Skip said. "Don't expect any grounders or fly balls out of me anytime soon though."

Les chuckled. "Well, it's football season now anyway."

Les stayed and visited for about an hour and the two of them got to be good friends. When Les told him he had to go Skip asked him to come back again soon, maybe even bring some cards or something. Les could tell he really appreciated the visit.

"I'll come back tomorrow, how about that?"

"Great," Skip said. Les told him goodbye and headed out for the twenty-minute walk home. It wasn't until he was gone ten minutes that he realized that neither of them had even mentioned what went on inside that old hospital after Skip got through naming off his injuries. Les figured he'd find out plenty of details soon enough.

The following day, Friday afternoon, Les went by to see Skip on his way home from school. Again, Skip was alone and Les could tell he had been crying. He figured the pain had gotten to be too much for him.

"You must be hurting a lot today," he said. "Are they giving you enough medication?"

"I suppose," Skip replied. "But if they really wanted me to heal faster they'd keep my old man out of my room."

"What?" Les said.

"He just left a few minutes ago," Skip continued. He looked at Les for a long moment, apparently pondering how much to trust him. "He asked me if I was responsible for Harry's death. Can you freaking believe that?"

"Wow", Les said. "That's messed up!"

"Yeah," Skip said, "how can he even ask that. I wasn't the one giving beer to under-aged kids. The only reason Harry and Don were at that frat party in the first place was because he and my mom ordered me to drop them off over there."

Les briefly saw and felt the downside of having a father in the home, something he'd missed since he was two. It was an unfamiliar feeling. "What else did he say? If you don't mind my asking."

"No," Skip said, "in fact, it helps to get things off my chest. He asked me if it was those fraternity pricks that killed him and Don. Then he said that the story I gave the cops just didn't cut it! That crap about little Indians and tomahawks and all that!"

"Is that what it really was?" Les asked him.

"Yes!" Skip said. "Every word I said to the cops is true. I know it's crazy but I know what I saw."

"I believe you," Les said. "Every word."

They sat silently for a moment before Les broke the silence. "I brought you a chocolate bar. Here, hide it where the nurse won't see it."

"Okay," Skip said, "thanks." He slid the candy under his pillow. "Want to go outside and walk around?"

"You sure you feel up to it?"

"Yeah, besides, I need some fresh air."

Skip got slowly out of bed and started getting dressed. They took the elevator to the ground floor and walked out to the court yard. Skip was limping and grimacing in pain with each step so it would be a short walk.

"Man these things itch!" he said, pausing to scratch his leg.

"What things?"

"These scabs." Skip sat down on a nearby picnic table bench and pulled up his left pants leg. What Les saw next terrified him.

Across the outside of Skip's ankle were three long cuts, each repaired with about fifteen stitches. The deep, dark-red gashes were equal distance apart and parallel.

"I don't believe it," Les exclaimed as he stared at the wounds. "Tommy and David both had leg injuries matching those exactly!"

"This is what those frigging midget Indians did to me," Skip said. "There must have been fifteen or twenty of the little bastards. Nobody wants to believe me but I swear to you that's what attacked me."

Les was still getting over the shock of seeing Skip's leg injuries. "What exactly happened in there?"

Skip looked at him for a long moment. "It's pretty hard to believe," he said. "I still can't believe it myself."

"Try me," Les said. "You said it was little Indians or something?"

Skip took several moments and gave him a detailed account. "When I think back to how I went in there all alone with just a flashlight and a switchblade, it makes my skin crawl," he concluded. "I wouldn't do that again for a million dollars and a keg of European beer."

"Skip," Les said, "I think I know who those midget Indians were."

"You do?" Skip's heart was pounding and he looked around nervously.

"Yes," Les said. "Now it's your turn to try and cope with the unbelievable."

Les told him about the Burial Ground and what Don and Harry had done. He told him all the details about Tommy and David's deaths, and their bizarre leg cuts that matched Skip's exactly. Les then told him about how he himself was the only remaining individual involved that had not experienced the curse in any form, at least up until now.

"I think you're in the clear now," Les told him. "If the little people had wanted you dead they would have gone outside and finished the job. My involvement is much deeper. I'm afraid it's going to be just a matter of time before they come after me."

"Maybe you're in the clear now too," Skip said. "All you did was maybe trespass. You didn't do any of the digging or take out any trinkets."

"True," Les said. "But David and Tommy didn't do that much either and look what happened to them."

"Those were accidents," Skip said.

"I thought that too at first," Les said. "Then I saw the cuts on their legs. And now the ones on yours. This curse is real. It's still out there and it has unfinished business with me. I can feel it."

Skip studied Les's face for a long minute. "You scared?"

"Hell yes, I'm scared," he said. "And I don't know where to turn to for help. I know better than to ask those police detectives that have been interrogating you. The only thing that would accomplish is getting my name on the suspect list."

"I see your point," Skip said. He sat staring at a grove of trees across the busy street in front of the hospital. He wasn't looking forward to another night in the noisy place.

"What do you plan to do now," Skip said.

Les thought a moment. "I don't know. Maybe I can do some research at the public library. I need to learn more about Indian legends and history. Maybe there's something I can do to stop this curse before it stops me."

"Hey, that's it," Skip said. "I'll bet if you return the skull and all the trinkets back to their rightful place it'll stop the curse. There's probably some kind of simple ceremony you could perform."

"That might work," Les said. "But it would involve going back to that Burial Ground again and that's the last thing I want to do."

"Even if it means saving your life?" Skip said. "I think you should at least consider it."

Les thought a moment. The very idea of going back into those haunted woods made him shudder. But that was only part of the problem. "I don't even know how I could get back up there," he said. "My mom would never let me use her car. I don't even have a learner's permit yet."

"That's no problem," Skip said. "I'll drive you up there. We'll go together."

Les turned and stared at him. "You'd do that for me?"

"Not just for you but for myself as well," he said. "And for Harry, Don, Tommy and David. Somehow I think none of us can rest in peace until this matter is settled. You go learn all you can and I'll finish getting healed."

Les thought a moment and then smiled. "That sounds like a plan." They got up and Les walked Skip back to his room. "I'll stay in touch," he said as he headed out. He then began the eight-block walk to the town library.

"We're closing in half-an-hour," the librarian told Les in a matter-of-fact voice as he entered. He looked at her and tried to respond with a perfunctory smile but found he couldn't manage one.

He looked at his watch. "Four-thirty," he muttered. "Got to move fast."

He spent the next few minutes searching a shelf with books about Native American tribes. He found several books that looked promising at first, but soon discovered that none of them held any information about curses. It wasn't long before he came to the conclusion that he was not going to get any help with his dilemma from any of the books in this library.

He stopped and thought a moment, then decided to turn his attention to the microfilm room. He stepped inside and looked around the shelves. Years and years of newspapers were stored here, some of them perhaps containing details of incidents at the old hospital where Harry and Don had met their end. He wanted to start immediately, searching for the truth and a way out of his predicament.

"Closing time," the librarian said from a few feet away.

"Okay," Les said. "Are there any weekdays you're open past five o'clock?"

"Nope," she said. "Same hours for the last fifty-three years. Nine to five Monday through Friday and nine to four on Saturday."

The following morning, Saturday, Les was waiting at the front door when the same lady opened up from the inside at nine-o'clock on the dot. He headed straight for the microfilm room and got one of the other librarians, this one younger and a bit friendlier, to show him how to use the equipment.

Within minutes he was rolling through the newsprint of the 1950's, one day at a time. About an hour later he discovered an article from 1954 about an incident at the old hospital. He had found the tip of the iceberg.

There had been a number of articles about the building of the hospital, originally called "Brady Hospital" after its founder, but later was simply known as "University Hospital" due to its proximity to the medical college. Very little was mentioned until one week in October, 1954 when it was the focus of a bizarre and heinous crime. Les felt his blood run cold as he read:

The Atlanta Daily Register
Monday, November 1, 1954

MURDERS AT BRADY HOSPITAL SHOCK NEIGHBORHOOD

Local residents were stunned Sunday morning when police vehicles began arriving at Brady Hospital to investigate a bizarre killing rampage. According to a spokesman, the distraught husband of a former patient is believed to be the culprit.

Police say 39 year-old Henry "Scout" Lee of Fannin County in northeast Georgia is believed to have entered the hospital with a machete around one a.m. killing a doctor and three night-duty nurses. One officer described it as: "the bloodiest mess I've ever seen".

Lee fled out a rear entrance on foot but was quickly arrested upon reaching his parked automobile by a motorcycle police officer who was in the midst of writing him up for being parked illegally. The officer saw that Mr. Lee was covered in blood and drew his revolver. The suspect was taken into custody without a shot being fired and is currently being held at the Dyer Count jail without bond pending arraignment.

The Police spokesman said Mr. Lee entered the hospital through the delivery entrance and made his way up to the fourth floor. There he allegedly killed the first person he saw, an as-yet unidentified nurse, beheading her with a machete. Police are still looking for the woman's head.

Mr. Lee then proceeded to the far end of the hall where he encountered another nurse just leaving a patient's room. He then allegedly demanded she point him in the direction of a doctor (whom police also refuse to identify pending notification of relatives) before killing her in the same manner.

"Apparently," one investigator said, "her scream alerted the doctor and another nurse down the hall who ran out of a room and attempted to escape down a stairway." Mr. Lee

then chased them to the third floor where he cornered them in front of a locked doorway.

> *A patient in room 337 told police he heard Mr. Lee right outside his room telling them he was avenging the death of his wife two weeks earlier and was "punishing" the doctor and the nurse for their negligence. He killed them both, then escaped through the door after breaking it down with his fists. Approximately five minutes later he was arrested by the policeman two blocks away. The four headless bodies were taken from the hospital to the morgue shortly after dawn Sunday morning as police continued to ask questions about who Mr. Lee is and why he committed the killings.*

Les sat horrified as the gruesome details of the thirty-year-old murder unfolded before his eyes. After reading the article again, he removed the microfilm and proceeded on to the next day's newspaper. This time the story continued on page one.

The Atlanta Daily Register
Tuesday, November 2, 1954

KILLINGS MOTIVATED BY REVENGE

> *Dyer County murder suspect Henry "Scout" Lee admitted to police during interrogation that he killed three nurses and a doctor at Brady Hospital over the weekend because "they weren't doing their jobs" the night of his wife's death two weeks earlier. Lee told investigators that the doctor (whom police still won't identify) was having sex with a night nurse in an empty patient room when Mrs. Lee hemorrhaged and died only a few doors up the hallway.*

> *Lee, 39, of Fannin County, Georgia is being held without bond in the county jail on four counts of first degree murder and is likely to face Georgia's electric chair if convicted. His arraignment is scheduled for Wednesday morning at nine o'clock.*

Les made notes as he continued through the microfilm. The last newspaper account on Mr. Lee ran the following August, the day after his execution. In an interview days before his death, Mr. Lee claimed to be a proud Indian of the Yuchi tribe and a descendant of a great chief.

"Yuchi," Les muttered, "I've never heard of them. I'll have to do more research on them later." He turned his attention back to the newspaper article.

In the significantly edited interview, Mr. Lee said his wife's death had been the "final straw" for him. He blamed the white man for what had happened to his people over the last two centuries. He said it was well worth his life to get even with those who allowed his wife to bleed to death like an injured animal.

Feeling he had about all the details of the killings he could stand, Les left the library and headed over to see Skip at the hospital. When he arrived at Skip's room, he found Skip's parents there. The four of them talked for a few minutes before Skip's mother said they had to leave to run errands.

Both of Skip's parents were polite to Les but not friendly. He could tell that they both were still mentally in another place.

Once the two of them were finally alone, Les filled Skip in on what he had learned at the library. "The murders back in 1954 are similar to Harry and Don's," Les said. "It even happened on the same two floors. It's almost as if Henry Lee's ghost was in that old hospital along with the little people that night."

Skip sat in bed without speaking, trying to digest all that Les was telling him. "The fact that Mr. Lee happened to be a Yuchi Indian just adds more to the mystery," he said at last. "It makes me wonder if the curse is tribe-specific. And if it can get to you no matter where you are."

"Exactly," Les said. "That's why it's critical that we get that skull and those trinkets back to the Burial Ground where they belong, and soon!"

"Well, the good news is they're letting me go home tomorrow," Skip said. "I figure I'll be able to drive by midweek. Do you think you can wait until next weekend to head up there?"

Les thought a moment. "I wish we could leave right now, but next weekend will have to suffice. I guess what I have to do now is figure out a way to get Don's parents to give me access to his room so I can search for the trinkets. That won't be easy."

"The trinkets are at my house," Skip said.

Les's eyes widened. "They are?"

"Yeah," Skip said. "Don made Harry take it off his hands. Everything they brought out of those woods is now hidden somewhere in my house."

"I don't believe it," Les said. "After all that bragging Don did about taking that stuff to school. Why did he give it to Harry?"

"I heard the two of them talking in Harry's room on Wednesday or Thursday morning after they got back from the camping trip," Skip said. "I can't remember which day it was. Anyway, I wasn't able to put it all together until you told me the particulars about the trip to the Burial Ground."

Les moved to the edge of his seat. "What did you hear them say?"

"It was real early that morning, maybe six o'clock," Skip said. "I heard a tapping noise at the window and got up and peered outside. A few feet away I saw someone standing in the bushes and rapping on Harry's window. He glanced in my direction without noticing me and I saw that it was Don. He was as white as a ghost. Harry must have opened the window and realized who it was. Next, I saw him disappear inside."

"What happened then?"

Skip scratched the scabs on his leg without looking at what he was doing or breaking his train of thought. It was obvious to Les that with several days of experience he had learned how to scratch carefully so as not to tear the wounds.

"I quietly stepped inside the closet in my room," Skip said. "With my ear to the wall I tried to hear what they were saying. It wasn't hard because something really had Don shook-up and he wasn't making any effort to keep his voice down. Harry told him several times to keep it quiet but I could hear every word."

"What had Don so spooked?"

"It must have been the skull," Skip said. "He told Harry he kept having terrible nightmares every night and that they were getting progressively worse. I don't think Harry believed him.

"Then Don got really panicky. He said the skull woke him up that morning. He said it was scratching the bare wooden floor and bumping against the wall.

"Don told Harry that he opened the closet door about an inch and looked inside with a flashlight. He said the skull was looking straight up at him and smiling. Then it began to hop around a little, like it was on a vibrating surface, turning its face from side to side like it was looking around for an enemy. Don slammed the door and leaned with his back to it. He said he could hardly breathe."

Les stared at Skip with utter astonishment. "You don't really think all that is true do you?"

"Don swore it had happened just an hour earlier," Skip said. "And I could tell by his voice he believed it. Trust me Les, he was genuinely terrified."

Les stared at the floor, his eyes darting from tile to tile in the brown and off-white checkerboard. "But Don was so cocky about the whole thing," he said. "Even after David got killed he still wasn't bothered by any of it."

"I think that was all a smoke screen," Skip said. "Did either of them ever bring any of that stuff to school like they said they would?"

Les thought a moment. "No. In fact, I remember sitting a couple of tables away from them at lunch that Monday, waiting to see if they were going to start any kind of disturbance, but they never did. To my knowledge they never took any of the stuff from that burial ground with them to school. I don't think they even mentioned it to anybody."

"They were too scared to," Skip said. "For legal reasons at first I suspect. Then later for different ones."

"Don went on and on that morning about how he had to get that stuff out of his house in the worst kind of way and Harry had to help him. Get this, he even went out to the storage shed behind his house a got a fish net to corral the skull off the closet floor. He told Harry he wanted to get it into a shoe box without touching it. He said he was afraid it might bite him."

Les chuckled slightly as he realized the strange way Don had applied some of his scouting training. "Unbelievable!"

"Harry finally told him he could stow the stuff in the crawlspace under our house and Don climbed back out the window," Skip said. "I stepped out of the closet and went to peek outside. I watched him grab a potato sack from the bushes and disappear down toward the little door just off our patio. My guess is that it's all still down there."

"I'll bet they were going to try and return it to the Burial Ground themselves," Les said. "But they didn't live long enough to do it."

"They probably were planning that," Skip said. "But I don't think Harry was as convinced as Don was that there was any urgency to it. I think that once they got the stuff hidden where nobody could find it they figured they were okay for awhile."

"At least until David got killed," Les said. "I wonder what they were thinking then. Whatever it was they didn't share it with me."

"I guess you knew too much," Skip said. "You knew they had the stuff and they probably figured if they didn't draw attention to it you might forget all about it. Then, sometime in the future, they could get it back to where it belonged and the whole episode would be over once and for all."

"I guess they knew they'd have to wait awhile for the furor over Tommy's death up in the hills to quiet down," Les said. "But in the long run they wouldn't have to admit to anyone what a big mistake it all had been. That is just so typical of those two."

Skip thought a moment. "Yeah, that sounds right. I guess they never figured they could get into such a deep mess as this."

"And now it's down to me to rectify the problems myself." Les thought a moment and began to feel overwhelmed. "I don't know if I can do it."

"We'll get it all straightened out," Skip said. "Don't worry. Next weekend we'll go up there and put everything back where you guys found it. That will put the curse, if it really does exist, back to sleep."

"Yeah," Les said. "All I have to do is remain alive until then."

He stayed a few more minutes before heading home. When Les was walking past the street corner one block up from the old hospital site he glanced over to see a county truck pull away from the curb. A new Historical Marker sign had just been placed there. Fear overwhelmed his as he read it. He reread the sign several times to make sure he had his facts right. Once he caught his breath, he rushed home to call Skip and tell him about it.

"Are you sure about this?" Skip said. Les could hear someone else in the background and realized Skip wasn't alone in the hospital room.

"Who's there with you?" he asked.

"A nurse," he said. Les paused a moment and heard Skip thank her for bringing him something to eat. He couldn't help noticing how much nicer Skip seemed to be treating other people lately.

"Okay, I'm back," Skip said. "Now, let me get this straight. You say there were some Indians massacred 200 years ago at the site of the old hospital?"

"That's what the new sign says," Les said. "There was an Indian community there back in the early 1800s and the local settlers took away their land."

Skip thought a moment. "I can't believe they'd put up a marker for that."

"The sign says the Indians defiantly refused to go west on the Trail of Tears," Les said. "The government ended up forcing them to go. Of course, the sign implies that the Indians had a choice."

"Sure they did," Skip said. "Just like they invited the Europeans to come take their land off their hands before they did something crazy with it like farm and raise families."

"I can't help but wonder if the same curse that inhabits the Burial Ground is also somewhere around that future city park," Les said. "I'm beginning to think it's all over town."

There were a few moments of silence. "This thing is really starting to get to me," Les continued. "I hope you'll hurry up and recover so we can take care of this problem soon."

"Hang in there," Skip told him.

Over the next week Les tried to go about his normal activities, mainly, going to school every day and trying to concentrate. His nights were reduced to a few short hours of restless sleep, frequently broken by noises from outside that made him think the little people were gathering beneath his window, preparing to burn the house down or massacre him and his mother. His first conscious thought each morning was that he had somehow made it through another dangerous night.

When the three-o'clock bell finally rang on Friday afternoon, Les ran home to get ready to hit the road with Skip. As he finished packing his backpack, his mother came into his room.

"So you're going camping with Skip? That's nice that you two are spending time together. I know it means a lot to him."

"I'll try to be home before dark on Sunday," Les said. He didn't want to even imply that there was any danger in what he was about to do. A good way to cover that was to change the subject quickly, he thought.

She continued to look into his face with her steel-grey eyes that exactly matched his. She had his hair too, which she kept shoulder-length. Over the years a number of his friends had commented to him how attractive she was.

"Mom, do you ever hear from Frosty these days?"

She looked at him for a long moment, evidently surprised by the question.

"Haven't seen him lately," she said. "You'll be careful won't you?"

"Always," he replied. Then he turned for the door. He walked as fast as he could the half-mile or so to Skip's house.

"Hey man," Skip said as he opened the door. "I'm almost ready."

"First things first," Les said. "Let's get into that crawl space and find the skull and trinkets."

"I'm a step ahead of you," he said. Skip walked into the next room and returned a moment later with a shoe box. "It was right where I figured it would be," he said.

Les took the shoe box with trembling hands and used a knife to cut the duck tape that was wrapped tightly around the lid at each end. He then slowly opened it and looked inside. The skull was there, wrapped in a dirty washcloth. There also was a strand of beads and some arrowheads. It looked to Les like all the artifacts that had been taken were accounted for. The skull showed no proclivity to initiate any movement on its own at the moment.

"I guess it's time to leave, Skip."

"That's going to take a little doing," he said. "My mom's not too keen on my going camping, especially with all the things that have happened lately."

Les thought a moment. "I think you should stress that you are trying to get some closure over Harry's death," he told Skip. "Maybe tell her bonding with me will help do that. What better way to bond with the most decorated boy scout in the state than to go camping with him. Tell her I need closure too, which is true. Want me to go out and talk to her?"

"That might not be a bad idea," Skip said. "She's out in the back yard hanging clothes on the line."

The two of them went outside and spoke briefly to Skip's mom. It was the first time Les had spoken to her since Skip had left the hospital and he could easily tell she was still far from starting to deal with Harry's death. She seemed distant and unemotional. Les was glad that she was aware that he had not been with Harry the night he and Don were killed. And if she knew about the skull and trinkets she wasn't letting on.

"Les and I will be back on Sunday," Skip told her as he attempted to conclude their two-minute long chat. He waited for her to respond with something he could take as an okay to proceed with his travel plans. She simply looked at the two of them with little expression.

"We're going to be okay, Mom."

"I guess I don't even need to tell you to be careful," she said. "Les, I expect you to look out for Skip. He's still not fully recovered from his injuries you know."

"Sure," Les said, trying to sound confident. "Skip's trying to deal with this as best he can. I hope spending time with me will help him heal. Mentally I mean."

"Well, I assume you've talked to your father about this," Skip's mother said.

"Yes, Mom. He said the same thing he always says; 'clear it with your mother'."

"Just don't be too late getting back on Sunday," she said. "You go back to work on Monday you know."

"We'll be back before dark," Skip said as they began walking away. Then to Les: "did you bring a tent?"

"It's still up at the clearing in the woods," he said. "We'll need Harry's tent for tonight."

"It's in his closet," Skip said. "Go inside and get it and I'll meet you out at the car."

Skip had packed everything he'd need into Harry's backpack which he had left in the driveway leaning against his car. He walked over to it and set it in the open trunk.

A moment later Les came out the front door and tossed the tent and his pack into the trunk before slamming it shut. He then got into the passenger side of the Charger.

"We need to get going before my Dad gets home from work," Skip told him as he started the noisy engine. Les looked over at him but didn't reply.

The first thing they had to do was stop for gas and snacks. Les had prepared by scraping together twenty-three dollars before leaving home. He handed Skip ten and said: "get as much gas as this will buy." A few minutes later they were on the interstate headed for the north Georgia mountains. As was his trademark, Skip was wasting no time.

They made one more stop for a fast-food dinner before heading into the wilderness. This guaranteed that they would be doing all of their hiking in the dark.

About a half-hour after leaving the restaurant they were parking the car off the side of the road where the river trail crossed it. "You're sure this is the right spot?" Skip asked.

Les took a moment to recheck the map. "Yeah, this is it. Let's try to hide the car as much as possible."

"Why?"

"Just an old habit of mine," Les said.

Skip laughed. "Old habit? You've never even owned a car."

Les looked at him and laughed too. Skip backed into a spot between a couple of trees and cut the engine. There were three other vehicles parked nearby. Fellow hardy souls, Les presumed.

They got out and put on their hiking boots and packs. "It's going to get pretty cold tonight," Skip said.

"It already has," Les said. He rubbed his hands together and noticed that he could see his breath now.

They got out the flashlights and started down the trail. "I'll find us a good camp site about half-a-mile up," Les said. "I brought a lantern so we will be able to see while we set up the tent."

Les had his map with him but never reached for it. Even in the dark the place looked very familiar. He and Skip talked a little at first but then hiked mostly in silence. They never saw or heard another person.

After hiking for almost an hour Les spotted a side trail. "Let me take a look up this way," he said. Skip waited a moment while Les's flashlight disappeared up the path. A couple of minutes later he came back out. "Yeah, there's a great spot to camp about a hundred-feet back. Just follow me."

They reached the spot and Les fired up the lantern. A few minutes later they had the tent up and a short time after that got a fire going.

When he finally had a chance to relax, Les noticed how different the forest looked with most of the leaves off the trees. The changes he and Skip had been through since his last visit to these woods were so vast that they didn't seem possible. It was hard to believe it was still the same year, or lifetime for that matter.

The two of them sat by the fire, talking and eating snacks for about an hour before calling it a night. Once they had the fire extinguished and were in their sleeping bags it seemed like no time at all before the sun was coming up. Les awoke and lay quietly for a minute before waking Skip. They had a very long and arduous day ahead of them.

CHAPTER 10

THE WHISPERING WOODS

Sunrise came late this time of the year. His watch read four minutes past seven. "Skip, wake up," he mumbled. After a moment he reached over and gave him a gentle shake. "Skip."

"Huh!" Skip jumped almost as if Les had poked him with a fork. "Now? It's still dark."

Les sat up and yawned. "Not for long. I'll boil some water for oatmeal and coffee. I want to be on our way in less than half-an-hour."

By ten o'clock they were nearing the side trail that would lead to the Burial Ground. Les had his map in one of his front pockets but still didn't need it. He remembered the area very well. Too well perhaps.

Skip got noticeably nervous when Les suddenly stopped walking and held up his hand and told him to halt. "There's the entrance to the trail."

Les watched the anxiety appear on Skip's face and suddenly realized his friend might not be as ready for this as he had thought. "You can wait here if you want to. In fact, I recommend it." Deep down he hoped Skip wanted to continue on with him. The thought of going it alone terrified him. Only the thought of not continuing at all scared him worse.

"I'm in this with you all the way," Skip said without hesitating. "Lead on."

Les turned and started walking with Skip right behind, off the main trail and uphill into the thick grove of bare trees. About five minutes later the same eerie feeling that Les had experienced weeks earlier came over him again as they crossed some kind of invisible boundary-line onto the Native American hallowed ground. Only this time the familiar sensation brought fear with it. And Les was fully aware of the real danger.

"There's the first marker."

"Where?" Skip said. He followed Les's point and spotted the carved tree stump some thirty-feet away. "Damn, it looks like a human head!"

They approached and Skip leaned over to examine it, making sure he didn't touch it. He looked at Les waiting for him to speak. Instead, he merely stared up the trail ahead.

"I wonder if we should have brought a peace-pipe or something," Skip said.

Les wondered momentarily if he was joking. By the look on Skip's face, he guessed not. "The clearing is this way." They resumed walking.

Les felt his heartbeat increase with each step they took. He knew it was going to be emotionally difficult, he just didn't know how bad. "Thanks for coming up here with me, man."

"No problem," Skip said between pants.

Les halted and stared ahead. "There's the campsite. What's left of it." Skip didn't reply as he watched Les walk slowly to the center of the small clearing and stand between the two remaining tents.

"Don took his tent down and carried it out with him when we broke camp. We used Tommy's sleeping bag for the stretcher. Otherwise, everything is exactly the way we left it. It doesn't even look like there's been any wildlife in here."

"Do you blame them?" Skip said. He walked around slowly and examined the hastily abandoned campsite. One of the two poles in Tommy's tent still stood, making it look like a small, tan-colored pyramid. Narrow strips of nylon that once made up the back of the tent fluttered in the breeze.

"Look at this," Les said pointing. "Tommy clawed his way out the back like a terrified animal to get away from Don and Harry. He tore through this nylon with his bare hands. As it turned out the real danger didn't come until about two hours later."

He glanced over at Skip. He appeared sickened by the sight.

Les walked over to the empty tent he and David had shared one last time on that fateful night. He felt a brief twinge of heartbreak when he spotted his late friend's meticulous knot-tieing of the cords that still firmly held the tent's corners to their respective stakes.

"Everything's just like it was when we left it last month," Les said. He paused while looking around. "Well, not exactly everything."

That comment caught Skip's attention. "What do you mean?" He paused a moment for Les to reply before his follow-up question. "Do you think whoever or whatever killed Tommy is still out here? Maybe even watching us right now?"

"I'm not sure," Les said. "Things aren't quite like I was expecting. Maybe we can negotiate with it."

He started walking toward the interior of the burial ground and Skip instinctively started to follow. "Stay there," Les said without turning around. "I have to do this part alone."

Skip started to protest but Les waved his hand at him to remain silent, the whole time keeping his eyes fixed on the deep woods before him. "It's not my call."

Les walked about thirty paces and began picking up strange images in his mind. Something told him the spirits of some long-dead Indian braves were gathered nearby, peering at him from behind the trees. Their leader the closest, preparing to pass judgement on a foolish young white man who had dared to be part of a raid on their sacred land. He was perhaps only moments away from a silent wave of his arm to tell them to attack.

A faint steady beat of tom-toms came to his mind's ears from deeper inside the Indian burial ground. The sound quickly faded into a soft rhythm of the few remaining crickets and tree frogs.

"What are you doing back there Les?" he heard Skip call out from a few yards down the trail. Les could hear his approaching footsteps in the underbrush.

The image came to Les's mind of an old Indian chief looking at him with an expression of anger and fading patience. Les immediately interpreted it to mean that if he was about to meet a tribal leader, he'd need to get rid of Skip in a hurry.

"Skip," Les said as he turned to face his approaching friend, "I need you to walk back to the clearing, have a seat and stay there until I come back for you."

Skip stopped and looked at him with an expression of amusement. Les knew that expression very well, having seen it many times on the face of his younger brother Harry. It was an expression that usually preceded a snide comment and an attitude of resentment.

"Whatever you're about to say, don't," Les told him in a firm tone. Skip froze and glared at Les. "I need you to turn around and walk back to the clearing, okay?"

Skip stood and stared at him for several long seconds. Then he began to look above and around them. Les hoped that some of the images he had been seeing might show themselves to Skip. If they did, Skip would no doubt exit quickly, probably running frantically.

Suddenly Les heard a voice in his mind whisper the words: "Get Out!" He was watching Skip's eyes at the moment and saw them dart back to his face.

"Okay," Skip said, as if he thought Les had said it. "I'll go wait for you at the clearing, you don't have to get nasty about it." Les watched silently as Skip turned in a huff and started back down the trail.

Once Skip's footsteps could no longer be heard Les turned and faced the trail toward the Burial Ground's center. A moment later the steady beat of tom-toms resumed in his mind's ears and he began walking again. He reached the top of the hill and again noticed the immense amount of standing dead trees and brush. After a brief pause, he started down the hill toward the grave sites.

A cold breeze blew through the leafless tree branches making a faint whistling noise. Les paused and listened a moment before he continued down the hill to the bottom, where he stood surrounded by the pock-marked grounds.

Up ahead he spotted the hole from which Don had excavated the skull with a small pile of dirt beside it. "Don didn't even bother to fill the hole back in," he muttered. "At least it makes it easy to find the right spot."

Les removed his backpack and unzipped the main compartment that held the shoe box. Carefully setting the box on the ground to open it, he took out the string of beads, the arrowheads and finally the skull and stepped forward. Then he bent down and gently placed the arrowheads into the hole.

At that moment a strong voice in his head told him not to bury the skull here. The same inner voice then told him to take the beads and place them around his neck. He stood, put on the beads, and absently reached with his right foot toward the pile of dirt to push it into the hole. Again the image of an old Indian chief appeared in his mind. Les froze, then got down onto his knees, reached over to the pile of dirt with his hands and gently covered up the arrowheads.

As he kneeled with his hands flat to the ground, Les felt as if he was falling into some sort of trance. He closed his eyes and saw with his mind. The first vision was of Indian warriors fighting in the surrounding woods. He heard loud "whoops" and cries of pain from wounds inflicted by rifle fire and tomahawks. Dozens of arrows whistled through the air over his head.

He saw Indian encampments ablaze in wildfire, buckskin-clad women and children scattering into the wilderness, running for their lives. He saw the sick and dying lying on the ground and a helpless medicine man going from person to person with his rattles and smoke, trying to stave off the inevitable onset of widespread death.

In a few fleeting moments Les saw hundreds of years of tragic history of the red man and his demise at the hands of the European invaders and their cruel guns and relentless diseases. The vision terrified him with its graphic realism and intensity.

He saw things that he had just read about in library books, suddenly taking on new meaning with their tragic senselessness. The images were frightening and sad. After a few moments, they began to fade, leaving him with a much clearer appreciation for what America had been in the centuries before the people from across the sea first arrived, and what it became for Native Americans in the decades that followed.

As the images played across his mind's eyes in this lonely, forgotten place, Les felt himself transformed from part of the problem to a vital part of the solution. It was the most life-changing, overwhelming emotional and mental experience of his life. Then, just as quickly as they had begun, the visions ended. Les opened his eyes and slowly stood up, a changed man.

He reached up to remove the beads from around his neck and again the image came to his mind to keep them on. I should keep the beads and the skull? he asked in his mind. The answer came to him. It was "yes". Les turned slowly and walked, shoe box in hand, back toward the clearing. When he arrived there he found Skip sitting on a log looking at him with a questioning expression, but not an angry one.

"How did it go?"

"I don't know," Les said. "I still have the skull."

Skip's eyes grew wide. "What? The main reason we came up here was to get rid of that nasty thing. Give it to me and I'll go in there and bury it."

"No," Les said. "It doesn't belong here. It never did."

"Now how do you figure that?" he asked. "This is where those Indians buried it centuries ago. Where else could it possibly belong?"

Les thought a moment. "I saw images in my mind while I was back there. Some of them I'd seen the last time I was there but didn't really notice." He gave Skip a confused look. "I don't think this is a burial ground."

Skip's eyes grew wide and his brows furrowed exactly the way Les had seen Harry's do on countless occasions. "Excuse me?"

"There were some conflicts among the tribes that once occupied this land," Les said. He pointed at the shoe box that now lay on the ground next to his backpack. "And there was a great deal of internal strife and hurt feelings over the burial of that particular man. I'm not sure what it all means but I have an opportunity to settle an issue that has been pending for over two-hundred years. If I can figure out what it is then maybe I really can put the curse to rest once and for all."

Skip stared at Les for a long moment. "Les," he said, "I think you've finally gone over the edge."

"No," Les said. "On the contrary, I now see this matter clearer than ever. This skull belonged to a high-chief, but not a member of the tribe that this sacred land belonged to. I don't think Indians buried him here."

"Well if they didn't then who did?"

Les looked up at the thick canopy of bare limbs overhead. "White settlers," he said. "Or maybe Confederate soldiers or even Indians from a different tribe, I don't know. Whoever it was they were killers. Murderers who didn't care about anything except taking what they wanted."

"You're scaring me," Skip said.

Les turned and looked him in the eye. "You should be scared. That Indian warrior never should have been interred here in the first place. He has to be moved to the correct location and buried properly. And it's up to me to do it."

Les could see the exasperation on Skip's face. "Don't worry, it doesn't have to be done today," he said. "In fact, I think I have until the Hunter's moon, at least that's what I read in some of those books at the library."

"Hunter's moon," Skip said. "When is that?"

"The full moon of November, which is still two weeks away. You ready to get out of here?"

"Yeah," Skip said. "Why don't we walk back out to the main trail and find a nice spot by the creek and camp there. It's a pretty nice day for this time of year."

"Sounds good," Les said with a smile. The smile quickly faded as he looked over at Tommy's torn tent. "I guess we have some work to do first."

The two of them quickly folded-up the remaining tents and gathered all the equipment that had been left behind by Les and his fallen comrades weeks earlier. They took down Tommy's tent first.

The hardest part for Les was untying the cords of his tent from the stakes that still held it firmly to the ground. He had personally taught David how best to tie the knots and his now-deceased friend had mastered the technique. David's signature handiwork was standard yet meticulous.

Les paused momentarily and whispered a brief prayer. Then, with tears in his eyes, he yanked the cords free and brought down the tent. He felt a thud in his heart as he erased the last imprint of David's hiking legacy.

"I'll help you with that if you want," Skip was saying. He was standing two-feet behind Les and was cramming Tommy's folded tent into his pack.

Les looked back momentarily and then politely refused. "This is the last tent David will ever pitch," he said. "I need to take it down by myself."

With that he stood and walked around to the other side. He then hastily pulled the remaining two cords loose and quickly gathered up the blue nylon fabric.

Less than three minutes later they were donning their packs. Without a word they headed for the exit trail and left the sacred ground for what Les hoped was the last time.

When they got close to main trail about half-an-hour later, Les noticed a strong sense of relief coming over him. He found himself and Skip talking more as they hiked and the conversation lightening-up as well. They got to within fifty-feet of the main trail with Les leading the way when he heard voices somewhere nearby. He quickly turned and motioned Skip to halt and remain silent.

Skip froze. "What's wrong?"

"Not sure," Les whispered. "Keep your voice down." He slowly approached the trail with Skip a few feet behind when they heard voices approaching. The two of them crouched down in the underbrush and watched the trail. Moments later a group of six cub scouts, boys about nine or ten-years-old, came walking along talking and laughing. They passed without noticing. The scout leaders, two men that were probably fathers of a couple of the boys, tagged-up the rear.

Once they had passed and were out of earshot up the trail in the opposite direction, Skip gave Les a comical look. "I don't think those kids were going to harm us," he said with a laugh. The two of them stood up and walked out onto the trail.

Les looked behind him and noticed for the first time that a new National Park boundary sign had been nailed to the big oak tree behind them. Obviously it had been put there to replace the one Harry had knocked down weeks before.

"If one of those kids had noticed us coming out of the woods back there and walking past that sign he probably would have made some kind of big deal out of it to impress his friends," Les said. "In a matter of seconds the whole troop would have been trying to make a case against us to make a name for themselves. That would have been the last thing we need right now."

"I see your point," Skip said. "Glad your hearing is better than mine."

Les walked over to the new sign and read it, including some fine print. "This one is updated from the old one," he said. "It even mentions fines and jail time for violators."

"Wow," Skip said. "I wonder why we didn't see it before."

Les stood under the sign and was gently rubbing his hand across its shiny yellow surface. "I think it just got placed here earlier today," he said.

"Maybe the Park Service knows what's really back there," Skip said. "They've gotten serious about keeping people on the trail and out of the woods along here."

"They probably did it in response to Tommy's death," Les said. "That and a phone call from a rural home-owner named George."

"Think so?" Skip asked him.

Les thought a moment before nodding in agreement. "Yeah, I think that's what happened alright. Let's go find a campsite and cook some dinner. I'm starved."

They hiked for about thirty more minutes until Les spotted a short side trail to the right. A quick inspection revealed that it led to a secluded spot next to the creek. Previous campers had built a fire ring about two-feet high a short distance from the shore. "This looks like a good spot," he said. They unpacked Les's tent, pitched it, then started cooking.

Darkness soon set in and the warm fire felt good against the cold night air as the two of them sat and ate a dinner of camp stew and mixed vegetables. "It's nice the way the trees keep the wind away," Skip said. "It's actually pretty warm close to the fire." He had finished eating and set the metal plate on the ground at the base of the fire ring.

Les stood and put his plate and drinking cup there too. "I'll wash those in the creek in the morning," he said. "I'm too tired to do it now." He sat back down on the log and started warming his hands.

"You bothered by having that skull in your backpack?"

Les looked over at him. "A little I guess. But I know we need it"

"I can't believe you're going to take that thing back with us," Skip said. "It really makes me wonder why we came all the way up here in the first place."

Les stared into the flames and thought about what Skip was saying. "I needed the knowledge I gained from being in these woods," he said. "I also think my mind is still processing some of it. Maybe my subconscious will analyze it tonight while I'm asleep and I'll know more in the morning. That happens sometimes."

"Just the same," Skip said, "I hope your not going to bring it into the tent with us."

Les looked up at the star-filled north Georgia sky. "No, I'll leave it in my pack outside tonight, that's no problem."

They sat silently for awhile, watching the fire die down to embers before heading into the tent for the night. Les put his pack against a nearby tree and used a shock-cord to hold it fast. He then climbed into the tent and zipped into his sleeping bag.

Several hours later he was startled awake by grunting noises coming from a few feet away outside the tent. His eyes popped open and he lay motionless as he heard something large moving about. The memory of Don and Harry invading Tommy's tent weeks ago came briefly to mind.

Suddenly he heard a loud roar identical to the one he had heard from one of those guys that night. He grabbed his flashlight and crawled out of the tent, half-expecting to encounter a ghost. When he got outside he shined the light toward the sound. Over next to his backpack stood a large black bear. The bear looked back at him, its eyes reflecting a dull-green shade.

"Hey," Les yelled at the bear. "Get out of here!"

The bear just stood and stared, showing no sign of either anger or fear. Les looked around him and spotted their dinner plates on the ground. Holding the flashlight between his teeth, he grabbed a plate in each hand and began clanging them together as he charged at the bear. The sound startled the animal and it quickly ran about ten feet into the woods before stopping and looking back.

Les clanged the plates together again and took several more steps in the bear's direction. He then took the flashlight in his right hand and kept it on the bear to see what the animal was going to do next. After a moment it turned and lumbered into the woods and disappeared.

Les looked back at the tent and saw Skip standing outside by the doorway. "Good job," he said. "Looks like you scared him away."

"I wonder what he wanted," Les said. "We didn't leave any food around."

"Probably smelled the dirty dishes."

"Yeah," Les said. "Except he wasn't near the dishes, he was over by my pack." He shined the light on the pack from ten feet away. It looked okay. "I'll check it closer in the morning," he said as he headed back to the tent. "It's too cold to be standing around out here."

Once they were back in their sleeping bags, Les started to get comfortable again. That's when a strange thought came to him. "I wonder why that bear isn't in hibernation yet?" he said.

"Maybe his calendar got lost in the mail," Skip mumbled. With that, the two of them went back to sleep.

The next morning Les got up and went to his pack to look for any damage the bear might have done to it. He immediately spotted several scratch marks on the outside of the front pocket where the skull was stored. Luckily he had stopped the bear before it ripped the pack open.

"It looks like that bear wanted the skull," Skip said from behind him. "So it wasn't the dirty dishes after all."

Les sat on the ground and stared at the scratch marks on his pack. "It does look like he wanted the skull."

Les rubbed his hand across the slightly-damaged side of his pack. "Why would that bear want the skull?"

He looked back at Skip a moment, then kneeled-down in front of the pack, rubbing the spot again.

"Bear," he muttered. "Bear. I had a dream about a bear." He sat and thought a moment longer, his mind searching for clues in the fading memory of his dreams.

"You had a dream about a bear?" Skip said. "That's odd, I had that dream too."

"Very funny," Les said. "No, I had a dream about a man named 'Bear'. The Indian chief whose skull is in my pack. The word 'Bear' is in his name. I don't know, Running Bear, Bear Hunter, something with 'Bear'." He looked at Skip as he continued to search his mind for answers. "I'll bet someone around here knows who I'm talking about. If we can find somebody who has lived in these parts for a long time then maybe they can steer me in the right direction. I need to find this Mr. Bear."

Skip thought a moment and Les spotted the slightest hint of the family smirk on his face. He secretly hoped Skip wasn't about to make a comment using the name "Yogi".

"Why don't we pack-up and get back to the car," Skip said. "We can drive around for a while before heading back. Maybe there's a gas station or store clerk around here that might know something about this 'Bear' dude."

"That's a good idea," Les said. They quickly prepared breakfast, broke camp and headed up the trail toward Skip's car.

Once they got out onto the main road they had to drive several miles to get down from the mountain ridge. There was a small community centered around a cross-road intersection with a gas station and a large building that housed a Laundromat, a pawn shop and a car wash, all of which were closed on Sunday.

Skip slowed the car down and they both looked in all directions. "Go right," Les said. "I think there's something down that way."

Skip turned and headed down the two-lane road. About a quarter-mile ahead they spotted several houses on the left and a convenience store/gas station on the right. "Let's try here," Les said and Skip pulled over and parked.

Les got out and went inside. A lady and two small girls were just leaving and Les held the door for them. He then headed for the counter and the lady behind it. "Hi there," he said. "Do you know of any Native Americans living in this area?"

The lady, a dark-complected woman of about forty stared at him with a confused expression. Before she could reply Les decided to be more explanatory.

"I'm looking for an Indian person," Les continued. "Maybe somebody that has lived around these parts for a long time."

"An Indian," she said. "You mean someone in particular or just any old Indian."

"Just any old Indian," Les repeated. "I know it sounds crazy. Maybe I should just try a library or something. I'm just trying to learn more about an old Indian Burial Ground a few miles from here."

That last statement seemed to strike a chord with her. "Burial ground," she said. "What the hell would you want with a place like that?"

"So you know about it then?"

"Sure," she said. "When I was in school the boys used to talk about it all the time. Some of them claimed they went up there on weekends to drink and make out but I think it was mostly talk. My father once told me that some kids went up there one night about sixty-years ago and never came out. Don't know if it's true or not. You gonna buy something?"

"Uh, yeah," Les said, spotting the grill behind her with several hot dog wieners spinning slowly. "Give me a hot dog."

She picked up a paper napkin and placed a bun on it while Les pulled out a dollar. After he paid her he walked over to the condiment table and began adding relish and onions.

"You don't by any chance know of anybody who lives around here that might know more do you?" he asked.

"What, are you trying to find it?" she asked. "Cause if you are you can get in a lot of trouble. I heard that a boy scout got killed up there a month or so ago. The local sheriff told me just the other day they're gonna prosecute trespassers in that area from now on. Wouldn't want to be the next person caught in there, that's for sure."

"No," Les said, "I'm not interested in going there. I'm looking for someone that might know the history of Native American's in this part of Georgia. I'm thinking of writing a book."

That last comment, totally untrue, came out of his mouth too fast for him to stop and think what he was saying. He took a bite of the hot dog. It tasted much better than he expected.

"A writer, huh," she said. "If I was you then I'd go up the street to the library and talk to Miz Peters. She's been here going on fifty years. If there's anyone that could answer your questions it'd be her."

"Hey, thanks," Les said, "you've been really helpful."

"Sure," she said. "Just come on back if you ever need a soda to wash down that hot dog." She grinned a tobacco-stained smile.

"I will," he said, and he headed out the door.

A black Toyota was just pulling up to the gas pump as Les walked back to Skip's Charger and got in. "I think I may have found a lead," he said. He told Skip about the library and how he wanted it to be his next stop.

"It'll have to wait awhile," Skip said. "I doubt the place opens again until tomorrow morning. Looks like we'll have to come back next Saturday."

"You're probably right," Les said. "Why don't we run by the place and make sure they're open on Saturdays?"

Skip drove awhile and within minutes they spotted the County courthouse with the library across the two-lane main street. On the glass front door was a sign giving the hours. "Good," Skip said, "they're open all day this coming Saturday, from eight to five."

Les shook his head. "I sure wish we didn't have to wait that long."

"I know," Skip said. "It seems such a long way off."

They barely spoke during the trip home, just mostly listened to the radio. Les thought several times that if he was going to keep hanging out with Skip he would have to try to learn to get used to hearing lots of heavy-metal music. Although the songs were unfamiliar they brought back unpleasant memories of the night he and the others had run afoul of the sword-wielding man called Snake the previous summer. The memory gave him the creeps.

Thinking back to the Snake incident made Les think of his only remaining close friend from that night, Ken. *What a great sense of relief it would be if Ken would come along with us next weekend,* he thought.

Les looked over at Skip. He liked to sit back in the seat while he drove, his right hand on the top of the steering wheel, eyes fixed intently on the road ahead. "Would you have a problem with my asking Ken from the scout troop to come along with us next weekend?"

Skip thought a moment. "I don't think I'm familiar with Ken."

"He's the black guy in the troop," Les said. "Harry may have mentioned him."

"Oh yeah," Skip said. "Harry told me the guy has a really smart mouth. I don't think he liked him very much."

"I think Ken felt the same way about Harry," Les replied.

Skip looked over at Les. "I take it you like the guy."

"Yes," Les said. "In fact, to be perfectly honest with you, I'm better friends with him than I think I ever was with Harry or Don."

There was a long pause as Skip took in what Les was saying about his late brother. "I thought you and Harry were pretty tight," Skip said at last. "At least I know you were as kids."

"Yeah," Les said, "but time changes people. I think that once Harry and Don got to be seniors they really felt the age-difference between themselves and the rest of the guys in the scout troop. Plus, that trip to the Burial Ground showed me just how different philosophically I was from them."

Les paused a moment as the two of them stared at the gray roadway ahead. "It's nothing against Harry," Les said. "He and I just grew apart. It's one of those things."

"Yeah," Skip said. "Change happens."

They finished the drive home without Skip's ever giving Les a final decision on whether or not he could invite Ken along the next weekend. He figured it wouldn't hurt to find out if Ken would even be willing to join them before he mentioned it to Skip again. After all, this had become a whole lot more than just another camping trip.

CHAPTER 11

THE SEARCH FOR THE TRUTH IN THE HAUNTED WOODS

Les usually saw Ken between his second and third classes around a quarter-to-eleven each morning. On this particular Monday, however he spotted him as they both were coming in the front door around seven-forty. "Hey Ken, got a second?"

Ken strolled over with a curious smile. "Man, what's got you so stirred-up this early? Biology class can't get here soon enough for you?"

"Ken, save it. You want to go camping this weekend?"

Ken straightened up in a snap. "Sure Man. I'd love to get away out in the woods this weekend. You want to leave Friday afternoon?"

"Yes, the minute the dismissal bell rings," Les said. "But there are a few things you need to know before you commit. Harry's older brother Skip is driving. The main objective of the trip, well, the only objective actually, is to return Don and Harry's artifacts to their rightful place."

Les watched Ken's face as a lot of serious thought ran across it. "I love to have you come along for additional moral support if you're willing. That, and to have an extra set of eyes watching my back. It's a trek with a pretty serious agenda. I'll understand if you want no part of it."

He continued to watch Ken's face. He had no idea what question he'd ask first. As usual, Ken surprised him.

"Skip? Isn't he just a bigger and meaner version of Harry? You know, same smirk, same attitude, not so keen on black people?"

Les thought momentarily. "I had that impression about him too before I really got to really know him. He's more mature than Harry was. Smarter too. And I think he's really a different person now since Harry's death. Not to mention his own near miss with the grim reaper."

It was obvious to Les that Ken needed some time. This decision was harder for him than he had expected. "Ken, Skip is doing me a huge favor assisting me on this. I really need him." He put his hand on Ken's left shoulder and looked him squarely in the eyes. "And I need you."

For the first time in his life Ken actually looked serious. Les watched his eyes dart about the hallway. They were standing in the middle of the large high school building entrance and multitudes of students were filing past them on both sides. Yet, for that brief moment in time they couldn't have been more alone.

Les, in deep need of a trusted friend's help, read some of Ken's thoughts and seemed to feel his emotions. He saw raw talent, innovation, and a truly loyal friend. He was also saw genius. Their friendship was true and strong, and couldn't have come at a better time.

The ten-minute warning bell rang suddenly and brought him back to the present. "You don't have to give me an answer right now," Les said. "Think about it and we'll talk later in the week."

He started to walk away and Ken grabbed his arm. "Hey Man, this is something serious, right?"

Les nodded. "Yeah, as serious as a heart attack."

Ken let go of his arm and patted his shoulder. "I'll have your answer for you today. Promise."

"Cool," Les said. "Whatever your answer, it's cool." He turned and headed down the hallway. He already knew what Ken's answer was going to be. The pat on the shoulder revealed it. Les smiled.

A few hours later Ken came up to Les while he was fishing through his locker for his biology book. "Hey Les," he said in an excited voice. "I've made up my mind. I'm in for this weekend. I know just what to say to get it past my parents."

"You're sure you are okay with all the bizarre circumstances?" Les asked him. "There's a bit more to this than just being out in those cold woods all weekend you know."

"Oh, that's fine," Ken said with a chuckle. "In fact, that's the best part."

"How sure are you about your parents being okay with it?"

Ken smiled confidently. "They won't be a problem. They were so impressed when you won that scholarship to Wilderness Unlimited that they think you can do no wrong."

"Wow," Les said. "That might be a tough act to live up to."

Ken laughed. "Not a problem, buddy. My parents both know that the safest place in a forest is three steps behind you. And I'll just promise them that it's exactly where I'll be the whole time."

An underclassman he knew greeted him as he passed by. Ken said "hi", then quickly turned his attention back to Les. "They would probably freak if they knew all the weird details, especially my mom. But we were out of town when your trip with Tommy went south. And they know you weren't around when Don and Harry had that, how would you say, bad night."

"Yeah," Les said, taken aback somewhat by Ken's odd wit. "I guess you could call that a 'bad night'. I'll feel a lot better having both you and Skip there with me so I don't have a bad one of my own. And three steps right behind me is as good a place as any."

Ken gave him a quick smile and stepped backward half-a-step. Les had seen this move quite a lot now and knew it was one of Ken's "soul moments", or whatever you might call it.

"I got your back, my white brother," he said at last. "Besides, that night we tangled with Snake was a real bash." He seemed to be reminiscing briefly as he stared down the hallway. Most of the other students were in their respective classrooms by now and the tardy bell was due to ring any second.

Ken's broad smile lingered. "I can still see that drunk redneck's face when he thought my ghost was coming to get him. I have fun when I'm with you, Les. I'm suprised you don't have multiple girl friends. Nobody can accuse you of being boring."

Les rolled his eyes just a bit. "I strive to avoid boring."

Ken laughed. "I don't think I'll have much trouble clearing it with my parents as long as I limit the details. My dad was in Vietnam, you know. There was a lot of 'weirdo' crap going on in that place. I believe he thinks you're macho. All those badges and stuff you've piled-up are what he terms 'earned, not given'. He seems to like the idea of having me hang-out with you."

"I'll try not to let him down," Les said. "I'll let you know a more detailed schedule once I talk to Skip."

That afternoon Les called him as soon as he got home. As expected, Skip had just a little hesitation about having Ken come with them. "You sure you want to bring Ken? I don't really know him that well. Besides, something could happen to him and then I'd get blamed."

"Nothing's going to happen to him," Les said. "Besides, if anything happens to anyone the victim will be me. I'm the one who's butt is on the line. Yes, I'm sure I want him along. The more trustworthy people that have my back the better."

Skip appeared to Les to be searching his mind for another excuse. Les briefly wondered if his main objection might be racial. "He'll help share the cost of gas, you know."

"Oh, yeah," Skip said. "My charger does drink the petrol. We could certainly use some help there."

Les smiled. "Now, you're thinking. Pick us up in the school parking lot Friday afternoon around a quarter-to-four."

After hanging-up from talking to Skip, Les called Ken. He was very happy to get the news that everything was a go.

The rest of the week seemed to take a month to Les. He continued to take nightly walks around the windows and doors, inside and out, hoping and praying there weren't any little red men peeking inside, waiting for him to fall asleep so they could take him out in a quiet, bloody manner. He did manage to start sleeping and by Thursday night was able to get a good rest. He was plenty ready to go on Friday when he went to the designated meeting place the school parking lot and found Ken and Skip already there.

The two of them had already gotten past the reintroduction stage. The trunk was open and Ken was loading his backpack and sleeping bag.

"You brought some cash, right Ken," Les heard Skip ask him. "We may do a lot of driving. Not to mention eating in some fancy restaurants." He paused a moment and then grinned.

Ken looked at him a moment and chuckled. "Fancy restaurants? How fancy can a place be that will let in the likes of you?"

"Did you bring yourself some money or not?"

"Yeah," Ken said. "I got some green-backs. You?"

"Oh, I'm set," Skip said. "But I'm doing plenty of work behind the wheel too."

"Not to mention scouting out all those fancy restaurants," Les said. They both looked at him and laughed.

Les tossed his backpack into the trunk and then opened the passenger-side door. He pulled the front seat forward so Ken could squeeze-in. Ken got in the back seat and quickly got comfortable in the middle. "Well if I'm paying you to chauffeur then you're going to have to put on a hat, Skip."

Skip looked at Les and smiled. "Got one right here," he said, putting on an old, worn Atlanta Braves cap and turning the bill around to the back. "Tips are always welcome."

"I'll catch-up with you at the gas station," Ken said. He laid his head back and closed his eyes. "Just wake me when we get there."

Les and Skip smiled at each other as Skip started the engine and drove quickly out of the parking lot. "This is going to be pretty cool," he said.

"Yeah, well just make sure you drive cool," Les said. "We don't need any speeding tickets or other road problems."

"Just relax, Les," Skip said, putting on some dark glasses. "Just because I drive a sports car doesn't mean I'm careless."

After a quick stop at Les's house for a cooler of food and drinks for the next two days, they headed up the interstate for the north Georgia mountains. "We might as well get dinner and gas at the last place we see before we get on the scenic highway," Skip said. He was driving without the sunglasses now and would soon be turning-on the headlights. "Nightfall is coming early these days."

"Not a problem," Les said. "One of the things in that box I had you put in your trunk yesterday is my camp lantern. Looks like we'll be doing our tent set-up in the dark."

After the dinner stop it was only another half-hour to the trail-head. Skip found a place to park in one of the more secluded spots in the small clearing off the road. There were only three other cars parked there. "I guess the hikers coming this weekend are waiting until tomorrow morning," Les said. "I would have thought this parking area would be more full than this."

"There might not be much interest after Tommy's tragedy occurred near here," Ken said. "And it'll be pretty cold this weekend."

They got out of the car and started getting the backpacks ready. "I don't think the tragedy has much to do with it," Les said. "It's been almost a month now and most backpackers have pretty short memories."

"And most of the people that hike this area have no idea where the Burial Ground is located, or that it even exists," Skip said. "But Ken sure is right about the cold."

Les finished adjusting his waist-strap and flicked-on his flashlight. He had put in fresh batteries and shined the wide beam of light down the trail to his left. "Everybody ready?"

They hiked a short distance and found the going slow with only their flashlights for illumination. "We don't need to go very far," Les said, "just out of sight of the road will do." About ten minutes later he found a good, level place.

Ken had recently gotten a dome tent big enough for all three of them and their packs. Even in just the light of a lantern they were able to pitch the tent quickly. Soon, all three of them were in their sleeping bags even though it wasn't yet nine-o'clock. The move was more for warmth than out of tiredness. At that point there was little else to do but lie in the dark and talk.

"So, what are we doing first tomorrow?" Ken asked from his corner of the tent. "Got any specific game plan in mind?"

"First stop is the library," Les said. "I figure there are some Native American families living somewhere around here that might know the background story of that burial place. Perhaps they would be able and willing to point me in the right direction of where to go with all this. The first objective is finding them.

"The gal at the convenience store last weekend said to talk to a Miz Peters at the library. She supposedly knows about everybody in town and maybe she can tell me who we're looking for. I just hope she's friendlier than some of the librarians back home."

"And maybe younger and hotter too," Skip said. They all laughed. They chatted a few minutes more but soon were asleep.

The next morning Les got up first, found Skip's keys on the floor beside his boots, and made a quick trip to the car to retrieve his cooler. He got back to camp with it and fired his two-burner stove at exactly one minute after seven.

One of the many things he appreciated about the first morning of a camping trip was the extra food selection. Unlike the rest of the hike, the first day's breakfast could be made up of foods that had to be used-up right away due to their perishability. For him that meant bacon and eggs. The welcoming smell of his cooking always brought his companions out of their tents without any prodding on his part.

"Better eat-up guys," Les told them as he poured himself some coffee. "You never know when we'll get to eat next so a good start is always crucial."

"You don't need to tell me," Ken replied, his mouth so full he could hardly close it. "I eat like this every morning."

"You mean like a pig?" Skip said with a laugh.

Ken finished his bite and grinned at him. "Sometimes like a pig. Sometimes something worse. Pray you never see it."

"Ha!" Skip said with a laugh. "I can probably challenge you good in that category."

"I pray none of us ever sees that," Les said.

After eating they broke camp at a few minutes after eight. It was a short hike back to Skip's Charger and soon after that they were on their way back down the mountain toward town, arriving at the library only minutes after it opened.

"May I help you find something?" a lady that appeared to be in her late-fifties asked them as they entered.

"Yes ma'am," Les said. "I'm looking for Miz Peters."

"I'm Mrs. Peters," she said somewhat sternly. "You are aware that there is no such word as 'miz' aren't you."

"Yes, ma'am," Les said. "Mrs. Peters, I'm trying to learn some of the history of Native Americans in this part of Georgia."

She looked at him and thought a moment. "Are you the writer?"

"Writer?" Les asked.

"Someone at the local filling station told me there was a young man who claimed to be a writer in town last weekend that might be looking for me today," she said. "I was just wondering if you might be he."

"Les," he replied. "Yes, it's me."

"It is I," she corrected. "You'll need to do some work on that grammar Les if you hope to make it as a writer in this day and age."

Les glanced over at his two buddies and saw them trying not to burst into laughter. He figured she'd throw all three of them out if they so much as snickered. He held his glare on them until both noticed him and straightened themselves up. Mrs. Peters had also observed the exchange and didn't appear impressed.

"So we know my name and that of Les here. Do you young gentlemen have names as well?"

Ken gave Skip a quick glance. "Ken," he said, holding out his hand for her to shake. She only glared at him.

"I'm Albert," Skip said without showing any expression whatsoever. "But you can call me Al."

Les and Ken stared at him in momentary disbelief. He continued to look Mrs. Peters in the eye and his facial expression didn't change. Les knew if she realized he was lying about his name she'd throw them out in a heartbeat. In his mind he briefly saw the image of them being taken out by the local police. He would proceed with caution.

"We have a section dedicated to Indian culture over this way," Mrs. Peters said. She began walking several aisles to her right and Les followed. Skip and Ken stayed put momentarily.

"You've got to watch what you say in here, Albert," Ken said, doing his best impression of Mrs. Peters, only in a whisper. "Or Miz Penis will pull out her trusty ruler and whack off your little white Johnny Cake."

Skip almost sprayed saliva as he struggled to hide himself from Mrs. Peters' view before breaking out laughing. Luckily she was too far away to notice him at the moment.

"Compose yourself immediately, Alberto," Ken continued in the funny voice and with a remarkably straight face. "Or I'll tack your little pocket-trophy on her private wall in the basement myself."

"Stop, you're killing me," Skip laughed.

Ken walked over and stood a few feet behind Les. Mrs. Peters was pointing out two shelves of literature on the subject of Indians. "The Cherokee books are on the left here. You can probably find something about other tribes on the right one."

When she noticed that Skip and Ken had joined them she looked at the them through the thick lenses of her horned-rimmed glasses. "Do you fellows have something specific you're looking for also? Or are the three of you some kind of a team?"

Skip laughed. "Oh, we're a team alright."

"That's right, ma'am," Ken added. "You see, we don't have a great deal of time and need to do the research quickly."

"I see," she replied. "Are you interested in any tribe in particular?"

"The Yuchi," Les said.

Mrs. Peters looked at him for a long moment. "The Yuchi," she repeated. "I don't know if you are aware of this but the Cherokee were the dominate tribe in this area. They had their own written language, schools and a high literacy rate. They also ran the only Native American newspaper. If you want a good deal of fine material to write about, then I would suggest making the Cherokee the topic."

Although her light brown hair and grey eyes didn't tell it, Les surmised that Mrs. Peters probably had some Cherokee blood in her. He also figured it was easily offended.

"Thank you for the suggestion," Les said, trying his best not to come off sounding smart-aleck. "But our research is more along the lines of hostilities, inter-tribal conflicts, Indian wars. I'm afraid the Cherokee were too refined a people for our somewhat crude research topic. Thank you for the suggestion though."

"Why don't you just come right out and ask her, Les," Skip said. His sudden outburst caught Les by surprise. It also hinted of impatience, a characteristic he didn't want out on display.

"Good suggestion Albert," she said. "Yes Les, why don't you come right out with it."

Les gave Skip a quick glare, then turned to face Mrs. Peters. "We're looking for an Indian man that may live in the area. The gal at the convenience store said you might know of someone."

"Oh did she now?" She reassessed all three of them with her eyes momentarily and Les detected that she was considering how much information to share with them for some reason. He worried that he might now be scaring her.

"Does this man you are seeking have a name?" she asked finally. "Or am I supposed to come up with that also?"

"Yes," Les said, smiling just a little. "We're looking for a man with the word 'Bear' in his name." She looked into his eyes and he looked into hers. He felt he was asking her to go somewhere in her memory she didn't like. This wasn't going well.

Mrs. Peters remained speechless a moment longer. Les doubted she was interested in wasting her time with anyone not bearing a valid library card. The local tax-payers didn't hire her to provide county services to the likes of these fellows. Her patience was now in overtime. He quickly realized that if he had a wild-card to play in this little poker game, the time for it was now.

"I may have some of the remains of one of his ancestors," Les said with a sad expression. Mrs. Peters' mouth fell open for a moment but she quickly composed herself. Meanwhile, Ken and Skip were staring at Les, wondering what he was going to say or do next.

"Someone I was once good friends with excavated a skull from the Burial Ground in the woods a few miles from here," he continued. Again, Mrs. Peters struggled to hide her shock. "I think it may have belonged to a chief or medicine-man, I don't know. Anyway, I thought it should be buried in a proper place and in a proper way. I was hoping someone like this 'Bear' person might be able to provide some guidance."

"A friend of yours illegally absconded with a human skull taken from an Indian Burial Ground," she said. "How charming. Your friend's name wouldn't happen to be Les would it?"

"No," Les replied with enough force that she actually was taken aback momentarily. "His name was Don. And along with the skull he also unearthed an Indian curse of some kind. A curse that ended up killing him."

"And three others along with him," Skip added. "Including my only brother."

Les watched her eyes dart about the room. He couldn't tell if she was going to help them or not. But the fact that she was an educator, someone professionally trained to help students in need, might aid his cause.

"This friend of yours must be the young man I read about in the local newspaper a few weeks ago," she said. "Not a very nice fellow I would say."

Les thought of Tommy momentarily. "You couldn't be more wrong," he said.

It was obvious to him that she only knew sketchy details about the incident, all of them slanted perhaps. He thought it would be best to only provide her more information if it became necessary to get her to answer more questions.

"You want to know the worst of it all, Mrs. Peters?" He said. "The part about the place having a curse. That one is true."

"I see," she said. Her eyes were probing him from head to toe. They seemed to be searching for dirt on his clothes and under his fingernails. Wondering perhaps if he had a little shovel out in the car, which of course he did.

"I know about the curse part in the worst way," Les continued. "First-hand."

She stared at him momentarily. "Well, if this 'curse' has already taken revenge on the grave-robbers, then why do you still have it?"

"You might say I inherited it," Les said. "Curse and all."

"And the curse isn't finished yet," Skip said.

Les glanced over at him. He was glad Skip didn't decide to add the word 'sister' to the statement.

"He smuggled it out of the woods," Ken said. "Don, I mean. The curse didn't get him until a couple of weeks later. Took one of his friends out in the same grisly fashion that same night. We just acquired the skull from his personal effects and are hoping to end this awful nightmare. Ma'am."

Les was pleasantly surprised by Ken's input. They needed someone to explain quickly and clearly what they needed from her and Ken did that like a television sports announcer.

"So you were with him that night?" she asked.

Les nodded. "I was."

Mrs. Peters glared at him with the slightest hint of fear in her eyes. After a brief awkward silence he continued.

"Look, we're trying to do the right thing here before something else happens. Are you able to help us or not?"

He again stared into her eyes and she into his. She wasn't ready to answer the question yet. Maybe she never would be.

Les glanced around them at the shelves of Native American books and the artwork adorning the walls. "What would the legacy of the proud Cherokee inside you tell you to do, Mrs. Peters?"

By now she was over being shocked by what she was being told. Les was in fear for his life, something she had actually only seen three or four times in 32 years as a teacher and guidance counselor. Les detected the slightest hint that she was going to relent.

"We'd really like to talk to this 'Bear' fellow if you know of such a person, ma'am," Ken said. "We don't plan to bother him if we can help it."

"Beartracker," Mrs. Peters said with more than a hint of frustration. "He lives in a trailer on one of the hillsides a few miles out of town. I taught his five children English many years ago, as best I could anyway."

"Can you call him for us?" Ken said. "We'd really like to meet him."

"And he'd like to meet us," Skip said rather sourly. "Trust me lady."

"I see," she said. "Why don't you use the office phone." She pointed at a desk twenty-feet away. "There's a phone book over there somewhere too." Then she took a moment to look them over again. "I hope you didn't bring that skull with you into this library."

"No ma'am," Ken said.

"It's in the car," Skip chimed-in. "Want me to go get it?"

"No," the three of them replied in unison.

"Just don't tell Mr. Beartracker you found him through me," Mrs. Peters said. "I've had enough dealings with that man to last a lifetime." With that, she turned and walked away.

Les took a moment to ponder why she felt the way she did toward Mr. Beartracker. It could be because she was a Cherokee and he was something else. Whatever the reason, he felt that they had gotten lucky to get as much information from her as they had, given the circumstances. It was now time for the next step.

"He's here in the white pages," Ken said excitedly as he held-up the thin local phone book. "Doesn't say anything about smoke-signalling. Guess he's not all that Indian?"

"Just dial the phone, dude," Skip said. "I'm ready to blow this place. Kind of reminds me of an old-folks home."

"Will you keep your voice down please," Les said. Ken dialed the phone and then handed the receiver to Les. It was answered after the second ring.

"Hello, Mr. Beartracker?" Les said.

"No, this is his daughter," came the reply. Her voice was quite deep.

"Oh, you're his daughter," Les said. "Sorry. My name is Les Harrison."

Skip started laughing and wisely turned his face away from Les's direction. "He couldn't tell if it was a man or a woman that answered the phone," he said to Ken. "We're in deep shit with the guy already."

"Could I speak to your father please," Les asked. She sighed but didn't reply. "It's about Chief Beartracker."

Ken and Skip both looked at him in disbelief. "Chief?" Ken whispered.

"What about him?" the woman demanded. "He's ancient history."

"My call is actually in reference to the curse of the Indian Burial Ground," Les continued. "I'm afraid some friends of mine aroused it and died because of it. Now I fear I'm its next victim if I don't talk to your father right away. May I speak to him? Please?"

There was silence for a moment and then an older man's voice came on the line. "This is Mr. Beartracker."

"Hello, sir," Les said. "My name is Les . . ."

"You knew the boy that died in the woods near here last month I take it," he said.

"Yes, that's right sir," Les replied.

"Native American curses can be strong and dangerous things. You are wise to have come to me, wise beyond your years, young white man."

"Thank you," Les replied, somewhat puzzled. "May we come see you today?"

Skip and Ken held their breath awaiting a reply. "What do we do for the rest of the day if he says 'no'?" Ken whispered. "Do you think Miz Penis knows if there are any casinos around here?"

Skip gave him a brief sneer. "Shut up!"

"He said okay," Les told them with his hand over the mouthpiece. He then turned his attention back to the conversation with Mr. Beartracker. "Great, how do we get there?"

Les paused and listened a moment. "Can't one of the people here at the library tell me how to find your place?"

"You don't want to be spending a lot of time around those people son," he said. Les looked around the desk and spotted a pen and piece of paper.

Once he began writing he wrote for quite a while. When he was finished getting directions he had a full page of notes.

"Thank you, Mr. Beartracker," Les said. "There will be three of us in a silver Charger. We'll be there shortly."

He hung up the phone. "We're in."

They headed for the door as Les glanced over toward Mrs. Peters, who had turned her attention to a girl of about six or so. She seemed to be strategically ignoring them as she helped the little girl find a suitable book.

Finally, she glanced up at him. Les quickly smiled and said the words; "thank you."

She didn't offer so much as a facial expression in reply and he didn't wait around for one. He turned and headed for the car, driving directions securely in hand.

CHAPTER 12

BEARTRACKER S FOREST—
A RED MAN S SANCTUARY

"So, how far are we going?" Skip said as he got into the leather driver's seat and started the engine. Ken found his way into the back and Les pushed the seat into upright position and got in.

"I think it's about twelve-miles," Les said. "But there are a lot of turns. It may take us an hour."

Les directed Skip back to the main highway and they headed in the direction of the trail from which they had come earlier that morning. They were soon passing the trail-head and continued on up the mountain from there. About three-miles later, Les told Skip to start looking for a gravel road on the left. They spotted it and pulled in.

"Okay," Les said as he tried to read his hastily-written directions. "We should see a gravel cross-road about another half-mile up. We go straight across."

"Man," Ken said. He was sitting on the front edge of the back seat and was practically between Les and Skip. "This cat lives out in the boonies."

"I just hope the road doesn't deteriorate any more than this," Skip said. "Chargers aren't four-wheel drive you know."

"It'll be fine," Les told him. "Here comes the cross-road."

There were no other vehicles in sight in either direction as Skip slowly ran the rusty stop sign. Another hundred-yards and the road took on a downhill slope and began to wind around.

"Get ready to turn right," Les said. "The road is hidden from this direction and is easily missed."

Skip slowed as they rounded a curve. That's when Les spotted it. "Right here!"

Skip turned them onto a dirt road that had a slight amount of mud on it. The car slid sideways just a bit before the big rear wheels dug-in.

"I'm not sure I want to do this," Skip said as they listened to the sound of road dirt being thrown up into the under-siding of the car. "I think it rained up here last night."

"Just a little farther," Les said. The road remained mostly level as they passed under very large pine trees and crushed dozens of large cones. There were two more turns to be made before they reached the dirt road where Beartracker's trailer stood off to the left.

"Guess this is it," Skip said, turning into the driveway and trying to avoid a large puddle. Two big, black dogs could be seen coming out from under the rickety wooden porch and approaching. When they got about thirty-feet away they began barking loudly and angrily.

"That must be the welcoming committee," Ken said. "Les, maybe you should be the one to go knock on the door."

Les looked back at him and smiled. "We are expected," he said.

A moment later they could hear a man's deep voice order the dogs to be quiet and the two animals immediately ran back under the trailer. He stepped out the door and stood staring at them. He had long, gray hair, parted into two braids, each adorned with colorful feathers at the tips. He wore a round, black hat and appeared to have few if any teeth.

"Man, that guy must be 110 years old," Skip whispered.

"Yeah," Ken muttered back. "Maybe we should find out if he's checking out soon. Then he could take the skull with him and save us the trouble."

He and Skip both burst out laughing. "Good one, dude," Skip said.

"Hey idiots," Les said. "This man is doing us a huge favor just talking to me. He doesn't have to and we don't deserve it. You will both show him respect and courtesy at all times or I will personally kick both of your butts. You get me?"

There was total silence for a moment as Skip parked the car. "Hey Les, we're cool," Ken said.

"Me too, man," Skip said.

Les relaxed a bit. "Good. Now, unlike when we were in the library, let me do all the talking. In fact, why don't you two just wait in the car."

"Works for me," Skip said.

Les got out and closed the door. "Hello Mr. Beartracker," he said with a smile as he walked up and held out his hand. "I'm Les Harrison. I sure appreciate your seeing me."

"Les," Beartracker said as he took his hand. After three firm shakes he held Les's hand for a moment longer, looking deeply into his eyes. It was a long moment before the elderly, Native American man spoke again.

"You are in a bad place," he said. "Very troubled and afraid. I detected as much when we spoke over the phone but not to this degree."

"That is true," Les said. "My dreams led me to you."

Beartracker smiled ever so slightly. "Confirms my Shaman status I suppose."

Beartracker's two black dogs came out and walked up to Les. He carefully patted them each on the head and both wagged their tails slightly, almost as if they had already met. This did not go unnoticed.

"Dogs are very good judges of a man's character. Scout and Nightsky seem to accept you. A very good sign."

There was a brief silence before Beartracker continued. "You said you have come concerning Chief Beartracker. He was my great-great- great- grandfather. Come, let us talk under the oak tree."

Underneath an enormous tree that looked to be as old as the hills themselves, Beartracker had built a long bench from split logs. The two of them sat down and Les took-in the magnificent view. Before him lay a long, smooth hillside with neatly lined rows at the bottom where crops had been recently harvested. Beyond the ten or so acres of farmland lay the forest, still displaying outbursts of fading yellow and orange leaves.

"This was once the land of my people," Beartracker said. "We took only what we needed from it and it provided well. The white man came and took our game, then he took our land. Finally, he took our very lives.

"Once there were many of my people living here. Today, I am the last. Life as the Yuchi once knew it is now all but forgotten."

"I know what you say is true," Les said. "I had never heard of the Yuchi until a week ago."

"That is because the things the white man knows as 'history books' do not include my people," Beartracker said. "Our history has been erased and left to fade into nothing. Only the hills have our memory now."

He sat and gazed into the distance as Les observed his face. He was very old, perhaps over eighty. His face was wrinkled and deeply tanned from years of sun. Beneath his brown eyes lay a man of pride and distinction, someone under-appreciated for his knowledge and wisdom in a world where his ancestors were not welcome. The feathers at the tips of his gray braids told of a heritage he was trying to keep alive.

"Tell me why it is that your have sought me out today," Beartracker said. "Your finding me must have been a bit like finding a needle in a hay stack as they say."

Les smiled. "It's kind of a long story."

"Then start at the beginning."

Les told him all the details of their night in the Burial Ground and how he was the last of the original five that was still alive. He told of the circumstances of his friends' deaths and of the similar slash marks each had on their legs.

"The curse is real and I'm afraid if I don't do something fast then it will get me," he concluded. "I know it's out there somewhere. I can feel it."

Beartracker paused a moment as he finished digesting all that Les had told him. "There were once more than two-thousand Yuchi in these woods," he said at last. "As recently as three-hundred years ago we farmed these valleys and raised our children amongst the hills. Our leader was a man named Tuskeneah. He was the first of my ancestors to observe that the white man said one thing but did another. He foretold our fate long before it became apparent to the rest of us."

Les looked away from Beartracker and toward the expanse of forest that began some one-hundred yards beyond where he sat. He invisioned the peaceful images as Beartracker described the gentle sound of tom-toms in a steady rhythm and the voices of children, laughing as they played together. A happy people, living in harmony with the animals of the forest.

"My people were the first to inhabit this land," Beartracker said, an air of pride in his inflection. "We built small homes along the river banks.

We set them in rows so they pointed toward the heart of our community which was a sacred square. It was not only the center of our town, but was the core of our spiritual lives."

Les sat quietly and felt a strong sense of peace come over him. In his mind he saw villages beside running streams where women gathered wood and kept the cooking fires burning while they awaited the return of the young braves with hunted game.

He saw Indian children braiding each other's hair and decorating their faces with crude, clay-based paint. They leapt to their feet and hurried excitedly toward the edge of the encampment to greet two young men who were returning with a freshly-killed deer.

The animal hung by its feet from a long stick that rested on the shoulders of the two braves. It had a large rack of antlers and its feet were tied together with a binding made from tree bark. The deer would feed all of them that day.

"One day around 1800 a white man named Benjamin Hawkins entered our camps," Beartracker continued. "He was a settler, unarmed and friendly, a more peaceful man than most of the native people of other tribes we often encountered. Mr. Hawkins led us to believe that all white men were harmless. He stayed for one day among my people, counting them, assessing them.

"A short time later the woods began to change. Within weeks there were many white settlers invading our land. They carried guns and used them at will, often shooting down my people like they were animals."

In his mind Les heard the sound of distant rifle fire, and saw the Yuchi running to the sanctuary of their encampment, gathering for safety in a circle. The surrounding forest, which once had been the site of sustenance, was now wrought with danger.

"My people soon joined forces with a neighboring tribe, the Creeks. Some of the other tribes joined American soldiers in an apparent effort to get into their good favor, but not us. We fought against all of them in the Creek War of 1813-14 on the side of the 'Red Sticks'. But their numbers were too great, and we were soon forced off of our land."

Les continued to stare into the distant woods, seeing in his mind the images Beartracker was describing. He began to see why the forest was now devoid of human inhabitants.

"The Yuchi and Creek were living as one the last few years that these hills still belonged to us. That was in the early 1800s," Beartracker said. "Although we maintained our uniqueness from the Creeks, we were banded together with them for survival. That lifestyle was maintained, for a while, by treaties we signed with the newly-formed United States government. We surrendered thousands of acres of land in exchange for the protection of our freedom.

"That freedom lasted just over twenty years, until President Andrew Jackson ignored the treaty signed by his predecessor, John Quincy Adams, and took the rest of our land."

Beartracker turned and looked Les in the eyes. "Like so many other dealings between native peoples and the government of this great country, betrayal, fraud and greed eroded our livelihood."

He stared into the distance where the mountains ended at the horizon. "Left with a choice of moving or dying, we were forced onto what is known as 'The Trail of Tears'. Thousands of Yuchi and Creeks were taken on crowded steamers up the Mississippi river to the Arkansas territory where we were forced to walk 300-miles to our reservation. Many weren't up to the journey and died along the way. Countless others reached the reservation only to linger and die from dysentery and cholera. Less than seventy-five years later a bill passed by the U.S. Congress rendered my people extinct once and for all with the wave of a pen.

"My family and I are perhaps the last of the Yuchi living in the state of Georgia," Beartracker said. He looked over at Les and studied his face. "But there are many of us buried in cemeteries all over these mountains.

"This land holds much history. I would be untruthful if I were to tell you there weren't native curses conjured-up against the white man in centuries past. After a long period of dormancy, one of them could have become aroused again. This appears to be what has happened in your case."

"Yes," Les said. "I had four friends who did a terrible thing. They found one of these burial places and unearthed remains. I was with them and am ashamed to admit I did nothing to stop them. Now they are dead, and I fear, so am I."

Beartracker studied Les's face but showed little surprise on his own. "Your friends unearthed our honored dead. That was a foolish thing to do. Very disrespectful."

"Yes it was," Les said, "on both counts. I tried to return the skull they dug-up to the same place where they found it but for some reason felt that it didn't belong there. Now, I need to know where it does belong and how exactly to place it there so that the curse can be put to rest. If that's possible." Les looked into Mr. Beartracker's dark, expressionless eyes. "Will you help me?"

"This sacred place your friends desecrated," Beartracker said, "is it near here?"

"Yes," Les said. He pulled out Don's old map and showed it to him. Beartracker studied the map a moment and Les watched his eyes grow larger with each passing second. After a moment he looked up at Les with a look of fear on his face.

"I am familiar with this location," he said. "It is a bad place indeed." He folded the map and handed it back to Les. "It is a cross-road. The curses of two tribes exist there, not just one." Then he took a long moment to think before speaking again.

"The curse of this particular place is one that originated from the strange collection of rites that developed when the two tribes, the Yuchi and the Creek, were merged against their will by the American government. Before the forced exodus west, when there appeared to still be hope of keeping our land here in the southeast, government social workers were sent to 'close the gaps' if you will, between the different lifestyles of the two tribes. They wanted to make the entire population of both tribes into one people of one culture, one set of leaders, one history. They were disrespectful fools.

"Over the course of a few years, these social workers became more and more hostile toward the people they had been sent to help. When it became obvious to them that the merger of the two cultures would never be acceptable to either tribe, they started to reveal through their actions exactly what it was that had been motivating them from the beginning. Their disregard for our language, culture and ancient ceremonies became more and more pronounced. They didn't really come to help. They came to get us out of their way in the shortest time possible. Their real intentions and prejudices did not go unnoticed by the tribal councils.

"Each tribe had its share of spiritual leaders who had witnessed the deterioration of our great cultures in the short time since the white man had arrived. They were not happy, and called upon the Great Spirits to come to their aid.

"A large gathering was called. The white man often refers to such a meeting as a 'pow-wow'. That's a generic term for any native ceremony in which a large number of my people assemble. Ceremonies are like the hills themselves, no two are alike. We gather to mourn, we gather to celebrate, we gather to worship. We have many different ceremonies, each with a different purpose.

"We respected the Creek, with their ceremonies and practices, and they respected ours. What we had in common was that the white man had no respect for either. This was the source of great anguish and disdain to both tribes. And it led to rebellion.

"The elders of the two tribes met in secret and discussed the situation for many days. We referred to this as the 'Red Stick Council'. It was this council that created the tribal army that attempted victory over the American government troops and their traitor Native American allies in the 'Red Stick War' that would happen several years later.

"Prior to that war, the 'Red Stick Council' had sent scouts to visit neighboring tribes, attempting to find allies who, along with ourselves, could rise up and defeat this massive invasion of the white man before it wiped us all off the face of the earth. These scouting missions failed, and further distanced us from the rest of the Native American world.

"This series of events led to a strengthening of the bond between the Yuchi and the Creek. It also led many of the elders of both tribes to foretell of defeat and death to come. Visions of the future that we now know all too well were accurate.

"Not long after that, our medicine men began to talk of a new set of spirits, evil ones that our people had never encountered before in the twenty-plus century history of our races. These evil spirits were diseases that we would later come to know as cholera, dysentery, small pox and diphtheria, all delivered to us by the white man.

"A new spiritual movement began within the merged tribes. The talk of a last defense, a powerful force with origins in the great spirits of the wind and land, permeated throughout the tribes. With the combined spirits of the recent dead, victims of the white man's onslaught whose numbers were increasing daily, a protective force could be conjured-up to shield our land, surrounding us, protecting us.

"The tribal council meetings continued in secret for weeks. Finally, they recessed for a fortnight, awaiting the full moon of the 'Night of the Hunter'."

"The 'Night of the Hunter'," Les said. "That would be the second full moon after the Autumnal Equinox. The so-called 'Hunter's Moon'."

"That is correct," Beartracker said. "The first full moon of the autumn is known as the 'Harvest Moon'. The 'Harvest Moon' has much tradition and significance to my people also.

"All of this is based on the ancient knowledge that the full moon always rises at sunset and sets at sunrise. During the autumn the cooler weather keeps the spirits of the rain and thunder away, making night bright enough for a man to continue harvesting or hunting all night long, in preparation for winter. Unfortunately, it also afforded the white man the opportunity to do other things in the bright moonlight."

Les couldn't take his eyes off of Mr. Beartracker. He was fascinating and at the same time frightening. There was no denying his wisdom, however. And he made Les feel a most welcome guest.

Beartracker stood and walked several feet to a rack he had built by nailing boards between two large trees that stood about three-feet apart. Inside the square area created by the boards stood several spears and long, carved sticks.

He removed one of the spears, a four-foot, multi-colored, neatly painted wooden shaft that was adorned with several feathers near its hand-crafted, arrow-head point. The spear, red and blue but mostly white, looked very ornamental with bright yellow feathers dangling from its end.

"This is a ceremonial war spear," Beartracker said. He held it up for Les to observe, though Les kept his hands in his lap. "It is passed around to each tribal council member at the beginning of the council session. Then it is placed in the front of the lodge for all to see while the session is taking place. After the ceremony, the war spear is returned to safe storage until needed again."

"You may hold it if you would like."

Les smiled and stood, reaching with both hands to cradle the relic. Beartracker gently laid it into his hands and he held it horizontal in front of his face. He closed his eyes as his hands tightened their grip around the narrow shaft of the spear. He let his arms drift down to his sides and he found himself holding it in a comfortable manner with the spear in a diagonal direction across his chest.

Les felt a warm sense of security come over him as he held the spear. In his mind he heard birds thrashing about in the woods a quarter-mile away. He heard a fish jump in a stream near some rapids that made a constant roaring sound as the water rushed down from the high country. He invisioned himself holding a brightly-lit cylindrical object that looked nothing like a spear, but more like a glowing stick of yellow fire. He felt the gentle heat, radiating from the spear he was seeing in his mind.

Les opened his eyes and handed the spear back to Mr. Beartracker. He took it in the same fashion as Les had moments before and held it before his face for a moment. Beartracker then walked over and set it back into the rack between the trees. The two of them then sat back down on the log seat.

Beartracker looked at Les with a stern expression. "The artifacts your friends dug-up in the sacred Burial Ground, do you have them with you?"

Les reached into his pocket and pulled out the beads which he now kept in a large pill-bottle. "I have these and a skull," he said. "The skull is in the car. May I get it?"

"Yes," Beartracker said. "I need to see it."

Les jumped up and hurried back to the car. The radio was playing at low volume and the two occupants were napping. Both awakened when Les walked up to Skip's window.

"Sorry to wake you sleeping beauties," he said. "I need the skull. Mr. Beartracker wants to see it."

"It's in the trunk," Skip said. He took the key out of the ignition, cutting off the radio, and handed it to him. Les walked back to the trunk, opened it, and found the shoe box containing the skull against the left inside wall of the car's trunk. He took out the box and closed the trunk. He then walked up to Skip's window and handed him the keys.

Skip took them and looked at him groggily. "How much longer is this going to take?"

"Yeah, man," Ken said. "We're getting hungry. I tried to get out of the car to come see how you were doing but those two dogs wouldn't let me."

"Yeah," Skip said. "They came out and growled at him as soon as he opened the car door. I'm surprised they aren't attacking you."

Les chuckled. "I think they like me."

"So what's the deal?" Ken said. "You going to be much longer?"

Skip slid his key back into the ignition and tilted it back to activate the radio. "Yeah, man. We're about ready to split."

"Just hold your horses," Les said. "I'm making great progress here." He paused as he stared at the faded brown trailer. There were many rust-stains along the front and one of the small windows was broken-out. Nothing but air stood between the outside and the faded white curtain behind it.

"Well, hurry it up," Skip said.

"I'll try," Les whispered. "Why don't you kids go back to sleep." He chuckled as he turned and began walking back to where Mr. Beartracker sat. He removed the rubber band from the shoe box and handed it to him as he found his seat.

Beartracker slowly removed the lid and peered inside the box. After studying the skull briefly, he lifted it out and held it at eye-level. After a brief moment he got a look of shock on his face. "Kiawampa," he said.

Les was puzzled. "Kiawampa? You know whose skull this is?"

Beartracker turned and looked at him. "Yes, my friend, you have found the skull of Kiawampa. His remains have been missing from my people for generations. This comes as a great surprise to me. It also may be more than mere coincidence."

Les silently watched him place the skull gently back into the box and set it on the seat beside him. He then put one elbow on his knee, his fist up to his chin and stared across the weedy yard, deep in thought. After a long pause, he spoke.

"Kiawampa was the warrior that rose to greatness during the 'Red Stick Council'. On that night, our great leader Chief Tuskeneah took a ceremonial spear, much like the one I just showed you, and handed it to the strongest brave of the tribe, designating him the warrior leader of our people. There were two such young men that exhibited the strength and courage for such a task, but Chief Tuskeneah could choose but one.

The two young braves were Kiawampa and Beartracker, my great-great-great grandfather. Perhaps because he was the older of the two, Chief Tuskeneah chose to give the spear to Kiawampa.

"The spiritual leaders from both tribes gathered around Kiawampa and told him to sit in the middle of the floor. Then they began a spiritual dance that I cannot describe to you because you are not of our blood."

"I understand," Les said.

Beartracker stared blankly into the distance as he told Les what came next on the fateful night two-and-a-half centuries before. He told it in such a way that Les almost wondered if Beartracker had been there himself. Sure looks old enough, he thought.

"The entire group of tribal spiritual leaders gathered around Kiawampa and placed their hands on his head, anointing him Supreme Warrior," Beartracker said. "Not only did it give him the strength to be a great warrior and leader, but it also bonded the two tribes in a way they had sought for years but never achieved. You see, Kiawampa was Creek and Beartracker was Yuchi. The two of them led us in battle with great courage. Unfortunately, it wasn't enough."

"What became of them?" Les said.

"The same thing that befell the rest of our tribe," Beartracker replied. "They vanished into the forest. None of those of us left behind ever really knew exactly what became of them. We only knew that the two of them and many, many other braves went courageously into battle that day and never returned.

"Kiawampa and Beartracker were the best of friends, brothers almost. I have long believed that they died side by side.

"Tell me, Les, how is it that you found the skull and then sought me?"

"My gift of extra vision led me to you," Les said. "Recently, while I slept in my tent the woods, a bear came from out of the forest and tried to get at the skull, which was in my backpack. I was able to follow some kind of mental trail that led me to a man with 'Bear' in his name. That led me to the nearby town and eventually to you."

Beartracker thought a moment. "You possess good tracking skills. But unlike other braves, you follow footprints in your head. I believe our spirits have led you. Strange, and you have no Indian blood in you?"

"Not a drop," Les said. "I'm new to this country. My mother is from the Eastern European nation of Hungary. I was actually born there and came to America when I was two."

"Amazing," Beartracker said. His gaze found its way back to the trees in the distance.

"Will you tell me more about Kiawampa?"

Beartracker nodded. "My people have many legends that explain our brave warriors' entry into the battlefields of the great beyond. Some say that you can hear Kiawampa's voice in the wind at night in these vast woods, calling upon the warriors of the tribes to rise up against the oppression that was encroaching upon us. Another says that he has been known to appear along with some of the tribe's elders when our land is invaded by an outsider.

"When Kiawampa died he was carrying the strength of many spirits, a force that no doubt lived on in some form or fashion long after he was gone. That spirit has been dormant for over two centuries. At least until now."

Les felt a cold chill at that moment. He remembered David telling him he thought he saw an apparition of some kind in that burial ground. Kiawampa himself perhaps. He realized now how subtle the warnings can be, even when the danger is strong.

"These stories I've shared with you today were handed-down to me by my forefathers. The curse of Kiawampa is what your friends uncovered when you unearthed his skull. Of all the Indian graves in this vast land for you to have chosen, you picked absolutely the worst possible one."

Les stared into the distant woods as he digested what he had learned today. "I think I heard Kiawampa's voice in the trees myself," he said. "In my mind I heard him warning us to get out of the burial ground. My friends had other ideas however."

"Too bad," Beartracker said. "It might have saved their lives."

Les looked at him and Beartracker saw the pleading in his eyes. He didn't even have to ask the next question, as Beartracker already knew what it was and had the answer.

"It isn't too late for you, my friend," he said. "There is still a way you can save yourself from the curse."

"Just tell me what it is," Les said. "I'll do whatever it takes."

Beartracker again sat and gazed into the distance. Les knew better than to interrupt his thoughts, so he sat quietly, watching the expressions on the old man's face, waiting for him to speak.

"The fact that you have located Kiawampa's remains confirms a fear that my people have had for over two-centuries," the elderly Indian man said. "Because none of the tribal elders knew exactly where Kiawampa was when he met the spirits of the great beyond, they were not able to bury him in a proper place and manner. This place in the mountains where you and your friends found his skull was not a sacred place to my people."

"It wasn't?" Les asked. "But what about all the carved markers surrounding the place? Don't those mean anything?"

Beartracker almost smiled. "Oh they have meaning alright. You see, the white men that defeated Kiawampa that day also no doubt killed many other braves as well. In fact, my guess is that it was a slaughter, with no survivors. The bodies were probably buried hastily in a shallow mass-grave. If they were buried at all.

"As was a common practice by our disrespectful enemy, no attempt was even made at a proper burial. They were too busy tending to their own dead and wounded to fret over the braves they had just defeated. So they just discarded their enemy in an out-of-the-way place and left.

"Had the situation been reversed, the victorious braves would have mangled the bodies of their fallen enemy. This is done as a safety precaution so they wouldn't come back for revenge in the afterlife."

Les wore a look of fear. "They take revenge in the afterlife? How does that work?"

Beartracker smiled briefly. "My people hold strong beliefs in the spirit world. Often, after victory in a battle the fallen enemy must be further disabled. If the body of an opponent has no hands or feet it cannot use them to retaliate in the spirit world where enemies may meet again. The same is true for eyes. It is easier to avoid someone seeking vengeance who cannot see you."

"Oh," Les said. "I am beginning to understand much now."

Beartracker paused momentarily to allow Les to absorb what he was being told before continuing. "As for the markers, they were placed there months or years later by other Indians, perhaps of a different tribe, who saw that land for what it was, a cursed and haunted place to be avoided. They would have seen or heard the spirits in the area and placed those markers as a warning to all to keep out."

He looked over at Les. "Indians, regardless of tribe, know to avoid such an ominous warning sign when they see it. If only the white man could be so wise."

Les now saw this whole ugly scenario for what it truly was. He couldn't help but wonder how he could have been so foolish.

"I guess that explains why the location of the Indian Burial Ground was actually printed on that old map Don had," he said. "Somehow, the person who drew it up knew about the place and its reputation, and put it on the map to tell people not to go there."

"I would say that is a correct assumption," Beartracker said. "Because no Native American would ever put such a place on a map, especially one that might fall into the hands of a white man."

Les sat staring toward the distant forest. "So just who are the Little People?"

"They are fallen warriors," Beartracker said. "Perhaps the spirits of the many braves who died on that terrible day so long ago. I am not sure. But whoever they are, their battle has not ended. They will continue to fight to defend their people and their homeland. In this lifetime or the next."

Les thought a moment. "You said it still isn't too late for me. I want to put this curse to rest."

"You can do that," Beartracker said. "Since you have discovered Kiawampa's remains, and since he never had the proper burial his spirit requires, you have an opportunity to right an ancient wrong."

He gave Les a long look. "You will have to bury him in the proper place and manner. And you will need to do it soon. Active spirits take to the war path at the time of the Hunter's Moon."

"I already tried to rebury him," Les said. "It didn't work."

"It didn't work because you were in the wrong place," Beartracker said. "You will have to travel to our original homeland in Alabama. Our honored dead rest in the last home of the Yuchi and Creek before the forced exodus on the 'Trail of Tears'."

"Where in Alabama?" Les asked. He looked at his watch, it was just past noon.

"Just over the Georgia state-line and north of the Talladega National Forest. The Burial Ground there is the rightful place for our great warrior, Kiawampa. I will provide you written instructions. They will include the words to say after you bury Kiawampa's skull in the sacred ground. The process will only take you a few minutes but it will provide a lifetime of peace for my people."

"I have to get there first," Les said. "Is it a long way from here?"

"I would say you could get there in less than two hours," Beartracker said. "You'll need detailed directions which I can prepare for you."

"That sounds promising," Les said.

"Unfortunately, our land is not as accessible to us as we would like. It is well-hidden, much like the other burial ground. But this one is surrounded by private property, making access to it difficult."

"Maybe we can get the land owner to cooperate," Les said.

"Perhaps, but time is short and the hour will be late when you get there if you are going now. What may work best for you would be to become an Indian brave yourself. Walk like the deer, silent and watchful. Hide like the fox, stay undetected and sly. Choose your steps wisely and you will succeed."

Les thought a moment. "Would you start writing-up those directions for me? I need to go tell my two buddies waiting in the car that we still have some traveling to do."

"Yes," Beartracker said. "I also have someone who can help you when you arrive there. He is my brother's grandson, Carl."

Les looked at him and smiled. "Carl? I would think he'd have an Indian name like yours."

Beartracker smiled, showing Les his stubby teeth for the first time since he had arrived at his home. "He does, his name is Carl Beartracker. My first name is English too, David."

Les was shocked. Beartracker had the same first name as his late best friend.

"I will write out the directions to Carl's home as well as the instructions you are to follow when you reach the burial site," Beartracker said. "I think I should phone him right now as well."

"I'll be out at the car," Les said. He stood and reached out his hand to shake. Beartracker took it and shook it firmly twice. "Good luck, Les," he said. "If you are brave and do not let the weak spirits within you to guide your path, you will be successful."

"I will be brave," he said as he turned for Skip's car. Beartracker went inside his trailer to the phone.

CHAPTER 13

ALABAMA RED
STICK COUNTRY

"It's about time," Skip said when he saw Les walk around the side of the trailer and approach the car. He and Ken had gotten out to stretch their legs and were keeping an eye out for the dogs. "I was beginning to think you were never coming out."

"We can't leave just yet," Les told him. "It should be just about ten more minutes."

"We've been here almost two hours already," Ken said. "Can't you just say goodbye?"

Les opened the passenger door and Ken knew that as an invitation for him to get in the back seat. Instead, Ken pulled the front seat forward and gestured with his hand for Les to get in first.

"Get in the back seat, funny man," Les said.

Ken laughed, then crawled in. Les got in the front seat and closed the door. He then explained the situation to them.

"You mean we have to drive all the way to Alabama now?" Skip said. "That's a long way."

"Mr. Beartracker says it takes less than two-hours," Les said. "We can stop to eat on the way and still get there well before it gets dark.

He's arranging for us to meet his great-nephew when we get there. Once we are done, we can find a place to camp and sleep, then go home tomorrow. We'll be home and done with this whole mess before the end of the weekend."

"Sounds doable," Ken said. Les was glad to hear some encouragement from one of them for a change.

Beartracker came out of his trailer a moment later and walked up to the car. He handed Les a sheet of paper with lengthy directions neatly printed by hand.

"Nice handwriting," Les said as he inspected it. "I should have no trouble reading this."

"My grand-daughter writes well," he said. "I just phoned Carl and he will be looking for you when you arrive. It would take too long for me to write down the ceremony you will need to perform. Carl is doing that now. He will instruct you when you get there. The rest is up to you."

Again Les extended his hand through the open car window to shake. "Mr. Beartracker, I can't thank you enough."

"My thanks to you as well my friend," he said. "Tonight will be a monumental time for my people. Finally, many spirits can be put to rest."

Skip started the loud motor at that point and slowly began backing out of the dirt driveway. Les waved one last time as they pulled away. A half-hour later they were on the main highway heading west.

They soon stopped for a fast-food meal and to gas-up Skip's Charger. It was almost four o'clock in the afternoon when they reached the Alabama state-line.

"Set your watches back an hour," Les said. "Central time zone, we all just got younger."

"So let me get this straight," Skip said. "We're going to have to go into the woods to the real Indian Burial Ground and plant this skull with a proper ceremony."

"That's about the size of it," Les said. He was looking at the map and trying to figure out how much further it was to their turn-off.

"Are you sure you can handle all this ceremonial stuff," Ken said. "I'd hate to come all this way only to find out they don't let white guys in at this place." He and Skip both laughed.

"Not so fast, Ken," Skip said. "They may not let brothers in either."

"Oh, that sounds okay to me," Ken said. "We brothers know better than to go where we're not welcome. I'll be glad to stay back and guard the car."

"Knock it off," Les said. "I'll go in alone if you guys don't want to join me. It's my problem and I'll deal with it."

"I was just kidding," Ken said. "We're in this together."

"Me too," Skip said. "After all, they killed my brother and almost killed me. I want to put this thing to rest just like you do."

"Thanks guys," Les said. "When we meet-up with Mr. Beartracker's great-nephew Carl, he'll help us get through it."

"It might even be fun," Ken said.

Les looked around in his direction. "I just hope I'm still going to be alive this time tomorrow to look back and judge how fun it was."

"Here's the junction with highway 278," Skip said. "We're getting close." They were on a two-lane highway with a 55 speed limit and the traffic was light. The roadside trees were still dappled with some autumn colors which glowed magnificently in the golden afternoon sun.

"About ten more miles and we'll turn off onto a country road," Les said, rechecking his directions. "Looks like Carl lives out in the sticks just like Mr. Beartracker."

"I wonder if he has man-eating dogs too," Ken said.

A few minutes later they spotted the turn-off to the right and headed south. Les recited the directions as Skip drove, sending them along a number of turns over the next twenty-five miles until they finally saw the road sign pointing toward a small community called Dayton.

"Only about five more miles," Les said. The sound of his own words made him somewhat nervous.

They turned onto a dirt road and went two more miles before spotting a trailer that looked a lot like the one in which Mr. Beartracker lived. "Brown pickup truck out front," Les said, "this must be it."

They pulled into the driveway and immediately heard a large group of dogs barking. A man wearing worn-out blue jeans, a dirty white shirt and a baseball cap stepped out of the trailer and yelled at the dogs to be quiet. He then smiled and walked toward the car.

"This guy is an Indian?" Skip muttered.

"He looks more like a good-old boy to me," Ken said. "Les, better check his credentials." He and Skip laughed.

Skip killed the engine and the three of them got out. "You Les?" Carl asked in a deep, southern accent.

"Yes," Les said. "This here's Ken and the driver is Skip."

They all said their greetings and Carl invited them inside. "We're going to have to wait another hour for sundown before heading for the cemetery," Carl said. "That will give me some time to go over the ceremony details with you. Hope you guys can read in the dark." He chuckled.

They all stepped inside Carl's trailer and watched him chase a large black and white hound off the well-worn couch. "Get down Dozer," he said. Dozer jumped to the floor and laid down beneath a cluttered table.

The three of them sat on the couch, Les in the middle. Facing them was a new-looking television with several dirty dinner plates sitting on top of it. From somewhere further back they heard children.

Carl showed them where the bathroom was and then finished working on some written directions. Once the three of them were again seated, he sat down on a dusty, gray-colored easy chair facing them and started telling Les about the ceremony he would have to perform. "I talked to my Uncle David for a long time after you guys left his place," Carl said as he handed the sheet of paper to Les.

"We concluded that a basic, simple ceremony should put Kiawampa and his curse to rest once and for all. It will only take a couple of minutes. Just bury the skull exactly where I tell you, then step back several steps, stand facing the grave and read the words on the sheet." Les looked at the neat printing on the paper. He didn't recognize any of the language.

"I'll read the words to you and you write down whatever is necessary to remember how to pronounce them." Carl read aloud and Les wrote the words phonetically. He then read it back to Carl a couple of times to make sure he had it right.

"That's all there is to it," Carl said. "You sound like a pro."

"Okay, so I have the words down," Les said, "but what exactly is it I'm going to be saying?"

"You will be asking the Great Spirit to open the gates to the Great Beyond for our brother and friend Kiawampa," Carl said. "You will be freeing his spirit from the confines of this world and uniting him with those who have gone on before."

Carl studied Les's face a moment. "I'm trusting you can deliver the words with dignity and genuine feeling."

"Oh, I can do that," Les said. "Considering how much I have personally invested in this, I can generate a lot of genuine feeling."

"I believe you are ready," Carl said. "What about you?"

Les smiled. "Yes. "Ready as I'll ever be."

"How do we get to the burial ground?" Skip asked him. "Is it far from here?"

"The burial ground," Carl repeated. "Now that's a whole new can of worms."

"What do you mean?" Skip said. "It isn't going to take long to get there is it?"

"Oh I can get you close in only about fifteen minutes," Carl said. "But to actually get to it you're going to have to cross about a quarter-mile of private property. That's the hard part."

"Nobody's going to shoot at us are they?" Ken asked. Les saw the concern on his face again.

Carl laughed. "Not if they never know you're there. But if they catch you then yeah, probably so."

"You're kidding, right?" Skip said.

The smile left Carl's face. "No I'm not. I won't sugar-coat it boys. This isn't going to be easy."

"But you know them don't you?" Les said. "Couldn't you just call them and explain the situation?"

"That would be the worst thing I could do," Carl said. "You don't want these inbred freaks to know you're headed their way. They don't like Indians. They also don't like strangers, outsiders or city-slickers." He glanced over at Ken. "They don't like blacks either. Come to think of it, there are about a dozen different reasons for them to shoot at any or all of you. And only one for them not to, the fact that they won't know you're there."

Carl sat looking over his written instructions and Les studied his face. It appeared that Carl's confidence level wasn't very high.

After a moment Carl looked up at them. "You're going to have to really be careful. Just quietly go in and then back out like the wind and no one will be the wiser. And don't try to rush it."

"I don't understand," Les said. "Isn't this burial ground on state land?"

"State land," Carl said thoughtfully. "Yeah, I guess you could call it state land." He laughed. "Unfortunately, it's surrounded by unfriendly territory. And the woods are crawling with armed, good-ole boys."

He looked at the ceiling briefly, perhaps pondering some wild idea. He quickly dismissed it.

"If we had a boat I could take you there on the river and get you in pretty fast. But that would be dangerous in the dark and my boat's dry-docked right now anyway. No, this is the best way, if there is such a thing."

Carl pulled out a map of the area and laid it on the cluttered coffee table just in front of the boys' knees. "Here's the river," he said pointing. He then took a pencil and drew a circle beside it. "There's a cemetery right here," he said, tapping the point of the pencil in the middle of the circle. "Most of the graves have been there a century or more. There's even a Civil War general buried in a special section there. You'll see a wrought-iron fence around it.

"You boys will walk through the woods to the gravel road, follow it inside the cemetery, walk past the iron fence and go down a hill all the way to the back."

"To the back of the cemetery?" Ken asked. His eyes were wide and Les began to worry that he might be about to bail.

Carl nodded. "And even on past the back of it. The Indian Burial Ground is between it and the river. You'll have to go all the way through the cemetery to get there."

"How will we know when we get to the right place?" Les said.

"You'll see a short wall made of old river stones that encircles several graves all bunched together," Carl said. "These were the first settler graves to be placed in the cemetery. Just go about another thirty-feet past the wall and you'll be there. The Indian cemetery will be easy to spot because all of the grave markers are little wooden crosses. They're placed in a big circle and you'll just go to the stone marker in the middle."

"Then we just dig a hole and put the skull inside it?" Skip asked.

"The skull and the beads," Carl said. "Les must dig the hole alone. You'll then place the beads on the bottom of the hole and the skull on top of them. Then cover them with the dirt using your bare hands, not the shovel, and pack the dirt down gently to make it level.

"After that you'll stand and recite the words on the sheet to complete the ceremony. Once you're done, just retrace your route to the rendezvous point and I'll bring you back here."

"Sounds simple enough," Les said. "I think we'll be back here before ten o'clock."

"If all goes as planned," Carl said. "Since it's Saturday night, my guess is those country boys will be in town drinking. They probably won't be back home until the wee hours. That should give you plenty of time to get in, do the ceremony, and get back out really slick."

"You're coming in with us aren't you?" Ken asked.

"No," he replied. "I can't leave my truck anywhere in the area. It'll stand out like a sore thumb. If I keep moving and they pass me on the road then they probably won't recognize me. But if they see my truck parked on the roadside, they'll stop and investigate. We don't need that."

"I take it they don't like you," Skip said.

"Of course not," Carl said, "I'm an Indian. Some of the people in my family owned land adjacent to the cemetery as recently as twenty-years ago. But when my grand-parents died, those scum-bags swooped-in and bought it at auction before any of the rest of us could scrape-up the money to bid on it."

"But it's still public land, right?" Les asked.

"Yes," Carl said. "But to drive there you'd have to pass about half-a-dozen houses down near the main road. The people that live in those houses stay home all the time and always look outside to see who's passing through. If they see a strange truck go in they might call the sheriff. Or worse, they may just decide to get some shotguns and go check it out for themselves. It's a dead end down there." He smiled. "Pardon the pun."

Les stared blankly up at a stuffed deer-head mounted on the wall. "But it's public land," he said.

"Not at night it isn't," Carl said. "The state of Alabama has laws about going into cemeteries at night. And the fact that you boys are going to be carrying shovels says one thing loud and clear: 'grave-robbers'."

All three of them looked at Carl with stunned expressions. "We're not making a withdrawal," Skip said. "Just a deposit."

"Yeah, right," Carl said with a laugh. "I'm sure the local sheriff will be real understanding. The smile faded from his well-sunned face. "Remember, my Uncle David and I discussed this at length earlier today. There's only one way to pull this thing off. This is the way."

Les looked over at Ken and saw that he was shaking just a little. "Ken, you don't have to go in there with me if you don't want to. That goes for you too, Skip."

Skip gave him a startled look. "Are you kidding? "I didn't come all this way to sit on the sidelines. I'm in."

"I'll come too," Ken said. "That's what scouting is all about: teamwork."

"I really can use you in there," Les said, patting Ken on the shoulder. "While I'm concentrating on the ceremony I need someone to watch my back."

"I've got your back, my brother," Ken said.

"Me too," Skip added.

"Well it's settled then," Carl said. He looked at his watch. "It's almost six, we can go in a few minutes."

Carl got up to get his jacket and keys while the three of them stepped outside. The sun had just set, leaving bright patchwork at the western horizon. It would soon be a cloudy, dark night.

"It's going to get chilly tonight," Skip said. "Better get gloves and hats out of the backpacks." He walked over to the trunk and opened it.

"Everybody bring flashlights and I guess one of the collapsible shovels," Les said. "And refill your canteens at that spigot over there."

They got what they needed and closed the trunk. At that moment Carl stepped outside and let the screen door slam behind him. "You guys ready?"

The four of them piled into the cab of the old pickup and Carl cranked the engine. Les sat beside Carl with Ken bunched-in next to him. Skip sat by the window. Carl put the truck in gear and they all heard the sound of the gravel stones crunching under its weight.

Les sat staring ahead as the truck's headlights shone across the weedy yard and to the side of the rusty trailer as Carl turned around and headed toward the driveway exit. Although he was very tense, he had to keep reminding himself to take deep breaths and remain calm.

"Something else I forgot to tell you about the cemetery," Carl said as he drove. "When you get to the stone-walled family plot at the bottom of the hill you'll notice how it stands a little distance from the rest of the graves. That's a family that was massacred mysteriously around 1850. That's where most of the sightings seem to take place."

"Sightings?" Ken asked.

Carl glanced over at him but didn't reply.

"The whole family was massacred?" Skip asked. "By whom?"

"Nobody really knows," Carl said. "They lived in a farmhouse back when there was nothing along the shores of that river but trees and bogs. Somebody walking through the area found the house burned-down and the whole family dead. The local townspeople buried them right at the site where the house stood. The stone wall surrounding the grounds is all that's left of it."

"Was it an accidental fire?" Les asked.

"Maybe," Carl said. "But nobody really knows."

"Do they think Indians might have killed them?" Skip asked.

"That's the story the other white settlers spread around," Carl said. "But the Yuchi weren't that type of people. They were peaceful. I've always suspected it was other settlers that killed them, perhaps for their belongings and live stock. Then they made it look like Indians had done it."

He looked at the three teens sitting to his right in the cab of his pickup. "White settlers never had much respect for the red man."

They rode in silence for the next several minutes. Outside, the darkening landscape became more and more ominous as they neared their destination.

"The locals around here believe the woods are haunted," Carl said. "Ever since the massacre over a hundred years ago people have been seeing and hearing things back there. Especially at night."

"What kinds of things?" Ken asked. Carl had his undivided attention.

"Apparitions, drums, voices, and sometimes screams." They were back at the main road now and Carl turned right onto the pot-holed, gray blacktop.

"Ghosts?" Ken asked.

Carl glanced over at him and nodded. "That's what they say.

"A boy I knew in high school told me many years ago that the man who had lived in the house appeared to him one afternoon while he was fishing from the river bank near the cemetery. He swore the man just appeared at the edge of the woods about twenty-feet away and stared at him for maybe ten seconds. Then the man opened his mouth as if to say something and this eerie sound started coming out. Then he simply vanished. Scared the hell out of the poor guy."

"Did he say what the man looked like?" Ken asked.

"He said he was all white, appeared to be wearing overalls and a straw hat, and you could see right through him," Carl said. "The man seemed to be telling him not to fish at his private spot.

"I didn't believe the story but the guy told me he'd never go there again. And he didn't. I saw him in town one night years later and he still swore the story was true."

"Man," Ken said. "That would scare the hell out of me."

"I doubt the people who live up this way go in there much," Carl said. "That's why I don't think anybody will bother you tonight." He looked over at them and grinned. "It'll be just the three of you and the ghosts."

"Don't say that, man," Ken said. Les could tell he was really getting the jitters.

"So I just bury the skull and the beads and read these words," Les said, holding up the paper Carl had given him. "That'll put the curse to rest?"

"That's it," Carl said. "Oh, and one more thing." He paused as he looked for the gravel road that branched-off to the right. While he looked straight ahead, all three of them were looking at him.

"I don't think you'll meet-up with any long-dead settlers," Carl said, "but it is possible you may hear some things while you're performing the ceremony."

Les swallowed hard. "What sort of things?" He could feel his heart pounding and noticed a crack in his own voice. The others no doubt noticed it too.

"Legend has it that those who have already passed on to the other side sometimes attend burial ceremonies," Carl said. "They gather at the holy crossroads to welcome a strong spirit to the afterlife."

He paused a moment to look each of them in the eye. "You may hear faint drums or chanting, whispering voices, that sort of thing. I doubt it'll happen but that's what the legend says. I figure I'd better warn you just in case there's some truth to it."

"Hey Ken," Skip said as he jabbed him lightly with his elbow. "Maybe the settler's ghost will distract them and they won't mess with us." He laughed.

"That's not funny, man," Ken said. "I'm already so scared I don't know if I'll be able to walk straight."

"Just relax, Ken," Les said. "You'll be fine."

Carl gave them a confident smile. "That statement might not be as far-fetched as you think Skip. If the legend is true, and there's a good chance that it is, although I haven't seen it personally, having some spirits show up would be a good thing. Remember, you three are the good guys in all of this."

He glanced over and looked each of them in the face for an instant. "If I were you I'd expect anything. But remember, you'll be strongest and safest on tribal land."

At that moment Carl slowed down and pointed out a gravel road on the left as they passed it. This one featured a small green sign that read: "Cemetery Road."

"That's the entrance," Carl said. "The cemetery is about a half-mile down." With that, he sped on past and drove into dense forest.

"You boys are going to have to really be sharp tonight," Carl said. He looked over at them and made eye contact with Les. In the faint light he looked Native American to him for the first time since they first met almost two hours earlier. It was subtle, but it was there.

CHAPTER 14

THE CEMETERY

Carl drove about two more minutes before speaking again. "There is a sunken area in the woods on the right side of the road up ahead," he said. "It's a great hiding place. We'll make that the rendezvous point.

"You guys can hide there when you come back out. Then just wait until I return. I'll park and show it to you. We'll have to make it quick though. People out in these parts tend to investigate parked vehicles with rifles in hand."

He pulled over to the right side of the road and parked, leaving the lights on. Ken grabbed the folding shovel and all four of them had flashlights. They got out of the truck and began walking into the woods. Somewhere in the distance hounds could be heard baying.

After about twenty steps Carl stopped and pointed his flashlight into the hiding place. It looked to Les to be just big enough for the three of them. The ground at the bottom was level and lay about four-feet lower than the surrounding forest floor. There also were some bushes and a few young saplings around the edges.

"This is a good spot," Les said as he glanced around. "Once it gets completely dark out here it will make a perfect place to hide."

Carl stepped down into the small trench. "The three of you can sit at the bottom of this little ravine and stay well hidden," he said. He squatted down and looked back at the truck. "You get a good view of the road from here too. Just sit here and watch for me to return. You'll easily see me coming. I'll flash my lights so you'll know it's me.

"I'll drive by every hour on the hour starting at nine o'clock. When you see me, first make sure it's me, see my lights flash, then come out and get in the truck fast. That's how you'll get out from this point."

"How did you happen to know about this particular spot?" Les asked.

Carl took a brief look above and around. "I used to play here as a boy. Seems a hundred-years ago now." Les watched his eyes dart in the direction of the road. It was all clear.

"Coming here is a risky thing for me now. That makes me very sad."

"How do we get to the cemetery from here?" Les asked.

"Just walk over to where the truck is parked and go straight across the road from there," Carl said. "There's an old wagon path that will lead you in the right direction into the woods. Use your compasses and flashlights and go straight east. After about a hundred-yards or so you'll come to an old, rusty fence. Get over or through it and keep going straight. Just don't use the flashlights after you get past the fence. Nothing gives away your position in dark woods worse than a flashlight, except maybe a campfire.

"After another two-hundred yards or so you'll come to a gravel road. That's a driveway. It leads to a house at the bottom of the hill to the right with the river beyond that.

"First, make sure nobody is around before you venture out into the open. Then go straight across the driveway and into the woods on the far side.

"After about another hundred-yards you'll come to the gravel road that leads into the cemetery. You will be past the last house on the road at that point so there won't be anything between you and the entrance. It will be to your right. Just go straight in and follow the instructions I gave you earlier."

"Then once we're done we come back out the same way to this ravine," Les said. "Sounds simple enough."

Carl nodded. "Exactly. Then wait for me to come through at nine o'clock to get you. We'll hustle out of here and be done with the whole thing lickety-split."

"Then if we miss you at nine, you'll be back around at ten?" Skip asked.

"Right," Carl said. "And at the top of each hour after that all the way up to dawn." He laughed. "If you aren't out by daylight then I'll just figure you aren't coming out at all."

Les, Ken and Skip all looked at each other but didn't say anything. Somehow, this little mission seemed very doable.

"Be sure you don't approach any vehicles that you may see through here if it's not right at the top of the hour," Carl said. "Even if they flash their lights for some reason you can be sure it won't be me."

From somewhere in the distance they heard the unmistakable sound of a gun firing. Everybody but Carl jumped.

"What the hell was that?" Ken asked.

"Shotgun," Skip said. "Pretty close-by too. I'd say less than a mile away."

"It's a lot closer than that," Carl said. "It's probably somebody firing off a celebration shot. Whatever it is they're going to do on this Saturday night, it's about to get underway. I wouldn't be surprised if they came driving through here in a few minutes. I'd better get going." With that, he headed toward his truck.

"Why don't you three hide in the ravine for a little while to give it time to get good and dark," Carl said as he walked away. "Then get moving when the moment feels right."

"Good idea," Les said. "Waiting a few minutes will give our eyes time to adjust to the dark. See you in a few hours, Carl."

"Okay," Carl called back. He got into the truck and started the engine. Then he turned back in the direction from which he had come and drove off into the quiet Alabama night.

Les stepped into the ravine and looked around with his flashlight. Ken stood looking at the woods surrounding them. "This is one spooky place," he said.

Skip had stepped a few feet away to relieve himself and came running over toward the ravine. "Somebody's coming," he said. They all got into the ravine and squatted down. A moment later an old, light-colored car came up the road from the right and drove past. They could hear several people talking as it went by, and a few moments later the smell of burning marijuana could be detected.

"Looks like somebody's off and running tonight," Skip said. They sat quietly for another twenty-minutes and debated when to get started.

"When do we go Les?" Ken asked. "It's getting cold out here."

"Just a few more minutes," Les said. "I'm waiting for the moment that it just feels right."

"Okay," Skip said somewhat sarcastically. "But can it happen before we all freeze?"

"Patience", Les said softly.

About ten minutes later they heard several vehicles in the distance. The sound of their engines carried well through the dark woods but no sign of them could be seen. After about a minute the sound was completely gone.

"Alright," Les said, standing and stepping out of the ravine. "I was waiting for a clue like that. Some people just drove from our left to our right a quarter-mile or so away. There's nobody on the left now and that's where we want to go. The time has come."

The three of them started walking toward the road and looked in both directions before leaving the safety of the woods. "All clear," Skip said in a loud whisper.

They crossed the road and spotted a trail that led into the woods. "That must be the path," Ken said. Once they had gone fifty-feet or so they turned on the flashlights and began a slight uphill walk. After another twenty-yards, the trail faded out.

"Okay", Les said, "be looking for the rusty fence, that'll be a property boundary."

"Here it is," Skip said. He shined his flashlight so the others could see it easily. The old, rusted wire was still sturdy and taunt.

"Don't anybody cut yourself," Les said. "No injuries tonight."

He found a weak spot between two rotten, wooden posts and pushed the fence down to the ground. Skip stepped over and Ken followed. Ken then held it down while Les got clear.

Les stepped a few feet past the fence, took out his compass, held it up to the flashlight and flicked it on. "What are you doing?" Ken asked him.

"Juicing-up the compass' night-glow properties," he said. "For the next couple of hours I'll be able to read the compass without having to use the flashlight." He held the light to the face of the compass for a few more seconds before turning it off and putting it in his pocket. He then held the compass out for Ken to see.

"There," Les said, "nice and bright."

"Hey," Ken said. "You can really see it good in the dark now."

"Okay guys," Les said, "no flashlights from here-on. Talk only in whispers. I'll lead, why don't you guys take turns tagging-up the rear and watching behind us. If we do this right it should come off without a hitch."

"You got Carl's instructions for the burial ceremony?" Ken asked.

Les patted his left front pocket. "Got them right here." He took a moment to look at the pitch-dark woods surrounding them. It was deathly quiet.

"Beware of the fact that the leaves are going to crunch under your feet with every step you take," Skip said. "And these woods are full of freshly fallen leaves."

"That's right," Les said. "If you spot another person or even think you do then go totally still. Silence is our biggest ally right now."

"Just like Carl told us," Ken said. "We go in and come out like the wind."

Les started leading the way with Ken behind him and Skip at the rear. Following the compass straight east, they made their way through the quiet woods.

"All things considered, I'm seeing pretty good without the flashlights," Ken whispered.

"Yeah, me too," Skip said. "And we'll get some help from that bright moon when it comes out from behind the clouds."

Up ahead, Les saw what appeared to be a clear area. When they reached it they saw that the woods ended abruptly at a wide, grassy field. About twenty-feet ahead of the tree-line lay the long gravel roadway that ran downhill from the left.

"Here's the driveway," he said in a low voice. "I'd guess it's about seventy-five feet to the woods on the far side."

"That's a pretty wide gap to cross out in the open," Skip said. He was standing next to Les and looking around. "We'll have to be quick."

"I can see the house down at the end of the hill," Ken said, pointing to his right. "The porch light is on."

"I'd say it's at least eighty-yards away," Skip said. "No way they could see us way up here from there."

"Let's move," Les said. With that he started jogging forward and the other two came right behind him. In less than a minute they were across the gravel driveway and into the woods on the other side.

"Piece of cake," Skip said as they stopped under the canopy of trees and looked around. From somewhere down toward the house they could hear the barking of a large dog. Other than that, it was totally silent.

"Okay," Les said, "we continue straight east, parallel to the river through these woods and we'll come to the gravel road that leads to the cemetery."

"Out of the frying pan and into the fire," Ken said.

"Remember," Les said. "Any time you guys want to stay put just say so. I can take it alone from here."

"I'm okay," Skip said. He looked over at Ken. "How about you."

"These woods are really spooky," Ken said. "But I'll just stick close to you guys. There's no way I'd want to be out here alone, even for a minute."

"Just remember to stop in your tracks and hit the ground if you see or hear anything," Skip said. "And let the rest of us know. Team work is everything right now."

"That's right," Les said. "It's absolutely imperative that nobody, and I mean nobody, knows that we were ever here." He briefly checked the compass again. "This way," he said. "Be careful not to let any tree branches hit you in the face."

They walked in silence for several more minutes before reaching the gravel road. "Here it is," Les said, "Cemetery Road." He looked back in the direction of the main road that lay a few hundred yards to their left. He saw no houses or any movement in the empty roadway. There was nothing but dark woods in all directions.

"Wow," Ken said, "what a lonely stretch."

"Don't forget spooky," Skip said with a chuckle.

"Oh, I won't forget it," Ken said. He knew Skip was playing with him but didn't mind. Constant reminders that he wasn't alone out here were fine with him. Getting teased a little in the process didn't bother him at all.

Les headed to the right and the three of them walked a short distance before spotting two brick pillars on either side of the narrow road. They entered without breaking stride.

"I guess this is the cemetery entrance," Les said. A few feet inside the entrance the gravel road forked. Beyond that, about a dozen large headstones could be seen on both sides and straight ahead. Les pulled out his flashlight and turned it on.

"Do you think it's a good idea to shine the light around?" Ken said.

"Yeah, it's okay," Les said. "We're not on private property here and there's nobody around for probably a mile or so. Besides, we'll never find our way around in the dark."

"Guess you're right," Skip said. He pulled out his flashlight and turned it on as Ken did likewise. Once they had some light, they could see about forty or fifty graves.

"I've got to spot the stone wall Carl told us about," Les said. "It should be straight back this way." He pointed the beam of his light toward the back of the cemetery and saw where the gravel roadway ended about another twenty-yards ahead. The road made a long oval with several large oak and cedar trees standing in the middle.

Skip walked to the left side and began reading some of the inscriptions on the neatly-carved monuments. "Here's a couple of graves that have been here just since the late seventies," he said.

Ken walked toward the middle section of the cemetery and read some of the grave-markers. "Looks like this section was open for business in the fifties and sixties. A friend of mine refers to them as 'Underground Condos.'"

"Sick son of a bitch," Skip said with a laugh.

"Hey, keep it down guys," Les said. "There's one over here that dates back just to last month." Ken and Skip walked over to look where he was pointing his light. "That one is so fresh the grass hasn't even taken root yet."

Ken read the date on the headstone aloud. "October thirteenth, 1984. You're right, just last month."

"I don't believe it," Les said. The others looked at him. "That was the night I was in the Indian Burial Ground when this whole ordeal began. That's a bizarre coincidence."

"Sure is," Skip said. "Let's see what's down this way." He walked to the end of the gravel road and pointed his light into the wooded grounds that lay beyond it. Here was a large field with perhaps as many as a hundred gravestones in it. As they shined their lights around this part of the cemetery, they noticed that the gravestones were smaller and less-fancy. The farther they got from the entrance the older the graves became.

"Notice how there's just this dirt road running through the middle of the cemetery here," Les said. "A long time ago they probably delivered the coffins to the grave-site using a horse-drawn hearse. Once this part of the cemetery filled-up they abandoned the road. Now all that remains is this wide path."

"And they're using the gravel road now to bring the coffins in," Skip said. "This cemetery is incredibly historic. It dates back two centuries and is still being used."

He walked over to one of the small, brown headstones before him and read the inscription. "Wow," he said. "This grave was placed here in 1898." He walked a bit further and looked at another one. "And this one is dated 1873. The people in this area lived during the Civil War. I can't believe it!"

"Can we get going?" Ken asked. "I'd really like to catch the nine o'clock shuttle back to Carl's place if we can."

"Yeah," Les said. "Let's keep moving." He walked down the hill on the abandoned wagon roadway to where the ground leveled-off. To his right was the wrought-iron fence Carl had told them to find.

"Here's the Civil War officer's monument," he said. He stepped through the open gate and shined his light on a granite walkway that led to a small courtyard. There was a large headstone in the middle of the courtyard with a neatly engraved inscription. "Major Bishop Rogers Colquit-Civil War Hero," Les read aloud.

"I'm confused," Ken said. "Does that mean that he was a major and a bishop or was his name Bishop?"

Les scratched his head and thought a moment. "Well, I've never heard of a major bishop so I suppose his name was Bishop."

"They sure have him buried far from the beaten path," Ken said. "Maybe he grew up in this area."

"I'll bet the place hasn't changed much since the 1700s," Les said as he looked around the dark cemetery. "Talk about the middle of nowhere."

"Kill your lights and drop," they heard Skip say in a loud whisper. Les and Ken immediately turned off their flashlights and squatted down. They were all silent for several moments as they listened for any unusual sounds. Only the quiet of the woods could be heard.

"What is it, Skip?" Les whispered as loudly as he dared.

"I hear something moving around down at the bottom of this hill over here," Skip whispered back. He was standing a few feet away with his back against a massive oak tree. "I think it's a person walking around."

Without using the flashlights, Les and Ken hurried back out to the path and down to where he stood. "Right down there," Skip whispered and pointed. "There's somebody down there!"

The three of them crouched and stared at the dark area that lay down the hill before them. Nothing could be seen but they did hear something moving about in the dry leaves.

"Oh hell, it's Kiawampa's spirit," Ken whispered. "Coming here was a bad idea."

"Quiet," Les said. He flicked-on his flashlight and began shining it around in the direction of the sound. Two green eyes reflected back at them in the light.

Les felt Ken's hand on his shoulder. "Oh shit, it's him."

"It is not," Skip said. "It's some kind of an animal. Humans can't maneuver around thick woods in total darkness, it's impossible." He snapped his flashlight on and a moment later Ken did his as well. In their combined light they saw a large deer standing motionless, staring up at them. After a few seconds the animal turned and slowly disappeared into the woods.

"Oh, what a relief," Ken said with a sigh. "Skip, don't scare me like that."

"I wasn't trying to scare you," Skip said. "We just can't be too careful out here."

"No we can't," Les said. "And good work noticing the deer, Skip. Next time it may be something else."

"Yeah, like Kiawampa's spirit," Ken said.

"Will you shut-up already about Kiawampa's spirit," Skip said. "You're just scaring yourself. We'll come across an owl or a raccoon next and you're going to shit your pants."

"He's right, Ken," Les said, trying not to laugh. "Kiawampa is the least of our worries right now. The real danger out here comes from the things that walk on two legs."

"And that's another thing, Les," Ken said. "What made you so sure it was okay to go shining our lights down there before we knew what it was we were dealing with? If it had been one of those locals with a rifle he could have just shot at the light and hit us."

"Nobody in his right mind is going to be walking around in this cemetery on a cold, dark night," Skip said. "I'm sure they have better things to do."

"There could have been a guy down there stalking that deer who had his light off at the moment," Ken said. "Some people don't care about hunting laws, they'll hunt any time of the year and any time of day or night."

"Now you're just talking crazy," Skip said. "I think this place is starting to get to you. You're losing it. Be sure to keep several feet away from me. These are new shoes I'm wearing."

"Very funny, Skip," Ken said.

"Hold it both of you," Les said. He paused a moment to allow the silence of the woods to recapture its dominance. "You are both right," he whispered calmly. "We have to take precaution with anything and everything we see and hear, whether it's a poacher, a bear or something else. Ken, I need you to get control of your emotions, okay?"

"No, I'm cool Bro, really."

Les put his hand on his shoulder. "Are you sure?"

"Yeah,' Ken repeated. "I'm okay now."

Les smiled and patted his shoulder twice. "Good. Now, let's keep moving."

"Les," Skip said. "What time is it getting to be?"

Les hit the light button on his wristwatch. "A little after eight-thirty," he said. "I don't know if we're going to be able to catch Carl at nine. Guess we'll have to shoot for ten."

"Well let's be sure and catch him at ten," Ken said.

Les started down the hill and the other two were right behind him. When they reached the bottom where the ground became completely flat, Skip walked over to the right and spotted the stone wall.

"Check this out," Skip said as he pointed with his light. "There's the stone wall." He then raised his light slightly. "And there are the graves of the massacred family."

Two large headstones surrounded by several smaller ones lay bunched together in the small plot. Les and Ken waited as Skip walked over for a closer look.

"The only inscription I can read on any of these graves is on this big one," Skip told them. "It just says: 'Father'. Any other wording that may have once been on any of them is long gone, eroded away by the elements and the years."

Les walked over and inspected the inscription. "Man, look at how crude this is. It looks handwritten. And these stones weren't carved into headstones, they were just large rocks that happened to be the right shape."

"I'll bet they date back to the seventeen-hundreds," Skip said. "This place is amazing."

"And notice how far from any other graves they are," Ken said. "It's like they were segregated as if it might be a bad omen to be buried near a family that was massacred."

"I doubt that's a coincidence," Les said. He stepped out of the family plot and back onto the main trail. He then shined his light into the woods ahead. "I guess all that remains is the Indian burial ground. It must be straight back there."

"Wait a minute," Skip said. "There are some more graves in here. And these are fresh!"

"What?" Les asked. He stepped back inside the family plot and looked where Skip was shining his light. Some thirty-feet back from the original set of graves stood five small headstones lying side-by-side. Four of the graves had a distinct pile of red dirt, indicating recent burials. The fifth grave sat empty.

"Those graves are new," Skip said. "Just like that recent one up front."

"You're right," Les said. "And yet they are the same crude, unmarked stones as the others in this family plot. That doesn't make sense."

"Who's graves do you suppose they are?" Ken asked.

"I think they're symbolic," Skip said. "They don't actually contain bodies, they're here to represent the latest victims of the curse."

"You mean Tommy, David, Don and Harry?" Les said.

Skip gave him a frightened look. "That's exactly what I mean."

"But what about the empty one?" Ken said. "Who's grave is that?"

"That one is intended for me," Les said.

"But that's impossible," Ken said. "This isn't even the same state."

"It's the same tribal area," Les said. "White man's boundaries don't mean a whole lot here."

Skip patted Les on the shoulder. "We're here for you man," he said.

Ken stood shining his light into the empty grave. "This is just too freaking creepy!"

"Forget about it," Les said. "I need to do the ceremony while the words are still fresh in my mind." He stepped back out of the family plot and looked toward the river that was now less than fifty yards away.

The trail they had been following had gradually shrunk from a gravel road at the cemetery's entrance to a dirt road and then to a narrow path. Les led the way to where it ended and shined his light into the woods. About ten-feet in front of him lay a group of old, wooden crosses.

"This is it," he said. "Here's the Burial Ground." He pulled out his backpacker's shovel and folded it into working position. Skip and Ken held their flashlights on him as he dug. In about two minutes he had a medium-sized hole in what appeared to be the very middle of the small Indian cemetery.

"That should be enough," Les said. He handed his shovel to Skip, then reached into his pocket and pulled out Kiawampa's skull. He then took out the beads and dumped them into the hole, carefully placing the skull on top of them. Then with his bare hands he gently filled the hole and patted down the dirt with his palms.

Les then stood back. "Okay," he said, "I need the two of you to walk over to where the path ends and stand with your backs to me."

Ken and Skip did as Les asked, leaving him alone in the Indian cemetery. Les stepped three paces back and took out his flashlight and the sheet of paper Carl had given him.

Facing Kiawampa's burial site that had lain empty for almost three centuries, Les began to recite, speaking in a conversational voice for the first time after an hour of whispering. Almost immediately he began to hear sounds coming from the surrounding woods.

The first thing he heard was what sounded like the faint trampling of many pairs of feet on the hard-packed dirt, forming a wide circle around him. Strangely, there were no sounds of crunching leaves, despite the fact that they covered every square inch of the dark forest.

He then became aware of faint chanting and soft drums. Although Les couldn't tell if he was hearing all these sounds in his head or in the distance, the one distinct thing he was sure of was that the drums were being played by hands, not drumsticks.

It took only two minutes to read all of the words on the sheet. Les read steadily, not missing a word or pausing in his delivery. As he read, the sounds around him grew louder and more intense, reaching a crescendo on the last two or three sentences. Without looking up or hesitating in any way, Les read the last of the words, turned off his flashlight and then stood with his head bowed and his eyes closed.

He stood motionless, listening to sounds of movement all around him and letting the sound drive the images in his mind. He saw himself at a funeral ceremony from another time and place. Something perhaps that no white man had ever seen before.

The cold night had become a warm, beautiful, summer day. The leaves on the trees were green, the hillsides were dotted with mountain laurel, colorful and fragrant, and songbirds chirped and moved about the surrounding brush.

In his mind he saw more villagers approaching in canoes on the big, clean river less than a hundred feet behind him. They pulled up onto shore and dropped their paddles in their boats. Approaching the holy grounds with anticipation and reverence.

Facing Les were tribal elders wearing elaborate feathered headdresses and full war-paint, standing proudly and expressionless. They stood in a row just on the other side of Kiawampa's grave.

Behind the proud warriors stood several women, some very old and gray, others young and lovely with their long, black hair in braids adorned with colorful feathers. Standing with the women were several children, silent and dignified. All wore brown, deer-skin clothing and moccasins. Each stood with their hands folded in front of them and their heads bowed.

The steady beat of tom-toms continued for several seconds, then began to fade into the distance. The image Les saw in his mind of the small band of Yuchi, gathered to pay final respects to their great fallen leader, began to disappear. The sun set behind him, the green leaves disappeared from the trees, darkness engulfed, and the drums became the hoofbeats of a lone horse, galloping into the distance.

The sound of hoofbeats made Les tilt his head back, eyes still closed, facing the dark canopy of trees high above him. What he imagined next was a strong, muscular Indian chief riding on the back of a galloping stallion. The stallion had large wings that flapped slowly and silently. The chief wore a long headdress with hundreds of feathers, so many that they dangled amongst the horse's long, flowing tail.

Les watched in total awe as the image, bright white and ghostly, soared upward and through the bare branches of the trees. He opened his eyes as it faded into the sky and became a lone star, whose light somehow penetrated the thinning cloud cover.

Along with the fading visual image, the hoofbeats drifted away as well, momentarily becoming the rhythm of chirping crickets before disappearing into total silence. Les stood mesmerized, staring at the star above and trying to take in all that he had just experienced. Then the most relaxing, comforting feeling of peace he had ever experienced covered him like a warm blanket.

"The curse is lifted," he muttered. "I can feel it!" He turned and walked toward Ken and Skip who were still standing with their backs to him. Both were staring up the trail that led to the cemetery's exit.

He smiled with a mixture of relief and accomplishment. "I guess you guys heard all the sounds from the forest."

"Yeah," Skip said, "we heard everything you said."

"I meant the drums and the chanting and the footsteps."

Both Ken and Skip stared at Les with bewildered expressions then looked at each other. "No," Skip said. "We only heard you. Everything else was in your mind or something."

"Yeah," Ken said, "the only sound I heard was you saying 'the curse is lifted'."

"Same here," Skip said.

Les thought a moment. He remembered what David Beartracker had told him about becoming part of the tribe. Then he understood what that meant. Les would experience things non-tribal members would not.

"Yeah," he said at last, "I guess I just imagined the rest. Sure seemed real though."

"You feeling alright Les?" Ken asked.

"I'm feeling great," he said with a smile. "Now, how about we get out of here."

CHAPTER 15

THE INTERRUPTED RETREAT

From somewhere in the distance the sound of gravel being crunched under automobile tires made its way to their ears through the silent woods. "I think we are getting finished here just in time," Skip said.

Ken took a nervous look around. "You done here, Les?"

"Yes," he replied. "Mission accomplished."

"Good," Skip said. "It's time we high-tailed it out of here." He handed Les back his shovel.

Les took it and glanced at his watch. "Nine-fifteen. Maybe if we hurry we can catch Carl at ten."

"Well what are we waiting for?" Ken said. "Let's boogy."

They started walking briskly up the hill and a few moments later were back in the main part of the cemetery. "The road looks empty," Ken said. "I doubt that car or truck we heard is headed this way."

"Let's keep our eyes and ears open just the same," Skip said. "And watch out when using a flashlight."

"We'll get some help from that moonlight," Les said. He looked up to see if Kiawampa's star was still overhead. It was, but it had become lost in a sea of hundreds of others, all now being overwhelmed by lunar brightness.

"Another couple of nights and that thing will be full," Ken said. "The Hunter's moon."

After walking a short distance along the gravel road, Skip, who was leading the way, suddenly stopped. "Do either of you remember where the trail is?"

"Seems like it was just up ahead here," Les said.

"No, I think we passed it," Ken said as he pointed behind them. "Isn't it back there?"

"What difference does it make?" Skip said. "Les, just check your compass. We head due west."

Les took a moment to shine some light on the compass to refresh its glow-on-the-dark quality, then pointed them in the right direction. They bore left off the gravel road and began hiking through the woods.

"Okay, whispers only," Les said. "Remember, silent, like the wind."

They made their way quickly back onto the private land, stopping briefly at the edge of the woods and the knee-high grass that covered the plain between them and the driveway. It was totally silent.

"All clear," Skip said as he glanced around. With that he started walking out into the open.

As Les was walking he turned and looked toward the house. "Oh no," he exclaimed softly, "we came out of the woods in the wrong place. Look how close to the house we are."

"Man, that place looks run-down," Ken said. "But check out the cool motorcycle. At least they have some taste."

At that moment the barking of a large dog could be heard coming from inside the house. All three of them jumped.

"I hope that dog can't get out," Ken said.

"We shouldn't be this close to the house," Les said. "Let's walk up the driveway and get back to where we can find the old wagon road."

"This way," Skip said in a casual tone as he started walking.

"Keep your voice down," Les whispered. "Just because it's dark and quiet doesn't mean nobody's home."

"Nobody's home, Les," Skip said, a little quieter this time. "Just fifty-yards or so up the driveway and then we're out of here for good."

At that moment Les felt his heart jump into his throat. "Somebody's coming!"

Both Ken and Skip looked back at the dark house. "I don't see or hear anything," Skip said.

At that moment they all heard crunching gravel. Les looked up the long roadway. A bright light illuminated the hilltop.

"You're right Les," Ken said. "Somebody's going to top that hill in just a few seconds. The headlights are going to shine right where we're standing."

"Oh shit!" Skip said. "We're out in plain view!"

"Let's hurry to the woods!" Ken whispered frantically.

"No!" Les said. "There's not enough time, the clearing is too wide here. We've got to hide!"

"But where?" Skip said. He looked up and saw the bottom of the beam of light slowly descending toward them. "We're going to be visible any second!"

"This way," Les said. He ran back across the driveway and into the knee-high grass that lay on the hillside there. Then he dove head-first to the ground and lay on his stomach. Ken and Skip followed suit and hit the ground next to him.

The instant they all got down, a car roared over the hill and rushed down the driveway. A few moments later it drove past them less than twenty-feet away. Two more followed right behind it. One of the cars threw a small chunk of gravel that hit Les right on top of the head.

A young man who appeared to be around twenty stuck his head out the back window of the third car and yelled loudly into the night. For an instant Les thought they had been seen. The cars continued on past and rolled to a stop in front of the house. Eleven people got out of the three cars and began strolling inside.

"We're really close to that house," Skip whispered quietly.

"I screwed-up the directions," Les said. "My bad."

"Too late to worry about that now," Ken said. "It's all about damage control from here."

"Good point," Les said. "I think they're all going inside. Once they do we'll take off." The three of them remained completely still, hidden by the surrounding high grass. A moment later they saw the last person enter the house and let the screen door slam behind him.

Les stood up. "Okay, it's clear", he said. "Let's go quickly and quietly." The other two stood and started following Les. They each took about five steps toward the driveway when they were suddenly illuminated by bright floodlights coming from the house.

"Everybody down!" Skip said in a loud whisper. Les and Ken were side-by-side and Skip was about five-feet away. The three of them dropped in place and again laid on their stomachs. The screened-door swung open and several people came walking out onto the deck, each popping the tops of drink cans.

"I'll bet those aren't soft drinks," Ken said in a faint whisper.

"And I'll bet they aren't the first drinks of the evening for this crowd either," Skip quietly added.

"Hopefully that will play to our advantage," Les whispered. They continued to lie motionless, all eyes on the house.

A stereo was turned on and the sound of country-rock music emanated from inside. It had a familiar ring to Les's ears for some reason. The music wasn't terribly loud and the voices of the people on the porch could be faintly heard over it.

Les tried to peer through the bright flood of light at the silhouettes of the people on the porch. He estimated that they were about sixty-feet away. Because of their vertical alignment on the hillside, the floodlights were practically aimed right at the three of them.

Fortunately they were far enough away that the light wasn't extremely bright. It was enough however that would make them visible if they moved when someone at the house happened to be looking their way. "Everybody just remain perfectly still," Les told them.

"I'm glad these people aren't sticklers for mowed grass," Ken whispered.

"Quiet," Skip said.

From where Les was lying, he could see three people on the porch in front of the house. It looked like three guys, two of them wearing baseball caps turned around backwards. One of them was a rather scrawny fellow that had the short sleeves rolled up on his tee-shirt. The temperature had cooled to the low-forties and the guy appeared to be quite comfortable. Les figured he had to be loaded. There was also something eerily familiar about him.

"They'll go back inside the house pretty soon as cold as it is out here," Skip whispered from his spot several feet away. "Just don't anybody sneeze."

"I just hope they go in before the sun comes up," Ken muttered. "I'll bet we've missed Carl's ten o'clock pickup haven't we?"

Les glanced at his watch. He could see it clearly with all the light. "Yeah, we've missed him," he said.

Les kept his eyes locked on the porch. The door opened and two more people came out. The dog they had heard barking earlier walked past the door but remained inside for the moment. It appeared to be a big, black hound.

"I hope they don't let that dog out anytime soon," Skip whispered.

"Really!" Ken said. "Hopefully not for a long, long time. We're not going anywhere anytime soon."

The minutes dragged by as the three of them remained as still as possible and watched the house, waiting for an opening to run to the woods. Dew was starting to develop on the grass around them, making it colder. Overhead, bright stars dappled the moonlit Alabama sky.

For the next twenty-minutes the five people milled about on the porch. Two of them appeared to be women but it was hard to tell. They could have been guys with long hair. After about fifteen minutes two people went inside. More time passed. The stereo played on. Then one of the remaining people went inside, leaving only two outside. "Only two to go", Les whispered. "We're getting close."

At that moment the door opened and two more people came out. This time the dog came out the door with them. "Uh-oh," Ken muttered. They all shared the sentiment.

They watched as the dog wandered over to one of the trees in the yard and watered it. He then sniffed around the perimeter of the house for a couple of minutes before returning to the deck.

"Can anybody see what that dog is doing?" Ken said.

"He just laid-down at the feet of one of those guys on the porch," Skip said.

"It sounds like one guy is bragging to the others about a wild sexual encounter last night," Les said. "I can make out about every third word."

"Must have been pretty good," Ken said. "Those other guys sure are laughing a lot."

"Let's hope it stays that way," Les said.

They watched as the dog stood and walked off the porch. Then he began sniffing around in the yard, gradually working his way further and further from the house. Les followed the animal's progress as it steadily got closer. They were deathly silent and perfectly motionless, yet painfully aware that their position was about to be compromised.

When the dog got about twenty-five feet away it stopped dead in its tracks and began looking around and sniffing the air. Les watched the dog look right at him and make eye contact. It then just stood and stared at him for a long moment, pointing. Les thought the animal was trying to decide if he was seeing an intruder or not. He glanced over at the house and saw that the four guys were still embroiled in their conversation, totally unaware of what was about to transpire in the yard.

The dog suddenly started walking slowly right toward Les and Ken. A moment later a low, guttural growl could be heard. It sounded like a distant garbage disposal, steady and dangerous. Apparently the dog had no idea he was about to walk two-feet in front of Skip, who was preparing to give him a swift kick.

Skip carefully positioned himself to hit the dog with the bottom of his shoe when he passed by. Sixty-feet away one of the guys on the porch stepped inside and came back out with a deer rifle. The others started admiring it and began taking turns pointing it at the sky and gazing through the scope.

"You ever hunt game, Snake?" one of them asked, handing over the rifle.

"No," he replied. "I'm fourth-generation Confederate Colonel. Always trust my sword first. Nice gun, though."

"She's high-powered."

Snake looked through the viewfinder. It was too dark to really see anything. "I'll try a practice shot."

Les and the other two were lying prone and ignoring the conversation on the porch. All three of them had their eyes trained on the approaching dog. "I don't think he's spotted you guys yet," Les whispered, getting to his feet.

When the dog saw Les stand any uncertainty it had about who or what he was approaching apparently disappeared. He snarled and began growling loudly, now bounding toward him in full attack mode. Les got into a place kicker's stance to defend himself.

The dog, intent on going for Les's throat, trotted right past Skip without even noticing him. At just the right moment Skip kicked and planted the sole of his right shoe on the side of the dog's head. It went down with a loud yelp and landed in a daze. In mere seconds, it got dizzily back to its feet and ran quickly away.

Snake jumped from his seat and nearly dropped the rifle when he heard the dog's yelp. "What in the hell is going on out there?"

"Cruiser?" the dog's owner called out as he scanned the yard. "You okay boy?" At that moment he spotted Ken crouching down in the high grass about a hundred feet away. "Hey, we've got a trespasser!"

Snake immediately set the rifle down in the chair and reached for his sword. He instinctively unbuckled his belt and slid the sheath with the sword in it onto his left hip. Then he grabbed the rifle and cocked it. "Well he sure picked the wrong night to show up here!"

Les had gotten back down into a prone position and could see three men heading in Ken and Skip's direction. They hadn't spotted him yet, but he knew it would only be a matter of time before they did.

"Hey you, don't move!" one of them yelled at Ken. He then saw Skip a few feet away. "You stand fast too, mister!"

Their cover blown, Les stood. "We've got to get the hell out of here guys!" At that moment a shot rang-out and they all three ducked.

"Don't shoot man!" Ken said as he raised his hands high. "We surrender." He glanced over at Skip and whispered: "not really. You guys start running."

"Like hell," someone shouted. "We shoot trespassers around here, boy. Think you can down him from there, Snake?"

"Hell yeah!" Snake replied. He took aim with rifle again. Les and the others ducked into the high grass as the wild shot came nowhere close to hitting any of them.

"Snake," Les said in amazement. "Where have I heard that name before?" After a few moments it registered. "I don't believe it. Snake?"

"You know that guy?" Skip said. "What, you've been hanging out in biker bars without telling me?"

Les continued staring at Snake as the three of them began backing up the hill and keeping their heads down. "I think it's that same scrawny freak we dealt with in the Chattahoochee Wilderness last summer. How'd he end up here?"

"I think you're right!" Ken said. "I had high hopes of never seeing his sleazy ass again." He looked at Les in disbelief. "What the hell is he doing here in injun country?"

Les glanced over at him and then back toward the porch. "I guess Carl's been asking that same question for years. A lot of hate there."

As the wheels turned in his head he continued to search for Snake's motive. Then it hit him with a jolt.

"It's still not over!" he said in a whisper. "I see it all so clearly now. The rebels and the Indians, the fight over the land and the resources. After all these generations, it's still not over."

"Jimmy, I think this sight is crooked," he heard Snake shout. "I can't hit these shitters worth a damn!"

"That's our cue to run!" Ken said to Skip as he tugged on his shirt. "Let's hit it!" With that he turned and bolted up the hill toward the woods to his right. A few seconds later he entered the woods and disappeared. Skip began jogging in the same direction. "What do we do now?"

"We need to split-up," Les said. "I'll head in the opposite direction and try to get Snake and his rifle to come after me. Then I'll shake him in the woods. Once I've done that I'll meet up with Carl at the rendezvous point. You guys go hide in the cemetery and just lay low. Once it's all clear Carl and I will come find you. Remember to watch for a flash of the headlights."

Another shot rang-out and they both ducked momentarily. "Okay," Skip said. "Good luck!" He then ran for the woods to follow Ken.

From his crouched position Les watched Skip vanish into the trees and then looked back toward Snake. He was waving the rifle around and appeared to be trying to take aim for another shot. The rest of the group was coming toward him again and were now only about twenty-yards away.

"Don't fire, Snake," one of them yelled. "You might hit one of us good guys."

Snake hesitated a moment, then lowered the rifle. "Okay, but stay on those bastards! Any sign that they're getting away from you and I'll start shooting again."

Here's my chance, Les thought. He bolted for the woods to his left as fast as he could. In less than a minute he reached the tree line.

Snake hurried down the porch steps and started heading in Les's direction. "I'm going to get this guy myself," he muttered to no one in particular.

Les continued along the edge of the woods until he spotted the trail they were supposed to have been on in the first place. He jumped behind a large tree and peered around it to see what his pursuers were going to do next.

"You guys get those two assholes if it's the last thing you ever do," he heard Snake shout from twenty or so yards away. "The blond-haired one's ass is mine." Les could faintly see him making his way up the hill.

This guy's fast, he thought. And he seems to know right where I am. He turned and began running along the trail as fast as he dared. The dry leaves crunched loudly beneath his feet.

The footsteps gave away his location and Snake spotted him. "You're dead, scum-bag!" The rifle fired again and Les heard the bullet hit a tree somewhere behind him.

Without breaking stride Les continued running toward the hiding place where Carl would look for them at the top of each hour. About ten-minutes later he got close to it and stopped short, jumping quickly behind a large oak. After pausing briefly to catch his breath he peered around the wide tree trunk, looking and listening for any sign of Snake. After a moment he figured that he was alone, for now at least.

I'm glad he's a smoker, he thought. Seeing no sign of Snake, he ran the last fifty-feet to the sunken-in hiding place at the rendezvous point, entered and crouched-down. Trying to be as quiet as possible he gasped to catch his breath.

He glanced at his watch. Eleven-oh-six. Great, he thought, I just missed Carl. He decided to sit for awhile, carefully crawling around periodically to peer in all directions through the surrounding brush to look and listen for Snake or any of his buddies. The next half-hour passed uneventfully.

CHAPTER 16

KEN AND SKIP FEND
FOR SURVIVAL

Having successfully escaped, Ken waited behind a tree for Skip to catch-up to him. After about two minutes he spotted him coming through the woods. "Over here, Skip," he said. Skip rushed over to him and put his hand on Ken's shoulder while he gasped for air.

"How far behind you are they?"

"Not sure," Skip said between pants. "Not far though."

"Let's take the gravel road to the cemetery," Ken said. "If they're still tracking us we can hide in the trees or behind some headstones. Maybe they'll get creeped-out before they find us."

"That might work but I don't know," Skip said. "They're pretty pissed about me kicking their dog. I think they're going to be persistent. Just give me another minute to rest."

"Okay, but just a minute. It'll give me a little time to think."

"Think like a scout," Skip said. "Isn't that what Harry always used to say? I heard that at least fifty times so I know you must have too. And I was never even a scout."

"Yeah," Ken said. "A good scout, who really trusts his ears and his outdoor instincts can disappear in the darkness and do it safely. Nothing against your brother but I learned that from Les. You about ready?"

Skip looked all around them. "I don't hear anything. Yeah, let's go."

Ken started jogging as quickly as he dared in the faint light with Skip right on his heels. After about a quarter of a mile they reached the gravel road. "Stay to the side of the roadway," Ken told him. "If you hear or see anybody, duck into the trees and get down all the way to the ground."

"Okay," Skip said. He looked back and thought he saw a flashlight shining around in the woods a hundred-feet or so away. "We've still got company."

The two of them hurried down the gravel road about another two-hundred yards before Ken turned into a gap in the trees to his right. "Let's take this trail," he said, turning on his flashlight. "It leads in the general direction of the back-most part of the cemetery."

Skip glanced behind them and then back at Ken. "I'm glad you know where we are. Just be careful where you shine that light."

They jogged about another fifty-feet and were starting to get a good pace going when Ken suddenly stopped dead in his tracks. "Whoa!" he exclaimed, placing his hand out toward Skip's chest to stop him. "What the hell is that?"

A large, white object, over three-feet high, stood motionless on the trail before them. In the dim moonlight it looked to Ken like a child wearing some kind of a skeleton Halloween suit. He was afraid to move.

"What do you suppose it is?" Skip whispered, his voice quivering. "A ghost?"

For a long moment the two of them stood motionless, trying to decide what to do next. The mysterious object moved slightly and rustled a few leaves. Several voices could be heard from somewhere in the distance behind them.

"Aww, screw it," Ken said. He turned-on his flashlight and aimed it at the mysterious object. They both breathed a sigh of relief when they realized it wasn't alive. "It's a kite."

"A what?" Skip said. He was standing behind Ken and was peering over his right shoulder.

"A kite," Ken repeated. "A big, fancy one. See the long tails at the bottom?" He walked over to it.

Skip looked up at the thick canopy of tree limbs overhead. "How do you think it got out here?"

Ken picked-up the kite and gave it a quick visual inspection. "Some kid must have been out in a cornfield around here flying it really high and the string broke. It probably drifted on the wind for a long way before dropping through these trees. It's pretty torn-up."

"I could have sworn it was alive when I first saw it," Skip said. "I thought something had us."

From behind them they heard voices again, closer this time. "I think they came this way," they heard someone say.

Skip looked toward the voices and then back at Ken. "We've got to keep moving. They're almost on us."

"Hey," Ken said, handing Skip his flashlight. "I just had a great idea. Hold the light on the kite. We need it and all the string we can find."

"What?" Skip said. "Are you crazy? Those freaks are going to be here in about one minute."

"We thought the kite was alive when we first spotted it, didn't we? So will they. I'm taking it with us."

Skip positioned himself so his back was in the direction of the voices he had just heard. Cradling the flashlight in his stomach he turned-on the light and shined it on the kite. "Whatever you're going to do make it fast."

"Here's the string," Ken said. "And there's a good twenty-feet of it." He began carefully gathering it from the surrounding brush and wrapping it around his left hand as Skip illuminated his fingertips with the light. "And what a break finding this thing right now."

"Will you hurry up," Skip said. "What the hell do you want it for anyway?"

"This kite and string is just what I need to haunt a cemetery." He paused momentarily to give Skip a sly grin. "Okay, you can kill the light. Pardon the pun. Let's go!"

They got moving again with the sound of numerous pursuers thrashing through the woods somewhere behind them. Ken carefully steered the kite around from side-to-side as he walked to prevent it or its long tails from getting snared in the underbrush.

A couple of minutes later he spotted the wrought iron fence bordering the back of the Civil War General's grave site. "We made it," he said.

"Great," Skip said dryly. "What now?"

At that moment they both heard a loud truck driving on gravel somewhere in the distance. It sounded like it was heading away from them.

"Hear that?" they heard someone say loudly in the distance. "I think our trespassers just left."

"I don't think it was them," another said. "That could have been somebody else."

"I don't know," the first one replied. "It's clouding-up and the moonlight is fading. It's getting too dark out here to do much of a search. And we still have another twelve-pack in the cooler at the house. They're gone. I say we head back."

"You heard what Snake said about us catching those two assholes," said another. "If we give-up now what do we tell him?"

"Tell him the truth, they left."

"Hold it a minute both of you," another said. "Let's check the cemetery to be sure. Then we'll head back."

"Uh, you know it's against the law to go in a cemetery at night," one of them said.

"Shit, Dooley," said another. "You haven't cared about what the law said since you was eleven-years-old and shooting road signs with your pellet gun. I think you're just yellow."

"Okay, so what if I am? Got some law against that? You've heard the stories about this place."

"Shut-up both of you. I'm going in, you guys follow me." The voices went silent after that.

Ken and Skip were standing in the shadows of some large cedar trees at the cemetery's entrance hearing all that was being said. "Damn, I was hoping they were about to give up," Skip whispered.

"Well, at least they have their doubts now," Ken said. "It was a lucky break that that truck drove past when it did. Let's head down the hill to where the frontier family is buried. We can hide there and hopefully wait them out."

"I guess it's worth a shot," Skip said. "Maybe the farther back we get the less likely they are to keep looking."

"It's about our only chance," Ken said. He led the way past the modern graves and back to the old wagon road that led down the hill. As quietly as possible they walked through the freshly-fallen dry leaves that covered the ground.

Moments later the group of drunk, angry country boys now numbering four, arrived at the cemetery entrance. "I've never been to this grave yard before," one of them said. "Sure is creepy looking."

"That's what I've been trying to tell you," Dooley said. "Now whose getting yellow?"

"Bite my ass, Dooley!"

"Quiet," another one said. "If they're here we'll find them. And they've got nowhere else to go. This little road dead-ends into the river."

"We've got them now," said another. "Whoever they are."

"Doesn't matter who they are," said another, holding up a rifle. "Those trespassers hurt my dog and we're gonna find them! Everybody spread-out."

One of them was shining his light around the grave stones. "Hey' what's that over there?"

"There's a Civil war hero buried back here," Dooley said. "This place dates back two-hundred years. Snake told me once that this general is his great-great grandfather."

"You guys think he was as big an asshole as Snake?" one of them said in a low voice. They all laughed.

"Better not let Snake hear you say that," Dooley said. "He'll cut off your ear with that evil sword of his."

"I know," said another sarcastically. "So why don't we not tell him, Dooley."

"I learned a long time ago not to tell Snake anything unless he asks. And then just the bare minimum."

Meanwhile, at the bottom of the hill, Skip was inspecting the group of headstones in the old family plot. Only the largest one was big enough to provide him a hiding place. "That's a precarious place at best."

"It should suffice," Ken said. "But let's increase our odds. Here, take some of this kite string and tie it to a small tree or some other bushy vegetation that can be easily moved with a few tugs." He measured out about ten feet of the kite string, cut it off with his teeth and handed it to Skip. "If anybody gets close to you pull the string a few times and shake things up. Maybe we can scare them away."

"Okay," Skip said. He spotted a small bush a few feet from the largest headstone and tied the string to one of its middle branches. He then uncoiled the string and got down as low as he could behind the grave marker.

Ken took a moment to look around for a hiding place of his own. Suddenly he had a brilliant idea. There was a medium-sized oak tree to the side of the little graveyard with limbs about ten feet above the ground.

After quickly tieing the kite string around his wrist, he jumped up and grabbed hold of the lowest limb in the tree. He then swung his legs up and spun himself on to the top of the limb. From there he was able to reach higher branches that eventually lead him to a large, flat branch about twelve feet above the ground. He then carefully maneuvered himself onto it and found a comfortable place to stand.

Ken then pulled the kite up and held it against his chest so it wouldn't catch in the breeze. From some fifteen feet below him he heard Skip whisper: "nice work."

They were both in position now. It was time to wait, hope and pray.

Several minutes passed as the search party roamed around the cemetery near the top of the hill. They seemed to be losing their concentration, especially when the big black dog, sporting a nice bump on the side of his head, came up to his owner and licked his hand.

"You okay Cruiser?" he asked in a gentle voice. The dog whimpered once but appeared to be recovered. As he spent a moment alone with his dog, the others began reading the gravestone of the war hero, as well as some of the other monuments. At the bottom of the hill the minutes felt like hours for the waiting Ken and Skip.

As he stood quietly in the tree and watched the beam of the distant flashlight, Ken began to like their chances that their pursuers were going to give up soon and go home. From his vantage point he could see them fairly well.

Suddenly the flashlight shined right on him and stayed there for an eternity of a few seconds. Ken felt his heart jump up into his throat as he tried to assure himself that there was no possible way they could be seeing him from so far away. Still, the light stayed on him. Finally it moved away and he breathed a sigh of relief.

"Let's see what's down here," someone said. A moment later the entire group could be heard coming down the hill.

Skip and Ken were out of options now. With their backs literally to the river they had to hope the hiding places they had chosen would be sufficient.

Skip had been up on his knees peering over the top of the big gravestone. When he saw the first figure approaching he quickly squatted back down.

The four of them walked up to the family plot and gathered some ten feet in front of the graves. They were on the path looking up to the graves which stood on slightly higher ground. The stones were about chest-level to them. One read the inscription "Father" aloud. "These graves are so old that the wording on the headstones is hand-carved."

"This must be the grave site of the frontier family that was massacred in these woods back in the seventeen-hundreds," Dooley said. "I knew the graves were somewhere around here but I didn't know just where." His accent said deep south and he slurred quite noticeably.

"Massacred?" another said. "By whom?"

"Indians. Some of the old folks in town claim the woods around here are still haunted by their spirits."

"That's a bunch of crap," said another. A gust of autumn night wind blew through the woods at that moment, shaking hundreds of dry leaves from the trees overhead. It brought with it a brief, biting chill.

"I don't know," one of them said, "we all heard that truck leave a few minutes ago. I think it was those trespassers. There's nothing keeping us here, Snake will just have to understand. Let's go back."

"I'm not so sure . . ." one of the others said. "There are a lot of hiding places . . ."

At that moment Skip let out a long, low groan. It startled Ken because he didn't expect it. Apparently, neither did anyone else.

"What the hell was that?" one of them exclaimed. They still had the light on the large headstone and Skip had to remain crouched as low as possible to stay hidden in its shadow. He tugged on his string and the nearby bush shook slightly. The flashlight immediately shifted to the bush and Skip let it go still. It moved just a little in the light before returning to its naturally still state.

"Was something in that bush?" one of them asked. Skip decided not to pull the white string again for fear they might spot it. Instead, he continued to lie motionless, trying to keep his breathing as quiet as he could.

From his vantage point in the tree Ken began to fear for Skip's life. They seemed to be standing their ground more bravely than he had planned. Got to think up something fast, he thought. The idea came to him right away and he almost smiled.

"Who-o," he groaned in a ghostly voice. "Who-o killed me-e!"

"What the hell was that," one of them mumbled. His voice indicated that he was getting edgy.

"Sounded like a ghost," said another.

"Who-o killed me-e," Ken groaned again, this time louder and with more anger. The four country boys stood motionless and quiet. None of them seemed able to tell that the voice was coming from the tree.

Skip decided to join him sounding childlike. "Who-o killed us-s," he groaned from behind the headstone. He was doing his best impression of a little girl with a high-pitched, eerie voice. "Who-o killed us-s. You-ooo!"

"I . . . I don't think I like this!" one of them exclaimed. At that moment the bushes started shaking again.

The one with the rifle aimed at the headstone in front of Skip and fired. The bullet ricocheted loudly, leaving an inch-long shiny nick in the grave marker. "You're dead," he yelled. "You can't talk, you're dead." It came out sounding more like "day-ed". He pulled the trigger again and the gun clicked.

"Oh no," one of them said in a frightened voice, "we're out of bullets! What'll we do now?" It sounded to Ken like they were about to lose what little nerve they had left.

"Hold it just a minute," another one said. He boldly started walking toward the headstone and Skip. Ken knew that if he took just a few more steps he'd spot Skip and their cover would be blown.

These rednecks are probably football players or weight-lifters, he thought. They can still swing sticks and throw punches. I've got to do something fast.

In a last-ditch effort to distract the bravest one Ken began lowering the kite down by the string as quickly and quietly as he could. Nobody noticed it being lowered until it made a nice rustling sound when it landed in the dry leaves, startling everyone.

The one nearing the big headstone stopped in his tracks when he heard the sound a few feet to his left. "What the hell was that?" The one with the flashlight shined it toward the spot.

Luckily it caught his attention when it did, Ken thought as he watched from his perch in the tree. The guy was only about three-feet from Skip, who was still crouched behind and against the headstone.

"Who-o," Ken groaned as he started pulling the kite string. From ground level the kite appeared to be rising from directly behind one of the headstones. The flashlight, now dimming noticeably from weak batteries, found its way onto the rising kite, which didn't look much like a kite at all. A breeze blew a little and the long tails dragged amongst the dry, brittle leaves.

"Oh shit!" one cried out loudly. "Something's rising from a grave!"

"Who-o," the two of them groaned as Skip rustled the bushes again. "Who-o, who-o, who-o!"

The one that had approached the gravestone began to back away slowly, keeping his eyes on the kite as it dangled several feet above the ground. "I . . . I didn't mean any disrespect or nothing," he muttered.

"You-o killed me-e," Skip repeated in his child-voice. "Murderer!" Then he let out a high-pitched scream so terrifying that it even startled Ken.

The one holding the rifle dropped it absently at his feet. The resulting sound of it hitting the ground seemed to be the final straw for all of them.

"I'm getting the hell out of here," said the one nearest Skip. With that he bolted for the exit trail.

The others quickly followed suit, bumping into each other as they scrambled to get out of the cemetery as fast as possible. Ken and Skip remained motionless in their respective hiding places as they listened to the fading footsteps. Within one minute they were gone.

Ken dropped from the tree and walked over to Skip who was slowly getting to his feet. "Those stupid losers," he said with a laugh.

"Nice work, dude," Skip said, patting Ken on the shoulder. "That kite did the trick."

Ken chuckled softly. "The kite helped but it was that little girl scream of yours that finished them off. It scared me so bad I almost fell from the tree."

"Yeah," Skip said, finally allowing himself to relax just a bit. "That one just sort of came to me."

"It worked just in the nick of time, too." Ken looked up and around the now quiet woods and smiled. "Nothing like fun in the old bone yard with some drunk white boys on a Saturday night."

Skip gave him a quick dirty look, then laughed. "The cemetery is all ours. What do we do now?"

"Let's head to the front and find a good hiding place to wait for Les and Carl," Ken said. "Hopefully they won't be long."

"I hear you," Skip said. "This place is starting to creep me out too."

CHAPTER 17

THE LEGACY OF THE HAUNTED WOODS

Meanwhile, Les had time to catch his breath at the rendezvous point as he hid under the dark branches of the mostly bare trees. The moon moved from cloudy to clear sky at irregular intervals, causing him to constantly remain vigilant of his visibility.

The chill of the night was tempered somewhat by the many large trees which shielded the area from the wind. Most of the wildlife was in hibernation now and the forest was deathly quiet.

Occasionally Les thought he heard a twig snap or leaves rustling in the distance like someone was walking around. There were a lot of dead limbs in the trees and it seemed one was always dropping somewhere nearby. Each of the sounds was followed by several moments of silence and he was able to dismiss it.

Half an hour had passed since the last sign of Snake and it was beginning to appear that he had given up the chase and had perhaps gone to assist the others in their search for Ken and Skip. He could only hope that his friends were making out okay.

After a few more quiet minutes Les felt sure Snake was no longer looking for him. He decided to carefully exit his hiding place and walk quietly up the road to look for any signs of activity.

He stepped out onto the worn asphalt and looked in the direction of the cemetery. The only sound to be heard was the occasional movement of tree limbs in the breeze, followed by the raining of leaves. He started walking in the grass along the shoulder of the road so he wouldn't create the sound of footsteps. It's a lonely stretch on this road to the cemetery, he thought. Suspiciously lonely.

Suddenly he heard the sound of an approaching automobile. A moment later he could see headlights flickering through the trees as a pick-up truck navigated the road about a quarter-mile away. He spotted a large tree at the road's edge just ahead to the left and ran over to hide behind it.

A minute later the truck drove slowly past. There were two or three people inside, Les couldn't be sure. The truck kept going and its tail-lights soon disappeared. Les stepped out into the road and watched as the truck vanished in the distance. When he turned around to look in the other direction there was a lone figure standing in the road about fifty-feet away.

"So there you are," he heard someone say.

Les immediately recognized the voice. "Snake!"

"That's right," Snake said. "It's legal to kill trespassers in these parts you know." He lifted a rifle and took aim.

Les felt sure he was in no immediate danger. Snake had already demonstrated that was a lousy shot. Snake pulled the trigger and the empty gun clicked harmlessly. Snake paused, then tossed the rifle to the side of the road and pulled out his sword. "Guess I'll have to do this the messy way."

"Since when does it matter to you whether or not something is messy?" Les said. "Or legal. Your rap sheet is so long I wouldn't think such minor details would make any difference anymore."

"You don't know anything about me," Snake shot back. He was walking toward Les now, smiling broadly. "Who the hell are you anyway?"

"The name's Les. But you'll come to know me better as your worst nightmare."

"I hate nightmares," Snake said. "And I'm going to end this one happily right now." With that he started running toward Les.

Les instinctively turned and ran along the road in the opposite direction. He heard Snake whistle so loud it was almost deafening. Snake whistled again and again. The loud, piercing sound echoed off the surrounding trees. Les had never heard anyone who could whistle so loudly.

Moments later Les saw the pickup truck that had just driven past approaching from ahead of him. The engine was gunning and the truck was coming fast.

Got to hide quick, he thought. He saw what looked like a trail off to the right just ahead and ran straight for it. He bolted down the trail a short distance and jumped behind a tree. Peering back toward the road he saw the truck stop and heard Snake talking to the occupants.

"He went down this trail here," Snake said. He won't get far though. Nothing but woods ahead of him. You still got your hound dogs?"

Les couldn't hear the men in the truck but figured the answer to Snake's question was affirmative.

"How long will it take to go get them and get back here?" A muffled reply came next.

"Yeah, I can wait ten minutes," Snake said. "Go fast."

The truck drove quickly away and Les tried to see what Snake was doing. Now that the truck's headlights were no longer a factor he couldn't see Snake at all.

Les took a few seconds to run through years of scouting and survival training in his mind, trying to come up with just the right solution to his predicament. A moment later the answer came to him. Slap him with a tree, he thought, smiling slightly.

Stepping out onto the trail Les began walking farther into the forest, glancing from side to side in the shifting moonlight. Up ahead he saw exactly what he was looking for, a thin tree about ten feet tall that stood a few feet to the right of the trail.

He walked over to the tree and, reaching as high as he could, pulled it down until it bent about waist-high. Then, holding the tree top in front of his stomach, walked it around until he reached another small tree. He then took off his belt and made a loop around the tree that would become the catapult.

Les was then able to pull the other end of the belt around the stationary tree and hold it steadily there. He then sat on the ground behind the larger tree and leaned against it.

From where he sat he could see up the trail about thirty feet. It wasn't more than a minute before Snake came walking down it. Les got ready to release the belt at what appeared to be the right moment. If his plan worked he'd send a startled Snake flying several feet with the tree across his chest or face.

Snake slowed his pace and almost seemed to Les to be aware he was being watched. He walked to the edge of the small clearing and stood peering. For several long seconds he stood motionless. Come on, Les thought, just take a few more steps you crazy freak.

Snake remained motionless, looking all around. The bent tree was trying its best to pull the belt from Les's hands and was starting to burn his palms.

The others were due back any minute with their hunting dogs, very experienced ones no doubt. Les knew if he couldn't escape right now then he probably never would. He wouldn't be able to hold on much longer.

Finally Snake began walking slowly, stepping out into the moonlight at the exact spot Les estimated the tree would swing through when released. He let go of the belt and watched as the tree swung back to its original position with a lightening-fast snap. "Whoa," he heard Snake shout.

Snake managed to turn his face and spin slightly away as the tree came at him. The tree's cluster of branches caught him in the middle of his back and knocked him several feet into the woods. Les heard him cry out as the tree smacked the wind out of him. Wasting no time and ready to slap Snake with the belt if needed, Les ran past him and back toward the road. Putting the belt back on as he trotted, he scampered up the hill to the roadway. At the very moment he reached it a pickup truck was coming around the corner just fifty feet away.

Les found himself a deer in the headlights, momentarily not knowing what to do or where to run. "Les," he heard someone shout. He looked up and realized that it was Carl's truck. Carl passed him and hit the breaks.

"Get in the back of the truck, quick!" he said through the open middle window of the rear windshield. "There's a truck-load of hillbillies coming this way."

Les rushed over to the truck and practically threw himself into the bed. Carl started driving down the winding road at medium speed.

Les grabbed hold of the side of the truck and held on. "Those other guys went to get some hounds to help them track me down."

"That must be where they were going when they passed me headed the opposite way," Carl said. "I sped-up when I saw them turning around in my rear view. Then you picked the perfect time to come out of those woods."

Les turned and looked back just in time to see a pair of headlights appear in the distance. "Oh no," he said.

"Hang on tight, buddy," Carl said. "Things are about to get rough!"

The other pick-up truck drove up to the roadside by the trail from which Les had just emerged and stopped. Snake came staggering out of the woods, wiping his face with the sleeve of his shirt. "Get those sons-of-bitches!" he shouted. "Get them and make them hurt!" A moment later the pick-up began a hot pursuit. Les heard the screeching of rubber on the asphalt behind them.

"Carl, let me get up front with you," he shouted. "I'm going to get killed back here."

"If I so much as slow down we both are going to get killed," he shouted back. "There are some nylon straps clamped onto the hooks in the corners right next to you. See if you can hook them onto your belt loops. That'll hold you in."

"I don't see them," Les said. He was now holding onto the doorway of the dog kennel with both hands and the wooden door was opening and closing with every move the truck made, pounding his wrists again and again.

"You've got to strap yourself in," Carl said. "Them boys may have shotguns. Our only chance is to outrun them."

Les felt something slap him across the neck and looked over to see one of the nylon straps. He grabbed it with his left hand and worked his way to the end. He was able to hook it into one of his belt loops and pull the tightening device to make it taunt. He then spotted the other strap, got hold of it and hooked it into another belt loop. He was then able to close the dog kennel door and slide up against it. He then finished tightening the two straps.

"Okay, Carl," he said, "Get us out of here."

"Not a moment too soon," Carl shouted back. "Hang on tight."

Les looked up to see that the other pick-up truck had closed the distance on them. He watched in horror as the truck got right up on their bumper. A bearded man wearing overalls and no shirt leaned out the passenger-side window with a shotgun and began aiming it at him.

"He's going to shoot, Carl," he shouted. Les could see the man that was about to kill him smiling broadly. His long brown hair stood straight back in the wind and there was a dark gap in his smile from a missing front tooth. The man squinted with one eye and looked down the sites with the other as he aimed the twin-barrels right at Les.

At that moment Carl turned the truck sharply to the right, almost throwing Les out. He felt the jolt on his waist as the nylon straps held him fast. Next came the sensation of being airborne momentarily as the truck descended down an embankment.

Les saw a bright flare of sparks from the shotgun muzzle as the buckshot went harmlessly into the dark Alabama night. An instant later he was slammed back-first against the dog kennel and his seat pounded on the truck-bed. Pain shot through him from head to toe.

Behind them the pursuing truck was skidding to a halt and scrambling around to get onto the dirt road that Carl was driving them down at breakneck speed. Les lost sight of them and decided it was time to try negotiating with Carl for a better seat. "I'm getting pounded to death back here!"

"There's a flat stretch of road just ahead," Carl said. "Unhook yourself and crawl into the dog kennel."

"Are you crazy? I'll get shaken to death in there. Stop the truck and let me get in the cab."

At that moment the headlights reappeared. The country boys were back on their trail.

"I'm telling you, get inside the dog kennel," Carl said. "The floor's padded and they won't be able to see you. Plus, you can push against the ceiling and sides so the ride isn't so rough. You're going to have to trust me here."

"Okay," Les said, "I trust you. Just don't get me killed." He pulled the hooks out of his belt loops and opened the dog kennel door. The opening was narrow and with the rocking from side to side it was a difficult effort. Got to get in there without a head-bump, he thought.

He ducked his head inside the doorway and began crawling on his hands to the left. Once he reached the end he was able to pull his feet inside and point his toes toward the other end. He then got centered and pulled the door closed.

Dog hair began filling his nostrils and heavy dust popped out from underneath him with every bump taken by Carl's old pickup truck. The padded floor below him was smelly, but had a nice cushion to it.

A loud shotgun blast came at that moment from what sounded to Les like only fifteen feet away. Pellets could be heard hitting the side of the truck and rattling around inside the body walls for a few seconds. "Damn you sons-of-bitches," Les heard Carl yell.

Les then felt the truck brake hard to the left. He had to push his hands firmly into the ceiling to steady himself before he slid head-first into the end-wall. A second later came another hard jolt as the two trucks made contact with each other. He then heard several men cry out all in unison, followed by them fading in the distance somewhat. Carl then took a right turn and drove quickly for about two minutes.

After several more turns Les felt the truck slow down and then come to a complete stop. He took the respite as a welcomed moment to relax and catch his breath. He never could have imagined that a foul-smelling, well-used dog kennel could be so comfortable.

"Come on out, quick," he heard Carl say. "Les, you okay?"

"Yeah," he said. "Back hurts, but I don't think anything's broken."

Carl opened the gate and crawled up to the kennel door. "Try to squeeze out feet-first," he said as he pulled the door open as wide as it would go.

Les got his feet out and worked himself through. Carl then helped him up and they got out of the truck bed. "Get in," he said, closing the gate.

Les ran to the passenger side as Carl jumped in and put the truck in drive. He drove forward for a hundred feet or so, then spun around and faced the other way.

"You're heading back straight for them?" Les asked.

"Sort of," Carl said. He drove slowly forward to a wide, shady spot on the right and pulled over. "I'm going to park in this blind-spot off the roadway here," he said. "If they're still coming after us then hopefully they'll go right by and never see us."

"Good idea," Les said. He was reaching around with his right hand and feeling his back where the top edge of the dog kennel had left a painful horizontal stripe. "Can you see if my back is bleeding?"

Carl snapped on his flashlight and lifted Les's shirt. "No blood. Looks like it'll be a nasty bruise tomorrow but you're not cut." He placed his hand firmly on Les's back and pressed gently. "That hurt?"

Les winced. "A little, but not too bad."

"I think you're just bruised," Carl said, turning off the light. "Good thing you got in that dog kennel when . . ."

At that moment the other truck came flying past them on the road and kept going. Carl watched his rear-view as the taillights vanished into the darkness behind them.

"Worked like a charm," he said, starting the engine. "You just can't beat local knowledge." He gave it some gas and headed back toward the main road.

"Local knowledge?" Les said. "What's that?"

"I know these old logging roads better than they do," Carl said, tapping his index finger on his temple. "I've got fifty years' worth of local knowledge."

At that moment the other truck became visible in Carl's rear view mirror. "Damn," he said, "here they come again."

He hit the gas and roared out onto the main road. There were no other vehicles in sight.

"We can't go back toward the cemetery yet," Carl said. "The last thing we need is for them to figure out that we're going to try to pick up those other fellows. Plus, it's a dead-end."

The winding road through the woods had a speed limit of thirty five but Carl soon had them pushing sixty. The other truck was struggling to keep up.

"There are several side roads up ahead," he told Les. "I'll try darting onto one of them if I can just get far enough ahead that they can't see us make the turn."

"Where do the roads lead?" Les asked him.

Carl glanced from the road to his rear view and back to the road again. "Nowhere I'm afraid. But this road continues to twist and turn so there's a good chance they'd go another mile before they realize we've taken a different route."

Carl checked the rear view again. "I don't see them. Let's try this road here. Hang on." With gravel flying from the sudden deceleration, Carl whipped the truck hard to the right and plunged down a hill. After driving about a quarter-mile with no sign of being followed he pulled over and stopped. "I think we lost them."

Les leaned forward and looked nervously at the mirror outside his window. "How long should we wait before heading back for the cemetery?"

"We'll give them a few minutes," Carl said. "There are several dirt roads along this stretch. They'd have to get awful lucky to pick the same one I did."

He relaxed just a bit and looked over at Les. "So, how did the burial ceremony go?"

Les took a moment to mentally change gears away from their plight. "Oh, it went very well. While I was reading the script I thought I saw images of people standing around me. And I heard voices and faint drumbeats."

Carl's eyebrows raised. "Really? Wow, I'd say it went off perfectly. Better than I expected. That's the kind of thing I've only heard about in legends."

Les smiled, tempered somewhat by his nervousness. "I just figured it was standard procedure. Maybe I'm a member of your tribe now."

Carl patted him on the shoulder. "Our tribe, buddy."

Suddenly bright headlights shined on them from behind. "Oh hell," Carl said. "They've found us!"

With that he threw the truck in gear and hit the gas. A moment later a shotgun blast came and blew off the right side mirror. Instinctively, Carl swerved left onto a side road. "You assholes!" he shouted, shooting a nasty look into the rear view mirror.

With a trail of flying gravel and dirt, Carl soon had them going forty. "I should have gone back to the main road and headed the other way once they passed by," he said. "This dirt road is a dead end. Now they've got us cornered."

"How much farther does it go before it ends?" Les asked.

"A mile, maybe two. Hunters use it to get farther from the main road. There's nothing but a clearing where everybody parks their trucks at the end." He checked the rear-view again. "They've backed off a bit. I guess they know they've got us.

"I've got my shotgun on the floor behind you. Won't do us much good though, outnumbered like we are."

Les thought a moment. "I've got an idea."

"I'm all ears," Carl said.

"See if you can get a lead on them. Maybe try to get out of their sight. Once you do I can jump out."

"Then what?" Carl sped up and the headlights behind them faded somewhat.

"There's got to be a hillside above the road along here somewhere," Les said. "Maybe I can climb up over the road and find a large rock to throw down on them as they pass by. I might even be able to make them crash."

Carl glanced over at him. "Hey, that could work! See if you can spot a good place."

There was a short, straight part of the road ahead and Carl used it to push the speed up to fifty. Moments later he slowed down to around forty and began navigating some tight turns. The truck slid from side to side and Les feared they were going to sail into a tree at any moment. It was all he could do to keep from screaming.

"Look up ahead there," Carl said. "Think that hillside will do?"

Les could see the hillside Carl was referring to in the faint moonlight. "It's going to be a quick climb," he said. "That embankment has to be twenty vertical feet."

Carl hit the brakes and they slid to a halt. "Work fast, scout," he said. "Failure is not an option right now."

Les jumped out and Carl sped off before he could close the truck's door. He then scrambled up the embankment on the right side of the narrow road, reaching the top in about thirty seconds.

Got to find a big rock fast, he thought. He spotted one about the size of a basketball and rushed over to it. Disappointment hit him a moment later when he realized he'd never be able to pry it from the ground. He glanced down at the road and could see the approaching headlights through the trees. I've got less than a minute to come up with something, he thought. That's when he spotted the fallen tree. Oh, even better.

A few feet from where he stood the remains of a rotting tree lay flat on the ground, held in place by imbedded rock. He rushed over to the dead tree and rocked it back and forth with his foot. It moved relatively freely. Perfect, he thought. All I've got to do is get it over these rocks.

Les could hear the displacement of gravel under the tires of the approaching truck as he rushed to get on the ground behind the big, rotten tree. Thrusting with both feet, he pushed the tree over the rocks and started it rolling toward the edge of the cliff.

The oncoming truck was almost directly underneath it when the tree came plunging down. Les crawled to the ledge and watched as it fell toward the roadway. All three occupants of the truck could be heard crying out in unison as the driver hit the brakes.

The truck slowed as the tree landed right across the hood with a loud thud. The rear wheels left the ground momentarily and the truck spun, its momentum causing it to slide sideways. It then skidded into a bank of trees on the far side of the roadway, finally coming to a halt on its side. Within seconds, the woods were silent.

A few moments later Carl came around the corner and drove slowly past the wrecked vehicle. "Where are you, Les?" he called out.

"Up here," he replied as he ran along the embankment several feet above Carl's truck. Carl looked up and spotted him, then stopped the truck. Les got on his seat and slid back down the hill, landing with a thud on the roadside less than two feet from the truck. He glanced over to see someone trying to open the door of the wrecked vehicle.

"Get in the back quick," Carl said.

Les rolled over the railing into the bed of the truck and grabbed the two nylon ropes. "Hit it!" he said.

Carl floored it and they roared away. Les saw someone point a shotgun out the back window of the disabled truck and fire wildly into the woods. An instant later the whole scene faded into the distance.

"Okay, you can let me up front now," Les said. "That truck has chased us for the last time."

Carl stopped and Les jumped out. He then hurried up to the passenger side and got in. "Nice work," Carl said. "I don't know how you did it but you saved our butts."

Les was still catching his breath. "Those guys were playing for keeps."

Carl drove them back the way they had come and slowed when he approached the spot where the dirt road came out onto the asphalt. He turned off the headlights and peered over the steering wheel to look left. "Look down there to the right and see if you see any sign of anybody."

"All dark this way," he said. "What do you think we should do now?"

"Your buddies are still back at the cemetery I guess. Do you suppose we could run by and grab them?"

"We're going to have to," Les said. "Skip's car is parked at your place and they're stranded back there. I told them to wait and look for us. You'll just need to flash your lights and they'll come out from wherever they're hiding."

Carl pulled out and started driving cautiously up the road. "Only problem is we've got to be sure it's them we're flashing headlights at." He thought a moment and looked over at Les. "I don't suppose he left his key in the ignition."

Les gave him a momentary confused look. "No, Skip never . . . wait a minute. I have his keys right here. When the three of us got to the hiding place where you first dropped us off Skip told me he was concerned he'd lose his car keys so he gave them to me for safe keeping."

"So we can go get his car and come back to get them," Carl said. "That'll make a faster get-away for the three of you. Can you drive that Charger?"

"Not legally," Les said. "I don't have a drivers license yet but I think I could still manage."

Carl turned off the road they were on and headed back toward his trailer. "I've got a better idea. I'll drive Skip's car and you follow me in the truck. She's an automatic and will be easier for you to handle than that stick shift."

"You trust me, a first-time driver with your truck?"

"Ain't got much choice. You had any drivers ed at all?"

"Well, yeah," Les said. "But only the classroom part. Although I have driven a tractor a couple of times."

"She's just a tractor with a roof on her," Carl said. He had stopped the truck now and was looking Les in the eye. "David Beartracker told me over the phone today that there was something special about you. I can see it myself. You are a brave now, and a damn good one. You can pull-off just about anything you put your mind to. You can drive this truck."

Les looked at him for a long moment. "I just wish I shared your confidence."

"You just don't give yourself enough credit," Carl said. "A common trait among young scouts. It will come in time." He turned and started driving again. "Now, let's get the three of you the hell out of dodge."

About five minutes later they pulled-up beside Skip's car parked under the big oak in Carl's front yard. "Slide over and get comfortable behind the wheel," he said as he stepped out.

Les got over to the driver's side and felt the pedals. "I think I can drive her."

Carl walked alongside and instructed Les with driving basics as he drove the truck slowly up the driveway. In no time he had the hang of it.

"Give me Skip's keys and follow me," Carl said. Les handed them to him out the open window and watched Carl get in Skip's Charger. The noisy engine started, the lights came on and the two of them headed for the rendezvous point with Carl in the lead.

They saw nobody on the road and most of the houses they passed were dark and quiet. Once they got less than a quarter-mile from the cemetery Carl pulled off to the left shoulder.

Les stopped the truck and watched him back the Charger into some bushes. A few more feet and the car disappeared into the brush. Carl cut the lights and the engine and walked over to the truck. Les put it in park and slid over to the passenger-side.

Carl got in and drove a few feet forward before turning the truck around. "Why don't you get out here," he said, handing Les Skip's keys. "Go get them and drive as far from here as you can get before sunrise."

The suddenness of Carl's statement momentarily took Les by surprise. It took several seconds for it to sink-in.

"I'm sorry to have to say goodbye like this," Carl said. "Maybe in a year or so you can give Mr. Beartracker a call and let him know how you're doing. But no contact until then, none at all. Got it?"

"Yeah," Les said. He shook Carl's hand and hastily got out of the truck. "It's not safe to hang around here. You'd better go right now!"

"Be brave," he said. Les slammed the door and gave Carl a wave before he drove quickly away. He then stood in the roadway and watched as Carl's tail lights vanished in the distance. Seconds later he heard voices as several men came walking quickly out of the cemetery. Les ran into the woods over to where Skip's car was parked, got behind it and peered over the roof.

"Man, that cemetery really is haunted, just like the locals have been saying for years," Les heard one of them say. They didn't see him or the Charger as they walked past only about ten feet away. Les could clearly see all four of them in the moonlight. They were acting as though they hadn't heard Carl's truck pulling away.

"It sure was haunted tonight," said another. "I'm going to come back first thing in the morning though. I've got to get my rifle before anybody else finds it."

"Quiet," another said. "Whatever you guys do don't tell Snake that we almost got them. The less he knows, the better."

They continued walking up the road and were soon out of Les's earshot. After another minute he stepped out of the cover and headed quickly for the cemetery.

Once he reached the entrance and started walking past the first rows of graves he thought he saw two figures fifty feet or so ahead. "Who's that?" he heard Ken whisper loudly as they all spotted each other simultaneously.

"It's okay guys, it's me, Les."

"Oh, Les, thank God," Skip said as the two of them came running up to him. "Where's Carl?"

"He's gone," Les said. "Just like we need to be. We moved the Charger." He pulled out the keys and handed them to Skip. "I got her parked a couple hundred yards up the road."

Skip absently took his keys from Les as he slowly digested what he had just been told. "You guys drove my car?"

Les looked at him with sheer astonishment. "Our asses are on the chopping block right now and all you can think about is that somebody drove your precious Charger besides you?"

"Yeah, Skip," Ken said. "Maybe when we get home you and your car can go someplace quiet and have some quality time together. You know, just the two of you and a greasy tailpipe."

Skip gave him a nasty glare. "Ken, why don't you kiss my ass."

"Hey," Les said. "Let's just get to the car and get the hell out of here. You two fruitcakes can work out your other problems when we're safely away from this creepy place."

"Then let's go," Ken said. He turned and started walking quickly and the other two were close behind. When they got up to the entrance and out into the main road Les glanced at his watch. "Quarter past two. It's getting really late."

"Where's my car?" Skip said.

"Just up to the left. Right over . . ." At that moment a lone headlight snapped on in the road ahead of them.

"Oh, hell," Skip said, "what now?"

Ken squinted as he peered into the light. "Is it Carl?"

"I told you, Carl's gone," Les said. "And that's not a truck, it's a motorcycle. Snake's motorcycle!"

"You assholes just stand fast right where you are," Snake said. He had coasted quietly down the road with his headlight off and had literally come right up on top of them.

"Run!" Les said. The three of them bolted back toward the cemetery with Les in the lead. Snake started the engine and revved it momentarily as he watched the three teens run toward the dead end of the cemetery. After a moment he threw his head back and laughed maniacally.

Les led them straight to the family plot where they stopped and looked back. The engine of the motorcycle could be heard slowly approaching.

"I'm getting sick of this place," Skip muttered. They each got behind a headstone and tried to hide.

"We're sitting ducks behind these headstones," Ken said.

Skip glared over at him. "You got any better ideas, jackass?"

Ken whinnied like a donkey. "I'm thinking."

"Come on out, the show's over," they heard Snake yell from a short distance up the hill. He turned off the motorcycle engine and the woods went quiet. All that could be heard next were some muffled footsteps in the dry leaves.

"What's our next move, Les?" Skip asked in a faint whisper. "No rush. Anytime in the next three seconds will be fine."

Before Les could reply, Ken spoke up. "I've got it! Les, summon the help of the little people."

"Summon their help?"

"You still have the words to that ceremony you did earlier, don't you?"

Les felt his pocket. The folded paper was still there. "Yeah, I've got it."

"Well, pull it out and start reading," Ken said. "What have we got to lose?"

"That's right," Skip said. "Remember what Carl told us about the safest place out here being on tribal land? That's where we will be at our strongest."

"I guess it's worth a try," Les said. He took the folded paper from his pocket and thought a moment.

"I need to get back down there to the same spot where I was before," he told the two of them. "You guys hide somewhere."

"You Girl Scouts should know I've got you cornered," they heard Snake say from somewhere in the darkness. He sounded maybe seventy-five feet away.

"Make this easy for me and I'll kill you quick and painless. Make it hard and I'll bleed you slow. You'll see daylight before you finally die. It'll be the longest night of your lives. It's up to you. These are my woods and you boys ain't going nowhere. Not alive anyway."

"Who-o," Ken said from somewhere. He had relocated his kite string and was shaking the bushes. He couldn't tell if Snake even noticed.

Les was kneeling behind a tree and couldn't see or hear Snake anywhere. He was taken completely by surprise when Snake came walking out of the woods and spotted him peering from behind the tree.

"There you are!" Snake said, pointing at him with his sword. "Come out into the open."

Les stepped out from behind the tree and the two of them stood facing each other some twenty feet apart. The almost-full moon was out now and they could see each other well in the bright light. "Les," Snake said, "my worst nightmare." He turned his face and spat tobacco juice on the ground.

Les sneered. "Perhaps."

"Perhaps?" Snake said. "You're mighty confident for someone who is unarmed and in the wrong."

"In the wrong?" Les said. "I'm not the guy who murdered Earl."

Snake's face quickly turned to a scowl. "You don't know what the hell you're talking about, boy."

"I'm talking about the drug deal that went bad a couple of summers ago," Les said. "Your big score. The one that led you to kill Earl and throw him in the trash bin. Earl was part of the tribe. My tribe. The Yuchi people have a bounty on your head, Snake. And I'm going to be the one to collect it."

"You've got shit for brains, Les!" Snake said. "And who the hell are the Yuchi?"

"The people you've wronged on many occasions," Les said. "You and a lot of other ignorant rednecks just like you. These aren't your woods, they never have been. This is Yuchi sacred land. And you've wronged us yet again just by coming here. And tonight you've done it for the last time."

Even in the faint light Les could see intense rage come over Snake's face. He gave a sudden rebel yell, then started running at Les, holding the sword in front of him, charging like the Confederate soldier he apparently thought he was.

Les bolted to his right and started running toward the Indian Burial Ground. "I'm gonna cut you into so many pieces it'll take a vacuum cleaner to gather you up," Snake said as he ran. He moved tree branches aside with his free hand and cut others from his path with the sword.

Ken and Skip came out of their hiding places and began running after Snake. "Hurry," Ken said, "he's going to kill Les!"

"I'm gonna cut your damn head off you son-of-a-bitch," Snake could be heard yelling as he ran after Les. "I'm gonna bleed you like a pig and piss on you while you die."

Les smiled as he ran. His primary objective was to anger Snake as much as possible. That was the first tactic in defeating him. "You've got to catch me first you redneck bastard," he hollered back. "You can't do it, you're too yellow-bellied. I'll bet you got a short dick too, don't you Snake? Or are you more like a worm?"

He could hear Snake breathing heavily, so heavily that he couldn't muster the strength to yell anything back. Chain-smoking idiot, Les thought.

He reached the Indian Burial Ground and ran to the same spot where he had performed Kiawampa's ceremony hours earlier. Stopping there, he turned and looked back at Snake.

Snake ran through the graves and stopped just a few feet away from where Les stood. "Dead-end," Snake said through heavy breaths. "Just the way I like it."

At that moment Ken and Skip reached the bottom of the hill and saw Snake and Les facing each other from ten feet apart. "Don't come any closer," Snake shouted back at them. "If you're smart you'll run for your lives right now."

"Like hell," Ken said, and he began looking around for a large stick. "I'll show your narrow, white, redneck ass."

He found a large hickory nut the size of his fist and picked it up. Throwing it as hard as he could he hit Snake in the side and caused him to almost fall to the ground.

"Damn you son-of-a-bitch!" Snake turned and pointed the sword in Ken's general direction. "Where are you?"

Les crouched down, ran over to the middle of the burial ground and hid behind a small headstone. He felt a sharp twinge from his sore back as he held up the printed ceremony instructions.

Tilting the sheet so as to catch as much moonlight as possible, he began reciting from the beginning. He kept his voice low, hoping Snake wouldn't hear.

Les heard Snake shout at Ken. "Come out and face me like a man you coward." A moment later Snake cried out as another hickory nut struck him. A long string of obscenities followed.

Les realized Ken was risking his own life to allow him the time to start asking their Indian spirit friends for help. He didn't know if it would do any good but they were down to their last prayer. He decided to proceed quickly.

After quietly saying the first few sentences as best he could from the phonetically-written Indian language he began to understand what some of the words he was saying meant. He stopped reading and began searching the entire page for key words he needed for the circumstances. He was able to identify some of the critical words like "warriors", "fathers", "gather" and "battle". Les asked in the loudest voice he dared for the spirits to surround him.

Drumbeats could be heard coming from the darkness. The shuffling of feet followed and he sensed a tribe of invisible braves awaiting his next command. He stopped reading then and looked up, startled by what he saw. It was a great spirit. It was telling him he was the current heir, the Kiawampa of the present day. Yuchi legend was great once more, perhaps for the last time in history. But one more time than had ever seemed possible.

Ken had hidden behind a large tree in complete darkness and rested momentarily to catch his breath, confident that Snake had no idea where he was. An instant later a knife stuck into the tree just inches above his head. He whirled around to see a smiling Snake standing only ten feet away. "You got lucky just now," he said, raising the sword. "But not again."

Snake took two steps toward him but stopped suddenly and looked around as the sound of drum beats began coming from somewhere in the deep woods. Within a few seconds they surrounded them.

Ken took the momentary confusion on Snake's part to bolt into the woods. Snake reached up and pulled his knife from the tree, then turned his attention back to Les. That's when he became aware of numerous footsteps around him.

Something was surrounding him, something creepy and strange. Whatever it was he wasn't going to let it stop him from finishing Les.

He held the sword firmly in his right hand and walked toward the center of the burial ground where Les stood waiting. He could hear faint footsteps moving about on both sides and behind him. He looked around but saw nothing. Another faint sound came from several feet to his right. He swung the sword toward the sound but hit nothing but air.

"Drop the sword," Les said, when he spotted Snake. "Drop it and we'll let you live."

Snake smiled. "The only thing that exceeds your luck is your nerve. Smart people know better than to try any shit like this with me. Too bad you're going to learn that the hard way. Just like that coward Earl."

"You just stand right there," Les said. Snake paused and glared at him, rubbing the blade of the sword across his worn jeans. He turned and spat-out a wad of chewed tobacco.

"The Red Stick council has determined that you can accept the white man's justice and we will be done with you," Les said. "You'll stand trial for Earl's murder and serve a just sentence. Otherwise, you die. Right here, right now."

Les stared Snake in the face. For a fleeting moment he thought he saw fear. Then Snake's snide grin reappeared.

"You think you can pass sentence on me?" he said, raising the sword. "Out here in my own territory. Nobody will ever do that to me, you cocky prick." He started walking toward Les. "This is where someone dies alright."

A small red warrior ran out from behind a stump and whacked Snake across the side of his right leg with a tomahawk. The thump was loud and crude. Snake cried out and staggered, struggling to remain on his feet. "Damn you," he said, swinging the sword blindly. Les heard a faint laugh as the attacker disappeared into the brush.

"Where are you?" Snake shouted. "Come out you little bastard."

Another warrior came from the other side and pounded the same leg an inch higher than the last strike. A third one came right behind and slashed just above that. This was the first attacker Snake actually saw. He screamed and hobbled over to a large tree, leaning his back against it for balance and swinging the sword around in front of him. More faint laughter could be heard as he hit only air with the sword. "Come out and fight like a man you little pricks. I'll dice each and every one of you."

That comment hit a nerve with Les. Snake was threatening his people. In the time it takes to blink he felt an awakening within himself. He realized at that moment that he had become a Yuchi warrior chief. The weight of the people who truly belonged to this land, the ones on the other side of the open gate he had seen earlier tonight, were behind him, surrounding him, within him. The curse of the Little People and the tribe itself, were now at his command.

"It's over Snake," he said. "Surrender now."

"You're out of your mind," Snake yelled.

"Earl was a Native American from a family named 'Black Paw'," Les said. "He was the great-great-grandson of a Yuchi warrior named Kiawampa. Unfortunately, Earl made some bad decisions in his short life, the biggest of which was getting involved with white trash like you. All he was interested in was making some money to feed his family, it didn't matter how. He was desperate, and you lied to him to get him to help you in your illicit business dealings. Once he had served his purpose for you then you stabbed him in the back like the coward you are."

"He deserved it," Snake said. "Earl was a snitch. He said he was having second thoughts, that maybe he had made a mistake getting involved. I knew what he was going to do next. He was going to the cops. I had to waste him."

A that moment a small red warrior ran out from behind a nearby outcropping of rocks and came at Snake with a tomahawk. Snake saw him coming and swung the sword, knocking the tomahawk from his hand and sending him to the ground with a whimper. "Any more of you little freaks feeling lucky?" he shouted.

"You didn't know what Earl was going to do next," Les said. "He was going to give you all the drugs, the whole thing. He just wanted out and was going to walk away with nothing. It would have been all yours anyway. But you never gave him the chance."

Snake stared at him and snarled. "How do you know all of this? You weren't there. You didn't even know Earl."

"I didn't have to," Les said. "One of my people was there. You see, Snake, all this time you thought that Earl was the unlucky one because he got involved with you. But actually, the opposite is true. It's you that is the unlucky one."

"Is that so?" Snake said with a smirk.

"Yes," Les said. "As you know I have the same mental power that you do, only stronger. It's stronger in me than it is in you because you use it for evil purposes. You are an evil man, Snake, and tonight you're going down. Now drop the sword and lie face down on the ground. I'm turning you in to the law."

"The hell you are you city slicker piece of shit," Snake said. "Nobody is ever taking me back to jail. Never!"

Les looked around them. The Little People were numbering in the dozens by now. They were wearing their feathers and war paint proudly. Their tomahawks were clean and sharp. The odd part was that Snake seemed to not even be seeing them.

"Hear those drums?" Les said. "They're war drums. It's war against you."

"That's just your heartbeat," Snake said. "You hear it because you know you're about to die."

"I'm giving you one last chance, Snake," Les said. "Drop the sword and lie on the ground."

The most intense rage Les had ever seen in a man's face came over Snake at that moment. He raised the sword above his head, gripped it with both hands and began charging at him with a loud scream, limping badly as he tried to run on his bloody leg.

Les stepped back as the little people came running out from their hiding places and attacked Snake as a group. It was their fight now.

Snake began yelling obscenities as he swung the sword around blindly. The little warriors began screaming war whoops as they came swarming from all directions. Les thought they were so loud they could be heard a mile away.

Struggling to stay on his feet, Snake continued to wave the sword around in vain. "Die, die, die," he shouted as he swung it about wildly.

Les was horrified as he watched the warriors attack Snake in a mob. They chopped his legs and jumped on his back, cutting him on all sides like his whole body was made of rotten fire wood. Snake screamed and fell to the ground, his sword sailing from his hand and landing harmlessly in a pile of leaves. A few muffled cries were all that could be heard from Snake for the next few seconds before he was snuffed out permanently.

Les hid his eyes from the gruesome sight. His blood ran cold and his feet felt like they were in blocks of ice. From above him he heard a voice from inside the gates. He looked up and faintly saw Kiawampa's face in the white mist against a starry background.

"Go in peace now, white brother," Kiawampa told him. "Soar like the eagle. Accomplish great deeds! The legacy of our people is alive in you."

Still not knowing what to do next, Les looked up at his two friends standing just outside the confines of the Burial Ground. "Come on, Les," Ken was shouting. He and Skip both were waving their arms frantically. "Hurry!"

Les ran to his right, avoiding the melee that was starting to look like a small tornado in the middle of the Burial Ground. "Don't even look," he thought, "just run."

He hurried to his two friends and together they began running up the hill. As they ran through the cemetery and out its entrance, the sound behind them took on a life of its own.

Les heard the war whoops of hundreds, maybe thousands of braves. Horses whinnied and arrows could be heard sailing through the air. The pounding of the drums was deafening. And this time, the good guys were winning.

Les took the lead as they ran. Within a few moments the loud noises behind them faded into the normal sounds of the deep, Alabama woods. That told Les it was okay for them to slow down to a brisk walk. "We can take it easy from here," he said.

"I was beginning to think you were going to stand around in that burial ground all night," Ken said. "I wanted to come grab you by the hand and lead you out but some kind of invisible barrier seemed to be keeping me back."

"That was just your own fear," Skip said. "I felt it too."

"It was Kiawampa telling me to go that finally got me moving," Les said. "That and seeing his face in the sky."

Ken and Skip both stopped walking. "What?" Ken asked. "Who's voice and who's face?"

Les looked at each of them and saw in their expressions that they were suddenly questioning his sanity. "Kiawampa. You guys saw him didn't you?"

Neither of them replied. They just went on staring.

"Tell me you heard him," Les said. "You had to have heard something."

"All I heard was you," Skip said. "And Snake's screams when those little people attacked him."

"So you did see the little people," Les said. "I'm glad I'm not the only one who did."

"Oh I recognized them right away," Skip said. "Remember, I'd seen them before in the old hospital. Right before they almost killed me."

"I saw them too," Ken said as they resumed walking. "Hopefully for the last and only time."

"We can never speak of this to anybody," Les said. "Not a word to anyone ever. Got it?"

"Sure," Skip said. "Scout's honor."

Ken gave him a smile and slapped him on the back. "You were never a scout."

"He was tonight," Les said. "That goes for you too, Ken. This has to remain our secret."

"Okay," Ken said. "Now let's get out of here before a bunch of country cops show up to investigate the noises in the cemetery and decide to treat me like it's still the 1950's in these parts."

"Stop being so dramatic, Ken." Skip looked over at Les and smiled briefly. "But you're right about one thing. We do need to get our asses out of here."

When they reached the Charger Les climbed into the back seat. Ken took the passenger-side seat up front and buckled-in as Skip cranked the engine and started driving. When they reached the turn-off toward Carl's trailer he stopped. "Should we go say goodbye?"

"Can't," Les said. "Let's go home." Skip drove on.

"What are you talking about?" Ken asked, turning around to look at Les. Then to Skip, "We can't just leave."

"It has to be this way," Les said. "Carl may have to do some scrambling to cover his tracks tonight. And I have a feeling the local sheriff is going to be visiting the cemetery early in the morning, right after his coffee and doughnut stop. Heaven only knows what he'll find. We need to be long gone from the state of Alabama by then."

"You think the law would have any reason to come looking for us?" Skip said. He checked the rear view and saw that there wasn't another vehicle in sight.

"I doubt it, Skip," he said. "The police aren't going to be looking for us. Why should they? We weren't the ones firing shots. And not one of us ever laid a hand on Snake."

"Yeah, but I got the closest," Ken piped-up. "I nailed his ass twice with hickory nuts." They all laughed.

"You sure did, my brother," Les said. "You are truly a loyal brave. You probably saved my butt."

"You're right though, Les," Skip said. "He got himself killed. The gun and sword lying back in the cemetery don't have any of our fingerprints on them. And Carl doesn't really know us. In fact, he doesn't even know our last names."

"Or how to contact us," Les said. "Our disappearance should be pretty easy." He sprawled-out across the back seat. "I'm going to catch a little rest if you guys don't mind. Think you can keep each other awake long enough to get us home?"

"Yeah," Skip said. "I'm still plenty awake. I must have seen my life pass before my eyes four or five times tonight."

They drove in silence for about half-an-hour before getting completely out of the Talladega woods and onto the interstate. Ken and Skip soon heard light snoring coming from the back seat.

"Guess it's time for me to tell you a few funny ones," Ken said. "Got to keep you alert."

"Fire away," Skip said.

Ken cracked jokes for the next hour, keeping the punchy Skip in stitches. They arrived at Les's mother's house at a little after seven o'clock Sunday morning. Les said his goodbyes and staggered in a daze to the front door. He hit the bed a short time later and wasn't conscious again until early afternoon.

At a little after seven that night he got a phone call from Ken. "Go take a look at that full moon just coming up," Ken said.

Les looked out the window and saw the enormous, reddish-colored moon just above the horizon. "Wow," he said.

"It's the 'Night of the Hunter'," Ken said. "The full moon of November."

"It sure is," Les said with a smile.

"How you feeling?"

"Great," Les said. "My mom bumped into Frosty at the grocery store yesterday. They stood in the soap aisle and talked for half-an-hour. He's coming over for dinner tomorrow night."

"So everything's okay then?"

Les smiled. "Never better my friend. Never better!"

Afterward

Although the "Whispers" saga is fictional, there are many parts of the story that are historically accurate. They are presented in the dialog of David Beartracker. While Mr. Beartracker is also fictional, many of the accounts he describes to Les actually happened. I felt it was essential to deeply research Georgia history to add to this manuscript, not only for the realistic feel, but also to document the plight of some of our Native American predecessors before they are further forgotten in the abyss of passing time. Sometimes the best way to pass down the truths of the past is to pepper it with fiction to make it memorable and, hopefully, exciting.

Mr. Beartracker's account of Benjamin Hawkins (the government scout) is true. The forced merger of the Yuchi and the Creeks happened just as described, as did the Red Stick War and, sadly, The Trail of Tears. The physical layout of Indian villages were as described. Tuskeneah was real, although Kiawampa is a character I created to further the story of Tuskeneah's unknown fate. All references to US Presidents and treaties are true and correct as well. I feel that this gives the novel a well-grounded base from which to build the story. It is also important to me, as the author, to show my deep respect and admiration for the thousands of original inhabitants that lived their lives in this great land. May they never be forgotten.

I hope you've enjoyed the adventure. Thank you for coming along.

All my best!

Terry Sweatt

Made in the USA
Columbia, SC
18 June 2022

61909125R00171